Praise for
The Vampire Files

"The story shifts easily between comedy and mystery, and Elrod's treatment of the practical aspects of vampirism is clever and refreshing." —*Booklist*

"Echoes of Hammett and Chandler abound, but the novel succeeds in its own right as an entertaining exercise in supernatural noir." —*Publishers Weekly*

"Plenty of action, full of twists and betrayals, and the quirky characters and many touches of period flavor keep things amusing." —*Locus*

"Very entertaining." —*Mystery Scene*

"So fast-paced and so involving that you won't put it down." —*Romantic Times*

"Fast . . . intriguing." —*Midwest Book Review*

"An entertaining blend of detective story and the supernatural . . ." —*Science Fiction Chronicle*

continued . . .

‑ The Vampire Files ‑

THE DARK SLEEP

P. N. ELROD

ACE BOOKS, NEW YORK

THE DARK SLEEP

An Ace Book / published by arrangement with
the author

PRINTING HISTORY
Ace hardcover edition / June 1999
Ace mass-market edition / May 2000

The Penguin Putnam Inc. World Wide Web site address is
http://www.penguinputnam.com

Check out the Ace Science Fiction & Fantasy newsletter
and much more on the Internet at Club PPI!

ISBN: 0-441-00723-6

ACE®
Ace Books are published
by The Berkley Publishing Group,
a division of Penguin Putnam Inc.,
375 Hudson Street, New York, New York 10014.
ACE and the "A" design are trademarks
belonging to Penguin Putnam Inc.

PRINTED IN THE UNITED STATES OF AMERICA

10 9 8 7 6 5 4 3 2 1

With thanks to Kevin, Teresa, and the Tuesday night gang for handling the usual hair-tearing with their usual aplomb.

Thanks to the real Mary Sommerfeld for the high bidding (you too, Randy Paterno!).

And a very special thanks to
Nigel Bennett,
Jim Byrnes,
and John Kapelos,
three extreme and inspiring talents.

1

Chicago, April 1937

NORMALLY I wouldn't be caught dead—or even undead—in this kind of eatery anymore, but my partner
Charles Escott needed my help with a case. He had a
skittish client who insisted on being along for the ride
and wanted someone to hold her hand and keep her out
of trouble—that is to say, out of his hair—while he
worked.

I looked across the table at Mary Sommerfeld, and
tried to give her a reassuring smile, but she wasn't having
any of it. She kept darting nervous glances to her left, my
right, and several times I had to stop myself from doing
the same. If I wanted to see what was going on there, I
could use the pocket mirror cupped in my palm.

"Keep your eyes on me," I muttered. "Try to eat
something." After all, I'd bought her the more expensive
fifty-five-cent dinner (beverage extra), and I hated to see
good food going to waste. I assumed it was good,
anyway. My judgment on fine dining was no longer
reliable. The only thing that didn't smell nauseating to
me in this joint was my untouched coffee.

"But he's not *doing* anything," she muttered back.

I took her to mean my partner. "Mr. Escott's had lots of experience at this kind of thing. Give him time, he'll come up aces for you."

She grimaced and seized a fork, glared at it, and made a point of wiping it thoroughly with her napkin, which I thought unnecessary. Granted, the joint wasn't the Ritz Hotel, like what she was used to, but then it was a few steps above a greasy spoon, like what I'd been used to before I stopped eating solid food. It was clean and well lighted, with no lip-rouge stains on the glasses, and the ashtrays were emptied regularly. Not my kind of place these nights, but still fairly respectable.

Escott had chosen it because you could seat yourself, hence my place in a booth with Miss Sommerfeld, and his at a table twenty feet away with Jason McCallen. From my vantage I could easily block the front and back exits in case McCallen decided to hoof it before our business with him was done.

Our client wasn't too happy being so close to him, but with her short dark hair hidden by a gray cloche hat and the rest of her covered up with a matching coat and galoshes, she looked like a thousand other Chicago women for this time of year. Besides, McCallen was angled away from us, and would have to turn to spot her.

I'd tried to dress to blend in as well, leaving my pricey double-breasted suits and silk shirts in the closet in favor of a nondescript jacket and slacks, both in dark blue. My newsboy's cloth hat was stuffed in a pocket, and I wore black shoes with gum soles. My hair was trimmed, combed, and slicked straight back from my face. The impression I hoped to give was that of a laborer taking his girl out on a Friday-night date. Nothing fancy, but not insultingly cheap.

Miss Sommerfeld pushed her vegetables around and savagely speared a single kernel of corn. She shoved it into her mouth and chewed on it for half a minute.

"Stop staring at me," she growled.

I broke off and looked down at the mirror. Instead of paying attention to business, I'd been distracted by how long it took her to eat the corn kernel.

The tiny image in my hand shivered and settled. It was the same as the last time I'd checked, with Escott and McCallen at their table facing off over cups of cooling coffee. My partner was lean and tall, beak-nosed, dressed neatly in a stuffed-shirt sort of way, looking like a fussy bank teller. McCallen was just as tall, but more massive, with at least an extra fifty pounds of solid muscle riding easily on his shoulders and arms. He was big, hairy down to his knuckles, and dressed like a longshoreman. I couldn't blame Miss Sommerfeld for seeking help with the Escott Agency in dealing with him.

According to her story, McCallen had taken away an envelope of papers that were not his. They were worth a lot to her, enough to hire us to get them back again. She didn't want publicity, so the theft went unreported to the cops, and her lawyers had no clue about the incident.

When she first came to Escott's office early this afternoon to rent his services as a private agent, he made a good stab at trying to find out the contents of the envelope, but she clammed up and shook her head.

"It's personal and private," she told him. "Nothing illegal, I assure you, but they don't belong to him. Will this cover your fee?" Then she put five matching pictures of Andrew Jackson on his desk and that was that.

He called home at sunset to give me the short version of the deal and what sort of help he would need from me if I was available. I was—at least until around two in the morning when my girlfriend got off work.

"Are you out of your mind accepting a case without knowing the whole story?" I asked, running a hand over my beard stubble as I leaned toward the mouthpiece of the kitchen phone.

"Miss Sommerfeld's within her rights, Jack," he said lightly. "And it's not as murky as you think. I happen to have more background on her than you do."

The background being that she was an heiress to a fortune in saltine crackers. No, really. McCallen had been a foreman in one of the factories or plants or bakeries or whatever it is you call a place that makes crackers. He'd been romantically linked with Mary for a couple of months, until her parents in Michigan heard what was going on and packed her off to Europe. A little hobnobbing with other rich kids in the south of France had done the trick. Mary found herself accepting a marriage proposal from some minor prince and returned home in triumph.

"It is my opinion," said Escott, "that the diamonds on her engagement ring could easily buy my house with some considerable change left over for lavish decoration."

"So you do a good job for her and maybe she recommends you to rich friends in need?"

"That's always a possibility." He made no effort to dampen the smug satisfaction in his tone.

"What about the papers? Got any idea what they might be?"

"From her manner I'm assuming they're indiscreet

love letters written to McCallen when things were still amicable between them. She must have gotten them away from him at some point, then he thought better of it and stole them back. Her royal engagement could go up in smoke if he decides to use them against her."

"Where do you come by that?" I shifted from one bare foot to the other. He'd caught me just as I'd opened my eyes for the night. I'd launched straight out of my basement lair to catch the ringing phone and had only thin pajamas between me and any lurking draft. I don't feel the cold like I used to, but I hate drafts.

"She's both angered by and frightened of him," he answered. "I also believe there is more than a touch of guilt involved. You'll see for yourself when you meet her."

Which I did after catching a shower, shave, and dressing according to his suggestion. I arrived at Escott's office ready to play muscle for him should the need arise during his negotiations. He introduced me to Miss Sommerfeld as his assistant. She gave me a regal nod, perhaps practicing for her future life with her prince, then insisted on coming along to supervise. Escott started to object, but bit it off. I could almost hear him thinking about the hundred she'd dropped on the desk. With that kind of money involved, the customer is always right.

Earlier that day he'd worked out a money deal with Miss Sommerfeld and arranged a meeting with McCallen by telling him he would hear something to his advantage. The idea was simply to buy the envelope and contents back from him. If McCallen decided to be cooperative, all was well and good, and we could close and tie it up in a bow tonight; if not, then Escott would have to get sneaky and really put me to work.

Knowing a thing or two about human nature, I figured McCallen to be a blackmailer. All he had to do was sell what he had to any of the more jaundiced tabloids and he'd not only rake in a pile of dough for himself, but break up his old girlfriend's pending marriage. That was the lesser of two evils, though. Another strategy would be for him to wait, then quietly squeeze money out of her over the years, which would pay a hell of a lot more in the long haul. Either way, Miss Mary Sommerfeld was in for a rough time.

"Well, Mr. Fleming?" she asked through clenched teeth. She'd resisted looking across the room for several minutes now.

"They're still talking. Eat some more. You don't want to draw attention."

She subsided and pushed her food around. No one was paying any mind to us, but I wanted her quiet. The place wasn't noisy, but there was enough conversation going on to make it difficult for me to pick out Escott's voice from the rest. A couple at a table in between us finished and left, and once the busboy had cleared things I was just able to eavesdrop on my partner's negotiations.

"It's a perfectly fair offer," he said in his most reasonable tone.

McCallen, whose voice started somewhere near his feet, rumbled a response. I couldn't catch the words.

"I cannot answer that," Escott replied. "I'm only acting on her behalf, a neutral go-between and nothing more. All she asks is that you return the entire item, no questions asked, in exchange for a substantial reward."

"The goods belong to *me,*" said McCallen, loud enough for anyone to hear. Mary gave a little jump, and I put up a warning hand. She'd gone beet red from suppressed fury and her eyes glittered. It was even money whether she'd break into tears or charge across and attack him with the steak knife she clutched in one shaking fist.

"Let Escott do his job," I said in a soothing tone. "He's just getting warmed up."

She finally put the knife down and drank a gulp of coffee. It could have been sulfuric acid and she probably wouldn't have noticed.

I checked the mirror again and listened hard, but now Escott was talking low and quiet, leaning slightly forward. He must be to the point of laying the law down for McCallen, letting him know that petty theft was one thing, but extortion quite another. McCallen's face was hidden to me, but the set of his shoulders screamed alarm bells.

"One hundred!" he yelped in disbelief. "That's ridiculous. It's worth far more than that!"

His outburst drew notice from the other patrons and even the sleepy girl at the cash register bothered to look up from her receipts. McCallen had no mind for them, though, only his own troubles.

"I refuse, categorically," he said. "You can tell her that, or better, I'll tell her myself." Now I picked up a distinct Scottish accent. I wondered if Escott's own English accent was working against him for once. I'd read somewhere that the English and Scots didn't get along too well.

Mary started to gather herself to rise, but I fastened her with a warning look. I didn't put anything behind it and was doubly gratified when she chose to stay seated in reaction to my one raised eyebrow. I took it for granted that I might have to make my next suggestion a little stronger, though. She seemed ready to boil right over.

But Escott was still talking and McCallen still listening, which was a promising sign. He must have wanted more than a month's good wages out of the deal. Mary had authorized a payment of up to five hundred dollars to get the stuff back, which was a hell of a lot of dough for anyone's pocket.

McCallen was shaking his head. It wasn't just an ordinary refusal, but something in that categorical class from the way he wagged back an forth like a bad-tempered bear. He sneered at Escott's latest offer. "Two hundred—it's worth ten times that much and more. Greedy? I'm not being greedy, only practical, and if she'd wake up she'd see it herself. No, sir, I'll not be listening to you or to anyone else she sends. Tell her to call me when she comes to her senses and not a moment sooner."

Everyone in the joint heard him and paused in their eating to stare. Escott started to speak, but McCallen was already boosting from his chair and turning to leave. He had a solid square face, piercing brown eyes under thick brows, a grim set to his mouth, and looked about as easy to stop as a runaway bulldozer.

I pocketed the mirror and slid to the edge of the booth to be ready in case Escott wanted me to do anything, but Mary was faster. She tore out and put herself right in McCallen's path.

"You're not going anywhere, Jason McCallen," she snapped.

He stopped in his tracks, surprised by her sudden appearance, and looked down at her, for she was tiny next to him. "Well, well," he said, a bemused smile supplanting the irritation on his mug. He spared a quick appraising glance for me as I stood by her, and evidently decided I was no real threat, then pressed his full attention on the girl. "Mummy and Dadums let you out with only two chaperons? You *are* taking chances."

"I want those papers back. You must give them to me."

"Oh, I must, eh? Or what, you'll throw a tantrum?"

"They're not yours!"

"They were the last time I looked."

By now Escott had come up to join the party. He didn't appear too ruffled. "Perhaps if we adjourned elsewhere we could settle all this tonight without getting acrimonious," he suggested.

"Give them back!" insisted Mary, ignoring him.

McCallen only grinned. It was in the wiseacre class, with intent to annoy. "No, I won't."

"You have to."

"Girl, I don't have to do anything—except this." He seized her head in both his hands, bent low, and planted a kiss right on her mouth. She struggled and beat on him, but he just as quickly released her, grinning ear to ear.

Bad idea to let her go like that—she cut loose with a scream. It was short, but made up for its brevity in loudness and outrage. She took a swing at him, which he blocked like flicking off a fly. Then Escott stepped between them. I didn't have time to tell him that that was also a bad idea, and if he'd bothered to think it over he would have agreed with me. Instead, he charged into the thick of things and landed one solid punch against McCallen's jaw, which wiped most of the grin away. McCallen staggered back a step, but swiftly came around and went under Escott's guard, catching him in the gut. The force of the blow knocked him smack into me, and we both went tumbling down. I heard several women screech at this, but ignored them because the back of my head cracked against a table as I fell.

A very *sturdy* table.

Suddenly boneless, I dropped the rest of the way to the floor and stayed there, half-blinded by the intensity of the pain.

God damn *it, that hurt!*

I couldn't do much, only put my hand on the blazing sore spot and curse the pain. Any other man might have been knocked cold, but no such luck for yours truly. I stayed conscious through the worst of it, aware of the uproar and gaining another bruise or two as Escott scrambled off me to go after McCallen again. Too late, through slitted eyes I saw he'd already made it to the front door. He turned and flashed his teeth, barked a single laugh, then out he dashed to lose himself in the evening crowds.

Escott looked winded, but rounded on Miss Sommerfeld, either to breathlessly reassure her or to apologize. She didn't give him the chance. She shrieked one more time, embarrassment, anger, and massive frustration all packed into one short outburst, then tore off in tears for the ladies' room, rubbing at her mouth with the back of her hand.

He looked down at me, wheezing and a little doubled over from the punch he'd taken. "That didn't go too terribly well, did it?"

"Uh." I grunted in agreement from the floor. Damn, damn, damn, damn, *damn*, it hurt.

"Jack? You all right?" he asked, peering at me.

I held the back of my head hard, as though to keep my

brains from leaking out, shut my eyes, and tried not to swear too loud.

"Was it wood?" he continued, not without sympathy.

"Uh."

"Fortunate, that."

"Uh?"

"Were it metal instead, it might have been a bit awkward if you'd disappeared in front of everyone."

At the moment disappearing was one thing I wanted to do, but couldn't. Wood injuries have that effect on me. It's stupid, but nothing I could do anything about. "What 'bout you?" I asked between one wave of crashing pain and another.

"Winded only. Can you stand?" He helped me up, but I was still unsteady. When I staggered against him I figured out how he'd missed more serious damage. He was wearing his bulletproof vest. He usually did while working a case. In the winter he claimed the layer of small overlapping steel plates kept him warm by cutting the wind. McCallen was probably nursing some knuckle bruises himself for his punch.

"Charles, this stinks," I groaned, fighting for balance.

"Indeed. I believe the management is about to ask us to leave."

That was putting it mildly. The manager stormed up just then and told us to get the hell out or he'd call the cops. Lots of other people were talking at once, wanting to know what was going on and if there would be more of it. One couple ducked out, forgetting to pay their bill, and that set up a squawk from the girl at the register. Escott was on top of things, though, and waving a five-dollar bill under the manager's nose to catch his attention.

"I believe this will be more than sufficient to cover the various damages, sir. I'll just retrieve our lady companion from your powder room and we shall be happy to vacate the premises." He put the five in the man's hand then tottered toward the back to bang on the door, calling for Miss Sommerfeld to come out. He was careful to use only her first name. She eventually emerged, sniffling and red of eye. He took her arm and swept her away, urging me to hurry as well.

I heal pretty fast, even from wood, but it still hurt like the devil as I stumbled out after them accompanied by laughter, hoots, and other verbal disapproval from the café patrons. Not the best of exits, as Escott might have said. He'd parked his big brown Nash fairly close and was handing Miss Sommefeld into the passenger seat as I came up. I crawled into the back and resisted the temptation to lie down again. The change in elevation I endured while standing up had been enough sick-making fun for one life.

Escott hit the starter, flicked on the lights, and shifted gears, easing us into the traffic. He threw a wry look at the café front as we sailed past. "I'm glad that's not a place I normally frequent lest I should regret its loss. I fear we none of us will be welcome back there again."

It didn't matter to me: I'd stopped eating—so to speak—last August. Miss Sommerfeld had probably never been in such a place before and likely never would be again. We'd come out ahead on that, at least.

She seemed pretty much recovered in terms of self-possession, but was in need of outside repairs. Her lip rouge was smeared across her chin and her mascara had melted and run down both sides of her nose. She was also very much on the boil.

"Now what?" she demanded, her voice thick. "He's still got my papers."

"Mr. Fleming and I shall recover them," said Escott, sounding more confident than I felt. I noticed my specific inclusion on the deal. He had some dirty work planned for me. That's how it usually worked when something went wrong.

"How? Jason knows about you and will be on guard. He's sure to move them, or put them in a safety-deposit box."

"Not to worry. We'll merely fall back, regroup, and plan the next attack."

"You're not going to hurt him, are you?" She sounded excited at the prospect.

"I doubt that will be necessary. Have you his home address?"

"Yes, of course, but—"

"Excellent. As you stated, he will be on guard, but in a day or two he will relax and be more vulnerable to—"

"A day or two? Do you have any idea of the kind of damage he could do in that time?"

"Yes, Miss Sommerfeld, but he appears to be an intelligent man. He's not going to spoil his opportunity to profit from his situation. Am I correct in my assessment that we are not dealing with a merely greedy man, but a man who has been seriously injured in an affair of the heart?"

Her mouth popped open, then she looked down. I didn't need the occasional flash from a streetlight to see she was blushing. "He took my engagement to Prince Ravellia pretty hard and wants to get back at me. That's why he's being so mean about this."

"Then it is not so much money he wants from you as revenge?"

"He's a pigheaded idiot!"

I could almost say the same for Escott. The bonfire in my skull subsided enough to allow me to think again, and react, and I wasn't too happy with him. He should have let me handle McCallen, and not just from when things fell apart, but from the very first. I could have looked him right in the eye, told him to hand over the stuff and walked out, saving us a load of bruising and the client a truckload of annoyance. I'd tell Escott so, too, but not in front of Miss Sommerfeld.

It would be a repeat of what I'd said to him many times before and probably have the same impact as ever— none at all. His agency was his business; he called the shots. I was, in a manner of speaking, only the hired help and did what was asked of me. Though I could do a hell of a lot more and with much less risk, the danger was what he loved about his work. All it did for me was inspire a lot of hair-tearing worry that he'd someday get himself killed.

Ninety-nine percent of the time business was of the quiet sort; only rarely did things get rough, but when they did, Escott always put himself in the middle of it. He used to be an actor once upon a time; maybe he'd never gotten over that craving to be stage center with the spotlight burning on him. The trouble with that is you can't see who in the audience is about to toss the first tomato.

We made it to his office, and as though to put the last nail in our coffin, the wind had changed, saturating the area with the unique stench of the nearby Chicago Stockyards. Mary Sommerfeld wrinkled her well-bred

nose and hauled out a sodden handkerchief to block the
stuff. As usual, I just stopped any pretense of breathing.
Escott was on his own. After all, it was his office. At least
the rent was cheap.

Our client decided to hop into her own car and go
home. Escott's talk on the drive back had persuaded her
to keep us on for one more try. She threw a hasty good
evening to us, hurriedly revved up her brand-new Pierce-
Arrow, and sped off into the night. I hoped she'd think to
roll the windows down to flush the inside air once she
was upwind.

Escott was already trudging up the steps to the
second-floor rooms that were the official address of the
Escott Agency. The name itself was neatly painted in
gold and black lettering on the pebbled glass insert of the
front door. He unlocked and walked in, shedding his hat
and topcoat, placing both on a hall tree just inside.

The front room was small and plain, with durable
furniture and blank white walls. He had his operator's
license framed and standing on one of the file cabinets,
more as a declaration of his legal right to work than as
decor. He claimed that clutter was a distraction to clear
thinking, both for himself and the customers. If they had
nothing interesting to look at, then they could better
concentrate on their business with him.

The place had been tossed over by some mob goons a
couple of months back, but you couldn't tell it now.
Escott was ferociously neat about his person and surroundings. His desktop was bare except for a receipt
book and an ashtray. He put the book away in a drawer
and hauled out some paper from another, then pulled out
a fat-bodied fountain pen.

"Jeez, you still carrying that?" I asked, gesturing at the pen.

"War booty," he said.

It gave me the heebies just looking at the thing. Though it could write same as a regular pen, it also had a trick reservoir inside that had once held cyanide, not ink. Push a catch on it and out came the hypodermic needle that delivered the poison. Not too long ago the damned contraption had caused yours truly a whole lot of grief that still made me shudder whenever I thought of it.

"Jack, you look as though you've bitten a bad lemon, and we both know the impossibility of that," he said, scribbling the date at the top of the first page.

"Only because we both know I could have handled this without the fun and games. If you hadn't stepped in like that, I could have fixed a whammy on McCallen and had him purring like a kitten."

He shrugged, quite unconcerned. "When he so grossly insulted Miss Sommerfeld I just couldn't help myself. I do apologize for your bang on the head, though. Most unfortunate."

"It's part of the game, but about me taking the lead on some of these . . ."

He paused in his writing and lifted his chin, one eyebrow going up and the rest of his face like Fort Knox.

I sighed in disgust and turned away to look out the window. The blinds were down, so I didn't see very damn much. "Cripes, Charles, I thought the idea was to deliver what the client wants, not get ourselves killed."

"Too late for that—at least in your case."

I ignored that one. "You know that in a deal like this I should have been the one talking to McCallen."

"First come, first served."

"Huh?"

"I was the one to set up the meeting with him in the first place. He would deal with me because he'd know my voice. Having another man to reckon with might have scared him off."

"Nothing short of an earthquake would have scared that bruiser off."

"True, but I didn't know that until I saw him. Next time *you* set up the appointment, then you can make the negotiations."

"Not fair, you know I'm out of things during business hours. How about we take turns?"

He didn't say no right away, but pulled his pipe out and took his time getting it stoked and smoking. "I'll think it over," he finally said.

"Bullshit, Charles."

"I beg your pardon?"

"That's another way of saying no."

He gave a mild scowl. "I'm discovered, then. Very well, I concede that you have a valid point about raising the success and efficiency of this firm by making use of your abilities, but I was under the impression you were reluctant to do so. After the incident with that woman—"

"I was stupid and made a mistake. I'm past that now." Stupid and greedy and out of control with my appetite. The woman he referred to had recovered from my feeding, thank God, with no memory of what I'd nearly done to her, but the whole thing was burned forever into my mind. It would never happen again.

"Right, then. We'll take turns, providing your involvement is appropriate to the situation."

"What d'you mean by that?"

"Should the next case be the mere delivery of an item,

such as the last time, I should think you'd feel rather wasted. It required a cross-country train journey, which for you is a rather complicated."

"What complication? I just lock myself into my trunk and have it shipped to the right city."

"Really, Jack." He sounded pained.

"Yeah, I know, the porters could load me onto the wrong train and I end up in Cucamonga instead of Boise. Okay, I'll concede some as well, but if we get in another like this one, you put me on the front lines."

"Done and done, but the final decision is mine."

I wanted to argue him out of that one, but held off. It was his agency, after all. I could count myself lucky to have gotten this much from him and quit while I was ahead. "Okay. What else do you have planned for tonight?"

"Writing out a report on what happened for the files, then I'll probably go home." He opened a panel in his desk and drew out a portable typewriter.

"Have you eaten lately?" Sometimes he needed reminding.

"I'll pick up some Chinese on the way back," he said absently, fitting two sheets of paper and a carbon into the carriage.

More than once my girlfriend, Bobbi, had insisted that the odd plate of chow mein did not make for a good diet, but Escott seemed to thrive on the stuff. He rarely cooked for himself beyond opening a can of soup or beans, more often than not eating the stuff cold from the can. Only his passion for neatness kept the kitchen from collecting cobwebs.

"Will you be going to the club as usual?" he asked.

"Yeah. Bobbi's been rehearsing that new show all

week and it opens tonight. You're welcome to come along; she'd love to see you there."

"Tomorrow, perhaps. Let them work out of their opening-night jitters." He spoke from experience.

"I guess. She said the last rehearsal was a disaster, people missing cues, sets falling down . . ."

"Really?" He looked up from the typewriter, his expression warming. "Excellent."

"Excellent? How can you say that?"

"Because tradition has it that when you have a smooth dress rehearsal, the opening will be a flop, but if it's a string of disasters, then success is guaranteed."

I digested that one. "I'll let her know."

"She already does, I'm sure. Do give her my regards."

A clear signal for me to remove my charming self so he could get to work. "Right, see ya."

I shut the door and went downstairs to my waiting car as he began hammering away on the machine, which was something of a reversal for us. At home I was usually the one doing the typing, with him providing the interruptions. I harbored a dream of becoming a writer of fiction, having until some months back been a writer of fact in my career as a newsman. I'd worked for one of the minor New York papers for several years, fighting for bylines, fighting for this, fighting for that, before deciding that I needed a change; hence my move to Chicago.

Most of it had been inspired by the disappearance of my girlfriend at that time, Maureen. Hell, we were lovers, passionate, devoted lovers. She was a vampire, though that had never been an obstacle to either of us. The lovemaking was incredible and created the potential for my own possible conversion. Then one night she just wasn't there, and the cryptic note she'd left me about returning when things were safe nearly drove me out of my mind with doubt, worry, surmise, betrayal, and a hundred other forms of self-torture. My one defense against them was the solid knowledge that I *knew* she loved me and that only something very extraordinary had to have come up for her to leave as she'd done.

And so I waited for her to return, placing ads in all the papers for her every week like clockwork. I waited for five goddamned years before despair finally set in and I decided to move and start fresh in Chicago. There were too many memories in New York, too many people who knew my problem, too much cloying sympathy from some or exasperated chagrin from others who thought I was a sap and wasting my time. I left plenty with forwarding addresses in case Maureen returned, and she knew my parents' address in Cincinnati. If she wanted to contact me, she could.

She never did, but other things happened to keep me busy. My first day in Chicago I got caught up in some mob business and shortly thereafter was murdered because of it. But Maureen's unique gift to me during our many exchanges of blood allowed me to come back from death. I suppose some might think it a ghastly life to return as a vampire, but for my money it beat the hell out of a cold unmarked grave at the bottom of Lake Michigan.

While I was attempting to wreak havoc on my killers, I met Escott and not long after started rooming with him, eventually becoming his mostly silent and, when required, invisible partner. To earn my living I provided occasional supernatural muscle, and he gave me protection while I was helpless during the day; it was an arrangement that suited us both.

As for what happened to Maureen, that's a dark story I've told elsewhere. Look it up sometime.

I climbed into my Buick and headed home to change clothes. Though I had the pull to get into the Nightcrawler Club as is, it would hardly be, as Escott might have said, "the done thing." Tonight was the opening of a brand-new show, *The Shanghai Review,* starring Bobbi Smythe. My girlfriend. My lover. The light of my otherwise murky life. I wanted to dress up sharp and do her proud.

The review was an important step up in her career. When we'd met she was the top singer at the Nightcrawler Club—and also the mistress of its mob manager. He was dead now, replaced by another mobster named Gordy, who was more of a protective big brother toward her than anything else. He didn't have a problem with me courting her, which was fortunate for us all. I considered Gordy to be a friend by now, and I don't hypnotize friends into being cooperative to my wishes.

Not unless it's absolutely necessary, of course.

Bobbi's singing earned her a steady living at various Chicago clubs, but she wanted to move up in her corner of the world. Last fall she'd been featured on a nationwide radio broadcast, but she and her agent waited in vain for fresh offers to come in afterward. She went back to nightclub singing, but during the day invested in dance lessons and an acting coach. Her dream, like others before her, was to take on Hollywood and win, but she knew she'd have to work for it.

"One step at a time," she said. "First the clubs, then some shows, mixed with more radio to get noticed. One step at a time, but walk fast."

She wanted to be in films, but going out to California

and knocking on studio doors like five thousand other girls wasn't her style. Bobbi was a bombshell with lots of talent, but she knew she'd get lost in the crowd unless she could get herself established, recognized by the right people, and specifically invited. She was now walking very fast indeed, because at twenty-five, she worried that she might be getting too old to be considered for movie work.

I parked the car as usual on the street in front of Escott's house. The garage in the alley running along the back of the house was for his Nash. I didn't mind, it only meant I could come and go that much faster. One of our neighbors walked past and threw a half wave at me. I responded in kind and decided not to go transparent and slip through the cracks between the door and its frame as I sometimes did. Key in the lock like everyone else this time.

Inside, I turned on a few lights, not that I really needed them, but so things would look right, then went upstairs. Escott had done a lot of work on the place, knocking out walls here and there, making small rooms big. The building was old and a couple decades back had been a brothel, and while a chamber just big enough to hold a bed and a night table was all the management needed then, the new owner had other ideas.

Escott had picked up a lot of carpentry skills during his acting days and put them to good use knocking through walls. He made himself a princely suite at the far end of the hall with its own bath. My territory was just off the upper landing, slightly smaller because the bath was the next door down, but more than enough for my needs. The third floor he worked on when the mood struck and he had the time. I didn't know what he eventually planned to do with it.

My room had two windows overlooking the street, a bed that I never slept in, and a pleasant mess of magazines and books that had piled up during my occupancy. The closet and drawers were stuffed with clothing, most of it new.

Two months back, in the course of trying to prevent a gang war, I'd walked away with a sizable chunk of money that the mob didn't know existed. For all the crap I'd been through it seemed a fair enough compensation. At just a hair over sixty-eight grand, I was a rich man for the time being and still figuring out what to do with it. That kind of big cash could make for all sorts of problems.

There was Uncle Sam to be reckoned with for one. He didn't care how I earned my money so long as I paid the taxes on it, which I intended to do. Honest. But until I came up with a way of legitimizing the stuff, I pretty much had to sit on it. A part-time employee at an extremely modest investigations agency doesn't just walk into a bank with that kind of dough and no explanation, especially in this town. So I bided my time, bought a lot of pricey clothes, took Bobbi out to expensive restaurants, and generally celebrated my good fortune, albeit quietly.

With the window shades safely down, I took a moment to vanish, which cured my head of any lingering ache from the knock against the table. After that I changed into one of my two tuxedos. Yeah, I went nuts and bought two. The one with the snow-white dinner jacket was at the cleaners. The black one looked just as sharp, or so I'd been told since mirrors are as useful to me as a third thumb. Because of this handicap I had to make my best guess whether or not my tie was straight. I'd never been especially vain, but I did miss the satisfaction of seeing the final result once I was ready to leave.

The Nightcrawler Club was up on the north end of town and, museums, aquariums, and public parks aside, was still fairly close to the lake. It really shouldn't have been in the area, but when it was built the mobs were openly running things in this patch, and if they wanted something done, it got done.

It was both a showplace and a fortress, though most people would miss the subtleties of the latter. There were grilles set in the walls on either side of the entry where armed goons could keep an eye on things. The walls were angled to create a cross-fire area on the street and fitted with steel shutters. All the windows in the joint also sported steel shutters on the outside, though whoever built them did a damn good job of disguising them as ordinary painted wood. The glass was thick enough to be bulletproof.

The upstairs was sort of a free hotel to a few of the men working there, and sometimes a way station for guys passing through town. The previous manager used to live there, but not Gordy. He preferred to keep moving around. The basement had plenty of storage and a very well-concealed escape hatch leading to an ancient brick-lined passage that eventually emerged in a building some distance away. We'd used it once to avoid some crooked cops during a police raid.

Those happened more or less regularly because of the casino that took up half the ground floor. The room was invitation only. If the goon at the door didn't like your looks, you didn't get in. The raids weren't much of an

•

inconvenience to Gordy. He just rode them out, had his lawyers deal with the law, paid his fine out of petty cash, and was usually back in business a day or so later. Sometimes the interruption was mob-ordered to distract the public from some other embarrassment and to make it look like the cops were on the job. Gordy found the notoriety good publicity; the place rarely had a slow night.

The only thing they didn't think to do for the place was improve the parking, but the whole city was like that. Most of the customers were well-heeled enough to take a taxi or have their chauffeur drop them off. I wasn't one of them and circled the block a few times to find an open spot. Ordinarily I could could find one, but the papers had carried plenty of advertising on the show; it looked to be a full house for the nine o'clock opening. I finally gave up and used the valet parking, trusting the thin kid who took my keys would bring my buggy back.

I checked my topcoat and hat and threaded through the drinks crowd in the club's outer lobby bar to see if the hostess remembered to hold a table for me. In a black dress covered with silver sequins forming a spiderweb pattern, she wore a silly little hat made to look like a cheerfully smiling spider. The other girls had similar costumes, but with shorter skirts. The hat bobbed and the spider's googly eyes rolled as the hostess pored over her seating roster.

"I'm sorry, but we had to give your table to another party," she said, sincerely apologetic. "Gordy said it was okay and for you to find him so you can sit at his table." This drew the jealous attention of a few eavesdroppers who would have to wait for the second show.

Well, it sometimes pays to be a privileged character.

Not that I'd been worried or even annoyed about having my table yanked from under me. Being a familiar face here by now, I knew I'd easily find a spare chair with some acquaintance, but so much the better to get with Gordy as he'd have the best view in the house. And thanks to him I had the run of the place. After I saved his life a couple of times, he thought it was the least he could do.

The orchestra was Ted Drew's Melodians, and they were in full swing as I pushed through the dividing curtains into the club proper. They were ensconced upstage on risers overlooking the dance floor, which was surrounded by three ascending tiers of chairs and tables for the audience in a wide horseshoe shape. Gordy wanted an outrageously high cover charge of five bucks for tonight's show, but that didn't seem to deter anyone; the joint was packed. Dancing couples bumped shoulders in a haze of colored lights and cigarette smoke, and the padded walls were having a hard time muting the clamor of a large crowd trying to make themselves heard over the music and each other.

The sight of it jolted me like a physical force. The faces all seemed to smear and blend into one anonymous mass. The music and talk were unnaturally loud to my sensitive ears, and when I bothered to breathe, the smoke clogged my throat like a clenched fist. Most of the time I could ignore such distractions, but not now. The fancy clothes, perfumes, expensive surroundings, the clink of glasses, and shouts of laughter devolved into the sharp memory of a dingy dance hall, the bite of damp wool clothing, old sweat, and shuffling feet on an unswept floor. Then, involuntarily, came the next inner picture of that floor cluttered with fallen bodies, the blood spreading wide and far, and the stink of cordite hanging in the air.

I shut my eyes against the vision, willing it out of my mind. It had been two months, more than two months, since the killings at what had come to be known as "The Dance Hall of Doom" occurred. You'd think I'd be over it by now. I'd gotten away clean from the slaughter—except for the crap lingering in my head. The various investigations had pretty much closed the case; the smarter ones even hastened the closing lest some bright light decided the official version and the facts didn't jibe quite as well as they should. It was a shoot-out between law and crooks with both sides killing one another off, no survivors, and that was that. Several government agents gave their lives in the performance of their duty and were honorably laid to rest, their sacrifice held up as an example to their peers. Nobody needed to hear the true story; times were discouraging enough.

"'Lo, Fleming," said a deep voice above and behind me.

I gave a start in spite of myself. If my heart had been beating it might have gone on strike just then.

2

GORDY Weems, manager of the Nightcrawler and resplendent in the new tux he'd had tailor-made for the opening, loomed over me with a hint of smile on his normally phlegmatic face. "What's up, you see a ghost?"

"No, but you sure as hell move like one." He was a huge man, not fat, and amazingly light on his feet for his bulk. Despite the surrounding babble I *should* have been able to hear his approach. Maybe I was having a case of opening-night jitters myself. *Or more likely a hangover from a not-so-long-ago closing night.*

"You looked like hell for a moment," he said. "Anything I should know about?"

I shook my head. "Just remembering that damned dance hall."

What little hint of pleasure he'd shown instantly disappeared. "One rough job."

"And then some." He'd been along with me, and I'd helped him survive the killings and get away. Apparently he had his own bad memories to look after.

"Where's Bobbi?" I asked. I knew where she'd be, but wanted a change of subject.

"Backstage getting warmed up. Might be a good idea to keep clear."

"Yeah, I will." Better I stay out front so she could concentrate on her work. Bobbi would be nervous enough without having me underfoot. Besides, I'd already offered my good-luck wishes the night before, having Escott's answering service order a big bunch of flowers sent to her dressing room today. Daisies and carnations, mostly, her favorites.

He glanced at his watch. "We got thirty before the show, let's go upstairs."

"Won't you be needed down here?"

"Not unless there's a riot. The staff's got brains, they can handle anything short of that. The rest is the stage manager's problem."

I followed him off to the right toward a door marked PRIVATE, where we were nodded through by its tuxedo-clad (and discreetly armed) watchman. No cover charge was necessary for this area; if you knew about it, you were expected to spend your dough here. Inside, the din was much more subdued, as the crowd concentrated on their games of chance. The only real noise came from the cranking of the slot machines and occasional exclamation of joy or disappointment from the players at the craps or roulette tables.

A different kind of atmosphere held sway here, made up of hope, desperation, amusement, and terror, depending how the dice rolled or a card fell, often all four at once. From this nearly soundproof sanctum the booming band was distant background music; I relaxed, sighing out a breath I didn't know I'd taken.

We walked down the length of the tables, through another door into the back hall, then upstairs to Gordy's office, or rather his new office. It had been his dead boss's bedroom once upon a time, and Bobbi had had her own bedroom within the suite. All the sumptuous sleep furnishings had been removed from both, replaced by sumptuous office furnishings. The kind of people Gordy dealt with were impressed by the silent language of expensive trappings, so he had the decorator pull out the stops. The effect was rich, but not too gaudy, in some ways overwhelming, in others almost homey. All trace of his predecessor was gone; Bobbi's small room had been converted into an accounting office.

"Have a seat," he said, gesturing at a leather-upholstered monster that wasn't designed for sitting so much as wallowing. He made himself a drink, knowing better than to offer me anything, and eased onto the oversized sofa across from me.

"Looks good," I said, with a nod to the surroundings.

He grunted a thanks. "Yeah, you haven't been up here since the last raid."

The club had been turned upside down by the feds following the dance-hall deaths. Some of the gangsters involved had been seen at the Nightcrawler shortly before their demise, so it was a matter of guilt by association. The club had already been raided and everything reduced to a shambles, so Gordy kept his hands in his pockets, his poker face unchanged, and let them wreck what was left in their search for anything incriminating. In vain. All that had long been moved elsewhere. When the dust settled, he repaired the damage and opened for business as usual.

"I've seen the backstage area, though. Quite an improvement."

He crinkled the corners of his eyes. "That's Bobbi's

doing. She said if she was to come back, she wanted showers and heaters in the dressing rooms. The builder thought I was nuts."

"Is it paid off yet?"

"It took care of itself the first week of running the casino. That's where the real money is."

"But if you didn't have the casino, how long before it paid out?"

"Maybe eighteen months, call it two years to be safe. That includes the fact that not every night's a sellout. Why you want to know?"

I took a moment before answering, savoring the anticipation. Until now I'd kept my ideas to myself. "This is for this room only, not even Bobbi knows what I'm planning yet."

His brows twitched ever so slightly. Raging curiosity for him.

I took in half a breath, then plunged ahead. "I was thinking of opening my own place. Smaller, though, and no gambling."

Gordy gave nothing away, but I could tell he was surprised and thinking hard. "What sort of place? How small?"

"About a thirty-foot stage, tables for three fifty, four hundred, dance floor, bar, a kitchen to make hors d'oeuvres. Maybe expand it later to do dinners." Small compared to the Nightcrawler, but with the right trappings just as impressive. The main reason the Nightcrawler got hit so often was the casino. Every cop in Chicago knew about it, and not a few of the city and state politicians were its regular customers. The idea was for my place not to be such a conspicuous target. I'd have less profit without slot machines, but would get to keep it rather than plow it back in the business with repair work and rising bribes.

"I figured you for a tavern with peanut shells on the floor," he said after a long moment.

I spread my hands to indicate my new clothes. "Thought I'd move myself up a bit."

"That's a hell of a big stage for that size an audience."

"Not for the performers." Too many times I'd seen bands stuffed like an afterthought into a spare corner with hardly enough room to play in.

"Where's the money coming from?"

"Call it an inheritance." Which was close enough, since the gangster who stole it in the first place was dead.

He gave me a look to indicate he knew better, but wouldn't press. "How much can you put up?"

"Twenty-five grand."

"The wiseguys in town will want their cut for letting you operate."

"I'm figuring it in along with the taxes, permits, and licenses."

A slow nod. "You just might bring it in for that, but six outta ten places go bust the first year."

"Then I make sure this one doesn't."

"How?"

I had a specific idea on that, but didn't feel like sharing just yet, if ever. "By hiring in good acts."

"Like Bobbi?"

"You got it."

"She won't be around forever, y'know."

"What d'you mean by that?"

"She's moving up, too. Tonight's a big step for her. She's bound to get noticed."

"I hope she does, but she knows fame and fortune are

as hard to find as a lightning strike." We'd had a lot of
midnight talks about her dreams. She was realistic about
her chances.

"Unless you're sitting on a flagpole," he said, looking
mildly smug.

"What do you know I don't?"

"You'll see."

He wasn't the sort to give away a secret until he was
ready, so I'd have to wait it out.

He drained away half his drink. I got the impression it
was to cover an honest-to-God smile. If so, then he was
in a hell of a good mood. "Ike LaCelle," he said.

"What about him?"

"You want to open a club, you should talk to Ike. He
knows all the show people. He can introduce you
around."

"Great, more wiseguys."

He spread one hand, palm up, unoffended. "It's how
we do business in this burg, kid."

"What's he do?"

"He arranges things."

"That could mean anything from setting up a crap
game to taking someone for a long ride off a short pier.
What's his specialty?"

"More in the line of crap games and doing favors. He
makes sure the right people get together at the right time,
then takes a cut of the action. Mostly he's starstruck.
Likes to make friends with actors, showbiz types, then
show them off to impress others. Think of him as a
middleman who don't know he's a middleman. Once
you've met the talent, you can deal with their agents. For
my money I'd rather deal with the wiseguys, they're not
so dangerous."

Coming from him that meant something, but I quelled the tiny, rising doubt about my ability to make the club happen. Of course anything could go wrong and knock my plans flat, but if I could make enough things go right . . .

I'd been researching the idea of owning a nightclub since acquiring my windfall of cash. Though I'd have taken Bobbi out on dates regardless, for the last two months we never went to the same place twice unless there was something about it that appealed to me. Then I made a lot of mental notes to figure out what it had that I liked and how I could reproduce it, only better.

"I thought you wanted to be a writer," said Gordy, drawing me reluctantly back to the present.

"I do – that is, I am. I am a writer. I just haven't found a publisher yet who agrees with me about it."

"Don't you become a writer only after you sell something?"

"Already did that when I worked for the papers, but even without a sale I'm a writer because I picked up a pencil and started scribbling." It was something I'd read somewhere and fervently hoped was true. "That includes everyone from speechwriters to bathroom-wall poets."

He didn't look convinced, but made no arguments. "How's this club you want to start fit in with that, then?"

"It could take me years to get self-supporting as a writer, if ever. I like working with Charles, but the agency is his business, not mine. I want a place of my own, something for myself." Something that would provide me with a fairly steady income for decades on end and yet be interesting enough to hold my attention. It's a fever that runs in my family. My dad had never been content working at a hardware store until he was able to buy it and be his own boss. He had to work three times as hard, but never complained, he was too busy enjoying himself.

Gordy must have seen more than a hint of the need on my face. He nodded without comment. "I hope you can do it. If I can help . . ."

"I'd appreciate a word of advice now and then."

"That you can get right now: make sure the location ain't too close to this joint."

He got a laugh from me for that one, but I knew he was serious. Even if his place had been paying off like a triple bonanza, he wouldn't welcome any nearby competition. "You can make book on it." There was a big silver and black clock on the wall behind him, very modern, with symbols shaped like arrowheads where the numbers should be. "It's nearly show time. We oughta get downstairs."

"We oughta," he agreed. "Ike LaCelle's supposed to be here tonight. I'll introduce you. Make friends with him."

I took that to be more advice and resolved to do so.

We returned to the club proper again by way of the casino, skirting the whole backstage area. From what I heard coming through the walls, mostly voices of the chorus girls, it was barely controlled pandemonium there. They sounded more excited than panicked, though, a good sign.

Gordy had the best table, right in the center front of the stage off the dance floor. Some other people that I recognized as regulars were already seated and greeted us with louder-than-normal good cheer. They'd apparently kept the drinks flowing free for some time now. I squeezed in between Cathy Bloom, the buxom wife of

Gordy's lawyer, and a guy with buckteeth and blank eyes who was supposed to be an enforcer.

Ted Drew's Melodians had taken a short break, allowing the dance floor to clear. A guy I recognized as the stage manager emerged from the wings to check the area and exchange a few words with Ted, then ducked back again as the orchestra took their places and tuned up. Mrs. Bloom began telling me some story about Bobbi, so I lost track of things until the lights went down.

At Ted's cue, the Melodians' horn section crashed into a mournful minor-key overture. The audience hushed, except for a noisy drunk in the back who was wandering from table to table. His evening clothes were the worse for wear, and he had a three-day growth of beard. I wondered how he'd gotten past the bouncers out front, but figured the ones inside would take care of him pretty quick.

"You seen 'er?" he groggily asked some grinning patrons. He didn't wait for a reply, but staggered to another group to put the same question to them. "You seen 'er? Anybody here seen my Lil?"

He tottered all the way down to our tier of the horseshoe without getting caught. I glanced at Gordy, but he stayed in place without so much as a nod toward any of his people to take care of the problem.

The drunk made it nearly to the dance floor and stopped at the last table, leaning heavily on it. His hand groped for a customer's glass, and he raised and drank from it before anyone could react.

"Hey, you lush!" complained a man at the table. He grabbed the glass away, but it was empty.

"You seen 'er?" asked the drunk piteously. "You seen my Lil?"

The man got an unpleasant smile on his face and flashed it at his friends. "Yeah, I was with her last night. She was one hot pippin."

"Why, you . . . !" The drunk took a wild punch at him.

Gordy still wasn't doing anything, just watching. Everyone was watching, some were even laughing, including the bouncers.

The man ducked the punch, grabbed the drunk by the shirtfront, and swung him roughly around. He hauled back for a right cross and let fly, but from my angle it looked like he missed by a handbreadth. Still, the drunk went reeling back, down two steps to sprawl in an ignominious heap on the dance floor. To add to the humiliation some bozo in the lighting booth aimed a merciless white spot on him.

That's when the music came up in another plaintive crash and died down. The drunk on the floor wearily found his feet, squinted bleary-eyed at the audience, and began to sing.

Oh. He's part of the show.

I was very glad that light wasn't on me, because I felt myself going red. I'd been had. The hook, line, sinker, caught, hauled ashore, gutted, and scaled for dinner kind of had. It was a blessing I'd held off from attempting to do anything about the man before realization set in. Dammit, but I'd have to pay more attention to Bobbi when she talked about her work. I had a dim memory of her mentioning the prelude to the show.

The drunk turned out to be a sailor named Bill who had jumped ship to look for his girlfriend, Shanghai Lil, which also happened to be the name of the song he was singing. The plot sort of followed the specialty number that was in the Cagney film a few years ago, but without the fantastic set pieces or endless lines of chorus girls and other extras.

The Nightcrawler did a respectable salute to it, though. A line of about ten joss-house girls, complete with black bobbed wigs and exaggerated makeup to suggest slanting, mysterious eyes, emerged from the wings, dragging canvas flats painted to depict shabby buildings. They transformed the dance floor into a Shanghai street. The girls arranged themselves around the stage for Bill to inspect, but none of them was his beloved Lil. Their bright satin costumes were tight-fitting Chinese dresses, but with side slits all the way up the leg allowing them freedom to dance. You could also see the tops of their stockings and garter straps.

Not a bad show at all. And this was just the beginning.

Bill faded to the background while the girls swept around the floor with mincing little steps, waving painted fans and bowing. They took up the song, echoing Bill's words about his search for Shanghai Lil.

He wandered from one end of the canvas flats to the other and mimed knocking on doors, still looking, while the girls tried to interest him in their stunning charms. Bill tried a few dance steps with them, but at the last minute resisted temptation and got away from them. Ten more girls, costumed like American sailors, emerged from the doors and paired off to dance with their joss-house sisters, and was that ever an interesting sight.

Bill was still without a partner and drew a gun from his pocket. Just as he was about to end his lonely misery something like a shot went off, followed by several more in very rapid succession, like a miniature machine gun.

I sneaked a quick look at Gordy, but he was intently

watching the show, unmoved by the noise. It was just part of the act. In this place that was reassuring to know.

The gunshots turned out to be fireworks. The girls, both dancers and sailors, scattered, screaming in mock terror as a bloodred Chinese dragon lurched onto the stage. It snaked this way and that and ended up circling Bill, its head shaking and hinged mouth flapping up and down as though from laughter. This annoyed the hell out of Bill, who finally lost patience and lifted the head off the person who had been controlling it.

The puppeteer inside turned out to be Shanghai Lil, and Bobbi never looked so good. She beamed at the audience and threw her arms wide, as though to catch their wave of applause. Bill embraced her and some-how her red satin pajamas got ripped away to reveal a brief scarlet jacket and pants so short they might have well started as a bathing suit. She wore red tap shoes and stockings that went all the way up into the pants with no garters showing at all, which I thought to be a good trick. Topping her head was a black wig like the rest of the girls, but sporting red bows on either side of her face. She was also made up like a Chinese doll, managing to look virginal despite her joss-house past.

She and Bill sang the greeting part of the number to each other, then broke into a tap routine. Bobbi had not been wasting her time with all those dance lessons. She told me the key to selling a number was to make it seem easy while at the same time looking like you're enjoying yourself. She accomplished both goals so far as I could judge, and the audience seemed to agree with me and started applauding again before she'd quite finished.

Bill faded again, allowing Bobbi to do a solo dance, then she joined him so the chorus could come forward.

The "sailors" did a respectable hornpipe, which led to a medley of military type songs, like "Over There" and "Columbia the Gem of the Ocean," which got cheers from the veterans. Then the other girls joined in for several fast-moving bars of solid American swing that quickly turned into a jitterbug. I never saw so many legs moving so wild and fast. You sure as hell couldn't see anything like it in a movie now, not since Willie Hays had been called in to spoil everyone's fun.

The dance interlude was to allow Bobbi to catch her breath so she could belt out the closing of the number with Bill. They returned to the stage riding in a rickshaw pulled by four girls from the joss house, sang their piece, then rolled off in triumph, waving to the cheering audience.

The response was every performer's dream, not only a standing ovation, but one that started before the singers even came back for their bows. I yelled with the rest for an encore, and Bobbi must have picked my voice out of the crowd, for she looked in my direction, flashing the special smile she reserved only for me. I felt a lurch in my chest like my heart suddenly decided to start beating again, and had to sit down. God, what an effect she had on me.

Cathy Bloom looked in my direction. "It must be love," she wryly observed.

I couldn't deny it if I wanted to, and I sure as hell wasn't about to do that. I applauded until my hands stung.

The chorus and Bill vanished backstage and the lights brightened as Bobbi stepped up to a microphone near the Melodians so she could get her cue from Ted. They led off with a sprightly introduction, and she sang "Chinatown, My Chinatown." Not a real showcase for her voice, which was just beautiful, but it allowed her to work the personality angle. She really looked like she was having fun. Only I knew better. She was absolutely having the time of her life.

She bowed and hurried backstage while the applause was still strong and the Melodians' resident crooner took her place for a couple of songs. It also gave her a chance to change costumes. When she appeared a second time, she wore a delicately flowing set of pajamas in pale blue satin and held matching fans in each hand. Topping her black wig was a silly-looking hat shaped like a cup sitting on a saucer.

She did a few turns, waving the fans gracefully about, before being joined by six of the chorus girls dressed in similar outfits. They also used the fans, seeming to flutter and fly over the stage before bunching them all together like a giant flower. "Bill" suddenly burst from its center, dressed in a sailor suit now. He did a forward flip and landed lightly on his feet just as the Melodian crooner launched into "She Was a China Tea Cup, and He Was a Coffee Mug."

It was a very physical number for Bill, as he pursued his "tea cup" all over the stage, doing cartwheels and somersaults, all in time to the music. It looked to be a difficult piece to execute, but he hit all his cues and made it look easy. He got a special round of applause all for himself, and I wondered if he'd still be available for work by the time I got my own club up and running. It was something to dream about, anyway.

The show was an hour long, but seemed to flash by in half that time and ended with another standing ovation at the finale. The lights went out for the stage and came up in the rest of the house along with the level of conversation and activity. Orders for more drinks were requested at most tables; very few were being vacated.

"Looks like your customers are staying to see it again," I said to Gordy. "The ones in the lobby will be out of luck."

"There'll be other nights for them. In the meantime everyone's drinking. That's cash in the bank."

For him that was practically being garrulous. He was in a good mood.

Figuring it would be safe to see Bobbi during the break, I excused myself and headed backstage. I got caught up with the exiting Melodians, and for a few minutes the press was like Times Square on New Year's Eve. Mostly they were headed outside for a breath of air, some elbow room, and a smoke, since it was forbidden in the stage area, and I nearly ended up with them in the alley running behind the building. I fought clear and beat my way upstream until feminine voices predominated.

It was a lot more fun being surrounded by the chorus girls than the Melodians. Giggles and squeals of delight filled my ears, though it wasn't from my presence, but rather for the obvious success of the show. I wasn't the only boyfriend looking for his girl, but certainly the only one who could achieve a bit of privacy with her. The door to Bobbi's dressing room was wide open, unfortunately, and blocked with bodies, all of them giving her congratulations from the sound of things. I heard her laughter and knew without seeing she would be shining brighter than the spotlight out front.

And so it proved when I hacked my way through the mob. Some of the well-wishers knew me and simultaneously tried to get out of the way while pushing me forward. Every little bit helped. Suddenly I was next to Bobbi, grinning like an idiot. She let out a shriek of delight and threw herself in my arms. There must be a few things in the wide world that are better, but I sure as hell couldn't think of any. I planted a big kiss on her to the hoots of everyone in the room. Reaction seemed evenly divided from "Yeah, give 'er one for me," to "Jeez, throw a bucket of water on 'em."

Rachel, the woman who was in charge of costumes, read the writing on the wall and told everyone to clear out. "She's gotta rest and change for the next show," she bellowed to one and all.

"Tell us another," someone yodeled back as a challenge, but people were gradually leaving the room. It was small to start with, and with a dozen or more squeezed in, there was no room to turn. Most had to back their way out. Rachel was the last to go.

"Don't forget to lock the door, honey," she advised as she pulled it shut with a wink.

I practically pounced on the key.

Bobbi was executing a neat pirouette, arms up and her head thrown back, laughing. "Wasn't it just the best thing you've ever seen?"

"Only because you were in it, sweetheart." I leaned against the door and crossed my arms, enjoying my own private show. Now wasn't the time to attempt another kiss; she was all but bouncing off the walls from sheer excitement. It was her moment and more than fine with me just to be able to watch her have it. After a few minutes the excess energy ran down enough for her to throw herself in my arms again for a big hug. I lifted her high and made a slow spin, laughing because she was laughing.

She looked down at me and giggled. "Look at you, your face is covered with my makeup."

"Now, how in hell can I look at me?" I asked, and stepped before her dressing-table mirror. It reflected back an image of Bobbi suspended by some invisible support in midair. Generally I avoid mirrors; not seeing myself in them always gives me the creeps, but this was a whole different kind of reaction. I spun her again, faster. She yelped and wrapped her legs around me. I halted and considered the image. "*That* looks interesting, don't you think?"

"Oh, God, Jack!" Suddenly horrified, she started to let her legs drop, but I shifted my grip and hugged her close.

"Just a minute, baby, this has possibilities." I turned her one way and then another to get all the angles, and each one looked better than the last. She tried to catch sight of herself over her shoulder.

"What, with my butt hanging in the air like that?"

"Yeah, I like it."

"I thought you hated mirrors."

"I think I'm about to reconsider my opinion."

"This is wrinkling my costume," she said, eyes narrowing.

Never argue with a lady about her clothes while she's still wearing them. I set her down and forced myself to be patient until the inconvenient garments were hanging up in their tiny closet. For once she had on underwear, a brassiere.

"What's this for?" I asked, fingering a satiny strap.

"My breasts bounce around too much when I'm dancing. I don't want to be sore, especially there."

"Hmm, yes, but doesn't it restrict your breathing?"

She snuggled close. "Well, maybe a little bit. Besides, I'd like to find out how good you are at taking one off."

I love a challange.

"One-handed, from the front," she added.

"You are one hard-to-please woman," I grumbled, but went to work. She held still, but her hands were busy unbuttoning my pants, which made me squirm. Once they were unbuttoned, she started up a whole new kind of assault, which was extremely distracting.

"What's taking you so long?" she inquired, somewhat too innocently.

"I think it's welded shut."

"Keep trying."

"Ah! That tickles!"

"Does it? Oh, good, lemme try here . . . and maybe *here* . . ."

The damn thing finally came unhooked, allowing me to wreak the kind of revenge that left her gasping.

Someone knocked on the door.

"Later!" we shouted together at the offender. The knock was not repeated, and we got down to serious business.

In the cold light of practicality, it should be difficult, if not impossible, to shuck one's clothing while trying to give your partner a tonsillectomy with your tongue. Somehow, and I'm still not sure how, we managed.

I had some small section of my brain working on a related subject: the mirror. The aforesaid possibilities intrigued me. Since my change, all mirrors had ever aroused in me was annoyance—until I'd seen Bobbi suspended in midair and in just that position. Now it was arousal of quite a different sort.

When we worked our way down to the point that it was

skin to skin, I lifted her up again, cupping my hands to support her butt.

"Jack, you can't be serious," she protested, but she snuck a look at her reflection.

"Let's just give it a try. If you don't like it, I'll stop."

"Like has nothing to do with it, I'm just trying to get used to the idea."

I put my back to the mirror. "How do you like the view?"

"My God, I can see right through—oh, this is crazy!"

And, apparently, arousing to her as well, to judge by things. She locked her legs around my hips, and once we got ourselves properly adjusted, it went just great for both of us.

Her eyes were half-shut, and she was holding on for dear life. As if I could drop her at this critical point. "Jack, are you ready? I'm almost there—oh—it's—"

I'd been ready for this all night, every night, and every moment that I was with her. My corner teeth were out. I pressed my lips hard against the flushed and hot skin of her throat, drawing another moan from her. The timing had to be just right, but we'd had plenty of practice. I knew exactly when to bite down . . . she held in her scream—ecstasy, not pain—and spasmed against me. I'd turned sideways and now watched her writhing image in the mirror as the pleasure rolled over her, over us both. I drew gently on her life, extending the moment.

"It's too much," she whispered. "God, I can hardly . . . hardly . . ."

I knew better. She hadn't had nearly enough yet and neither had I. Nuzzling deeper, I took another sip of her red fire; she urged me to take more. I did, but very, very slowly.

She sighed, soft, shuddering breath warm against my ear.

I made it last for us both.

Then, enough. I didn't want to exhaust her for the next show or she'd kill me later. She was groggy from the exertion, though, as I carried her over to a sofa and stretched her out on it. The marks on her throat still seeped. I knelt and kissed them clean, tasting her makeup, the thin sheen of salty sweat, and the blood. Its flow finally stopped, and I held her close, my lips against her temples to feel the tickle of her pulse there. It gradually slowed to normal. I pulled a blanket down from the back of the sofa and tucked it around her. While she rested, I got dressed again, stealing looks at her the whole time. Her makeup was smeared and the black wig askew, revealing her platinum hair beneath, and still she seemed to be the most perfect angel, even more beautiful than the night I'd met her.

She stirred sleepily. "Why'd you stop?" she murmured.

"Didn't want to wear you out."

"I think it was more of a case of me wearing you in. Did I look good on you?"

"Magnificent would be the right word."

I wanted her all over again. Resisting temptation—this time—I pulled my pants up and made sure I got the buttons done up right. It wasn't that I was hungry for more blood—I could satisfy mere appetite feeding from the cattle at the Stockyards—I was hungry for more Bobbi.

Her eyes drifted shut, and I moved quietly, allowing her to doze. There was a covered tray on a table. I peeked, discovering a pile of sandwiches and a big glass of grape juice sitting ready. After such a demanding show, and certainly after what we'd done, she'd wake up ravenous.

I sat and watched her, and knew myself to be one hell of a lucky guy. Our first meeting hadn't gone too smoothly. She'd been told to lure me into a trap, which happened to be where I wanted to go, and though scared of the man who had ordered it, she'd tried to warn me away, to save me. Our first kiss had been my idea; I'd made it happen using hypnosis. I broke it off, though, knowing it was wrong. It felt wrong; it tasted wrong. But our second kiss had been her idea. And since then things had been nothing but right for us.

It happened fast, our romance, fast—without thought or plan beyond an immediate sating of physical and emotional need while we were both in a tense and dangerous situation. Things should have fallen apart for us afterward . . . but never did. That made me think that if we'd met in more normal circumstances, taken time to get to know each other first, dated, and talked like other couples, the same thing would have happened.

She was a wonder. Inspiring. I hadn't always been so uninhibited at lovemaking. I'd learned a lot from sweet Maureen, but Bobbi always seemed to push me further, and I would try new things, casting off old restraints. With her telling me what she liked and when, and me adding in a few variations of my own, we'd done better than all right by each other. It had taken us a while to get it right, though, but the best way to get good at anything is to practice, practice, practice. I learned how far I could safely carry things with her, how much to take, when to stop, when to keep going. What we felt was one long climax, but I took care not to go too far. If I truly abandoned myself to her whispered urgings, I could drain her too much, and the last thing I wanted to do was to hurt her.

She woke up suddenly, inhaling a sharp breath and looking wildly around. "The time . . . !"

"It's okay, you've got thirty minutes."

She visibly relaxed. "Whew, I thought I was a goner."

"Not while I'm around." I got the tray and put it on the low table in front of the couch. "Here, get this down."

"Just a little, I don't want to be burping through the next show. Is the juice room temperature?"

"'Fraid so."

"Good. Could you draw me a cup of hot water from the tap? It'll cut the sugar in the juice." The heat also kept her vocal cords from seizing up. Cold refreshments were only for after a show. I got her water from the bathroom sink while she ate half an egg sandwich, leaving the crusts on the plate.

"You need more than that," I said as she covered the tray up again.

"I'll have it later. This is enough to keep me from collapsing—oh, don't look so worried—but it won't slow me down. I can't be dancing up a storm if my stomach's busy trying to digest stuff."

"And you're going to be doing this twice a night for the next four weeks?"

"That's showbiz," she said brightly. "And in the final week I'll be rehearsing my next show here—unless something comes up."

"Something like what?"

"Oh, anything, really."

"Y'know, Gordy hinted that there was—does the name Ike LaCelle mean—"

"He didn't tell you, did he?" She looked dismayed.

"Who, Ike?"

"No, Gordy. What did he say about Ike LaCelle?"

"Only that he knew a lot of show people and might be here tonight. What's he to you?"

"Nothing right now, but through him I can meet people who really matter in the business, people who can do me some good."

This sounded familiar. "Good as in the big time?"

"Good as in the really big time, as in what I've been dreaming about since I first walked into a picture house. I wanted to tell you about it myself. Now, why are you so long in the face all of a sudden? I thought you wanted me to—"

"I do, honey. I want you up there, but sucking up to some mob middleman might not be the way to go about it. Who is he anyway? If he's expecting some kind of casting-couch shenanigans, I'll pop him into next Sunday."

"You're cute when you're jealous, Jack—"

"I don't feel cute."

"—but you don't have to worry about him. For one thing, I can take care of myself, and for another he's never going to cross Gordy, so you don't need to waste time frowning in his direction."

I was sullenly reassured. Having seen Bobbi in action with both a gun and a blackjack, I knew very well that she could take care of herself. I shrugged and nodded, letting it go. Anything else would annoy her, make her think I didn't trust her. The man she'd been with before me kept her on a leash so tight as to nearly strangle. After some of the stuff she'd told me about what life had been like with him, I privately vowed never to be so stupid.

"I see you got my flowers," I said, changing the subject.

She slid from the couch to come over and thank me. If she'd been wearing any clothes, I might have ripped them off her in response.

"They're beautiful, and in my favorite colors, and I loved the orchid." She sat before her dressing-table mirror and made a face at her smeared makeup.

"Orchid? I didn't order that."

"They all came in the same delivery, from the same florist."

"Where is it?"

"Over there with the rest somewhere."

She had quite a horticultural collection in the far corner from a number of friends, including an impressive horseshoe display on a tripod with a red ribbon sash wishing her good luck. That one was from Gordy, I noted with relief. I found a purple box with a cellophane window so you could see the perfect white orchid on its satin bed within.

"See who it's from, okay?" I asked, handing it to her.

"You're not jealous again, are you?"

"Not a bit," I lied, illogically wishing I'd thought to send such an elegant flower. Next to it the daisies and carnations looked a little on the plain side.

She opened the box, exclaimed over the orchid, and went all soft smiles at the card. "Oh, that's just so *sweet* of him!"

"Of who?" With much effort I managed not to pluck the card from her fingers.

She read from it. " 'My best wishes for a successful performance, break a leg, Charles.' "

Escott? Oh. Well. It was all right, then. I relaxed my

shoulders. "Yeah, that was pretty thoughtful of him. He never said anything about it to me."

"You know how he is. He likes me but just doesn't show it openly. If he wasn't English he'd probably duck his head and go 'aw, shucks' every time I said hello to him."

True enough. Charles did very much like Bobbi, but I could trust him to be a gentleman. "What's this 'break a leg' stuff?"

"It's one actor's way of saying good luck to another. I don't know how it started, but it's supposed to bring the reverse of what you wish for. Is he here tonight?"

"He had to work, but he told me to give you his regards. He'll catch the show later."

"I hope he doesn't leave it until too late. He gets so tied up in his work he forgets what month it is. What's he doing this time?"

"Getting love letters back from a blackmailer. I helped him out earlier, but it fell through. Tomorrow night he might have something for me to do."

She arched an eyebrow, but it had to do with her makeup repairs. "Burglary again?"

"Maybe. He'll figure some angle, he always does."

"So you're free the rest of the evening?"

"At your service, lady."

"Good. Gordy's having a private party after the club closes for the night. You're my date."

"None other, I hope."

"No chance of that, lover. Oh, damn, would you get the door for me?" She grabbed up a long silk dressing gown and pulled it on.

It was the stage manager calling the time until the next show. The now open door created a kind of burst dam effect, with people first trickling, then flooding in, all with business to accomplish in a very short time. Bobbi continued to repair her China-doll face and set the wig straight, an island of calm in the noisy waters. I waved mournfully at her from the doorway.

"After the show gimme a chance to clean up and I'll see you then!" she called over the press of bodies.

"I'll be here," I promised, and slowly made my way out front again.

There'd been a modest shift change in the audience as new customers were seated for the next performance. At Gordy's table the Blooms were gone, along with the bucktoothed assassin, a foursome having taken their place. A good-looking, sharply dressed man was in my chair. Next to him a strikingly handsome couple, and next to them a guy I recognized as one of Gordy's mob cronies. I'd seen him around the club a few times, Gil Dalhauser. He had something to do with running a truckers' union.

"'Evening, Dalhauser. Where's Gordy?" I asked, fastening on him as the only familiar face. The others studied me in a not unfriendly manner, especially the raven-haired woman.

"In the other room, some sort of business. He said I should introduce you around."

The other room meant the casino, and maybe not everyone at the table knew about it. That, or Dalhauser was just displaying the ingrained caution that came with his work. He was a tall, loosely built man in his forties with a mournful cast about him. He had thinning blond hair cut army short and steady, pale blue eyes, the kind that were shuttered so you couldn't see in, yet he was able to stare out, usually right through you. He duly made introductions.

The gorgeous woman was radio actress Adelle Taylor; I'd heard her name in lots of broadcasts from dramas to comedies, and currently she was a singing regular on the *Archy Grant Variety Hour*. She was about thirty or so, elegantly dressed in black velvet with leopardskin trim on the collar, cuffs, and hat. She held her head high like a queen, showing off the clean line of her chin and throat and the string of black pearls that dipped down out of sight between her breasts.

Her once-over of me with crystal cold baby blues was thorough, her response to my greeting polite but with a wait-and-see attitude. I could almost hear her thinking, Are you important? Do I need to know you? With some show business people this was necessary for survival, so I took no offense.

The handsome man with her was Archy Grant himself, looking the same as he did in the Sunday entertainment magazine inserts. He'd started out as a singer with a talent for comedy, and in ten years built up his reputation and following to the point of hosting, and starring in, his own show. He had a national broadcast once a week out of Chicago that I listened to more often than not. I got a firm, friendly handshake from him and a sincere hello in his familiar voice. He was stocky-framed, all muscle and energy, and his dark eyes were the kind that missed nothing. A useful ability to have, since he was famous for his ad-libbed patter.

Now that my mind was routed in that direction I wondered if he could be persuaded to perform in my club someday. That *would* be something to see, in which case a five-dollar cover would be entirely appropriate.

Get it bought and open for business first, Jack, I told myself, *then worry about what to charge for the acts.*

The last man was Ike LaCelle. He seemed as sharp as his clothes and had a good-natured spark in his eyes. His reddish hair was slicked back from his high forehead, but a stubborn cowlick gave the impression that he was more an overgrown schoolboy than a mobster. He pumped my hand, grinning broadly, and mentioned that he'd heard of me, and that it was fine, mighty fine, to meet me at last. I almost believed him. He gestured at Grant and Miss Taylor.

"Archy and Addie here thought they might like to see the show," he said. "I told 'em I could get 'em in, but they didn't believe me."

Adelle Taylor visibly winced at the shortening of her name, but did not correct him. She put an apparently careless hand on Grant's arm instead. He didn't seem to notice.

"That's the ticket," said Grant agreeably. "Ike said he knew the owner and could get us the best table for the opening. Took a while, though. Thought I'd drink myself blind at the bar." There was only a hint of a glaze on his face, so he was either exaggerating or had a high capacity for martinis.

"I happened to notice you in the lobby, Mr. Fleming, and saw you going right in," said Adelle in a tone to indicate she expected an explanation from me.

"Only because I'm a regular here."

"Ike said you're friends with the star . . . ?"

"Yeah, Miss Smythe and I have been dating for a few months."

"Lucky man," put in Grant, full of warm enthusiasm.

"I saw the portraits of her in the lobby. I understand she's also very talented."

"You'll see for yourself shortly."

Adelle's chin lifted very slightly and her eyelids dipped for an instant. I thought I'd caught the drift of things and put all my attention on her, smiling with vast appreciation. "It's such an honor to meet you, Miss Taylor. I hope you don't mind, but I have to tell you how much I've enjoyed your work on the radio. Your voice is so beautiful, and now to find that you're even more so in person . . ."

She beamed, obviously delighted at the topic shift, and I knew I'd called it right. "You *dear* man, how very sweet of you to say so. *Do* tell me more."

3

I asked Adelle Taylor if she had any new work coming up. Between that and the compliment, the conversation ran itself all the way through to the overture. She could talk fast, a necessary skill in radio, and filled my head with more information about herself than I could ever remember. It made the lady happy. The men were silent, though I caught Dalhauser giving me one of his long steady looks as if to say he knew what I'd done.

Ted Drew got his Melodians going for the second time, and the drunken Bill began making his rounds of the upper tier of tables. You could tell who in the audience had seen the show before and who was new by the grins on some faces and looks of embarrassed horror on others. The same guy knocked Bill onto the dance floor, starting the show in earnest.

Knowing what was coming added to my enjoyment, and the performance seemed even better than before. Everyone was warmed up, confident of their reception, and thus free to have fun. Bobbi's caperings as the Chinese dragon were broader and more bold, the dancers more in time with each other, the singing more expressive, the muggings at the audience funnier. The reward was laughter, applause, and another ovation. The latter was more raucous but shorter; the hour was late and everyone was pretty well-oiled.

I spared some attention for the others at the table, having the strong feeling that Bobbi might want to know Archy Grant's reaction to the show. He seemed to like it, laughing in the right spots, listening with concentration at others, particularly when Bobbi had a solo.

Adelle watched a little more coolly, turning away once to order a fresh drink. She asked everyone if they wanted another as well. Grant was the only one to say no, with an abrupt throwing-away gesture; the rest of us took a second or two to give her a whispered yes or no-thanks.

Ike LaCelle was so engrossed I thought he'd leave eyeball prints on the girls. He hung on every word, laughed the hardest at every joke, clapped the longest at every bow. He was trying too hard, but seemed unaware of it.

Dalhauser smiled a few times and applauded appropriately. Once or twice he'd throw a look of mild annoyance at LaCelle. He nursed his one drink through the whole hour.

As the lights came up and the applause died down, Archy Grant turned around to the table, a big grin lighting his face. "Well, as the man said, she is one hot pippin—if you don't mind my saying so, Mr. Fleming."

"I'll pass the compliment on to her. She won't mind."

Adelle and Dalhauser both noticed what I had not said about who minded what. She made a tiny smile, hiding it by taking a drink from her empty glass. He shifted his gaze to me for a second and the corners of his mouth twitched ever so slightly. He had my number all right. Archy was a good-looking SOB, famous, and apparently taking the stunning woman next to him for granted. If he was the predator I pegged him to be, then I was more than prepared to keep him a good arm's length away from Bobbi when she came by for the after-hours party.

Ike LaCelle looked like he had similar feelings for my girlfriend, and though he was also good-looking, I had little to worry about. Bobbi had met hundreds like him since she started singing and knew how to deal with them.

By now I'd long figured out that Archy Grant's presence at the club was no happy accident, and that he was certainly on the list for the party. Most likely Gordy had invited LaCelle and asked him to bring Archy. The lovely Adelle was a bonus. How Dalhauser fit in, I didn't yet know, or if he was even part of the group. He and Ike were certainly acquainted, but whatever other links they had, I'd have to learn from Gordy.

Our host had been completely absent throughout, which was not too surprising. He was usually a busy man.

The paying audience thinned and departed, as did most of the performers, though a number of the Melodians and costumed chorus girls remained to keep the place from echoing. Hot food appeared on a line of tables, and everyone but me gorged like starving lions.

"You sure can tell the talent from the rest," said Archy, nodding at the line. "Never get between an actor and his food."

I knew that the general idea applied for most other professions as well, but just to be friendly, I agreed with him.

"Are you an actor, Mr. Fleming?" he asked.

One of Escott's favorite sayings came to mind. "We're

all poor players on the world's stage, aren't we?" I asked, quoting him exactly, but without the English accent.

Grant froze for the briefest moment, his lips compressing into a thin line before he forced them into a brief, tight smile. My apparent youth was working against me again. I was probably his age in years, but my condition had shaved a decade or more from my face. Maybe he saw me as some smart-ass kid. Well, he was half-right, and not about the kid part.

Ike LaCelle laughed more than was necessary at my observation; even a chuckle would have been too much, but he didn't know that now. He'd been packing the drinks away like Prohibition was about to come back, and though he must have had a hell of a capacity, the load was starting to show. He was a happy drunk, though, if a bit boring for Adelle. For the last half hour he'd been trying to tell her some involved story featuring an encounter he once had with Laurel and Hardy. I think she stopped listening after he began with the question "Did I ever tell you about the time I met . . . ?"

"I'm curious, Mr. Fleming," Grant continued. "What's your line? I mean, besides playing escort to one of the most beautiful women in Chicago." He added a laugh, the same distinctive one he used in his radio show. Several heads turned in our direction and some people laughed as well, though they couldn't have heard anything. Grant had been recognized, and those in the know quickly informed the rest.

"A lot of different things," I answered, trying to decide how much he needed to hear.

"Yes, I suppose a young man like yourself has all sorts of prospects ahead of him. It might be hard to choose."

Great. Friendly words, condescending delivery. If I'd

really been the age I looked, I might have picked a fight with him.

"Archy, dear," said Adelle, smiling steadily at me. "You might take a moment to notice that Mr. Fleming's tuxedo is worth at least a week's pay."

"Leave it to you to count how much money a man has, darling." He said it like a line for his *Variety Hour* and made his signature laugh to let people know he was only kidding with her. There was just enough edge underneath not to be funny, but Adelle went along with it. Her smile did not reach her eyes.

Before anyone else could fill in the gap a cheer and applause went up across the room. Gordy appeared from the right-hand wings with Bobbi on his arm. She beamed and delivered a mock bow in acknowledgment. There was some hooting from a few, but it came from the other performers in the show and was of the good-natured sort.

I excused myself to one and all and made my way along the tables to meet them as they crossed the dance floor. Bobbi looked spectacular in a deep blue dress with a high collar and long sleeves that opened at the shoulder and closed up again at the wrists. It was in a floaty, clingy fabric that made her look like she'd wrapped herself in a slice of midnight sky. She wore a silver necklace with a modest sprinkle of tiny diamonds to serve as stars against the blue background. The only thing about her with more gleam and glitter was her soft cap of platinum hair, where she'd pinned the white orchid Escott had sent.

Wow.

"Something wrong?" she asked, stepping up to me. She had on a special rose-scented perfume that went right through my skull—in a nice way.

"Don't tease 'im, Bobbi," Gordy advised. "The poor schmuck's ready to keel over."

I woke up fast. "Not tonight, I ain't. Bobbi, you look . . . you . . . I mean—"

"Just as I said." Gordy again.

She slipped from his arm onto mine. "Keep looking at me like that and you don't have to say anything, lover."

Just as well. I couldn't think of any words that could come close to saying how I felt. And I had delusions of being a writer.

"I gotta do some business tonight, Jack," she said by way of a warning. Gordy had gone ahead of us; Ike LaCelle was busy introducing him to Adelle and Grant.

"I figured as much when Archy Grant turned up at the table."

"It was Gordy's idea to get him here to see me."

"I figured that, too. You angling to get on the *Variety Hour*?"

"Exactly. He's probably aware of it, so I can't be too anxious or obvious."

"Scheme away, my lovely. Make yourself rich and famous, just don't forget your old friends."

She planted a peck on the edge of my jaw. "Have you met Archy? What's he like?"

"He's okay, I guess."

"I thought you enjoyed his show."

"I do, but the jury's still out on whether I like him or not." Privately, I'd already pegged him as an asshole, but there was no need to prejudice Bobbi against him. She had enough to think about. "On the surface he's smooth enough, but he doesn't give much of himself away."

"He is pretty famous. Some people have to close

themselves off like that to keep everyone from taking away pieces. You've seen me do it."

"I have. But the jury's still out." After all, it wasn't like I was starstruck around him, as other people were. I'd met celebrities before. Hell, once I even lost twelve bucks playing pinochle with Chico Marx. "Grant seemed very interested in you—"

"Was he?" That pleased the hell out of her.

"—but if he gets fresh I'll see to it his face makes friends with the sidewalk."

"Oh, Jack!" She squeezed my arm. "You are so damn cute when you get jealous."

"I'm not jealous, just looking out for your interests."

"Well, thank you, but—"

"Okay, I know, and I'll back off. It's not that I don't trust you; it's all the rest of them. They should look at you with respect, not like you're a piece of fresh meat."

"You'll hate this, but Marza said nearly the same thing earlier today."

Marza Chevreaux was Bobbi's accompanist on the piano, and she had no liking for me at all. The feeling was mostly mutual, but for Bobbi's sake we lived by a sort of half-assed truce, only drawing blood when she wasn't around to hear us.

"You called it right, sweetheart. Me and Marza agreeing on something? Did hell freeze over and I miss it?"

"She's like you in wanting to protect me from the cruel, cruel world, but there's no need. After all the stuff I've been through, I think I can handle most anything."

"I bet you could."

"I know I can—but it's nice that you want to cover my back."

That called for a kiss. A peck on her forehead seemed the most appropriate, so I delivered.

She straightened my tie a little. "Now, where Mr. Archy Grant is concerned, it *is* strictly business. I'll charm his socks off, but that's as far as the undressing goes. Besides, he's sort of engaged to Adelle Taylor."

That surprised me. "Engaged? Jeez, the way he treats her I thought they were married."

"Oh, yeah? Tell me—no, never mind. Gordy's waving. It's show time."

She didn't really square herself as others might have done to face an important situation, but a subtle change did take place in her. I could almost feel the electricity she could generate suddenly building to charge through and around her like a small, intense storm. I don't know what it was she did or how she knew to do it, but when she went into it she seemed bigger and brighter than before. She radiated enthusiasm and energy and people got caught up in it in spite of themselves. Some liked it and hung around like moths wanting to burn themselves up, and others gave her a wide berth, but one way or another everyone felt it.

She was different than she'd been when I'd first met her. The potential had been there, but she was so under the control of her mob lover she didn't dare use it except onstage. Once clear of him, and once she understood I wasn't about to make his mistakes, she cut loose and really pressed ahead with the serious business of being herself. It was a wonderful process to watch, and God help anyone, myself included, who dared to interfere.

Of course, I still had a protective streak toward her that was a few miles wide. I couldn't pretend otherwise, but kept it well in check. If there was one thing she couldn't stand, it was having anyone looking over her shoulder for her own good.

With this in mind I hung back by half a step once we reached Gordy's table. As host, he presented her to them all. The men stood and acted suitably impressed, even Dalhauser. Adelle shook hands with a big, sincere-looking smile and complimented her on the show, giving the rest the signal to fall over themselves delivering their own praise. Ike had the most to offer, comparing her to Ginger Rogers and Carole Lombard, both of whom he just happened to know. We took our seats, and Grant spared us from another of Ike's involved reminiscences.

"This is a quite a change from that jungle review you did for the Top Hat Club a few months ago," he said to Bobbi.

"Goodness, you saw that? Thank you for remembering."

"Not at all. You showed then that you have the rare quality of good comedic timing; that's something you have to be born with."

"So I've been told."

"After this club date, what are your future plans?"

"That depends on what my agent turns up for me." It was her standard reply for anyone who bothered to ask. This time she did not follow it up with further information, such as what she expected would come her way. That was to be Grant's job if things worked right.

"What would you like to do?" he pressed.

"Anything that pays."

"*Well,* now . . ." he began, doing an Eddie Cantor roll of the eyes.

She picked up on it and laughed. "Anything with singing and dancing, I mean."

"You *are* versatile." He milked it for exactly two seconds, then damped it down to a more serious level. "Would you be interested in singing on my show?"

"Who wouldn't, Mr. Grant?" She beamed him her sunniest smile.

"Archy, please. If we're going to work together it has to be first names all around. Isn't that right, Adelle?"

"Perfectly right, darling," she said, unconcernedly taking a cigarette from a gold case with her initials engraved on it. Gordy, sitting between her and Grant, offered her a light.

"So, Bobbi, you think you could have something ready by this Tuesday? I know it's very short notice, but—"

"Oh, I could do it, but I don't know how to work it into my schedule. Your show's on at the same time I'm doing mine."

"You don't have to sing in the studio. We could set something up to broadcast right here from the club. With Gordy's permission," he added.

Gordy gave a slow nod. "It'd be good publicity for everyone."

Things moved pretty fast after that; even though I was stone-cold sober, I couldn't keep up with it. I had better luck paying attention to what was going on beneath the negotiations and planning.

It seemed clear to me that Grant was attracted to Bobbi, but smart enough not to move on her in an obvious way. All he really had to do was play up his brand of charm, flash the perfect teeth, and be vastly amused at anything witty she said, using his familiar laugh. It went without saying that he was very famous and in a position to do her a lot of professional good. Most other girls would have been dazzled and eager, but

Bobbi wasn't of their number. If any dazzling was to be done, that was her job. Ike was thoroughly caught up in her spell, and even Dalhauser looked more animated than was usual for him.

Throughout it all she would occasionally slip her hand under the table, find my knee, and give it an affectionate squeeze. It was an unconscious gesture on her part, for all her concentration was on Grant, but because it was unconscious it meant more to me than anything she could have done on purpose.

I also got the impression that Grant was out to annoy Adelle in a not-too-subtle way. She tried hard to pretend not to notice anything. Gordy wasn't blind and leaned over to whisper something in her ear, which resulted in a smile from her. Not a big one, but after that some of the stiffness left her shoulders. When the business talk died down Gordy signaled someone behind me, and one of the staff brought over a tray stacked high with fancy sandwiches and caviar. Someone else delivered more drinks. Bobbi had another grape juice, this time chilled.

"Aren't you eating, Mr. Fleming?" asked Adelle, sliding black fish eggs onto a cracker. I wondered if it had been baked by Miss Sommerfeld's family.

"I had something earlier." Actually, I'd fed heavily at the Stockyards last night, but she didn't need to know that. Bobbi's hand happened to be on my knee again. She gave me a playful pinch.

"That's a very smart outfit, Adelle," she said. "Is it a Schiaparelli?"

"No, a Banton. Is yours a Greer?"

"An Adrian."

This set off an intense discussion as they batted names like Chanel, Irene, Orry-Kelly, West, and Tree back and forth. The men, myself included, looked either bewildered, bored, or blank. The end result for the women was a date for lunch and shopping tomorrow.

One of the braver chorus girls, egged on by her giggling sisters, approached Grant and asked for an autograph. He flashed her his public smile and troweled on the charm. This brought more girls, one by one, all smiling, maybe hoping to do what Bobbi had just accomplished. Things were too crowded, and the stink of the food was getting to me. Bobbi still had more talking to do, so I quietly excused myself and slipped away to more open spaces. Gordy managed to do the same thing and joined me.

"That went like you wrote the dialogue," I said, straddling a chair up on the empty second tier.

"Better than planned," he agreed, leaning on a rail to watch things a few steps below.

"What if Grant hadn't been interested in putting Bobbi on the show?"

"Then I'd drop a word in Ike's ear so he could suggest that Grant get himself interested."

"Ike doesn't strike me as the kind who would have much influence with too many people."

"He's got plenty."

"How so?"

"Ike's cash and connections is what got Grant started back in New York in the first place. They been thick for years."

"So that's why Grant puts up with him."

"Don't underestimate Ike. He's starstruck and likes dropping names, but he knows how to do tough."

"And I should be friends with this guy?"

"He's a handy shortcut to a lot of talent."

"How much of that talent owes him?"

"A few, but not in money. For them, he mostly does favors."

"When he's not setting up crap games?"

"You got it, kid."

"What kind of favors?"

"Nothing too illegal."

That covered a wide range of possibilities "Such as . . . ?"

He thought a minute. "There was some Broadway singer playing around with his costar in a show, only his wife in California don't know it. She comes to New York for a surprise visit. Ike got wind of it, got to the hotel first, and had the girl dressed and down the back stairs as the wife was getting out of the elevator. It saved the production from looking for a new leading man."

"So he and the costar are Ike's good friends now?"

He opened his hand, palm out, in a "what do *you* think?" gesture.

"Did Bobbi know you planned to have Ike promote her with Grant?"

"I told her. She didn't like it."

"But she went ahead anyway."

"She told me if she didn't get a job on Grant's show on her own, then I was to tell Ike to forget it."

"Would you have?"

He grimaced and finally nodded. "You gotta be honest with a gal like her. On the other hand, Ike would have gone ahead and told Grant anyway. Just look at him. He's goofy for her."

"That would let you off the hook."

There was a look of definite satisfaction on his mug. "I win both ways."

"So does Bobbi." Of course, singing "Chinatown, My Chinatown" on Grant's show was probably not going to make her an overnight sensation. She'd had more to do on another national broadcast last fall and nothing had come of it. But with Grant backing her she might get more recognition than before. I could hope so.

Down on the dance floor some of the band members brought their instruments out and started an impromptu session. They'd been fed and watered and this time were playing for the love of their craft, not the money.

"That's good," I remarked. "Seeing 'em do that."

"How so?"

"It means they like it here, feel comfortable enough to hang around to have some fun. It didn't used to be that way." The atmosphere of the club was different with Gordy running things. There was still an air of risk about the joint, but now it was more in the line of forbidden fruit, rather than the imminent danger of getting killed.

"I guess," he said, watching the dance floor. Some of the men were leading girls onto it. Those girls left over danced with each other.

"What guess? It's all your doing. This has become a class place. It's because of this club I want to try my hand at having one."

"Huh. It's because of Bobbi."

No disagreements there. If not for her, a lot of things would be different for me, and Gordy wouldn't still be alive. We both owed her.

"She won't be doing clubs forever," he added.

"So you've said." I felt a tug inside. Sadness and pride rolled around in my gut. I loved her, and knew she loved me, but if she was going places and moving up, I couldn't hold her back. To do so would be to lose her.

Archy Grant had Bobbi on his arm and was taking her down to the dance floor. I kept a wary eye on things, but he behaved himself and didn't hold her too closely. Good. He was either too smart to try anything with her, or had determined that she was unavailable. Or maybe he'd wait until her inconvenient boyfriend was out of sight. If he thought by having her on his show he could expect her to be grateful beyond just saying thank you, he had another think coming.

At the table Adelle kept Gil Dalhauser company; Ike was busy dancing with a chorus girl.

"Is Dalhauser in their group?" I asked.

"In a left-handed sort of way."

"I heard he's in the trucking unions."

"He works one. Coal hauling. Almost legit. His company sponsors Archy's show. Ike was the one to talk Gil into backing the *Variety Hour*."

That explained all the coal commercials during the station breaks. "Everyone in each other's pockets."

"It's the way things work, kid."

"Dalhauser don't look like he's having much of a good time."

"He don't have to. He's just keeping an eye on his assets."

"Then he must be blind. A woman like Adelle Taylor sitting right there and he looks like he swallowed a bad lemon."

"He's not moving in on Grant's territory, is all."

But Grant didn't act like he cared and seemed oblivious to everything but Bobbi as he floated across the floor with her. I couldn't blame him much, she was a knockout and then some. Adelle's gaze strayed to him now and then, but not in an obvious way. She would make an extraordinary poker player with that air of supreme indifference, except that a sharp person could see she was wearing it like a fur coat in the summer. All I saw in her eyes was pain.

"Later," said Gordy, excusing himself. He went back to the table and spoke to Adelle. She smiled up at him in a brittle way and took his offered arm. The music was down to a slow waltz, which suited him. For a big man he moved well, but anything faster might have strained his dignity. He led her around the floor, managing to look graceful rather than ponderous. Adelle's tension eased, and by the end of the dance she was laughing again. Who'da thought he had it in him?

I thought of cutting in on Bobbi and Grant, but held off. She looked past him and caught my eye, but only winked and smiled. If she'd wanted a rescue she would have mouthed the word "help" and made a face.

Which left me at loose ends, but not bored. From this perch it was like watching a fishbowl. People were still grazing at the food table and making serious headway in exhausting the supply of booze. This inspired louder-than-normal talk and laughter, but no one seemed to mind, even the bouncers looked relaxed, and a few of them had already paired off with some of the chorus. One little redhead was receiving more than her share of attention from two of the bigger guys and seemed to be having trouble making up her mind.

When the waltz ended and the band started up with something faster, Gordy escorted Adelle toward the wings. I wondered if he was going to give her a tour of the renovated backstage or give her the business. Maybe both. I wished him luck.

Ike LaCelle cut in on Grant and took Bobbi away for a few turns. Some of the extra girls threw hopeful looks at Grant, but he headed back to the table to finish his drink. He nodded at Dalhauser, who had not moved, and said something to him. Dalhauser's eyes flashed once in my direction, then moved on. Grant was a little too careful about not glancing my way.

I could figure that Grant was wondering who the hell I was in the setup of things, and any interest he had in me was linked to his interest in Bobbi. Dalhauser couldn't tell him much, only that I was a regular at the joint and for reasons unknown could see Gordy anytime I wanted. There were plenty of other wiseguys who would like to know how I managed that.

Fine, let 'em all guess. No one would believe the truth of it, anyway.

I saw Bobbi's face as she peered past Ike LaCelle's shoulder. He wasn't doing the fox-trot so much as dragging her around in time to the music. She raised both eyebrows high and showed her teeth at me in a kind of sickly grimace.

Jack-to-the-rescue time.

The song ended just as I made it down there; my cutting-in operation went so smoothly Ike didn't know what hit him. Before he could get wise, one of the hardier—or more-determined-to-further-her-career—girls found her way into his grip and off they went. Between the two of them I wasn't sure who was trying to lead.

"You drifted clear in a quiet way," said Bobbi, melting into my arms as we made slow turns.

"From the table? Well, yeah. You and Adelle started speaking in that foreign language."

"On the fashion designers?"

"Sounded like a bunch of passwords to get into a speakeasy to me." I led her gently to the left, looking over her head. Grant and Dalhauser were still talking. "How did you get on with Archy?"

"Do you mean did he ask me for a date?" She giggled at my reaction. "Yes, he did."

"And him engaged and all. He should be ashamed of himself."

"I don't think he knows the meaning of the word, but he did ask very nicely."

"What was your answer?"

"That I don't date guys I'm working for, and I gave Gordy as an example."

"Grant might think you'll date him after the singing job is finished."

"No, he was smart enough to get my meaning. After that he changed subjects. We talked about his work, then about my work, and eventually he brought it around to talking about you."

"*He* brought it around?"

"Took him a while, but he managed. Once I was onto his game it was quite entertaining to see him play."

"What'd you tell him?"

"Only that I thought you were terrific, but he wasn't interested in that."

"What then?"

"Where you came from, what you do. I said you were a writer from Ohio; it seemed the most harmless answer."

"Don't bet on it."

"I don't think he believed me, anyway. Did I do wrong?"

"Never. He probably thinks I'm a jobless gigolo living off my rich and famous girlfriend."

"I'm not rich and famous."

"Not yet, you aren't. After next week, who knows?"

"I can hope so. You going to tell him different?"

"No, if he's so interested in my life, he can ask me for himself."

"Maybe he wants to date *you*," she joked.

I gave her a cockeyed look. "Then you should introduce Archy to your costar."

"Not necessary. He does all right for himself." She nodded toward the remnants of the band. "Bill" was crooning a love song, but directing it toward the trombone player, not the dancers.

"Are they all . . . ?"

"Yes, dear. That's why they didn't want to go home. Lonely is lonely no matter who you are."

She had that pegged solid. I held her closer and counted my blessings. Somehow they all had to do with Bobbi. "This shopping with Adelle, is it part of your business deal?"

"No, just being friends, though it's not without ulterior motive—on her part."

"What does she want?"

"You know the saying about keeping your friends close and enemies closer?"

"Sort of. It sounds like something Charles would come out with."

"I got it from him. That's what Adelle's trying to do."

I swung to the left, then to the right, and realized I'd lost the rhythm. "Say that again until it makes sense to me."

"She sees me as a threat to her place with Archy. Making friends with me might lessen the danger."

"I think I get it."

"So will she. Before the day is out I'll make sure she knows I'm not after Archy and will discourage any move he makes in my direction. She'll be reassured and then we can be real friends."

"She's going to a lot of trouble for a guy who doesn't seem to care much for her."

"But she cares for him—in a big way. They're not officially engaged, that's just the rumor. I think she can do better for herself, but she's too scared to try."

"Scared? Her?"

"She's pushing forty, darling, in a fickle line of work, and unmarried. She's terrified."

"You're kidding. She couldn't be forty."

"It can't be too far off. She was doing movies back when they were shooting stuff in New Jersey. By the time sound came along she was still only getting bit parts. She's been out to Hollywood, but I heard all they'd offer her were chorus parts in one-reelers. The only close-ups she ever got was when they smacked a cream pie in her face. This job with Archy is her last chance to make a name for herself."

"She's doing what you're hoping to do." But Bobbi was much younger and more likely to get spotted.

"And I gotta do it faster or in a couple of years I'll be in the same boat as Adelle: background chorus work or character parts playing the star's mother."

I'd heard it all before during our long talks in the dark when Bobbi told me of her dreams for the future. According to the movies, all women were either young and glamorous or old, overdressed biddies.

"I can help you there," I said. More than once I'd offered to place my own talents at her service. "All I gotta do is have a quick word with Archy and you could be a regular on his show like Adelle."

"I know." The way she said it, so neutral, so closed off, made me lose step again.

"Or . . . I could go outside and jump in the lake. I've tried kicking myself, but it doesn't work so good."

"Oh, Jack, I appreciate you trying to help me with this, I really do—"

"But it's not the way you want to win."

"Exactly."

"Look, it's not that you won't win on your own merits, all you need is to get in front of an audience for five minutes and let them fall in love with you. What I'm thinking is that I just fix it so you have the opportunity to get in front of them in the first place." We'd had this talk time and time again. "It's not cheating for me to hypnotize someone like Archy into giving you a real break. Cheating would be for me to hypnotize everyone in the audience into calling for more, and that's something you do yourself."

She opened and shut her mouth once or twice, then sighed and shook her head, caught halfway between exasperation and affection. "You're a fast-talking nut, Jack, and I love you dearly, but no."

I knew when to back off. "Well, the offer's always there if you ever want to take it."

"Thank you."

"You won't forget?"

"No, not if you'll promise me something."

"Name it."

"That you won't do anything like that and keep it from me."

"But I'd never—"

"Promise?"

I could have gotten annoyed that she would think I'd do anything like that, but considering the guy she'd been with before, I couldn't blame her for needing the reassurance. Besides, when she looked at me like that I'd have gone over Niagara in a leaky barrel full of bricks for her. "Cross my heart and hope to—"

"Oh, jeez, pick another!" She stopped cold, eyes wide. She'd spoken loud enough to draw attention, but had no mind for anyone staring at us.

"—not spit in the wind," I finished lamely.

She stared for a second longer, then fought to relax. "I'm sorry. It's crazy of me to be like this, but—"

"Don't worry about it." We'd each skated too close to death on a couple occasions for any light mention of it to be welcome to her. "You're an artist and allowed to be a little bit crazy. Charles is the same way about that Shakespeare play."

Mentioning his name brought some of her smile back. "Yes, I've heard him talking about it—or rather not talking about it."

I pulled her close and whispered into her ear. "And I'm the one who's sorry. I've said enough dumb things tonight to be drunk. I promise I won't help you unless you ask me to. And I promise never to go behind your back." It was easy enough to say, and being a basically honest person, I knew I'd stick to it.

She drew away just enough to look at me. "Thank you."

"My pleasure."

"No," she said, a mischievous glint in her eyes. "*That* happens later."

"Ho-ho." I pulled her close again and we kept on dancing even after the music stopped.

4

BOBBI had been too optimistic about more romancing that night—or rather that morning. It was after five by the time we reached her hotel, and she was nearly asleep on her feet. Maybe Dracula liked his women unconscious when courting, but not me. I got my girl out of her expensive gown, took her shoes and stockings off, and slipped her between the sheets, thoughtfully tucking her in. She was still in a very affectionate mood, though, and wrapped her arms around me.

"Wish you could stay," she whispered, her eyes drooping shut. "I'd love to wake up next to you."

Not during the day she wouldn't, and we both knew that. Once the sun was up, I was literally dead to the world. I kissed her good morning, but she was already asleep. Nothing left to do but to close the curtains, let myself out, and drive home.

Though still full dark, the city was starting to wake itself, early risers making their sluggish way to diners and drugstores in search of a nickel's worth of hot steaming resuscitation and maybe a plate of ham and eggs. Only the coffee still smelled good to me now, but then it was the one thing that had always smelled better than it tasted. I'd wondered about the possibility of mixing it with livestock blood, whether it would be drinkable or a disaster. Escott was of the opinion that the blood would coagulate when heated enough to percolate through a coffeepot. Ugh. And here I'd only thought of putting the two liquids together in a cup.

Lights still showed at the house when I parked in my usual spot. Escott had either left them on for me or was still up himself. As I came in the front door I heard him call a muted hello from the dining room.

We didn't use it for dining. He'd turned it into a general work area for hobby projects. The big table that had come with the house was scarred but still sturdy. It was presently covered with newspapers, but some of the mess had spread to the floor. That was temporary. He was a fiend for neatness and always thoroughly cleaned up after himself.

"No sleep again?" I asked, slouching in and leaning against the archway that led to the front parlor. The radio there was on, but the music had given way to farm reports.

He grunted an affirmative. He'd wrapped his purple bathrobe over blue-striped pajamas and shoved his feet into brown leather slippers. Bobbi might have had something to say about his color sense, but the rest of the time he was nattily correct in his attire. His face was pale and drawn, with circles under his eyes. I felt bad for him. He looked tired to the bone and painfully sleepy, yet if he tried to surrender to it, nothing would happen. He said drinking booze never worked for him, and he'd sooner shoot himself in the foot than take a sleeping pill.

"How did the opening go?" he asked, without looking up from his work.

"Just great. You were right about a lousy rehearsal making for a great show. You gotta come see it. Bobbi was fantastic. She says thank you for the orchid. It really meant a lot to her."

"I'm very glad. It was my pleasure."

"And Archy Grant was in the audience. He wants Bobbi to do a song on his show this week."

"Who?"

"Archy Grant, the singer-comedian. You've heard his *Variety Hour;* I listen to it most every Tuesday. He's really famous."

"Indeed? I'll take your word for it."

Escott wasn't much for light entertainment unless he was an active participant in creating it, and that hadn't happened since he'd retired from the stage. His favorite shows were along the lines of *The March of Time,* though he usually listened to the *Mercury Theater* with me if I thought to turn it on. I think it was only so he could criticize the shortcomings of their literary adaptations afterward.

"What's the project this time?" I asked. He'd brought in two floor lamps from other parts of the house to give him plenty of light as he concentrated on his close work.

"As you see." His hands were busy, so he nodded. The tabletop was an almighty mess, covered with wood shavings, tools, sawdust, and a hot plate gently heating a disgusting-looking brown substance in an old, scoured-out paint can. When I bothered to sniff, the whole place smelled like a glue factory.

Before him were several crossbows, from a small model that shot little darts, to a granddaddy that hurled foot-long bolts. On the night he first introduced himself to me he'd had that one concealed under a newspaper on his office desk. He'd figured out that I was a vampire and had had it ready in case I proved to be an unfriendly master of the undead. The wood shaft of the bolt was the one item in his line of defense that could have harmed me. As for the cross and garlic cloves he'd had standing by . . . well, I'm not evil, and I don't need to breathe regularly, so folklore failed him there, and just as well for us both.

"Repair work, huh?"

"Yes. Those hooligans that invaded the house did some serious damage to some of my little treasures, so I thought I'd make a start on restoring them. This one's ready for target practice." He was working on the granddaddy, rubbing the walnut stock with lemon oil.

During his days with an acting company he developed a talent for prop making and weaponry and kept them well supplied for their historical productions. Anyone else would have just made something that looked like a crossbow, but not Escott; his props had to actually *work*.

"Looks like you're pretty much finished with all of them. You been at this all night?"

"Couldn't sleep."

I used to know what it was like to lie in the dark, toss and turn, give up, and put on a light hoping to read myself drowsy or take a few shots of booze to knock me out, or both. I'd done my share of pacing, cursing, and praying for sleep that would not come. "Jeez, Charles, I've got an excuse to be up, but you don't. You should see a doctor about this insomnia."

"It'll clear itself soon enough. It usually does."

And he was pretty much correct. He'd go for weeks sleeping soundly, and then hit a patch where all he could do was pace the hall or read or work on stuff like fixing crossbows. Even from my bricked-up sanctuary in the basement I could hear his restless meanderings far into the night. Early on when we started rooming together, I'd offered to hypnotize him into slumber, but he only thanked me and politely refused. When I asked why, he just waved it off like it wasn't important. Bobbi thought it was because once he was asleep he had nightmares. His reaction when I once tried to draw him out on the subject made me think she'd pegged it square.

"Well, try to catch a nap during the day, okay?"

"I'll try. It would make a poor impression on a client telling me his troubles if I nodded off in the middle of things."

"You got plans for the Sommerfeld case tomorrow?"

"Actually, it already *is* tomorrow, and I've nothing at the moment. That may be changed by the time you're up and around, so be prepared for some evening work."

"It's the only kind I know."

I pushed away from the arch and trudged upstairs to shuck my clothes onto hangers or into the laundry basket. I used to just drop stuff on the furniture, but now that I was buying classy goods I took better care of things. Some of Escott's passion for neatness must have rubbed off on me. I put on some pajama bottoms so as to be decent in case of a fire, then went invisible and slipped down through the floors to the basement.

My hiding place was just under the kitchen. It was an alcove bricked off from the rest of the basement; access to it for anyone who wasn't a vampire was through a well-concealed trapdoor under the kitchen table. Escott had built it all himself, and only he, myself, and Bobbi knew the trick of opening it. Most of the time it was covered by a throw rug. I never used the trap, it was easier to just filter down through the creaks in the joints as I did now.

I'd left a light burning to spare me from materializing in total darkness. Without any openings to the outside except for a narrow air shaft, my night-sensitive eyes were as useless as anyone's in this pit.

Actually, calling it a pit was unfair, for it was a rather comfortable refuge, and, despite my precaution with the pajama pants, fireproofed. For my daylight comas I had a sturdy cot topped with clean linen; beneath the bedding was a layer of my home earth between protective sheets of heavy oilcloth. Maybe it wasn't the Ritz, but since I was completely unconscious a real bed and mattress weren't a necessity to me.

Against the wall was a desk I'd set up for my writing, working down here so as not to disturb Escott in the wee hours. It held my battered traveling typewriter along with stacks of paper, pencil stubs, and a collection of rejection slips that increased every time one of my stories came back. I'd been a pretty good reporter, but the rules for fiction were very different, and I was still trying to figure them out. Some nights I felt like I was reinventing the wheel while everyone else raced along in new Cadillacs.

Escott had once suggested I write what I knew, that I should write a story about a vampire. I suggested, as politely as possible, that he try his hand at scribbling a detective yarn. He shot me a sour look that meant I'd made my point, and thereafter kept his brainstorms to himself. I suppose I could have made an effort, but it just wasn't a topic I wanted to tackle. My tastes ran more along the lines of *The Shadow* and *Doc Savage*. I'd sent proposals to the publishers of those magazines, but never heard back from them. I had a friend in the business who told me that becoming a house writer was anything but easy, but I was anxious to get something—anything— published.

Well, I *had* been anxious. After going through the wringer a couple of months ago a lot of the creative juice had been squeezed right out of me. I'd been threatened by, come close to, and even delivered death in a very short span of time, and the importance I'd once attached to my literary efforts had been seriously diminished by a brutal reality I still sometimes shuddered over. The anxious fire inside had either gone out or was buried deep under the ashes, and I was too tired to dig for it or light it anew. And maybe too rich. With the dough I had stashed away in Escott's safe I had no real need to write for extra cash; I was having too good a time spending the stuff I had. It helped me forget about the wringer.

As I lay back on the cot all the familiar excuses for why I'd not put any work in on the typewriter bubbled up inside all over again. I was too busy right now; I didn't feel inspired; Bobbi needed me; Escott had a job for me, and so forth. A litany of laziness—or so nagged an all-too-pragmatic voice in my head.

To hell with it. I'll deal with it tomorrow.

My last thought as the sun came up and stole away consciousness.

The fault-finding litany was also my first thought the following night, reinforced by opening my eyes on the unchanged room. It was almost as though I'd not slept at all, which was true in a way. What swept over me wasn't normal human slumber; anyone finding me would find a dead man until the sun went down. I was always physically restored, but mental rest was trickier to achieve.

Unless something especially disruptive intruded, whatever was eating at me when I conked out would still be gnawing away upon waking.

At least now I could escape the reminders of my failure for the time being. I vanished and floated up to the kitchen, leaving my typewriter and its stack of clean, unmarred paper behind to collect a little more dust and guilt. Come morning I'd face it again with another pang of conscience, but until then I could ignore it.

Escott wasn't home, but he left a note on the kitchen table asking me to come by his office. I phoned there to see if he was still in. He was.

"What's cooking for tonight?" I asked.

"Just a little reconnoitering at a certain gentleman's abode."

"The kissing bandit from the other night?"

"Exactly."

Out of habit he was usually pretty cagey over the phone on the off chance that it might be tapped. That had happened once. We hadn't liked it much. "Working clothes?"

"Yes, by all means."

Which meant no tuxedo. I rang off and went up for a quick bath and shave and pawed through my closet for appropriate attire. I found a black shirt that used to go with a snow-white tie, but Bobbi said they made me look like a cheap movie gangster. I thought I'd looked pretty sharp, but since I was handicapped when it came to mirrors, I usually took her advice on clothing. The tie got a bloodstain on it—I'd been careless feeding once—and I had to throw it out anyway. The shirt came in handy for jobs like the one ahead tonight. I pulled on some black pants and a wool pea jacket, leather gloves, a cloth hat, and my gum-soled shoes. Any cop worth his salt would look twice at me while I was in this suspicious getup, but I always took care never to be seen.

I locked the house, hopped in my Buick, and drove toward the office, taking a route that passed by the Stockyards. I could comfortably go two nights between feedings, three in a pinch, and four if absolutely forced to, but rarely pushed things that far. Every other night kept me sated and happy, and a lot less likely to make mistakes with people. I'd nearly gone over the edge once for lack of self-control. Never again.

Bloodsmell everywhere on the cold wind when I parked. You couldn't escape it any more than you could escape the perpetual stench of manure and churned-up mud. The nation had to eat and this was the place that turned Bossy into dinner. Though I kept clear of the processing areas, I knew it was basic, brutal, and organized into mechanical efficiency. If people had to actually see the procedures that brought a steak or pork chop to their table, they'd probably quit and eat Cornflakes instead.

I did what everyone did, though, and consciously ignored the smells and din and made my way to one of the holding pens. There I would always find a cow docile enough to stand still while I bit through its tough flesh, opening up a leg vein. If the animal was restive, my acquired talent for hypnosis usually worked to calm it down. The only time I had real trouble was during thunderstorms, but if the weather was rough I just skipped going that night.

Escott thought I should keep a bottle of blood in the refrigerator for emergencies, and I'd tried, but it wasn't too practical to acquire, and the stuff went bad pretty fast.

It was drinkable, but not all that satisfying. I preferred it hot and living from the animal, not siphoned off through a needle and rubber hose into a spare milk bottle.

Tonight's repast finished the job of waking me up completely as my body and mind flooded with the joyous heat of it. I always felt stronger, more alert afterward, making the trek through the appalling surroundings worth the trip.

But once finished, I quit the Stockyards gladly enough and finished my drive to the office. Escott's big Nash was the only car parked on the street at this hour. When the wind was blowing in the wrong direction no one working here lingered in the neighborhood if they could help it. Hell, even when the wind was blowing in the right direction everyone seemed to hoof it home fast. I hoofed it upstairs and let myself in.

God bless him, Escott was stretched out on the army cot he kept in the inner room for just such occasions. He wasn't fully asleep, though, just dozing. I could tell the difference by his breathing and heartbeat. Still, I hated to interrupt even this small a rest. He sat up slowly and swung his feet to the floor.

"You look like hell," I said amiably.

"No doubt, and you're looking disagreeably rested and fit."

I spread my hands, palms out. "What's the scoop for tonight?"

He went to the washroom and splashed cold water on his face, then scrubbed dry with a clean towel. "A little break-in job on our blackmailing fellow. McCallen will be out for the evening, allowing you time to make a thorough inspection of his flat and hopefully find the envelope containing Miss Sommerfeld's letters. When she called today she was somewhat less than pleased with my progress. I'm hoping your work tonight might improve her mood."

I'd done this sort of operation before, and because of it Escott's business had benefited to the point where he was considered to be something of a miracle worker. We were both well aware that it was completely illegal, but with me on the payroll the chances of our getting away clean were one hundred percent. On the one occasion when I had been surprised by a belligerent adversary, I not only hypnotized him into forgetting the whole thing, but persuaded him to turn over the item I'd been trying to find.

"When do we leave?"

"Now, if you're ready," he said, buttoning his vest and pulling on his coat.

"Fine with me, but I think you need some coffee."

"That might not be amiss, but I'd rather not squander the opportunity while we have it." He put on his hat and topcoat, locked the joint, and I followed him down to his Nash.

A special body shop had done a remarkable job at repairing the pockmarks left by a machine-gun strafing. The insides, protected by thick steel and bulletproof glass, were untouched, as was the motor, which started up smooth as a purring cat. Escott had bought it used from an old friend of his, Shoe Coldfield, who was now the head of one of the larger mobs in Chicago's Bronze Belt. The two of them had been in the same acting company in Canada years ago before drifting apart to end up on opposite sides of the law. How that happened I still wasn't sure, but I was glad of Coldfield's shady profession. Because of it, the protective refinements he'd added to his former property had once saved Escott's life.

Escott drove without hurry, but without wasting time or saying much. He still looked tired, and I wondered whether all of it had to do with the bout of insomnia or if it was boredom with the case. While Miss Sommerfeld was a more than generous employer, the job was not the sort to seriously challenge the resources of the agency— i.e., Escott himself. He craved mental stimulation and had a near addiction to physical danger, both of which were absent this time around. The closest threat we'd had was the scuffle with McCallen in the café—kid's stuff. Not that I minded having things this quiet. Maybe it contributed to Escott's insomnia, but at least he wasn't in danger of getting himself killed.

"How'd the day go?" I asked.

"The same as the previous one, but singularly lacking in new clients. I turned down yet another divorce case."

"You could get rich on those."

"Too sordid for my taste, old man. I think it would be better for society in general to do away with the whole business of marriage altogether. It would make things much simpler for the concerned parties to divest them-selves of each other without going through all that expensive hoop jumping to obtain grounds for divorce."

"There'd be hell to pay in other areas then."

"Yes, but the law courts would be freed up to try true criminal cases, and armies of lawyers would have to find some other type of work."

Just what the country needed—unemployed lawyers standing in the breadlines. "Well, maybe what they do in Reno will spread to the rest of the country."

"All unnecessary if a couple doesn't marry in the first place."

"It might be tough for their kids, though."

"Not if society accepts them as being no different from any other children."

I'd heard his opinion on the issue of marriage before. Some of it made sense, and some didn't. It mostly boiled down to the certainty that Escott wasn't going to commit that particular social crime if he could help himself. He touched on a few related subjects during the drive, and I gladly listened. It seemed to cheer him up to have someone around.

Jason McCallen lived near the University of Chicago, in a stuffy, tree-shaded neighborhood. The buildings ran mostly to two-story jobs, brick, and bunched close against one another. They looked cheap, but fairly comfortable. The fronts had a postage-stamp patch of dead grass and steps that went straight up to the doors, no porches. A narrow alley walkway led around to the backyards and most of those were blocked off by wrought-iron fences. The house we wanted was dark.

"Where's McCallen tonight?" I asked.

"He's a regular at a bar one block from here and spends several evenings a week there with his cronies. Miss Sommerfeld used to go with him and told me of his routine. He should stay until about half-past ten, walk home, go to bed, then drive to work at seven. That's his car over there." He nodded to a four-year-old black Ford parked across and down from us.

"What's he do?"

"He still works at the plant."

That surprised me. "I thought her family didn't like him."

"They didn't like the idea of their daughter associating with him, but he's good at his job, so they kept him on."

"That's pretty fair-minded. Ever think he might have something on her folks as well?"

"It's a possibility, but if so, then it's only enough to keep him at his present post, but not sufficient to promote him."

I got a flashlight from the glove compartment, went invisible, and floated across the street toward the house gate. I materialized long enough to get my bearings, then went up the steps and sieved through the cracks around the door. Good thing for me and for Escott's business that I didn't have to bother about getting an invitation before crossing any new threshold.

Once inside, I went completely solid and took a moment to listen on the off chance that Escott's information was less than perfect, but all was quiet. The shades were down, so my bobbing flashlight beam would be less likely to be seen by curious neighbors. I could have searched just as well without the flash, but I wanted to be thorough.

It helped that the house wasn't large, McCallen had few furnishings, and kept them basically tidy. Most of the stuff looked like it had come piecemeal from a secondhand store. Nothing matched, but it seemed to be of good quality. He bought what he needed and no more. A big chair with a floor lamp looming over it appeared to be his favorite roost downstairs. Within easy reach of it was a table with a radio. Scattered on the floor around was a stack of newspapers, another of magazines, and another of books. He had lots of those lodged in a number of bookshelves. I didn't bother getting nosy about titles; I was here to find the envelope, not a handle on his character. I flipped through the papers and magazines and turned out any books large enough to hide an envelope, then flipped the chair over and checked there. Everything went back the way I found it, and I moved on to other areas.

In ten minutes I'd given the downstairs a good once-over, hitting all the obvious places. Nothing jumped out at me, though I did startle a cat and vice versa. The thing hissed at me and shot upstairs, and if my heart had been working it would have given out just then. I eventually followed the cat, thinking that if McCallen had hidden the goods anywhere, it would be in his bedroom. I spent half an hour there, going through the bureau, the closet, every shelf, every cranny, under the bed, behind the bed, under the mattress. At the risk of getting caught I turned on the light for a second to see if he might have tossed the goods up into the suspended overhead globe, but it was empty.

That left the rest of the place to cover, and I was starting to get frustrated and was wishing that Escott was along. Maybe he couldn't disappear at the drop of a bullet, but an extra pair of hands and eyes would have helped speed things. I checked the undersides of furniture and drawers to see if McCallen had taped anything there and did a fine-tooth comb routine all around a desk. It was stuffed with all kinds of papers, mostly handwritten, but not the ones I wanted.

Once finished with that, I hit the ground floor all over again, getting more detailed. I even checked the sleeves to his phonograph records to see if all they held was music. They did.

The basement was next. This time I turned on the lights. It was dank and cool except near the furnace, with lots of crannies and dust, which proved helpful. Where it was thick and undisturbed I didn't have to look so closely. To judge by the footprints, he hadn't been down here in a while anyway. I went back up.

Two hours gone. I was nearly out of time and nothing to show for it. My guess was that McCallen had taken the stuff with him or hidden it in some other location, possibly even at his workplace. I'd looked at the tops of all the bookshelves and under all the rugs. The cat got over his fear of me and came out. While checking the icebox I found a plate of cooked fish and gave him a sliver or two. In a transport of feline affection he kept trying to turn figure eights around my ankles, meowing for more. A nuisance, but he gave me an idea, and I went up to the bathroom, where McCallen had a long flat aluminum pan full of sand for his pet. The envelope had been slipped exactly under it.

Feeling pretty cocky, I gave the cat another sliver of fish and quit the place a few seconds later. Materializing across the street in a dense patch of tree shadow, I walked up to the car where Escott patiently waited. I half expected him to be asleep, but he had his eyes open, keeping himself occupied by puffing on his pipe. He perked up when I waved the envelope at him. I opened the passenger door, letting out a cloud if tobacco smoke, and boosted inside.

"Excellent!" he said, looking pleased. "Are you sure it's the right one?"

"I took a gander and found a lot of stuff in a woman's writing. Didn't bother to read it."

He accepted the flashlight from me and looked for himself. "That's her hand all right." I told him where it had been stashed and he chuckled and congratulated me on the fit of genius.

"McCallen's gonna be madder'n hell when he finds out," I said.

"I've no doubt of that, but he won't be able to accuse Miss Sommerfeld of robbery without incriminating himself. If he becomes a nuisance, then your talent for persuasion might be necessary."

"Sure, just hope that he's sober." My hypnosis didn't work so well on drunks. "What now?"

"A swift delivery to our client and that should conclude things for us—if you have the time for it?"

"Yeah, sure. I always wanted to see how a cracker heiress lives." The evening was still young for me. Plenty of time before Bobbi's last show. If there was no party afterward, I could take her to some all-night place for food, and then back to her flat for a little drink if she was in the mood.

Escott put the Nash in gear and drove a few miles west. Miss Sommerfeld lived in what the fancier estate agents might call a honeymooners' cottage. It wasn't big, but had plenty of frills, standing on its own lot surrounded by a prissy-looking picket fence that wouldn't keep out a determined Mexican hairless. The shutters, which were for decoration only, were painted pink and had little heart shapes cut into them. The window set in the front door was also heart-shaped. I'd seen something like it in a cartoon. The architect must have tied one on during Valentine's Day and this was what he'd designed during the hangover.

She had a lace curtain covering the window and twitched it aside after Escott's knock. Her eyes went wide as soon as she saw us, and she instantly unlocked the door and welcomed us in.

"Good news for you, Miss Sommerfeld," said Escott, handing her the envelope with a little bow that only English guys can get away with and not look awkward.

She went nuts in a happy kind of way for a few minutes, squealing, hopping, dancing around, and breathlessly thanking him half a dozen times. When she calmed down enough to remember herself, she invited us into her living room and offered to make coffee. Escott accepted, and while she went to the kitchen to fix things, he dropped onto her couch and allowed himself to deflate a bit. I felt tired just looking at him.

Her place wasn't as fussily decorated as one might expect from its Swiss-chalet exterior. She had a few quality antiques mixed with quality modern, and the abstract paintings were expensive originals. When she came back with a tray of coffee and cookies, I asked if one of the paintings was by Evan Robley.

She was surprised and pleased. "Why, yes. You're familiar with his work?"

"I met him a few times before last Christmas. He's a nice guy."

"You *met* him! How interesting!" She launched into the source of the painting, some gallery I never heard of, and how she'd fallen in love with the colors and lines sprawling over the big canvas. "I can't tell you why I like it, but I just do. It is beautiful, isn't it? *Quite* my favorite."

I agreed with her and stood about ten feet away from the thing. As I'd thought, this was one of Evan's specialty works. From any other angle, from any other distance, it was an abstract, but if you looked at it just right and focused hard, the hidden image he painted into the thing would reveal itself. Or in this case *him*self. Evan favored doing highly disguised self-portraits of his favorite piece of his own anatomy. Escott raised one eyebrow, apparently recalling what I'd once told him about Evan's art, but I kept my mouth shut. Miss Sommerfeld's sensibilities were safe with me.

Escott accepted a cup of black straight and did not provide her with details on how we recovered her papers. "The method is not as important as the fact that they are now in your possession. Mr. McCallen will likely be furious when he discovers what's happened, so I hope you will take all necessary precautions to protect yourself."

"But he wouldn't hurt me . . . or do you think—"

"It has been my experience that when one has prepared a defense against the darker side of human nature, one never suffers regret when it attempts a mischief."

"Yes, I suppose he might try getting back at me."

"Are you armed?"

She blinked, slightly shocked. "I've got a .22 in the nightstand, but I don't think I'll need it against him. He's a lot of brag and bluster, but he would never hurt me."

"Famous last words," I said.

Her mouth sagged open.

Escott looked her hard in the eye. "Forgive my partner's bluntness, Miss Sommerfeld, but you should take what he says to heart. I would prefer you to be safe rather than sorry."

Some of the color went out of her and she stammered out a thin thank-you for his concern. After that it was a question of her signing a last receipt, and then we left.

Escott made sure she had one of his cards with the home, office, and his answering-service numbers on it.

"Call us if you feel uneasy about anything, and call the police instantly at the least sign of trouble," he said.

She promised to do so and firmly locked her door behind us.

"Think she bought it?" I asked as we settled into the car again.

"One may hope so."

"Are you really worried about her?"

"A little. She's all by herself." Escott had a streak of white knight in him. "Although my contact with McCallen has been brief, I would judge him to be too intelligent to make further trouble, but . . ."

"He could be Einstein and still fly off the handle and do something crazy," I concluded.

"Unfortunately, yes. I'll phone her tomorrow to make sure she's all right."

"Be careful. With all that attention she might dump that prince of hers for you."

"If you insist on being absurd, I shan't stop you."

"What about me discouraging McCallen?"

"Only if he becomes a nuisance."

"If I get to him first then he won't be."

"I'm willing to give him the benefit of the doubt."

"Famous last words," I said cheerfully.

Once we were back at the office, he counted out fifty dollars in bills and handed them to me.

I grimaced. "You know I don't need this."

"Of course you don't need it, but you have earned it. You did all the work tonight, and are more than entitled to your share of the payment. Take it so my books will balance."

I took it. "You heading home?"

"After a stop or two."

"Make sure one of 'em's an eatery. McCallen's cat is better fed than you."

He gave an amused snort and promised to see to his nutritional requirements before too much time passed. I wanted to tell him to get some sleep if he could, but bit it off. He could look after himself. Most of the time.

In my own car again, I drove a few blocks to a telegram office and bought a twenty-five-dollar money wire, arranging to have it delivered to my folks in Cincinnati Monday. The profits from the hardware business had dropped after the Wall Street crash, and Dad needed the help. My brothers and sisters had their own families and worries and couldn't spare much themselves; I was the happy exception and sent something every month. I had to be careful, though. If I sent too much too often, Mom would demand to know where it all was coming from, and I never did learn how to lie to her, not face-to-face. It was easier in a letter or over the phone.

So far as my family was concerned I'd quit the not-too-terribly-respectable newspaper game in New York and gotten a steady job in a Chicago ad agency, working at writing copy for the very eccentric Mr. Escott. He didn't give me much time off, so I couldn't come home for visits just yet, but he was generous with bonuses for good work. Whenever I got a bonus I'd send it home to Mom with my compliments and the assurance that I had enough left over to live on.

Not one of them knew about the vampire stuff, and I had no plans to ever tell them. I didn't know how. It was just too private.

The whole business about exchanging blood, getting killed, and rising from the dead was not something I could easily talk about to anyone, much less my parents. Sure, they loved me, but I knew them well enough to know they simply would not understand what had happened. It was completely outside their safe and sane world. Telling them would change things between us, and the change would not be to the good.

I'd done the same shut-mouth routine when I'd come back from the war. Some of the horrors I'd seen weren't worth recalling or repeating, so I just kept them to myself and told amusing stories about army life instead. To hear me talk you'd think I'd been on one long holiday. A lot of funny stuff did happen, so I wasn't lying, only leaving out what was bad. The folks were better off not knowing some of the things their youngest child had had to do then.

Of course, some of the things I did now weren't that much of an improvement.

There was one more place to go before I could run home, change to a suit, and get to the club and Bobbi. It called for a long drive, picking my way through block after block until I crossed into what was pretty much a separate city within the city—the Bronze Belt, as it was called by the white people, where Chicago's Negro population flourished. Whites did not venture here if they could help it, but I'd appointed myself the exception and sailed in.

Some spots were full of activity, taverns and churches mostly, not much different from any other part of the town. I drove past, stopped at the lights when I had to, and got stared at a lot. Most people were indifferent, a few were hostile, for which I had no blame. If times were tough everywhere, they were twice as tough here.

I found the place I wanted, but no close parking space. After circling the block once, I eased into an opening a few dozen yards away, got out, and locked up. A man jeered at me and another told him to shut up. There was definitely something to this dressing tough.

The building I wanted was old, like those surrounding it, and in just slightly better repair. Lights were on in many of the windows, spilling out onto the cracked pavement. It was surprising just how many people were taking the trouble to stop and watch me walk.

The door to the building got shoved open just before I reached it, and a large brown man emerged. He wore a white cook's apron covered with stains. He brought with him the smell of hot oil and raw onions.

"Hi, Sal," I said, putting my hand out to him. "Thought I'd come by for a visit."

Sal frowned at my hand and rubbed his own on the apron. "Miss Trudence is out on a call right now. You best come by another time."

His boss lady was a nurse and frequently away from the place. "That's too bad. I brought a little contribution to the cause. Will you give it to her when she returns?"

"She don't want no mob money."

"I know the rules, and it ain't mob money. I earned it fair and square doing a job for Charles Escott. She can call him and check if she wants."

"Got no phone here."

"I forgot."

"Maybe you should come back later."

"And maybe you got kids that need milk right now. Just give this to her for me, will you?" I took two tens and a five and held it out to him, better than a week's good wages in this neighborhood.

He scowled like I'd offered him a month-old fish. "How you know I won't just keep it?"

"Because you work for Miss Tru, and God help anyone who doesn't play square with her."

The scowl relaxed a little. "You say it's honest?"

"Word of honor. I've done this before. She knows I'm okay."

"Well . . . I guess." He took the cash and shoved it in a pocket. "You wanta come in or anything?"

Behind him was the unnamed haven Trudence Coldfield ran as best she could against the hard times and overwhelming odds. Her one-woman crusader's palace was usually crowded with women and kids, victims of hard luck, hard life, or both. She offered shelter, food, healing, and advice, and in return expected them to put work into the place as part of their payback. She'd helped me when I needed it once, but my payback took the form of cash donations. I wasn't sure how Sal fit into the picture, whether he was her boyfriend or just friend, but he did seem to be second-in-command of things.

"I might scare the kids," I said. His lukewarm attitude clued me on the proper response to his invitation. Inside I could hear people talking and a radio playing.

Sal unbent a little more. "Yeah, they might think you a ghost 'r something."

"Tell Miss Tru I said hello."

"Okay." He stood and watched as I went back down the street again. I couldn't tell if it was motivated by suspicion or to keep an eye on me. Not so many people stared this time.

"Hey! White boy! What business you got here? You looking to get your ass kicked?"

I would have kept going, but the voice was familiar and coming from a shiny new Nash that had pulled up behind and was pacing me. Shoe Coldfield was in the backseat. He'd partly rolled down a thick, bulletproof window to yell at me.

I walked over, grinning, and the car stopped. "Hey, yourself. How you doing? Isham, is that you?"

The driver turned enough to throw me a smile and nod.

Coldfield opened the back door, and I climbed in. "Isham, take us around the block a few times."

5

"How the hell you doing?" Coldfield asked, settling back into the thick upholstery. "And what the hell you doing at my sister's place?"

"Trying to give it a bad name. What's your excuse?"

"I got a call that a tall, skinny white guy dressed like a longshoreman drove into the neighborhood. Thought it might be you."

"The hell you say. You've got people watching the place?"

"'Course I do, but don't let Trudence know or she'll kill me."

To say that Trudence Coldfield disapproved of her younger brother's work would be an outrageous under-statement. He didn't seem to be bothered by her wither-ing opinion, however, mostly shrugging it off and acting humble when in her presence.

"Watching as in guarding?"

"You betcha. Lots of guys know we're related. If something goes bad against them from me, they might try to get back by hurting her. Tru's plenty tough, but there's some stuff goes on that would sink her in two seconds. She's about the only family I got left, so I look out for her whether she wants it or not."

"It must be quite a setup if it brings you around so fast."

"It is, but I was out and about anyway. Heard there was a good act playing at the Hearts Club. Thought I'd see if it was good enough for the Shoe Box." That was his own nightclub. He only booked the best.

"Is that why you're in the hats?" I indicated the derbies he and Isham sported. Each had a diamond-trimmed horseshoe pinned to the band. Al Capone's gang favored pearl-gray fedoras.

"Yeah. Gotta advertise now and then, just so people know I'm around and seeing to their interests."

"You're looking better than you did the last I saw." Back in February, Coldfield had been caught in the middle of a dozen or so pounding fists and kicking feet in a budding gang war that wasn't his own. I'd waded in to help clear things. He'd emerged out of it bruised and bloodied, but with some self-respect intact. I'd dragged back one of the fleeing mobsters so Coldfield could give him a lesson in fair fighting. We left what remained at a nearby hospital for repairs.

"I should hope so. Got a knot in one arm that's been slow to go away, but the rest healed up fine."

"Glad to hear it."

"How's Charles doing?"

"Same as ever. Not too happy about pitching out all the divorce cases that keep coming in, and he's been having another bout with the insomnia."

"He should see a doctor."

"That's what I tell him. He just changes the subject. Why's he so allergic to them?"

Coldfield shrugged. "He's not allergic, he just thinks he can handle everything himself, and most of the time he can."

"People don't have insomnia for no reason. I know what used to keep me awake. What's eatin' Charles?"

Another shrug. "It's his business. If he wants to tell you he will. Other than that, he's a private man. Respect it."

I'd heard that speech before. Coldfield had once suggested I get Escott stinking drunk if I wanted to hear him talk about himself. Not an easy thing to do with only one person doing all the drinking. Of alcohol, that is.

Coldfield told me Escott just needed to get out more. "Look, it's been a while since we all socialized, why don't you bring Charles over to the club this week for some food? I just hired a French-trained cook up from Orleans."

"Does he do blood pudding?"

He choked and shot me a sharp look at the reminder, suppressed a smile, then glanced at Isham. Isham did not appear to have heard. Coldfield knew about the vampire stuff and for some reason thought it to be completely hilarious that I should be in the dread ranks of the undead. "You can bring your own food," he muttered. "Or whatever."

"Or I can watch the show. Who you got in this week?"

He gave me the short version. The blues man playing there was good, but he did a couple numbers that nearly shut the place down. Some white cops had shoved their way into the club, having heard that obscene lyrics were being sung there. "Not what I would call obscene," said Coldfield. "Bo was doin' 'My Pencil Won't Write No More.' The cops were looking to make an arrest, but they listened to the whole thing and were so damned grass green that they didn't understand it."

I'd heard the song and it was plenty suggestive, but didn't have any actual swear words in the lyrics. "What'd they do?"

"Took ten bucks apiece from me not to break heads and went away. Wasn't even their beat. I made a phone call to the police captain I pay to keep this kinda thing from happening. He said they'd stay outta my territory from now on."

"Think they will?"

"If they know what's good for everyone. I can't have white cops taking graft that ain't theirs. It upsets the balance of everything when guys like that strike out on their own."

I made commiserating sounds.

"Besides, that captain knows if others come in an' take from me, then there's less to pass on to him."

"What a world."

"It's the way things work," he said, sounding remarkably like Gordy. "You wanta come along to the Hearts and see that act?" He knew I liked blues.

"I'm not dressed for anything fancy. I wouldn't want to lower the tone of the joint. Next time. We'll make a night of it."

"Yeah, being seen with you like this would be bad for my reputation. What's with the getup?"

"Charles had a job for me tonight. I finished, got paid, and swung by here to throw some cash at your sister's place."

"That's mighty nice of you."

"Bread on the water, I figure. She helped me in a big way that time. I owe her."

He snorted. "If she'd let me I could really help her with that half-assed soup kitchen she runs." Trudence had very strict rules about allowing riffraff into her haven, and that included her own brother. "She just can't see that it don't matter so much where the money comes from so long as it ends up in a good place. I tried telling her I was kinda like Robin Hood, but she wouldn't have any of it and told me I should leave Sherwood Forest and get a real job in Nottingham working for the sheriff. That· woman . . ."

"It might be a little difficult," I conceded.

"Ha! 'Cept for some acting experience and knowing how to shine shoes I got no skills the rest of the world wants, but I *am* good at *this*." He gestured at the car and the neighborhood beyond. I took it to mean his organizational abilities at running his gang. He could have taken those skills anywhere in the business world and done well for himself—if he'd been white.

Coldfield dropped me at my car and drove off after I promised to tell Escott about the French cooking. He was out when I returned to the house; the news would have to wait. I got into a suit, and went to the Nightcrawler in time for the last of the second show. Things were much the same as before, lively, but without the tense, worried energy of an opening-night crowd. The performance was getting good reviews and the customers were getting their money's worth, so everyone was happy.

Walking into the lobby, I skipped checking my hat and coat when I saw some familiar faces and spent some time saying hello. Most of them were mob and had business dealings with Gordy, but pretty nice guys when they weren't working. Gil Dalhauser was at the outer bar, his long frame slung onto a stool, his sleepy-looking eyes missing nothing. He nodded at me, so I went over.

"Have anything?" he asked, ready to signal the bartender.

"Thanks, but later. Can I stand you one?"

"I'm fine with this." It was a double, and he could nurse one of those for an hour or more. I'd seen him do it at the party.

"In for more fun and games?" I asked, meaning the show.

"I came with the others. They're inside."

"Who? Grant and LaCelle?"

Dalhauser nodded. "Came over here with the Taylor dame. Gordy took her into the private club an hour ago."

Interesting. "I heard she was engaged to Grant."

"She thinks she is."

"What's the real story with them?"

He shook his head, which said a lot to me, mostly that Bobbi had been right and Grant wasn't interested in Adelle. And that it was hard for me to make conversation with a man who was obviously related to a clam. Things might have been different if I could have joined Dalhauser for a drink, but that was impossible.

"I don't want to miss what's left of the show," I said. "I'll see you around."

"Fleming."

He stopped me just as I turned away. I turned back. "Yeah?"

"Watch out for Grant."

"How so?"

"Just keep clear of him. Consider it a friendly warning."

"You can't tell me something like that and not give details."

"Actually, I can." Nothing came out from behind those cold blue eyes. He took a drink and lowered the level in his glass by an eighth of an inch.

I looked hard at him. "Explain."

His expression clouded for an instant, then reasserted itself. Too quickly. Great, slow drinker or not, he'd had enough booze tonight to make hypnosis difficult. If I pressed any harder it would attract attention or put him on guard if I failed. I eased off, frowning.

"Only trying to do you a favor, kid," he said.

Maybe Gordy would have a line on this. "Yeah, thanks a lot."

I left him and went on into the club proper.

The lights were down except for those on the dance-floor stage. I didn't have much trouble navigating the smoke-filled dimness; I never do. Bobbi wasn't on just yet; the Melodians' crooner was doing his solo part, singing to some overdressed dowager who looked happy enough to burst. The teacup number was yet to come.

Gordy's table had a different set of people tonight. I didn't know any of them and figured he'd left it free for paying customers. Ike LaCelle had a spot off to the right on the second tier. There was a blond woman next to him who sort of looked like Carole Lombard but just a little plump. She was dressed flashy and laughed too hard at everything he whispered to her, and he laughed too hard back. They were having a fine time. I didn't want to sit just yet and parked myself behind an empty spot on the third tier rail to watch the show.

Just as I was wondering where Archy Grant might be and speculating why I should be wary of him, the crooner ended his song, and Ted Drew got his Melodians to strike up a familiar fanfare. The crooner turned and started clapping, looking upstage, and the spotlight swung from him to the right-hand wings. Archy Grant, looking fresh and thumbtack sharp, burst from them waving both arms and giving his signature grin to the rising applause as he was recognized. The music, which was the theme number to his radio show, faded as he stepped up to the microphone and introduced himself. To judge by the loud response, everyone knew him.

He explained how he thought *The Shanghai Review* was so good he had to get in on it to bring it down to his level. This got a laugh, then he said he'd wanted to join in on the fun for just one song if no one minded. Nobody did, and he launched into one of his standbys.

Grant was a good showman, practiced and polished, with a knack for making it look unrehearsed. He played to the audience, using his own brand of energy to get each to think he was singing only for them. By the time he finished the song most of the women looked like they'd just fallen in love with him. He bowed, grinned, and thanked everyone, then told them all to give a big welcome to the real star of the show, Bobbi Smythe. The lights went out, and when they came back, the crooner stood in Archy's place, ready to begin the teacup number. Bobbi and her sailor costar came out with the chorus and went to work.

I stayed and watched to see if there was anything new about it—there wasn't—and to just enjoy the performance. When it finished, I threaded through the crowd to get into the gambling room. Quite a few customers were ahead of me; the guard at the door just nodded as I eased past on the side.

While some were busy getting chips, I strolled by tables, checking for familiar faces. Adelle Taylor was at one of the roulette wheels, staring hard as it turned. She had quite a stack of chips before her, and her face was glowing. She had every right; at a rough count she must have had four grand in front of her. That struck me as strange, since the odds favored the house—in this place more than most. Then I spotted Gordy standing alone off to one side, watching her win his money. His normally impassive face bore a pleased expression.

So *that* was the way of things. I hated to interrupt his daydreaming, but went over.

"'Lo, Fleming," he said when I got close enough.

"'Lo, yourself. Another big night on your hands. I saw Archy Grant put in an appearance."

"His idea. I'm not gonna turn him down. How'd it go?"

"He livened things up. Made a big deal over Bobbi when he turned the stage back to her."

"Good. Real good."

"I saw Dalhauser. He gave me some kind of cockeyed warning about staying away from Grant. I tried to get him to explain why, but he wouldn't."

His gaze went from Adelle to me. "Warning?"

"He said for me to stay out of Grant's way, called it doing me a favor. The way he said it was like Grant could be a threat to me."

Gordy's mouth stretched slightly. Any more effort and it might have turned into a chuckle. "That'll be the day."

"Any ideas why Grant would have it in for me?"

"He likes Bobbi. You're her man. You wouldn't be the first guy he asked Ike to take care of so he could have a clear field with a woman."

"LaCelle an enforcer?" I snorted. "Come on, Gordy."

"Ike wouldn't do it himself, but he'd know where to find guys who would."

"Grant could have had his pick of any of the girls last night—"

"Except Bobbi."

"Except Bobbi. Are you saying he has guys killed so he can get dates?" I found that just too hard to believe.

"Not killed. Pushed around. Paid off. Nothing flashy enough to draw the law in."

"That's crazy."

He gave a minimal shrug. "I seen crazier. When he finds something he likes, he goes for it."

"Not this time he won't."

"No need to get on your hind legs for this. I'll have a word with Ike before he leaves. Make sure he knows not to do anything stupid concerning you. He can pass it to Grant."

"I'd appreciate it, but I got ways of dealing with Grant myself."

"Not for long term you don't." Gordy knew my hypnosis talent was powerful but temporary in its effect on some people. "Lemme handle it first. Ike has an interest in keeping his boy out of trouble. I'll let him know you would be six kinds of bad for Grant to tangle with, and this way Bobbi still gets to be on his show."

I let it sink in, finally nodding. Gordy was a specialist at getting people to do things for him, a real diplomat. He knew the players better, too. My skills were more in the sledgehammer line. "Okay. I'll be a gentleman. This time."

His lips thinned again. He was a mighty happy man.

"What d'you think?" He indicated Adelle Taylor. She had about five grand in front of her by now.

"I think you better buy her a drink before she breaks your bank."

The rear exit was for employees only, but that didn't apply to me. Another door and I was in the backstage area, fighting my way through a pack of sweating, chattering chorus girls. There are worse ways to spend an evening.

Bobbi's dressing-room door was shut, so I knocked a couple times. Rachel, the costume mistress, opened it. She had Bobbi's teacup pajama costume over one arm. Rachel's smile for whatever was going on within faded suddenly to surprise when she saw me.

"Hello, Jack," she said, just a shade too loud and clear, and stepped awkwardly back to let me through. "Look who's here, Bobbi."

Bobbi was at her dressing table in her kimono wrap, black wig off and her platinum hair fluffed and un-combed. "Hi, sweetheart," she called brightly over her shoulder to me.

Sitting comfortably on the couch against the far wall near her was Archy Grant.

Rachel looked at all three of us with a sick artificial smile, then scurried off, slamming the door.

Grant slowly stood and came over to put his hand out to me. "Well, if it ain't young Mr. Fleming. How you doing?" Perfect teeth, perfect grin, and an attitude calcu-lated to annoy.

I let him shake my hand. "Fine. I saw your song. It went over great." I looked at Bobbi. "You were terrific, angel."

She beamed and smeared some cream on her face to

take off the heavy Oriental makeup. "We thought it might be fun to have Archy make a surprise appearance at the last show. It's good publicity for the review."

"Very kind of you," I said to Grant.

"A pleasure and nothing but," he said, smiling warmly—at Bobbi.

Any other guy might have gone over to his girl, maybe put a possessive arm around her, maybe even landed a kiss on her mouth to let Grant know where and how things stood. I didn't have to do anything like that. Besides, the big makeup mirror looked over half of the room, and me not being reflected in it was not something he needed to notice. "Going to make any more appearances here?" I asked.

"Hmm?" He dragged his attention away from Bobbi. "Oh, well, that's always a possibility. Not too often or my agent will have fits. He likes me to earn money when I perform, but I make more than enough to keep me in champagne and cigars. How about yourself?" Those sharp brown eyes of his had already given me a once-over; he must have taken Adelle's hint about pricing the clothes I wore.

"I do okay. Just wrapped a job up tonight, so I've got some time off."

"What do you do?"

"I'm an errand boy." Yeah. Standing easy in a hundred-dollar suit with a silk shirt and tie. I could almost see the wheels spin in his head as he tried to figure it. The logical interpretation, given my surroundings and acquaintances, was that, like him, I was mob-connected and maybe dangerous.

Bobbi shot me an amused look to let me know what

she thought of my game and went on wiping cream from her face.

"Must be some company," Grant said.

"Yeah. I'm hoping to work my way up to the mail room before long."

His grin didn't falter, but something sparked in his eyes. He didn't like me, but wasn't going to make the mistake of showing it in front of Bobbi.

"Archy, tell Jack about the change," she said. It was her way of asking us boys to play nice.

I looked interested.

Grant looked vastly pleased. "Sure thing. Bobbi's going to be on my show next Tuesday for real."

"For real?"

"Yeah, not just some insert broadcast from the club. I've fixed things so she can actually be in the studio."

"What about the club act?"

"Adelle's agreed to take her place for that night as a favor to me."

I wondered how he'd managed it. For a woman like Adelle Taylor, doing a nightclub review was a step down and backward from her radio work. On the other hand, there was Gordy to be considered. Maybe she would see him as a step up from the indifferent Grant.

Bobbi finished with the face cream and turned around. "There's going to be a ton of rehearsing for us both. Adelle's got to learn the dance routines, and I've got to rehearse with Archy to get my lines and songs. Rachel has to make costumes for Adelle and—"

"It'll be fun," Grant said, all confidence.

"What a great break," I said. "What's Adelle think of this?"

"She's all for it."

"And Gordy? What's he think?" I looked at Bobbi.

"Oh, he thought it was a terrific idea. Not in so many words, but he gave us the go-ahead. So long as the review goes on, it's jake with him."

I'd bet it would be, having Adelle around for all that time.

"Tied up with a bow," said Grant. He put himself between me and Bobbi, took up her hand, and lifted it, looking deeply into her eyes. His voice got lower, more serious, and decidedly intimate. "Well, little teacup, I'll see you at rehearsal tomorrow at ten."

She smiled up at him. "Don't forget I'm bringing my accompanist."

"I look forward to meeting her." He bowed slightly and kissed the back of her hand, then gave it a friendly squeeze. On his way out he said he'd see me around.

"'Little teacup'?" I dryly asked, shutting the door.

"He thinks it's cute."

"What do you think?"

"That this radio show is the chance of a lifetime, so I'll put up with his snake-oil routine."

"Why was Rachel acting like she'd been punched in the gut?"

"Because she doesn't know you as well as I do and watches too many movies. She must have thought you'd go into some kind of fit at finding Archy and me so cozy here."

Bobbi's last boyfriend would have done the jealous-rage routine. "You know, Archy didn't make it easy on himself. Does he want me to take a shot at him?"

"I think he just likes flirting, but there's really nothing to it."

"There's something to it, baby."

"If there is, then it's directed at you not me."

"You saying he's like your costar?"

"No, I'm saying I'm not the real focus. He's using me to annoy you, which is too bad. If he smarted up, you two could be good friends. Wonder why he's doing it?"

"Look in the mirror, teacup, just look in the mirror."

"But he's not really after me, just the idea of me. I'm not real to him like I am to you. There must be another reason."

She didn't need to hear from me that Grant probably only wanted another trophy notation in his little black book. As smart as she was, she'd have already figured it out. "Some people don't need a reason to mix it up, they just want to see how far they can push others before getting pushed back. It happens. No skin off my nose, but I'll behave myself. I wouldn't want you to get thrown off his show."

I wasn't too worried about Bobbi. She could take care of herself. Grant may have been trying to play some kind of game to work me up the way some guys like to poke a stick in a tiger cage to get a reaction. With the bars in the way they feel all the power and are safe from reprisals. Bobbi's pending radio spot would do for bars to hold me back in this case. I could imagine his plan—he baits me so I get into a jealous fight with Bobbi, her begging me not to do anything against him, and then telling her boyfriend troubles to Grant, who would be so very, very understanding.

Yeah, I was probably putting too much into it, but underneath I did have to admit to a small but solid kernel of real worry. Grant was in the same kind of job as Bobbi and could appeal to her in a way I couldn't. He knew what it was like to feel the heat of a spotlight on his face and float on the applause of others, and that wasn't something I could give her or entirely share.

"Jack?"

"Huh?"

"You look like a week of bad weather. Archy Grant is convenient to me, but nothing more. I know I don't need to tell you that, but I wanted to say it anyway."

I went over and folded my arms around her. "Thanks. You, I trust; him, I don't."

She relaxed against me, hugging me back, and let out a long sigh. "I've missed this."

"But I was here just last night."

"Like I said: I've missed this."

She eventually put on a dress and hat, pulled on a long coat, and said good night to people as we strolled out. She hunched down into the protection of her high fur collar during the damp and chilly walk to my car.

"Want a late supper?" I asked, opening the door and helping her in.

"An early breakfast would be better. Take me home and I'll fix it there."

"You don't want to eat out?"

"Don't want to waste the time."

That sounded promising. On the other hand she had to get up early—for her—and go to that ten o'clock rehearsal. Grant would probably offer to take her to lunch. I knew if I had the opportunity I'd ask her, knowing she would be unlikely to turn me down. Maybe Marza the accompanist would take a dislike to him as she'd done to me and tag along. If she did, I'd send her a big bunch of flowers.

Bobbi's hotel apartment was dark and the curtains open. City glow illuminated her living room as we stepped inside from the hall. She shrugged out of her coat and told me not to bother as I reached for the light switch. She dropped the coat and hat on a chair.

"I like it this way, where it's all gray shapes and shadows," she said, stretching her arms high. She arched her back, and without thinking about it, my hands went straight to her breasts. The fabric of her dress disguised their texture but not their shape or firmness. She laughed softly and pressed close as I bent to kiss them. No brassiere tonight.

"I like your style," she whispered. "I don't have to offer you anything to drink first."

"It's called saving the best for last." I broke things off long enough to help unbutton her dress. She did the same for my shirt, and pulled on the tie until it joined her hat and coat.

"This way," she said, leading me toward the windows.

She'd originally lived on the fourth floor, but had moved up to the tenth when a suite became available. She'd wanted the better view. Right now it was a drab cloud-choked sky above and countless lights scattered below except for a thick slice of uncompromising black where the lake began.

Bobbi stared out, her face dimly reflected in the glass. "On nights like this I look down from here and feel like I own this town."

"You will own it." I stood behind her, arms wrapped snug around her slim body. The rose scent in her hair was enough to make me feel drunk. I let my hands roam free on her and kissed the back of her neck, taking my time. Before too long her dress slipped to the floor. She laughed again, raising her arms. "Someone will see," I cautioned.

"They'll need a telescope. And if they go to that much trouble, let's give 'em a real show to enjoy." She turned to face me and got me free of my clothes.

After that it was skin on skin and more laughter and touching and her brief, harshly drawn gasps for air. We ended up on the thick rug in front of her couch, limbs tangling and urgent. I pressed into her, giving her that climax, and then when she was starting to descend from it, I gave her another, much longer one. She didn't hold back her cry this time, just ran out of breath as I fed from the tiny wounds I'd reopened in her soft throat.

I lifted away. "You all right?"

"Yes, yes. Please don't stop, ple—"

She held me, arms and legs wrapped tight. I rode her gently, giving and taking all at once. My pleasure came from hers and from the blood she gave so willingly, from her sweet voice, sometimes moaning, sometimes begging me to go harder, to take more. I surrendered to it, to that blinding, white-hot, inside-out feeling, of being out of control and yet in perfect command. Surrendered, until I knew I had to go one step further to make it complete.

I rolled onto my back, pulling Bobbi along. I eased away from kissing her. "Your turn," I whispered.

"Jack, you—"

"Yes, now." I dug one nail into my neck on the left side. Couldn't feel much, only the sudden cool touch of my blood on my skin. *"Now."*

She began kissing me there, then licking, and finally drinking from me.

She held me fast, not letting go. I forced my hands away from her and down so I'd not hurt her, and then I was truly out of control, my body shuddering, writhing from the ecstasy. She took it all back again, the red life I'd taken from her. And with it she drank in the possibility of living as I did, beyond death. Because of it, I couldn't think, couldn't move, only feel the almighty delight of what she was doing to me.

It went on and on, getting better and better until it seemed like I couldn't take any more.

And when that finally happened, it didn't fade away— I did.

I came back to myself in the dark. In real dark, not the dim twilight that was usually like day to me. Something heavy was on my face. Hell, something heavy was on me all over, but it gave when I moved.

An abrupt ugly memory hit like an electric shock: of being tied head to foot in old carpeting, of weights against my chest, and the sudden fall to icy death in the free flowing water of that damned lake.

Half shouting, I clawed at the thing covering me. It dropped away easily enough, and I sat up, blinking.

I was alone on the floor of Bobbi's silent living room. The curtains were drawn, and she'd left a lamp on. A wall clock told me I'd slept the remains of the night and the whole day through. That was the only drawback to sharing blood with her. I tended to pass out and stay passed out unless she worked hard to shake me awake. Apparently she'd not bothered this time.

The heavy thing covering me was the thick rug on which we'd made love. She'd flipped it over my body to protect me from any sunlight straying in, and had shoved a small bag of my home earth under my head to act as a pillow.

Ingenious woman.

A sheet of paper folded into an A shape with my name on it stood on the couch seat where I would be sure to notice. I picked it up and read the letter.

> *Dear Sleepyhead,*
>
> *After that last turn down the road I knew trying to wake you up would be more trouble than it was worth, so I let you dream on. From the look on your face that dream must be wonderful, but then,* you're *wonderful. I called Charles's answering service and left a message that you were staying over for the day so he wouldn't worry.*
>
> *I had a beautiful sleep, thanks to you. I love it when you get jealous and try to spoil me for other men. It works every time.*
>
> *I love you — B*

I read the note several more times, folded it carefully, and realized I didn't have a pocket to put it in. Standing, I kicked the rug back into place and picked up the sack of earth, carrying it into Bobbi's bedroom. My clothes were hanging neat in her closet, looking sternly out of place amid the feminine froth. I put the sack in the back corner where she usually kept it, found a towel, showered, and shaved. My neck was all healed up.

There was fresh underwear and clean shirts in a bureau drawer she'd set aside for me, so I was soon ready for another night out. All I needed was a date. I called the club but Bobbi was already backstage busy preparing for the show. Fine, I'd catch up with her shortly. A call home went unanswered. On the slim chance Escott might be there on a Sunday, I tried the office. Nothing. Answering service. No message from him but they had one from Mary Sommerfeld. She said Jason McCallen had broken into her house that day, could Mr. Escott please, please help? She'd called several times in the last couple hours.

She must be scared as hell. As Mr. Escott seemed to be missing, it would be up to me to do something about the crisis. I grabbed my hat and coat and slammed out the door.

6

FORTUNATELY, I remembered how to get to her Swiss-chalet house. When I pulled into the street I saw that all its lights were on. Her form was clearly silhouetted in one window as she peered out, probably drawn by the sound of my car door slamming. Coming up the walk, I loudly whistled "Shanghai Lil" and called hello before stepping onto the porch, having not forgotten that Miss Sommerfeld was bound to be very nervous and owned a .22. It's a little bullet, but makes a mean hole.

"Mr. Fleming?" she called back. Her voice was on the high, quavery side tonight.

"I got your message and came right over."

She hastily opened the door and hurried me in, then locked it fast behind me. The whites were showing around her eyes, and she had a small revolver in one shaking hand. "Look . . . *look* what he did!" She gestured at her house, pretty much beside herself with fury and fear.

It had been turned over, not as messily as some searches I'd seen, but enough to let her know she'd had a break-in. Her paintings hung crookedly, books leaned to and fro on shelves, newspapers and magazines were scattered, throw rugs flipped up, that sort of thing. None of the stuff was damaged, no ripped cushions, but it was enough to let Miss Sommerfeld know about payback time for what I'd done to McCallen's place.

"Anything taken?" I asked. "Jewelry? Artwork?"

"No, he's not interested in those, only this." She pointed to a familiar envelope on her coffee table. "I've kept it with me the whole time today when I was out."

"Kept it? You should burn it, then he won't have a reason to bother you."

She looked outraged. "Burn it? I'm not burning anything. He's not going to beat me on this."

I went over the whole place and determined that McCallen could have used a thick piece of cellophane carding to slip the easy lock on the front door and then just walked in. Miss Sommerfeld listened carefully as I told her what kind of new locks she should get to prevent another invasion. She wrote it down. Then I tried to imitate Escott's "tell me everything" face, made her sit, and got her talking. She'd been out all day visiting friends and had an early dinner with them. When she got back around five she found the mess.

"Escott told you to call the cops first if anything happened."

"No. No police. I don't want my name in the papers over this. I don't want my family finding out."

I couldn't blame her; it might jeopardize her engagement plans with that prince. "So you called Escott?" I prompted.

"I tried. I left messages and have been trying the other numbers since. Then I happened to look out the window around six and saw Jason's car. He was just sitting in it, smoking and staring. When he saw that I saw him he started it up and drove off. I decided to leave the house again, but every time I got up the courage to go out, he'd come back, driving slowly up and down the block."

"He's trying to scare you, is all."

"He's making me mad. And scared. But mostly mad."

"Probably thinks he can get back at you."

"He wants the papers again, not revenge." She paced once around the room, pausing to peek through the lace curtains. Apparently the street was empty of big Scottish threats.

"I think he's after both. If you really want McCallen off your back for good, you need to burn them and send him the ashes."

She got a stubborn cast to her face. "That's *not* going to happen."

Never argue with a client. "When do you get your locks changed?"

"The man's coming tomorrow."

"No good. You got a place you can go to for tonight? Someplace Jason doesn't know about?"

"I was going to my parents' house."

"He'd know about that, you don't want him calling you there. We'll find a hotel for you. You got cash for it on hand? Good. Pack what you need and I'll get you out."

"But I don't know—that's so drastic."

"Miss Sommerfeld, a man has broken into your house. Do you really want to be here if he comes back? Even with new locks, all he needs is a brick to let himself in again."

She gulped and worked her mouth like a guppy for a moment as my words sank in, then finally nodded. "But what about tomorrow? And the next day, and after that? I can't very well stay away forever."

She was hinting around for the Escott Agency to do something about McCallen for her. I wasn't so certain that intimidation was quite in Escott's line, but I could be pretty good at it—providing the subject was sober.

"I'll talk to my partner when he turns up. I'm sure we can work out something to discourage McCallen."

"You're very kind. What will it cost?"

"If there's any charges, you can take it up with Escott. Now, is there someplace you've never been before?"

"Lots."

"Someplace you never mentioned to McCallen?"

"Well, there's—"

"No, don't tell me." Actually, she could tell me and it would be perfectly safe, but I thought she might enjoy the drama. "And don't tell your family and friends, either."

"But if they try to call or telegram me—"

"Get around that by phoning them as usual and pretend nothing's wrong. And you call the agency at intervals to see how things are going." Escott would love that one.

While she got packed I tried the office again, and then the house. Escott was finally home. He'd succumbed to cabin fever and gotten out to take in a movie, then visit some gymnasium for a workout.

"If you really want to build some muscles, our latest client needs some moving help," I told him, then explained the situation.

"I'll come right over," he said.

"I got things under control."

"No doubt, but one of us should stay in her house for the evening."

He said to give him half an hour and hung up. I called the club to leave a message for Bobbi that I was working tonight and might be late. Gordy would see that she got home all right.

McCallen drove by twice more.

Miss Sommerfeld had a guest bedroom window in front that looked on the street. I turned the light off there and opened the curtains just a crack to keep watch, and occasionally wondered why she hadn't destroyed her love letters. Either she was foolishly sentimental or maybe she was the one doing the blackmailing. That screwball thought entertained me until Escott arrived and she let him in. He was slightly informal with a golfing sweater pulled over his shirt instead of his usual coat and vest, so he must not have changed from the gym.

She'd cleaned a few things up during the wait, but there was still enough damage left for him to cluck over sympathetically. "Dear me, but this won't do at all. I think we shall have to have a little talk with Mr. McCallen."

"My thoughts exactly," I said, catching his eye.

Escott got my meaning, grimaced, but nodded. Maybe my hypnosis was temporary, but it would last long enough to get McCallen to cool down and find some other occupation besides breaking and entering.

While Escott and Miss Sommerfeld discussed the business end of things, I went back to my post at the window. Not too very long afterward McCallen cruised by again. When his Ford rounded the corner I went out front.

"He just left. Load the car now and go. You've got maybe ten minutes before he comes back."

I helped Escott play porter. For an overnight stay she had two large and remarkably heavy suitcases and carried a smaller case along with her purse. Maybe the hotel she wanted was in Europe. He assisted her into the backseat of his Nash and told her to lie down out of sight, then got behind the wheel and spun them out of there with eight and a half minutes to spare. I locked the house, for all the good it might do, and stayed outside, standing lonely under the thin shadow of a bare-branched tree, its trunk helping to conceal my still form.

McCallen pulled into the street pretty much on schedule. He slowed down as he neared the chalet, which suited me just dandy. I went invisible and shot over the pavement, aiming for his car.

Having no sight was a real disadvantage for this situation. I was aware of shapes around me, the press of the wind, and the low chugging hum of his car motor. It more or less gave me a direction to go to, and I did finally bump up against a solid, smooth-surfaced moving form. I tried to sieve through, but the metal was too dense, so I probed for cracks around the door and eventually found one.

The positioning of it seemed off to me, but I could feel McCallen start to speed things up as he passed by the house. Time to hurry. Once through the narrow crevice, I realized I'd gotten it wrong; the confined area I found myself in was too small. I'd managed to filter into the car's trunk.

Still invisible, I poked and prodded around for some means of entry into the front. My sense of touch wasn't the same as when I was solid. I'd not done any blind exploration in a while and was out of practice, but eventually I found a quarter-sized hole in the metal body that served. I smoked through, finding my way around the slab of backseat cushion, and finally settled like a pocket of fog on the floorboard behind the driver.

When I slowly materialized I half expected to find my hair rumpled and tie askew from all the effort, but nothing was out of place. As always, the image was strictly in my mind.

I took quick stock of my surroundings. The car was in steady motion, going at a moderate pace. McCallen wasn't about to break any speed laws. That suited me; I didn't want to break anything either, myself in particular.

While I kept quiet and bided my time, he made a few turns, but never stopped long enough for me to safely interrupt his driving. It's not a good idea to surprise someone while they're trying to steer a ton or so of car at thirty miles an hour; the property damage can be disastrous. I expected him to make some sort of a wide circle, then return to run past the house after a suitable period. Maybe he'd pull over and fill the time with a smoke. It'd be easy enough to make my move then.

Luck seemed to be with me; he made a slight turning and pulled up, but did not cut the motor. Instead he touched the horn briefly. A moment later someone opened the passenger door and climbed in and they took off again. I hunkered down even lower and let my ears flap.

"What's the story?" asked the newcomer, a man with a soft voice, like he had a cold.

McCallen growled and grumbled with displeasure. Even those sounds seemed to have a Scottish accent. "My lady Mary's barricaded herself in and called for help to come over. I caught a glimpse of her company. Looked like one of those gits from that so-called detective agency she hired. Couldn't tell which one, they both have the same build."

"Damn."

"Damn indeed. I should have gone in sooner, but all those lights, an' her neighbors are still up, she'd scream bloody murder."

"What about the cops?"

"She won't call the police if she can help it. But if I force things too much . . ."

"You won't be able to get it back from her." Soft Voice sounded morose. "I just know it."

"It'll just take me a wee bit longer than I'd hoped."

"Couldn't you just write the stuff out from memory?"

"That's next to useless, y' daft squirrel. What good's a copy? The original's what we need for the job."

"Well, it's only because she's not cooperating."

"Paterno, you give me just five minutes alone with her, and I'll have her cooperating beautifully. She'll be begging for me to—"

"Watch out!"

McCallen hit the brakes hard and we skidded. I braced myself, but no impact came. Instead he let forth with a forceful flow of volcanic cursing at some other driver.

"Damned drunk!" he concluded, brutally shifting gears and hitting the gas as though to make up for lost time. I braced again in the small space, glumly reflecting that I wasn't exactly getting paid for this little adventure.

"That detective she's got, he can't always be with her, can he?" asked the mystery man, Paterno.

"She's got money enough to hire a dozen watchdogs twenty-four hours a day."

"If you can't get past them—"

"I'll get past 'em, never you worry, and pay 'em back

double. Bloody bastards, tearing through my house like it was bloody Grand Central Station."

A gross exaggeration. I'd been very careful to put everything back again. Including the cat's box. McCallen hadn't been nearly so neat when he'd ransacked the Sommerfeld place.

"But when?" Paterno sounded impatient. "The people that want it won't wait forever."

"I said never you worry, I need their money too much to delay things. I'll keep an eye on her, bide my time, and then as soon as she's alone—"

"Bide your time?" Disbelief from Paterno.

"If that's what it takes, yes, and bugger the buyers. They know how valuable the property is. They'll wait if need be, but I promise you it won't be long."

"I should hope not."

McCallen made a sharp turn, slowed, and stopped. "Come on, I've a bad taste in my mouth that wants changin' for the better."

They got out, slamming the doors, leaving me in silence except for a few cars going by. I waited a few moments, then cautiously raised my head. I saw McCallen and a smaller, thinner man walking away down the sidewalk toward a tavern. They went inside.

I let myself out for a look around, finally getting a street name and block number from the sign at the corner. The neighborhood seemed familiar, the houses at one end all having the same age and look about them. McCallen had taken us toward his home. This was probably the bar where he spent his evening hours.

If he was drinking, then giving him my special evil-eye whammy wouldn't work. I decided to go into the bar anyway, just to try my luck. Maybe I could persuade him to step outside before he got oiled up. That would solve a lot of problems.

The street was lined with modest businesses—shoe repair, candy store, a clothing shop, and the like. The two largest were a drugstore on one corner and the bar on the opposite. All must have been there for a long, long time and verged on shabby, but weren't mean enough to have completely toppled into decrepitude.

The red neon sign behind the tavern's front window said MOE'S, in flowing script. I didn't think it had anything to do with the Three Stooges. I pushed through the door. Nothing pretentious here: peanut shells on the floor, the smell of wood polish, beer, and booze. The bar ran nearly the length of the dim room, which was wider than it looked from the outside. The wall between this building and the one next door had been knocked through; tables and booths were set up in the extra open space. For a Sunday night the joint had a good crowd, mostly young twenties, mostly male, though some had brought dates. They all had that wholesome-but-willing-to-be-corrupted-so-long-as-their-parents-didn't-find-out look of college students.

There was quite a knot of them gathered in one corner, where a man with a thick brush of salt-and-pepper hair perched on a tall stool and played his guitar. He was working a slow piece, crooning away in a whiskey-rough voice. No one listening to him moved a muscle.

I paused a moment. His song was about the Mississippi and lost love set to soft, evocative music that could break your heart. The words were poetry, the magical stuff that stops you in your tracks and stirs your heart until it turns inside out. I forgot all about chasing McCallen and drifted over to the crowd, easing down at an empty table on the edge of things.

My jaw was hanging by the time the man finished; he'd transfixed me so I was slow to come out of his spell and join the applause. I hadn't heard a voice like that since my last visit to Coldfield's place, but this guy was white. And yet it wasn't all to do with his voice, a lot of it was the feeling he put into his song. There was something special here; I *had* to hear more, and to hell with the Sommerfeld case.

The singer picked things up with a faster number. He went from brokenhearted misery to triumphant satisfaction, with everyone clapping a beat out for him, then traveled back to heartache again. That's what the blues were about, after all.

And then all too soon he was finished and passing a hat. I grabbed a business card from my wallet, scribbled a three-word message, and folded a five-dollar bill around it, dropping it in when my turn came. The other money was all quarters and dimes. The bill would get his attention.

When the hat got back to him his eyes widened with surprise, and he looked around the joint. I raised my hand slightly. He thought about it, frowning, probably measuring the five dollars against my flashy suit. I was the only one in the audience who could have given him such a huge tip. He finally nodded and set his guitar down, picking up a sturdy cane. There was something with his legs that gave him a stiff, strutlike walk as he came over to my table, and when he stood still he braced himself with the stick. He held my card and the folded bill between two fingers like a cigarette as I stood to greet him.

"'Come see me'?" he quoted from it. His speaking voice was just as husky as the one he used for singing. "If you're wanting company, I don't play that game." He put the card and bill on the table.

I chuckled once. "Nothing like that. My name's Jack Fleming."

"Jim Waters," he said, and briefly shook my offered hand. We sat down. He had to lower into his chair, stretching his legs out straight. "What do you want, Mr. Jack Fleming?"

"You don't waste time."

"A guy dressed like you doesn't walk into a place like this without some kind of angle; I'd as soon you get to the point so I can get on with my drinkin'."

"Fair enough." I started to turn for a waiter, but one was already on his way to the table. "What'll you have?"

Waters said he wanted his usual, and I asked for a coffee. The waiter came back with the coffee and a bottle of beer. I gave him a quarter and said to keep the change.

"You are a big spender, young fella," said Waters after taking a long swig.

"I like to make a good impression."

"You did that right enough. Was this a joke or is it funny money?" He held up the five. "If I'm lucky I might make this on a Saturday night after payday."

"It's not a joke. You impressed the hell out of me."

"Well, thank you kindly. But what's the angle?"

"First I want to know why I've never heard of you. I've been to just about every blues place in this town—"

"Except this one." His eyes crinkled.

"It doesn't exactly advertise itself. You only play here? Only here?"

"Why not? It's close to where I live and work."

"Where's that?"

"I got a little shoe-repair business up the street. Sweet, ain't it, a guy with no feet fixing shoes?" He tapped one of his legs in illustration.

"I guess it is. Was it the war?" I couldn't tell his age, he had one of those forty-to-sixty faces.

"Oh, yeah. Got in the wrong place at the wrong time. They give me a medal for it and a pension, but that ain't enough to get by these days, so I fix shoes and play guitar." His accent wasn't from Chicago, but from farther south, not too far. St. Louis maybe. That was a major blues town.

"Where'd you learn to play like that?" I asked.

"It's just something I picked up."

"And the songs?"

"Those are mine."

"My God."

"Impress easy, do you?" His eyes twinkled and he tilted his beer.

"Just the opposite, Mr. Waters. I've heard a lot of 'em. The best of the best in this city. I think you could hold your own onstage with any of 'em, and they'd agree with me."

"Well, that's mighty nice of you to say so. Now . . . you tell me your story."

I hesitated. The way things stood I didn't really have one. I'd just have to blunder through and hope for the best. "I'm going to be opening a nightclub and will need good acts to play there."

He snorted. "Uh-huh. An' you think you want me for your bill?"

"I know I do."

"Me and who else?"

"Ever hear of Bobbi Smythe?"

His disbelief wavered. "Yeah, she's one of the club singers around town. I seen her name in the papers."

"Right now she's starring over at the Nightcrawler, but when I get things set up she'll be starring at mine. That's the level of acts I'm putting in."

"Uh-huh. And when'll that be?"

I gave him a rueful face. "You got me there, Mr. Waters. Right now I've let my ambitions get ahead of my schedule, but I had to talk with you while I could. I can't give you an opening date for the place, but I would like to know if you'd be interested in playing once it got going."

He shook his head and shrugged. "Yeah, sure, why not?"

"You think I don't know how this must sound to you?"

"Son, at this point you are big bucketful of ifs." He drained away a fourth of his beer. "But for a tip like that and a cold one I can at least listen to you. You come back to me when you get your club going and we'll see about things then."

"Deal," I said, holding my hand out again.

He started to take it, then pulled back. "Hey, now, how much you plan to pay me?"

I calculated it against what I knew other singers made in the kind of club I planned to open and made him a generous offer. "That, plus whatever tips you get, and I have someone drive you there and home again."

He rocked back in his chair and couldn't talk for a while. "You crazy? You just walk in here cold, listen to a couple my songs, and give me a pitch like that?"

"You'll be worth it," I said. "Will you accept? I'll put it in writing later."

He laughed, shaking his head again. "Why the hell not?" And we closed the deal.

"Another beer?" I asked.

Waters didn't answer, but glanced sharply up and past my shoulder. I knew what was coming, and quickly stood to face it.

McCallen strode over fast. He had five or six friends behind him, emerging from a curtained-off opening in the back wall. It must have been a private-party room. He was the biggest in the pack, but the others made up for it with numbers. He stopped an arm's length away, eyes narrow, shoulders hunched, fists closed and ready to strike. The others formed an ominous half circle around us.

"I know you," he said, all menace. "What'd y'do, follow me here?"

I looked him hard in the eye, but had my doubts about being able to get past his anger, so I tried something else instead of hypnosis. "Let's talk outside. You wouldn't want to scare the ladies." People were staring, not the least of whom was Waters.

"Damn right we're gonna talk," McCallen rumbled.

I smiled reassuringly at my prospective nightclub star. "Mr. Waters, I apologize for the intrusion. This is a separate piece of business I need to settle with this gentleman, so I'll have to talk with you later."

Waters was obviously mystified and alarmed at why so many hostile customers were interested in me. "Later it is," he said.

I surveyed McCallen and his troops. They seemed to be young collegiate types except for Paterno, who was somewhat older. I recognized him by his coat and hat. He had thick black hair and glasses and watched me with high curiosity. I smiled at him, at McCallen. "Gentlemen? Shall we proceed out of doors?"

McCallen moved his big shoulders sideways by half a foot. It didn't give me much room, but it was enough. I nodded at him politely, still smiling.

Then I bolted past them all and slammed out the front door, running like hell.

A graceless exit, but better than getting pounded flat or having to vanish in front of a bunch of bewildered witnesses. The hoots and laughter that trailed me were soon replaced by a thunderous stampede made by a determined McCallen and his friends. He was close after me, cursing a blue streak. I shot across the street and past the drugstore and spotted the alley running behind it. Perfect. I ducked into it—and disappeared.

My momentum from running carried me forward a few yards. I eased to a halt and waited for them to rush in. It didn't take them long to discover their problem.

"Hey, where the hell is he?" asked Paterno.

"Hiding," snarled McCallen. "Come on, flush him out."

As though through a wall, because my ears weren't so good in this form, I heard the banging of trash cans as the men rooted around for me. A big dog began barking frantically at the noise. Other canines took up the boisterous chorus.

"Two of you run ahead in case he got to the other end," McCallen ordered.

"But he couldn't have. We were right behind him."

"He must have gone over the fence. Look in that yard."

"You kiddin'? I think Rin Tin Tin lives there, and he sounds pissed."

A woman's shrill and highly annoyed voice cut in on my fun. "Hey, you drunks! I'm calling the cops if you don't get out!"

That decided it for them. McCallen wanted to stay, but his friends persuaded him to abandon the search. If I moved that fast, they argued, I was long gone by now. Everyone withdrew, and I tagged invisibly along to see if I could learn any more about his plans for Miss Sommerfeld.

Most of them didn't want to go back to the bar minus their prize—me—and McCallen was in no mood to return either. After some discussion they settled things: they'd go to another place to finish their interrupted drinking. Everyone piled into McCallen's Ford. No one noticed me; I sieved into the trunk again.

The next ride was shorter, with no startling traffic encounters. When they stopped, I counted twenty and slipped from my hiding place, materializing crouched behind the car. They were all heading for a larger, brighter, and considerably noisier place, whose chief virtue seemed to be two-for-a-nickel beers. The music was raucous and loud. I could forget invisibly eavesdropping on McCallen and his group; I'd not be able to hear a damn thing. Ambushing him afterward I could also forget. Even that cheap a beer would make the job too difficult if he had enough of them.

I knew the neighborhood, which was only a couple miles from the Sommerfeld house. Flagging a cab was not a problem, as the dispatching office for a company was just down the block. I gave the driver the street, sat back, and listened to him talk about how he would fix things in Europe. He favored the idea of making the leaders all get into a prizefighting ring with baseball bats.

He had a point-and-handicap system all worked out so no one man would have the advantage. It made as much sense as anything I'd heard lately. I told him he should write to the prime minister of England with the suggestion.

"Why not to Roosevelt?" he asked.

"England's closer to what's going on. If that war in Spain spreads out, they'll feel it sooner than we would."

"Maybe I should write the king of England instead. Whoever the hell it is now," he said.

In summing up '36, the press had called it the "year of three kings" because of the old king's death, that business with the abdication, and the crown going to the next brother in the line. Escott had been singularly uninterested in any of it beyond a comment that the so-called scandal was nothing compared to those the previous generation of royalty had been embroiled in. To prove his point he related a few juicy stories that never made it to the history books, then went back to reading the papers without revealing his sources.

My driver got very detailed about his handicapping system, enough to keep me entertained on the trip back. I gave him a good tip when we arrived and checked the area on the off chance that McCallen had changed his mind and returned. The street was clear except for my Buick and the cars that had been there before. No Escott yet, so I let myself into Mary Sommerfeld's house and straightened books and paintings while waiting for him.

She had quite a collection of reading material, and just to be nosy I studied spine titles. She seemed to have a little of everything, from classics to the new stuff being touted as the next batch of classic literature. I had my doubts on that since I couldn't recall the name of last year's critically acclaimed opus. The fact that I'd not bothered to read it may have had something to do with the lapse of memory. My tastes ran to more lurid stuff. At least it could be relied upon to have a plot.

Once I tried to get through *Anthony Adverse* and finally gave up when I found myself passing over whole pages at a time to find plot developments. I didn't much like the ending either when I skipped ahead to read it. I fared better with *Gone with the Wind* because all the detail on the Civil War was pretty interesting. Bobbi had liked the book, so I read it to talk about it with her. She thought Scarlett should have wised up faster about Ashley and told Rhett Butler to jump in the lake at the end. I thought she should have picked up stakes and moved west right after Gettysburg and to hell with Tara. For that I got a pillow thrown in my face.

Mary Sommerfeld was also quite a theatergoer, to judge by her collection of old program books, many from New York. With her money she probably wouldn't think anything of hopping a train east to take in the Broadway season. She read plays as well, and had several books containing scripts of everything from Shakespeare to Goerge S. Kaufman.

Before I got too far in my cultural education I heard a car door slam. Escott was coming up the walk. I let him in and asked about our client.

"She's presently checked in under an assumed name in one of the upper floors of a hotel in the Loop, hopefully enjoying a room-service drink and a fine view of the lake. The more time she had to think about things the more agitated she got. I was wishing I possessed your powers of enforced persuasion by the time I had her settled in. She is not at all pleased at this turn of events."

"It's her own fault. You warned her, and tonight I told her she should burn the stuff, but it put her nose all out of joint. I've got a new turn for you, too."

"Indeed?" He dropped into a chair and stretched out his legs.

I told him about my hitching a ride with McCallen and his conversation with the new man, Paterno. "He sounded pretty thick with this bird. The impression I got was that Paterno was a go-between for some other players. McCallen's apparently trying to get the papers so either he or Paterno can sell them to an unknown party with plenty of cash."

"He did say it was worth ten times more than the two hundred I offered him," Escott recalled.

"Which is a lot of dough in anyone's bakery. Maybe it's a news outfit. 'Cracker Heiress Slums with Scotch Madman' would make a catchy headline for the seamier rags, especially if they had some purple-passion love letters to print with it."

He looked pained. "That's 'Scots.' Scotch is a drink."

"You catch my drift, though. McCallen's hurt feelings for her might translate into that kind of vindictiveness."

"For a mere two thousand dollars?"

"That's enough for anyone to start over anywhere and have plenty of fun along the way."

"I suppose, but it's just one possibility."

"You got others?"

"Suppose the family of her fiancé, Prince Ravellia, objects to Miss Sommerfeld as hers objected to McCallen? They might be trying to find a way of discrediting her in order to call off the marriage."

"I thought poor princes marrying American heiresses was still in fashion."

"Except that his family is not poor. Their objections could be based on the young lady's commoner blood-line."

"You're kidding. That's crazy."

"So speaks a man born in a democracy. But there are class issues to consider, and his family might think Miss Sommerfeld too inferior no matter how rich she is or will be."

I remembered about all the shock over the divorced American Mrs. Simpson marrying a king, and figured Escott had a point. We talked back and forth for a while, but came to the same conclusion in the end—I'd have to see McCallen.

"Fine," I said. "Invite him over to the office for a meeting. I'll deal with him there."

"Very well."

"Hey, Charles, I meant it as a joke!"

"Oh, yes, of course, but it is a most sensible suggestion."

" 'Sensible' is not the word. He was ready to break me in two tonight and would just as cheerfully fold you in half the wrong way if he got the chance. You're not inviting him over there unless I'm along to keep him in line."

"My dear fellow, I wouldn't think of depriving you of the opportunity. I'm well aware that he might be feeling a touch annoyed at your invasion of his house, but have no doubt you'll be able to sort him out."

"Good."

"And if I've not ascertained by then the identity of this Paterno fellow and his comrades, you can make inquiries directly with Mr. McCallen."

I was going to advise Escott to be careful, but bit it

back. He knew his business, and actually looked interested in it for a change. The case had some ups and downs, but it wasn't exactly riveting for him. Now that things had gotten more complicated, he'd have something to do tomorrow besides turn away divorce work.

We shut most of the lights off and hauled ourselves out of there. Escott locked up while I headed on to my car. I thought about going back Moe's to see if Jim Waters was still playing, but decided to leave well enough alone for the moment. I'd already made a hell of a first impression on him, anything more on top of it might make things worse. Better to try again another night, preferably after my talk with McCallen.

Remembering Waters sparked something else in my brain, though, and I trotted back to Escott just before he drove off. "I saw Shoe last night," I said.

"Really? How is he?"

"Doing fine. He wants us to come over to his club this week for dinner, maybe listen to the act he's got playing."

"A most generous invitation, but I—"

"He told me to say he's got a French-trained chef up from New Orleans."

That stopped him cold. "Well, I could hardly turn away from such a gastronomic opportunity. I'll phone tonight and see what can be arranged."

"Just not on Tuesday, okay? That's the night of Bobbi's broadcast and I'm gonna be busy with her."

"Right, I'll remember. It's a very exacting art, you know. French cooking. A matter of bringing out the taste and presenting it well."

"Even frogs and snails? What about that Cajun guy who eats things Shoe wouldn't step on?"

"The idea," Escott continued, nonplused, "is to eat

slowly and enjoy your meal in the company of friends. What a pity you can't join us for that. You miss so much good food because of your condition."

"Don't start that talk; I'm happy with what I've got." I'd tried frog legs once on a Paris furlough during the war and decided there was more meat to be had on a chicken. The taste was about the same, anyway.

Escott favored me with one of those piercing looks. "But the same thing, night after night after night?"

I shrugged. "I've tried to explain it, but it won't explain. To me the stuff always tastes just—"

He held up a quick hand. "No. Please. I'd rather you spared me the details." Escott was on the squeamish side.

"You two eat; I'll watch the show," I said.

"Another good reason to clear this case as quickly as possible."

"You said it, brother."

Going into the Nightcrawler lobby, I briefly wondered what I'd have done with my evening hours if there were no clubs. What did cavemen vampires do for entertainment while everyone else went to bed with the dinosaurs? Explore the caves? Had there even been such things as cavemen vampires? I sure as hell didn't know. Maybe one of these nights some guy with a low brow and knuckles dragging on the floor would materialize in front of me and explain the whole business. In fact, such a specimen did walk past, but he was one of the club bouncers.

The show was going strong, playing to a slightly smaller audience than the previous few nights. The bottom two tiers were crowded, but the population was more sparse in the third. Still, it was a good crowd for a

Sunday. Tomorrow the place would be closed and dark, with only the cleaning crew making noise while everyone else took some time off.

The intermission was about ten minutes away. I strolled into the gambling room and looked around for Gordy, but he was elsewhere. Just to keep in practice, I played a couple of hands of blackjack with my favorite dealer. He thought I had one amazing gift for luck, as I won more often than not. The luck had to do with my excellent hearing and his inability to control the beating of his heart when he had a good hand. It was a small edge for me, though a lot of it did depend on the fall of the cards and my own judgment. I won two hands and lost two, tipped him, and continued on to the backstage area just as the teacup number came to an end. Not long now. Soon I'd be seeing my best girl again.

Pushing open the door to Bobbi's dressing room, I discovered Archy Grant sitting on her couch flipping through a magazine with a drink in hand, looking like he owned the place.

7

HIS gaze hit mine and there was a definite air of mutual disconcertment and annoyance hanging in the space between us. His quickly vanished behind his signature grin, and he put aside the magazine to stand and walk over, hand out.

"Well, if it ain't young Mr. Fleming!" He really sounded sincere in his delight. "How y'doing?"

"Fine, thank you." I wondered if Gordy had had that word with Ike LaCelle and if it had filtered down to Grant yet.

He pumped my hand, apparently pleased to see me. The room seemed to get smaller with his presence suddenly filling the space. It was the same kind of thing Bobbi did when she tapped into her personal voltage in front of a crowd, and maybe Grant was doing it for the same reason; he wanted to be liked, and it didn't matter by whom. For him it must have been as automatic as breathing. Bobbi knew when it was appropriate, though, and when to switch it off and just be herself.

"I'd heard that you were working tonight," he said. "Glad you got finished in time to come by. I was going to take Bobbi to a late dinner, but now I can bow out—reluctantly, I will add—and turn things over to you."

"It's good of you to be looking after her interests," I said, determined to be gracious even if it choked me.

"My own interests, you mean. That girl is one talented ball of fire and it'll be a feather in my cap to have her on my show. I only want to keep her happy."

"That's good." Over by her closet stood a fresh bouquet of a couple dozen long-stemmed roses, and on the table in front of the couch was a huge open box of chocolates. He wasn't missing any of the traditional courtship gifts. In spite of my resolution not to give in to jealousy I couldn't help feeling a sharp warning stab. There was no reason for it; Grant's behavior wasn't Bobbi's fault. I knew that in my head, but it was harder to convince my gut.

He bounced cheerfully on his heels. "I'll stay long enough to tell her good night and be on my way. Have a seat."

"Thanks, I will in a minute. I want the leg stretch." And to avoid the dressing-room mirror.

He went back to sit on the couch and picked up his drink again. "What you been up to? If you don't mind my asking."

"A little interviewing."

"Bobbi told me you're a writer." The almost-but-not-quite-patronizing tone and the look in his eyes said that he remembered my errand-boy story from last night. "You doing an article on someone?"

"Different kind of interview. I write, but I also work for a private agent." That's the name my partner preferred over "gumshoe" to describe the job.

Grant let his forehead furrow, a comic exaggeration. "What's that? Insurance?"

"More like investigations."

"Detective work?"

"Something like that. The Escott Agency."

"Really?" He paused a moment, lips pursed. Maybe I didn't fit his idea of a detective. "The Escott Agency. Sounds . . . interesting."

"Yeah, sometimes it's a real riot."

He finished his drink, putting it on the table, and helped himself to a chocolate, chewing it slowly. Before he could continue his questioning, Bobbi came in, a noisy crowd at her heels.

"Jack!" Nothing false in her reaction of pleasure at seeing me. She gave me a light kiss, careful of her makeup.

"I got away from Charles sooner than I thought."

"Good! Look, Archy invited me to dinner, so why don't we all go out together? That is, if you don't mind, Archy."

He'd risen from the couch as soon as she'd come in and seemed nonplussed. "Well . . . ah . . ."

"Is there a problem?" she asked. "It's been a long day, maybe you're too tired?" Having quickly figured there was something wrong, she was trying to give him a graceful exit.

"Ix-nay on the inner-day," said Grant, abruptly switching on a rueful face and holding his palms out. "For now at least. After all, I was just pinch-hitting for the real thing. Your boyfriend's here to take charge, so I will diplomatically toddle off."

"But, Archy—"

"Three's one too many. Just be on time for tomorrow's

rehearsal, little teacup." As before, he bowed to kiss her hand, then swung past, wishing me good night with a quick nod and a forced smile. Even its pretense didn't quite reach his eyes.

The crowd of chorus girls hanging outside, attracted by Archy's brighter light and his loud, broad greeting to them all, went with him, and I shut the door.

"What happened?" Bobbi asked in the silence.

"Absolutely nothing. I came in to wait for you and found I had to get in line."

Her mouth sagged. "I hope you didn't mean that as some kind of crack." Her voice was oddly thin.

I realized just too late what I'd sounded like. "For God's sake, no. It's nothing against you, it's just him. He gets under my skin. I didn't expect him to be here."

"No need to worry, I'd have left the door open," she said, going to her dressing table and taking off the black wig. Her movements were alarmingly fast and jerky.

"Jeez, Bobbi, you can't think I'd think anything like that of you! And certainly not after last night."

She didn't make any reply. There looked to be too many of them hovering on her lips. She gulped, taking a few breaths. "Did you hypnotize him into leaving?"

"No! Of course not!" What the hell was going on here? "I promised you I wouldn't interfere, but you're making me worried. Did you really *want* to go out to dinner with him?"

"If I did, it would be for business reasons. But what am I to think when I come in here and see you looking like a volcano about to erupt?"

"That maybe your boyfriend is ticked off at another man who's trying to move in on you and pretty much rubbing my face in it. I thought I was cute when I got jealous."

"Not that way you aren't. For a minute you looked just like Slick used to."

The dawn finally came. A tightness I'd not been aware of eased from my shoulders, as everything made sense again. I walked toward her. "Come here." I opened my arms and pulled her close.

She stiffened.

"Come on, angel."

She resisted, trying to push away. "I'll get greasepaint on your suit."

"Another suit I can get. Another you would be impossible. Come here."

She allowed me to gingerly hold her and hiccuped a few times, but still resisted.

I whispered, "I'm *not* going to turn into Slick and never will. That's my cast-iron guarantee to you. If I should ever be so stupid, you kick me right in the pants, front or back, as high as you want to go."

Another kind of sound from her. Something halfway between a moan and a whimper. She hated to cry, but the tension had to go somewhere, so having it leak out of her eyes was the method this time. I could hold her closer now that she'd relaxed. "How come." She gulped. "How come. You're. So damned nice?"

I moved us toward the dressing table, scooped up a box of tissues, and eased my hug enough so she could get to them. She plucked several and blew her nose a lot.

"Because of this," I said. "The last line." From my pocket I drew out a slightly crumpled paper and unfolded it. It was the note she'd written me. "I believe what's here, especially the last line."

Maybe that was a mistake. She read it and then really started to cry. But she was laughing at the same time, and it gave her more hiccups.

After we traded sufficient hugs, kisses, and reassurances, I left so she could change and clean up in peace. I'd buy her that late supper at a place she liked, then take her home. In the meantime I asked around and heard that Gordy was at one of the back tables way up on the third tier. The view of the stage was so-so, but the location was dark and discreet. He and Adelle Taylor were working on what looked to be their second bottle of champagne, and whatever he was saying seemed to be pleasing her. She was elegant again tonight in black satin and diamonds.

I was going to ask him if he'd had his talk with Ike, but changed my mind. Far be it from me to interrupt a budding romance.

The crowd had thinned to diehards with the conclusion of the show, lingering over their last drinks and conversations. Someone in the sound booth had put a record on in place of the long-gone Melodians, and piped its music over everyone's head. Soft dance stuff, but no one was dancing. It was Sunday night and most would have to leave soon to totter off Monday morning to deal with short sleep, hangovers, and work.

To be strictly accurate, it was Monday already, but I'd never bought into that one-day-changes-to-the-next-at midnight thing. It was Sunday until I woke up tomorrow and not before.

On the other side of the room I noticed that Grant was still hanging around. He was at Ike LaCelle's table with Dalhauser and the Carole Lombard blonde. She looked sleepy and bored. The three men had their heads together; Grant did most of the talking, and did his talking to Ike. Ike had on a serious face and kept nodding to show he understood. Maybe I was flattering myself, but I thought my ears should be burning again.

The impulse came over me to vanish and float up there for some eavesdropping, but by the time I was ready to act on it, Grant and the others stood to go. LaCelle helped the blonde to her feet, but she was more interested in trying to get a grip on Archy Grant's arm. She woke up enough to keep flashing him an inviting, if bleary-eyed smile. LaCelle laughed and took the unsteady lead. None of them saw me as they went out, but then I was standing very still in a patch of shadow. They'd either forgotten about Adelle having been in their group or knew she was being looked after.

I kept an eye on them from a distance, but they only collected their coats and hats. LaCelle made a phone call, probably for a taxi, then they all went outside, sheltering under the awning from a sudden rain. Their pending departure didn't exactly make me sigh in relief, but I did feel better. The real relief would be when the radio show was concluded and things could get back to normal.

On the other hand, if Bobbi went over really big—and there was no reason to think she wouldn't—then she might have regular return spots on the show. Grant could become a chronic problem.

If I let him.

I'd promised Bobbi not to influence him concerning her career. I never said anything about curbing his romantic impulses. All I needed was a couple minutes with him to make him back off on the flowers-and-candy routine. If I was subtle about it, made it a gradual thing, even Bobbi wouldn't notice the change, and he sure as hell wouldn't be aware of it.

He'd underestimated me, Bobbi, and our connection to each other, which annoyed me more than anything else. Poking sticks at tigers was fine, but this particular tiger wasn't restrained by any cage.

After giving them enough time for their cab to come and go, I went out and brought my car around so Bobbi wouldn't have to walk far in the downpour. She had an understandable fear of catching cold. I put the heap in a no-parking zone right out the front, but one of the guys promised to watch it for me in case a bored cop cruised by. Fat chance of that happening here, most of the cops knew to give the place a wide berth so long as Gordy kept up with payoff money.

Bobbi emerged, all scrubbed and ravenous. It had begun to rain, so I hustled her into the Buick, and off we went to an all-night diner that, according to her, was both cheap and good. I bought her a meal, ordered yet another cup of coffee I would never drink, and worked hard not to breathe in the food fumes while she ate. We talked about this and that, and I was glad things were easy and fine between us again. I did not mention to her my decision about Grant, nor did it seem important to call her attention to the car that followed us from the Nightcrawler.

It waited across the street. From our rain-spattered window I could see it from the corner of my eye. Bobbi and I were in a well lighted booth, very visible from the street, but I wasn't worried about someone taking a shot at us. If that happened, the shot would be for me not her, and I was fairly certain there would be no shooting until and unless she was well out of the picture.

She filled my ear with what had gone on at the rehearsals that day, for she'd done two, one at the radio station and one back at the club, helping Adelle.

"Poor thing," she said. "It's exhausting. She has to memorize the songs and get the dance steps down in such a short time. The songs are no problem, she can do that at home, but the dance routines she needs to practice with the others to get the timing. Then she has to put it all together with the singing and make it look smooth."

"I thought it took weeks to do that kind of thing." I remembered all the work Bobbi had put into just this one show.

"It takes weeks to develop, but once a routine is set, then it's a matter of memorization and practice. Adelle got all that by the end of the day, she's a hell of a hard worker. Now she has to polish it."

"So it doesn't look like work?"

"Exactly. I've got it much easier with the radio job because I can have the music in front of me to read from, and I don't have to memorize the script so much as learn it enough to make sure the lines are funny when I say them."

"Adelle must be pretty good to pick it up so fast."

"Oh, she's wonderful. She was having a ball clowning around with that dragon's head. It's a different kind of comedy than she's used to doing, but she's great at it. Maybe I should worry about her turning out to be better in the show than me."

I told her not to worry. "How did she let herself get talked into doing this on such short notice? I mean, it looks like she's giving up her star spot to you."

Bobbi made a face. "It's complicated."

"I'm reasonably smart."

"And it brings up a sore subject."

"I expected Grant to be involved. Go on."

"The story I heard was that he got to talking with Gordy about my radio spot, then had a brainstorm about Adelle taking my place for the night of the broadcast so I could be free to do the whole thing."

"And you got this story from . . . ?"

"Gordy. Of course, Archy didn't really get the brainstorm right there and then. He'd obviously thought it all through. Gordy knew better, but let him play it out and agreed to be the one to talk Adelle into it. Apparently he didn't have to talk much. He made her a generous offer for the loan of her talent to the club show, and she's going to get her pay for the broadcast as well."

"How is that possible if she's not in it?"

"Her contract. She gets paid whether she appears or not. I just gotta get the name of the agent who made a sweet deal like that for her. I'm getting money for the broadcast, but forfeiting one night's pay on the show. Not that I mind, the radio work pays lots more."

"So what's the story with Gordy and Adelle? I saw her winning a wheelbarrow full of money from him in the casino, and he looked happy about it."

"With Gordy it's hard to tell, but I think he's head over heels."

Gordy Weems in love. My mind boggled. "What about Adelle?"

"It may take her a little longer to figure it out, but right now Gordy's giving her the kind of attention she used to get from Archy. That's got to count for something. For her career, Archy is still the better deal, though, so I don't know what's going to happen."

"It could work out as a fair trade. Archy gets you and Gordy gets Adelle."

"Not funny."

"Yeah, I know. But tell me, if I wasn't in the picture, if you hadn't met me, you think you'd go for Archy?"

Another face as she thought about it. "Oh, he's fun to flirt with, and very attractive, but no, absolutely not. He'd use me up and spit me out like a piece of old gum."

"Don't sell yourself short, angel. It could have been the other way around, and you'd be breaking his heart."

"You're sweet to say so."

"You don't believe me?"

"If anyone else but Archy was involved, I would. He's too sharp to let himself lose his head over a girl. Like I said, he's after the idea of me, but not me. I'm a prize, nothing more. He probably doesn't even realize it himself. I don't think he could even talk to a girl in a normal way; it'd all have to be flirting. For instance, I couldn't have this kind of conversation with him—he wouldn't know how—but I can with you."

She made a lot of sense, and this was so different from how she'd been acting earlier. The man she'd been with before me had done a lot of damage. She was pretty much over it, but in odd moments, when something sparked an unpleasant memory for her, she'd slip and give in to the past. Her behavior then was how she'd survived. These days it tended to trip her. But that was okay, I was good at catching.

I had my eyes open for the mystery car, and it was still there when we left. The driver was slumped down in the seat, so I couldn't get a good look at him. I drove Bobbi home and tried not to watch the rearview mirror the whole time. Whoever it was followed at a good distance;

this late at night he could afford to do so. As I walked Bobbi into her hotel, he parked half a block away from my spot, cutting his lights.

After a long day of practice and performance she was nearly asleep on her feet, so we limited ourselves to a chaste good-night kiss in her doorway, though I did set a date with her tomorrow night for a real dinner out after rehearsals. I'd take her to a nice place with tablecloths, crystal glassware, and a wait staff with foreign accents.

After the elevator dispensed me in the lobby, I departed by way of the hotel's back entrance, taking to the service alley that ran through the center of the block. Buildings loomed tall and sinister on either side, but I eventually emerged unscathed onto the street and cut right. When I rounded the corner I was exactly behind my shadow's parked car. It was a Buick similar to mine, but a different color. One man was behind the wheel, and now and then a plume of smoke came out the half-open driver's window as he puffed on a cigarette. As I'd hoped, he'd been content to watch my car, not me.

I walked soft, getting fairly close, knowing the rearview mirror would be useless to warn of my approach and the rain would cover any noise. When I got even with the back bumper I vanished and worked my way around to that open window and slipped in. The only hint of my presence to the driver would be a feeling of intense cold as I passed. Escott said it was the kind of chill that went bone-deep. Just to be mean about it I hung close to the driver until with a violent shiver and a curse he suddenly rolled up the window.

I was laughing when I materialized in the passenger seat and laughed again at the look on his mug when he turned to face me. If anyone could really jump out of his skin, this guy would have been the one to do it. He also let out with quite a yell of terrified surprise. Startled as he was, he had enough presence of mind to claw inside his coat for a gun, which I took away from him without much trouble. He threw a wild punch in my direction, then hit the door handle and shot out, running as his feet hit the pavement. I shoved the gun away in a pocket and vanished again to ease my own hasty departure.

Ghosting after him at a pretty fast clip, I got right on his heels, then poured back into myself. I also landed running, but didn't have to go far. I clapped a hand on his shoulder and spun him off balance. He yelled again, making an echo off the buildings. I got a solid grip on him, put on the brakes, and dragged him over against a wall.

He put up a good struggle, or did until I lifted him clean off his feet and pinned him against the bricks. He started up with more noise, but I cut that off with a hand over his mouth. After that I got his full attention and told him to pipe down and cooperate.

We were close to a street lamp, giving me sufficient light to make a firm impression. He got quiet in a magically short time, so I let go my grip. No running away now, he just stood there looking like a beached fish. That's the chief drawback for me whenever I put anyone under—that dead look they get in their eyes.

"What's your name, mac?" I asked.

"Shep Shepperd."

Well, if his parents had inflicted that one on him, no wonder he'd turned to crime. He had a thick body wrapped in a none-too-clean topcoat that was too big for him. He smelled of stale tobacco and garlic, but no alcohol. "Who sent you after me?"

"Ike LaCelle."

That I had expected. As soon as I'd seen the headlights I remembered the phone call LaCelle made before leaving the club. It sounded like Gordy hadn't gotten around to that talk after all. He'd probably been too busy with Adelle Taylor. What the hell, she was an understandable excuse.

"What did Ike tell you to do?"

"Follow you, find where you lived, where you work, who you—"

"I get it. And then what?"

"Then tell him."

"So he could tell Grant?"

"Who?"

I let it go. There was no need for LaCelle to fill one of his soldiers in on the background. "Did Ike say what he was going to do after you found out all this?"

"No."

"You done this kind of thing before?"

"Yes."

"What usually happens afterward?"

"This!"

The reply did not come from Shep.

Someone punched me one hell of a hard one in my right kidney. I couldn't help but drop. What wind I had in me for talking whooshed right out and wouldn't come back. He followed up immediately with a sharp, brutal clip behind one of my ears, and that sent me plummeting the rest of the way to the sidewalk.

My near-automatic reaction to escape such pain was to vanish, but it didn't happen. He'd used wood, then. Some kind of club. Just enough force to knock me down but not out, and it hurt just as much as it would a normal man. Lucky me.

The initial shock faded slowly as I lay on the wet pavement with the rain hammering my back. When things eased enough for me to start moving again, my attacker used his foot to turn me over. I squinted up at him, not liking him much.

He was bigger than his friend, with prizefighter ears and a beat-up face to match. He looked too old for the ring, though. Maybe he sparred for a living when he wasn't out in the middle of the night helping Shep tail a vampire. He was well armed, competently cradling one of Colonel Thompson's .45 caliber specialties. It was fitted out with a fifty-shot drum and a fine stock that looked to be made out of walnut. In my opinion, that was overdoing things.

I sat up, testing my recuperation, and rubbed the sore spot on my head. I'd had worse. "Dr. Livingston, I presume?"

He either didn't appreciate my humor or didn't get it. He balanced himself to aim a kick to my gut, but I made a fast lunge and caught his leg in both hands, turning it hard. He gave a surprised grunt and toppled, arms flailing out to save himself. The machine gun clanked heavy as it landed in the streaming gutter.

His recovery was quick; he must still have had some speed in him left over from the prize ring. He twisted, trying to get to the weapon before I did. We each scrambled hastily across the walk on all fours.

I won by half a second and managed to violently shove the gun a good five yards out of his reach. Instead of going after it, I got to my feet, pulling Shep's gun from my pocket, and aimed it like I meant it.

"Hold it right there, Ace," I told him as he lurched up. "I'm a rootin' tootin' son of a gun from Arizona, so don't dance with me."

"Yeah, sure, with the safety on," he said, grinning and moving forward in a fighter's crouch.

I twitched the muzzle in a threatening movement that made him stop. "It's a revolver, Ace, and we both know they don't bother with pesky things like safeties. Next time try teaching your granny to suck eggs, you'll get fewer laughs."

He scowled mightily.

"In fact, this is a sweet little double-action model, so I don't even have to cock it to make big holes in your skull, so why don't you back off and stand over there with Shep?"

He growled something under his breath about my mother that I pretended not to hear, but did as he was told while I retrieved the machine gun. Shep had woken up from his trance at some point and stared, still looking like a fish, just slightly more animated.

"What the hell happened?" Ace demanded of his friend. "I go off for one minute to take a leak and—"

Why Ace needed a machine gun along for that errand I didn't want to know.

"Gah!" Shep's memory had evidently caught up with him. He pointed at me with a quivering hand. "This guy got inna car, right inna car with me! You shoulda seen! He was just *there!*"

"Shep," I said calmly, looking hard at him. "Take a nap."

His eyes rolled up, and he slid to the sidewalk.

Ace's own eyes went wide, staring at his unconscious friend, before he turned them on me. It was all I needed, just a little of his undivided attention to put him under as well. I gave him the same questions I'd put to Shep and got the same answers. Ike LaCelle was accustomed to hiring them for odd jobs at odd hours, so when he called with instructions for them to get over to the club and follow me, it was nothing out of the ordinary. Night work was one thing that gangsters and the undead definitely had in common.

They were usually told to rough up the bird they were after, but not this time. I supposed LaCelle just wanted information to start with, then he'd send in his boys to discourage me from seeing Bobbi again. Maybe I was to come home one evening and find them waiting for me with brass knuckles and big grins.

Fat chance.

When I'd finished with them both, they'd have to report a dismal failure to LaCelle. I primed them to say they'd followed me diligently, then lost me sometime after I crossed the state line into Wisconsin. In fact, at three in the afternoon tomorrow they would make a collect long-distance call to Mr. LaCelle from wherever they happened to be in that state to let him know about it. I walked them back to their car, saw them tucked in all cozy, and waved good-bye as they drove off.

I hoped they had enough gas for the trip. I'd forgotten to tell them to stop for it.

The house was dark when I got back, though Escott had left the upper-landing light on for me. For once I was sorry that he was attempting to get one up on the insomnia; I'd wanted to tell him about my little interruption, and let him know about Ike LaCelle's bullyboys.

Just because I'd taken care of the two he'd sent didn't mean he couldn't find more.

I sieved upstairs lest the creaking of the house's old floorboards disturb my sleeping partner and shucked out of my thoroughly soaked clothes. Maybe I could get LaCelle to pay the cleaning bill.

Having changed into pajamas and a robe, I went silently down to the kitchen and spent some time scribbling Escott a letter on the situation, adding in the news about Bobbi being a full-fledged guest on the *Variety Hour*. He also had an invitation to come to the studio and watch—Bobbi's way of thanking him for the orchid. I left the note on the kitchen table with the revolver and machine gun, wishing I could see the look on Escott's face in the morning when he saw them.

It'd be a beaut, I was sure, especially before he had his coffee.

There was still a big slice of waking night left. My condition wouldn't allow me to cheat and go to bed early, so I caught up on reading the papers. Escott had gotten to them first; some were in tatters from his habit of cutting out any articles that caught his eye. He'd left the clippings on the coffee table; I didn't miss much. They were mostly concerned with crimes. I skimmed those enough to know what they were about then moved on to other news, little of which was good. The civil war in Spain was going great—for the side that the Nazis were backing. The word "atrocities" was used a lot, but the paper either wouldn't or couldn't get more specific than that.

I got sick of it and the state of mankind in general pretty fast and gave up on current news, trying a magazine instead. The first page I turned to informed me that dynamite was the preferred method of suicide in a Montana mining town. That was enough to send me back up to my room to find a book. I spent the remaining hours reading about a detective who talked tough, got hit on the head a lot, and planned to marry the girl right after the case was finished. He shot several gangsters stone dead and sent the chief bad guy plunging into a cement mixer, none of which brought any objections from the grateful cops. Not a bad life at all.

It occurred to me at several points in the story that I could do a better job of writing myself, but I just couldn't trouble myself enough to go down to the basement and prove it. I finished the book off, tossed it on a pile of others I'd gone through, and stared at the ceiling, not thinking about much of anything except Bobbi for a long while. I'd let her read some of my stuff, and she'd said it was good and that she'd liked it, but I wasn't all that sure myself. She was a singer, not a writer; I needed someone in the writing business to look at it. Since no editors were knocking themselves out to make appointments with me, the only course left was to get to work, finish something, and send it in.

Which I'd have to do some other night. The clock said I had just enough time to get to my basement sanctuary. I did exactly that, and for my last moments of consciousness I concentrated hard at not looking at my abandoned typewriter.

It was still in the same spot when I woke up, but I had a busy evening ahead and cheerfully quit the chamber to join Escott upstairs. He sat at his ease at the kitchen table surrounded by several empty cartons of Chinese food and sipping a gin and tonic. He was doing the newspaper crossword puzzle with that damned hypodermic pen.

"Cripes, it's the easy life for you and no mistake," I said, knotting the tie on my bathrobe.

He was fairly used to my sudden materializations by now and hardly bothered to look up. "Yes, it's been so dull here lately I was thinking of spending the next weekend in Cuba."

"Didn't you like the presents?"

Now he managed to crack something close to a smile. "Rather. Especially the machine gun. I took it out to the firing range today and had a bit of fun. The stock got slightly damaged from that roughhousing you described in your note, but it is a very fine weapon, indeed."

"You sound like you're keeping it."

"Why not?"

"Because it might have been used in a crime. The cops could be looking for it."

"Not to worry, I'll turn it in when I've finished playing. It's not often I get a chance to make so much noise in so short a time. You'd be surprised at how quickly one can empty those drums. It's a pity the Treasury Department has such a tight control over those things; I should like to have one for myself."

"Maybe you could ask that mug where he got it."

"I meant legally. I doubt *he* paid much attention to the restrictions."

"Yeah, crooks are funny that way. Where is it?"

"In the basement behind the safe's alcove. The revolver's there, as well."

We were the only two people on the planet who knew how to open the trick wall that hid the safe. "How're things going with the Sommerfeld girl?"

He made a sour face and capped the pen. "They're not. She's all right, or was so when she phoned this afternoon to check on me. In fact, she's phoned several times today, according to my service."

"Getting antsy?"

"That's an accurate enough description for her growing impatience."

"What about that guy Paterno? Find him?"

"No," he said, which really surprised me. Escott was capable of tracking down a black cat in a coal mine without breaking a sweat. "I tried asking at the tavern McCallen frequents, and several other leads, but nothing turned up concerning his mystery friend. The single name you provided could be a first name, an alias, or a nickname. Whichever it might be, he's never broken any laws using it."

"I'll do what I can to clear the books tonight when I see McCallen."

"Which may not be possible."

"Now what?"

"He did not go in to work today, nor was he at home."

"Where, then?"

He shrugged. "My guess is that he's either hiding out from us or devoting his time to searching for Miss Sommerfeld."

"That's just great."

"Yes, it *is* rather disappointing."

"I don't figure him for hiding out, though. There's probably nothing better he'd like to do than find us. He was steamed hot as hell about my going through his place."

"So you've said, but he avoided the office—at least when I was there."

"You mean you've been waiting for him?"

"Well, I did give the correct name of the agency when

I first contacted him for that café meeting. If he remembered it he need only look in the telephone directory to find the address. I did rather expect him to walk in at any time today, but . . ." He made a small throwing-away gesture.

"I hope you thought to—"

"My dear chap, I'm no fool, I took suitable precautions to arm and protect myself."

"There's a relief. I just wish you'd told me—oh. You couldn't."

"You do miss a few things with that daily coma of yours."

That called for a snort. "Now what?"

"It depends how much time you have to spare tonight."

I knew what he wanted me to do. "Not much, at least early on. I'll drive over to McCallen's, see if he's there. If he is, then the problem's solved; but if not, then I can't wait around. I promised to take Bobbi to dinner."

"How is Miss Smythe? She must be most pleased with the turn of events you mentioned."

"She's fine, all excited about the radio broadcast tomorrow. There're tickets reserved for us at the studio, and we're to go to the party at the Nightcrawler afterward."

"That is most generous of her, but I—"

"Charles, she likes you. It'd really make her happy if you accepted her invitation."

He bounced one eyebrow. "And I thought it was Mr. McCallen who was the blackmailer. What about this LaCelle and his toughs? Will he be at this event?"

"Probably."

"Then I shall be happy to attend."

"Great, just don't tell Bobbi you're there adding to your rogues'-gallery files."

"Certainly not. You do seem determined to fill up my social calendar this week. I phoned Shoe, and we've an appointment for dinner and to see the show playing at his club on Wednesday."

"You can have my plate of snails."

"If Shoe is not merely boasting about this new chef he's acquired I just may do that."

As this was the first real date Bobbi and I had had in a while, I put a little extra effort into making myself presentable. The tuxedo with the white coat was back from the cleaners, but I double-checked it for any sign of dark lint, just in case. Though I couldn't see anything in a mirror, I at least felt like I looked damned sharp. Escott glanced up long enough to say that I'd outdone myself, wished me and Miss Smythe a most enjoyable time, then went back to his evening papers. Unless work beckoned, he was more stay-at-home than Emily Dickinson ever thought to be, but minus the poetry writing to distract him. He had other activities to fill the hours.

His latest project with the crossbows appeared to be complete. The dining room and its big table were all cleared and cleaned, and hanging from its walls like trophies were the weapons he'd repaired. He'd been doing some practice with them, too. At the far end of the downstairs hall he kept a bale of old rolled up carpet about two feet thick and four feet square bound tight with rope. Most of the time he threw a tablecloth over the ratty thing to conceal it, but that was off now, revealing the target he'd tacked on the side. The red bull's-eye center was nearly eaten out by holes made from crossbow bolts.

Everyone should have a hobby. Besides, this beat the indoor pistol firing that had come before the crossbows. The neighbors had had fits complaining about the noise until I persuaded him to start going to a real shooting range.

I hopped in the Buick and went straight to Jason McCallen's place. It didn't look too promising; all the lights were out and his car was gone. On the slim chance that he might be playing games and skulking inside, I did another break-and-enter routine, though with me it was more of a vanish-and-slip-in-through-the-cracks act.

The living room was very still and dim. I listened hard before moving, but couldn't hear anything. My flashlight brightened things considerably, but did not reveal the presence of the owner, though it flushed the cat out as I went searching. The bedroom was in order, the clothing in the closet and bureau undisturbed, so McCallen hadn't packed for a lengthy trip—unless he planned to buy what he needed along the way.

In the kitchen the ample food in the cat's dish was still fresh, so the animal was in no danger of starving. It reassured me more than anything else I'd seen here that McCallen planned to return. He could have dropped in at any time today to feed his pet, who was presently trying to leave a coating of shed fur on my tux pants as he rubbed against me. I found the phone and called Escott. He took the negative news with a kind of verbal shrug.

"Nothing for it then but to get on to the rest of your evening."

"I'll try here again later. He has to come back to sleep sometime." I had the idea of waking McCallen in the wee hours to deliver my message. If I did it right he wouldn't even remember it as a dream.

"Only if it's convenient to you," said Escott.

I hung up and vanished, which scared the hell out of the cat, to judge by his hiss and yowl as he tore from the room. Animals are usually fine with me until I try disappearing. Maybe they don't like the cold in the space I occupy. I floated all the way across the street to the car, filling back into myself right in the driver's seat and feeling pretty smug about my ability to do so. Of course, I'd have felt a whole lot more smug if I'd actually reappeared in my *own* vehicle. The damp wind from the north had caused me to drift too far to the left. I was in somebody else's Studebaker.

A nice car, but my key wouldn't fit. I sieved out and humbly walked to my Buick.

A short drive later and I found a parking space no more than a dozen steps from Moe's tavern. Maybe I'd have better luck than Escott at finding McCallen here.

The main room held only a scattering of couples, but no sign of McCallen, Paterno, or any of the others who had chased me. I crossed to the curtained-off area they'd emerged from, but no one was there either. The only familiar face in the joint was Jim Waters, who sat sideways at one of the tables so he could stretch out his legs. I had time for a short visit, so I went over, said hello, shook hands, and apologized for my swift exit the other night.

"What was that all about?" he asked after inviting me to sit. "What did you do to get that big guy so mad at you?"

"It's a long story with no payoff. I need to settle something with him, but not when he's surrounded by a crowd."

"Well, I'm glad you got away. Leastwise, you don't

look worse for the wear, so I'm assuming you got away." He gave my duds a thorough eyeballing. My topcoat must have represented a month's earnings for him, even with an army pension.

"I'm taking my girl someplace fancy tonight," I explained. "Buy you a beer?"

He had one empty bottle on the table by him. "I won't say no so long as I buy the next round."

I lifted the bottle so the waiter at the bar could see and he nodded back. "This'll sound crazy, but I can't drink alcohol."

Waters laughed once. "I knew there was something wrong with you. You under the age limit?"

"No, it's just bad for my insides. Makes me sick as a dog, but I don't mind watching someone else enjoying a cold one." The waiter misunderstood my order and brought two bottles. Waters assured me he could make a home for the spare. I let him clear his throat with a good swallow of brew. "That big Scotsman, you know anything about him?"

"Thought he was your friend."

"No friend. It's a business deal with us, and I don't know him that well, or the people with him."

"I see him here a few times a week with his crew. They don't mix much with the rest of the crowd, mostly stay in the back."

"They must be tone deaf. What do they do there?"

"Talking and drinking. Once in a while I hear them arguing about stuff when I'm trying to sing. I usually just do a louder number."

"Arguing?"

"Donno about what, I don't pay 'em much mind.

Weird-looking bunch. Couple of 'em have that hungry, mad-at-the-world look. Maybe they're communists."

That caught my attention. It might explain a few things about why someone was willing to pay McCallen a couple of grand. Maybe he'd gotten Miss Sommerfeld to join the communist party and instead of love letters the envelope was full of papers proving it. That would break the engagement to her prince fast enough. If there was one thing royalty hated more than rioting peasants, it was rioting communist peasants.

"Does anyone else here know for sure? The staff? The owner?"

"I doubt it. Moe lets 'em have the room so long as they keep buying beer. He doesn't ask questions unless somebody starts busting furniture."

Since this seemed to be the limit of his information I asked him about his music. "Singing tonight?"

"It's early yet. I like to have some kind of a crowd before I interrupt their talking. You still serious about that nightclub?"

"Yeah." But I could tell he wasn't quite buying it yet. I wanted very much to convince him what I had planned was more than just some kid's ambitious pipe dream. "Look, how would you like to meet Bobbi Smythe? She's going to be on the *Archy Grant Variety Hour* tomorrow night and afterward there's going to be a celebration at the Nightcrawler Club. I'll introduce you."

"I don't know if that's my kind of party—"

"You need to meet her anyway. Once my club's up and running you'll be working together."

He hemmed and hawed until I was tempted to give him a little hypnotic nudge. Then: "Is she as pretty as she sings? I've heard her on the radio a few times."

"Brother, she's a knock out."

"Well . . . I *think* I could be persuaded to—"

"Great, I'll have a paid-up cab outside your store tomorrow at seven-thirty."

He gave me a startled look and chuckled. "You don't want me to change my mind, do you?"

I grinned back. "Nope."

He shook his head and started on the second beer. "This club of yours, where you setting up?"

I gave a shrug. "The best location I can afford."

"Well, you look like you can buy the best. Is it your money or the mob's?"

Maybe I'd been hanging around Gordy and his friends too much. Something of them must have been rubbing off onto me. On the other hand, in these hard times the only people with bucks were the racketeers. "I earned it, and I pay taxes on it." True statements, but both avoided a direct answer about its source.

He nodded, a wise gleam in his eyes. He was on to me all right, but willing to let me keep my secrets. "You got a name for this place yet?"

I'd been sitting on that one for a long time. The name had come to me one night with no effort or thought, yet it struck me as being absolutely perfect. "Oh, yeah. I do."

"Ready to share it?"

I had to grin again, I was so pleased with myself. "Club Crymsyn."

8

"A blues club named Crymsyn?" Waters gave me a cockeyed smile of wry doubt.

And spelled funny to boot. I figured it'd be memorable, not underwhelming, but he wasn't going to see me falter. The name was good luck, and I knew it. "The club won't be strictly blues. I'm planning to have in all kinds of music, lots of other talents."

"What? Like magicians and dog acts?"

"Only if they play good music and can sing to it."

That got a chuckle. "Then I'll allow as you just might get away with it."

I decided he wasn't trying to throw a blanket on things, only being innately cautious. He didn't know me from Adam, after all. I could be some crazed eccentric out to impress a stranger before disappearing into the crowd never to return.

There was one sure way to dispel that impression; all I had to do was find the right location to put the joint.

He sipped his beer and we talked about some of the other singers and bands in Chicago that would fit the bill for Club Crymsyn. He'd been to the Shoe Box a few times with friends, and was impressed when I said I knew the owner.

"He has some prime talent playing his place, but I heard Shoe Coldfield himself was a killer," he said.

"That I wouldn't know about. He's always been straight up with me. Pulled me out of a couple jams a while back."

"What kind of jams?"

Sometimes I talked too much. Not wanting to scare him off, I trimmed the complicated and violent past down to essentials. "I had trouble with some guys not unlike this stuff going on with McCallen. Shoe came by and helped peel me off the sidewalk."

He sat back, looking shrewd as Solomon. "There's a lot you're not telling, son."

"When I know you better. And when I have more time. For right now, what I do know for sure about Shoe is that he's a businessman looking after his part of the world."

"But he's still mob."

"Does that make him much different from a banker foreclosing on a widow? He's legal, but it's wrong. Shoe looks after his own."

"Meaning he might shoot the banker but not turn out the widow?"

"Why don't you come meet him sometime and judge for yourself?"

Waters gave a good-natured shrug. "I won't say yes or no."

"Maybe I can bring him here some night. I'd like him to hear you sing."

"What you planning on? Some kind of audition?"

"That's up to Shoe. I can't make promises for him, but

I think it'd be a hell of a thing to have you playing at the Shoe Box."

"A white guy at a colored place?"

"If Shoe says you're in, you're in. Turn the lights out and your music still hits the heart same as the rest."

He flapped a hand. "Sure thing. Bring him anytime you want, there's no cover, but I don't know if Moe might have a problem with a colored guy coming in here."

I smiled. "I'll have a little talk with him. He won't mind."

"Jeez, boy, but you are sure of yourself."

"That's the best way to go in this town." Of course, it does help to have a hypnotic edge over people.

"You know what kind of odds are against you for success with a new club?" he asked.

"I've been getting a pretty good idea from others in the business."

"Getting's not the same as having, and you gotta pardon me if I think you look too young to have much experience for this sort of game."

I nodded, giving him that point. My apparent youth would probably always work against me. I was getting used to dealing with it. "I know, but it's my investment to risk, my dream to bring about. Besides, I know enough to hire people who will be experienced."

"That's half of it, and I wish you luck."

"Hey, if I get artists like you coming in regular, the luck's already there."

He did enjoy hearing sincere praise. I got the impression he didn't receive a lot of recognition for his work. Maybe he'd become a fixture in this place, and no one paid him much mind because he was so familiar a sight. That would change if I had anything to do with it.

Time was short; I told Waters I had to leave and would see him tomorrow, then paused long enough at the bar to ask after McCallen. Neither the waiter nor bartender had anything useful to share about him. He came in often, usually had two or three beers along with his friends, all gathering to talk in the back room. The waiter thought they did a lot of speech making. Often when he went to check on them there would be one man reading aloud from some papers. They seemed to take turns, then argue with each other about whatever they'd heard. The waiter never paid attention to them beyond the fact that they were lousy tippers. It was a sliver more of information than Escott had, and it reinforced Waters's communist theory. Whether it proved to be useful remained to be seen.

And that was as much as I wanted to put into the McCallen problem for the present. For the rest of the evening I had better things to do.

Bobbi looked like one hundred percent nitro when she greeted me at the door wearing a blazing red dress with a band of gold sequins that spiraled up around her figure from hem to neck. It had some kind of matching-scarf things trailing from the shoulders that she wound in a repeat spiral over her arms and acted like sleeves. If she slipped them off her arms, they trailed gracefully down her back. She said it was another Adrian, and I asked if dresses came in models like cars.

"That's the designer's name," she told me, getting her big coat with the high fur collar.

"So's Ford's Model A."

She shook her head and gave a little eye roll, like I'd never really get it. "Adelle helped me pick it out when we went shopping. I've decided to wear it for the broadcast."

"It's too bad only the studio audience will see. If everyone else could you'd be a star in the first minute. Now, how do I get it off you?"

"Later, Mr. Caveman. Take me to some food, I've been singing all morning and helping Adelle with the dancing all afternoon. I'm completely starved."

I took her to one of our favorite dinner-and-dance places. She wasn't in the mood for dancing, not after all the rehearsal, but the food—she assured me—was marvelous. Last night I'd called Escott's answering service and told them to make an eight-thirty reservation for me. There shouldn't have been a problem as they were usually very efficient, but something had gone wrong. I went through variations of my name and even Escott's with the hostess, who gave me an apologetic smile and said she did not have any of those in her book for this evening. A table *might* be made available in another hour if the gentleman and lady would care to enjoy cocktails in the bar.

She had a glacial face, but I melted it with a long, steady look. "I think if you'll check just one more time you'll find my name listed." I released her from my concentration and waited.

She checked, and her smile got very sunny, indeed. She led us in triumph to a table overlooking the dance floor and saw that we were comfortably seated.

Bobbi managed not to break up until the woman was gone. "It's *spooky* when you do that—but so conve-nient," she whispered.

"Saves on bribes, too."

A waiter with an accent soon swooped in and out with Bobbi's order. I asked for only a cup of coffee, which seemed to worry the man, but I didn't owe him any explanations. To make things look all right, Bobbi occasionally sipped from the cup so he could refill it. She was very well accustomed to the fact I would never be able to join her in eating a normal meal. On the other hand, what we often shared between us afterward more than made up for it.

"Won't that keep you awake?" I asked, indicating the coffee.

"I thought you preferred me alert."

"And kicking, but you need your rest for tomorrow."

"Then you'll just have to get me to bed early and exhaust me."

"Whew. I'll do my best."

"As always."

The restaurant had a live orchestra, not as brash as the Melodians, but good enough to get the point across for listening as well as dancing; just in case she was up to it, I asked Bobbi if she wanted to take a turn around the floor, but she shook her head.

"We can find another floor to turn around on at my place," she said, then attacked her steak like she had a grudge against it.

When we went out to eat I usually did most of the talking to start with until she'd worked her way past the food. She would nod and make encouraging sounds to hold up her part of the conversation, then have a turn later. I told her about the Sommerfeld case and the possible communist angle.

"You make it sound sinister," she said. "Lots of my friends are communists and they're perfectly nice people."

"Even Madison Pruitt?"

"Okay, there are exceptions to everything, but it's more of an intellectual choice for them. He and the others aren't exactly building bombs in an attic."

"I doubt he even knows how to change a lightbulb."

"Oh, be fair. He's not dumb, just irresponsible."

"Which is curable, only he doesn't want to be cured."

"Maybe you could ask Madison if he knows anything useful for your case. He'll be Marza's date at the party."

"How peachy," I said.

Madison Pruitt was heir to a whopping fortune and a devoted communist—very distressing to his rich and straitlaced family. He was as passionate about his politics as he was short on social graces. He knew about manners, but eschewed them as concessions to the decadent oppressors of the workers of the world. In a young man a little rebellion is to be expected; in a guy well past thirty it's downright embarrassing. But Bobbi had a point, so unless something changed in the case tonight, I'd have a talk with him tomorrow. I don't know what her accompanist, Marza, saw in him, unless it was that fact that she was too intimidating for most men, and Madison was either completely oblivious or immune to her sandpaper personality. Though he had money enough to attract the most determined gold digger, he was fairly oblivious to them as well. His passion was for politics and food, often not in that order, depending when he'd last eaten.

"Is Charles coming to the broadcast?" Bobbi asked.

"I talked him into it."

"Good! How did you manage?"

"I told him how hurt you'd be if he didn't turn up."

"Oh, Jack, he should come to it because he wants to, not to keep from hurting my feelings."

"He knows better, honest—but this gives him an excuse to be persuaded. I think he's practicing to be a quirky curmudgeon."

"Why is he so shy about having a good time?"

"I don't know. Maybe it's that British blood of his." And maybe he really was shy. He was sure of himself in lots of areas, from delivering a Shakespearean soliloquy to an audience of drunken lumberjacks to facing down a roomful of armed mobsters, but the idea of going to a party just might petrify him. Gordy would be there, though, so Escott would have someone besides me with whom he could talk shop.

By the time Bobbi had reached the dessert stage, I'd figured out how to get the dress off her. There was a line of tiny hooks going up one side—difficult, but not impossible. It would require a careful, light touch. The last thing I wanted was her having a conniption if I pulled a thread.

Wrong, I thought, looking up. *The last thing I want is to see Ike LaCelle coming to my table.*

Bobbi followed the direction of my frozen gaze. LaCelle had his hand out and a big grin on his mug. She smiled and I smiled, though it was probably rather fixed for us both.

"Well, if it isn't Miss Bobbi Smythe lookin' like a million bucks," he declared loud enough to turn heads.

Bobbi murmured something gracious while he bowed and made a big deal out of kissing her hand. She'd already gone into her voltage routine, but keeping the power low, and put on her public face for him. He turned on me next, briefly. I stood to shake hands, but didn't invite him to join us, hoping he'd get the hint. He didn't, being content to keep me standing while he gave more greeting to Bobbi. If he was steamed about me taking on his boys and winning, he kept all signs of it to himself.

"I heard that the rehearsals for the show are going great," he said to her. His pitch was such as to let people know she was some sort of celebrity. "Think you'll be all set to take America by storm tomorrow night?" Why didn't he just say she'd be on Archy Grant's *Variety Hour* and get the advertising out of the way?

"I think so. It should be fun."

"Fun! Sugar, this is going to put you on top. I wouldn't be surprised if there was a movie deal at the end of it."

"That would be nice." From her expression I could see she was well aware he was laying it on with a trowel. Some of the people nearby seemed to be thinking along the same lines. He wasn't doing Bobbi any favors now.

"What a beautiful dress, you need to show that off. Will you do me the honor of giving me one little dance before I go?"

The "before I go" was a good touch, implying that we would soon be rid of him if she complied. I wasn't so sure, but gave a slight shrug to let her know it was all her decision. She managed another smile and said that would be lovely. It was delivered with a damning-with-faint-praise attitude, but LaCelle ignored it. On purpose, I was sure. No one was that dense.

LaCelle was somewhat better at a slow waltz than a fast fox-trot, so Bobbi fared better on the dance floor with him tonight than at the Nightcrawler party. I watched them and boiled for a few minutes, since I'd been very blatantly ignored by him, but hauled it all in.

There was no point getting angry with LaCelle, not when I knew I could take care of him as easily as I'd done his goons. If I was in a really good mood I'd only send him off to Wisconsin; if not, then he'd wake up and find himself stranded somewhere in the Canadian wilderness with no topcoat.

The waltz faltered and stopped. Laughter rippled through the crowd, and I guessed what was coming before I saw it. The smiling orchestra leader was in the process of stepping down, having just given his baton over to a broadly grinning Archy Grant, who looked like he owned the place.

The dancers also faltered, first turning to see, then applaud as they recognized him. Grant called something to the musicians and they started up with the sprightly theme song to his show, confirming to one and all just who was in charge of things. The applause became more pronounced, and Grant waved like he was having the time of his life. The good feeling spread throughout the crowd. To give the devil his due, he knew how to play to them.

He called something else to the musicians, they nodded back, and he returned the baton to the leader. Grant stepped up to a microphone and began singing a love song. LaCelle slow-danced Bobbi over close, allowing Grant to sing the song just for her. All they lacked was a spotlight, though it was hardly necessary. They were very much everyone's center of attention.

If Bobbi felt unsure about the manipulation that was going on, she didn't let it show. It looked like a crazy publicity stunt, and I might have approved but for knowing better. The whole romantic business was designed to bowl Bobbi right over, and might have worked a dream on any other girl but her.

Grant came to a stopping point in the song lyrics, but signaled for the music to keep going. "Ladies and gentlemen, I'm Archy Grant. I just had to stop in and say hello and introduce you to my beautiful guest for tomorrow night's *Variety Hour*—Miss Bobbi Smythe!"

Several photographers appeared out of nowhere and flashbulbs went off, freezing the moment. I had no doubt some of those pictures would find their way into tomorrow's paper.

She gave a bow, and people cheered like they knew who she was, and maybe some did if they'd been to see the club show.

As though he'd rehearsed it, LaCelle bowed and stepped away from Bobbi, applauding. Grant bounded lightly off the orchestra steps and caught her up in his arms, taking her for a smooth spin around the floor. Other dancers fell back to give them room, like it was a Fred and Ginger movie. Bobbi looked delighted with things, but that was still her public face. She played along with Grant's game as they danced, but I knew the difference between her real smile and the one she used for a performance.

Too bad Grant didn't.

I heard someone approach and looked up. Gil Dalhauser slid his long form uninvited into Bobbi's chair. It was shaping up to be a perfect evening. He didn't say anything for a while, just watched me steadily with those soulless arctic-blue eyes.

"Yes," he said to my unasked question. "Ike arranged all this."

"Just to get Grant next to Bobbi?" I supposed the

rehearsals weren't as good a setting for romance as a pricey restaurant.

"It's gonna happen whether you like it or not, kid," he said with a minimal nod toward the dancers.

"What about whether Bobbi likes it or not?"

"She'll like it well enough. Archy can boost her up the ladder a lot faster than you ever could."

"That's nothing to do with this."

"It's everything to do with it. All she has to do is make Archy happy and he gives her a hand up. Happens all the time."

"And she's got no say in it?"

"She'll know what's good for her and say yes."

"She'll tell Archy to go to hell."

"Not before the broadcast she won't."

He had a point there. Bobbi would be able to hold Grant off for that long, but afterward he could make a nuisance of himself. "If he gets insistent, she'll let him have it between the eyes. I've seen her in action."

He was amused. "*That* would be a career killer."

"She can survive it. Archy Grant's big, but not that big."

"But Ike LaCelle is. He knows everyone in show business, kid, who hires, who fires. If that girl makes the wrong move, he'll put the word out against her. She'll be lucky to end up as a singing waitress in a chophouse."

"Why should Ike go to so much trouble for Archy?"

"They've made each other a lot of money. Archy's been a good investment for Ike, so Ike's gonna keep him happy."

"Regardless of what Bobbi thinks of the deal?"

"She's just another broad. There's more where she came from. When Grant gets tired of her, he'll give her a diamond bracelet and say good-bye. But I guarantee you she'll be better off than she was before. He always leaves them happy. He's nice that way."

"A real saint, I can see it from here."

"And if you know what's good for you, you'll just back off until it's over. You'll get your girl again. And she'll be a lot more rich and famous."

"Or Ike'll send more goons like Shep Shepperd and his boxing friend after me?"

Dalhauser's cold eyes flickered.

I'd hit him square with that one. They were probably still wondering how I'd managed that little gag. "Maybe you should have a talk with Gordy, then instead of wasting time warning me, you can be telling Ike and Archy to lay off."

"Think you're hot stuff, do you?"

I didn't bother to answer. He wasn't the only one who could stare for effect.

He blinked once, slowly. "I got news for you, Ike's already spoken with Gordy. He said you were trouble and not to mess with you, but I wouldn't put much stock in his protection. Ike's got a lot more friends, and they're pretty powerful. You wouldn't stand a chance."

"Did Gordy make it clear that he didn't want Miss Smythe to be bothered by Archy?"

"He did. But if she's willing to go along, that's her business, isn't it? I heard she's done it before with Slick Morelli, so this won't be anything new to her."

"She's changed. And Slick's dead, you know."

"I think you're getting the wrong message out of this," he said, leaning forward on his elbows. "I'm still trying to do *you* a favor."

"Oh, yeah?"

"Mostly to cover things with Gordy. That way he can't say I didn't warn you."

"I'm touched."

He snorted, all contept. "Listen up: I've seen hotshots like you trying to go up against Ike. He looks soft, but he isn't. They always lose and they lose bad. Those two mugs he sent before are Boy Scouts compared to the real muscle he can call in."

"I'm sure they are. It only means I need to talk with Ike myself, then we can all avoid having problems."

He sat back. "Okay. Go ahead. He's not against a little payout to the boyfriend if it makes everyone happy."

I went very still. Inside me something colder than death and full of abrupt rage twisted like a stung snake. I had to struggle to hold it in check or Dalhauser would have a broken neck before he took another breath. He must have seen it in my face, because he suddenly went pale and straightened, his hand going inside his coat. For the first time since I'd met him he seemed alarmed.

Then I remembered who I was dealing with and made myself calm down again. He was a mug, a little smarter than most, but still in the same club, and to mugs Bobbi was just a piece of goods to be bought, used, and sold. He didn't know any better and never would.

"I want to talk to Ike," I said very softly. "Just talk. Go tell him."

Dalhauser didn't relax one inch. Still staring at me, he slipped from the chair and went away.

Bobbi and Grant continued dancing. Whenever he turned her in my direction she shot me a serious look, the rest of the time she smiled. Holy Hannah, but even from here I could see she was mad enough to chew nails. It must be costing her one hell of an effort to pretend to be having fun.

Ike sauntered over from wherever he'd been and looked down at me in a benevolent way. This time I didn't bother to stand, but did motion for him to take the empty chair.

"Gil tells me you're a little upset about the way things are going," he said with a sympathetic smile. We were such good friends now. "Did he explain it all fully?"

"Yeah. My girl sleeps with Archy and he gives her the world on a gold plate. Meaning you're the pimp?"

He only hooked one side of his mouth in brief amusement. "I'm just doing a favor for a friend."

"Then do Archy another favor and tell him to back off."

"Hey, I don't tell him what to do. If he happens to see something he likes, I just grease the wheels."

"Ike, look at me and listen hard: you're going to tell Archy to back off."

LaCelle's face went blank for a moment, then he shook his head, fighting my influence. "Who the hell do you think you are, punk?" he demanded, but his words were slurring.

"I'm the son of a bitch who's gonna turn your face inside out if you don't fix things the way I want." I locked my gaze onto him again and stepped up the pressure until it felt like a rope was tied tight around my head. "You hear me, Ike? You hear my voice? You can only hear my voice now, can't you?"

His mouth sagged. Dead-fish time. And I had him hooked solid.

I gave him the works. Not too easy at first, because I'd gotten hot under the collar, but I kept it under control.

The more orders I gave to LaCelle, the better I felt; there wasn't much danger of me driving him insane. That was a distinct problem if I hypnotized anyone while I was angry.

When I finished with him everything was crystal clear in his mind about talking Archy Grant into cutting short his Romeo act with Bobbi. He could be friends with her, joke and flirt if he liked, but anything more than that would only bring him grief. If Archy had any questions on this change of mind, he could come to me for answers. The same went for Dalhauser.

And the radio show would go on with Bobbi as scheduled.

I was skating close to the edge with that last one, considering the promise I'd made to her not to interfere. But in this case I was only making sure things stayed as they were, not changing them in her favor.

LaCelle was as primed as I could make him. I let him go and checked the dance floor. Bobbi and Grant weren't there. A wash of unease went through me because I wouldn't put it past him to actually kidnap her. It changed to vast relief when she came back to the table from a different direction. Her color was high and she was seething so much she trembled.

"I'm ready to leave," she whispered, holding tight to a thin, unnatural smile. Her public face, because people were still looking on.

I tossed an outrageously generous ten on the table and escorted her out; we retrieved our coats, the valet brought my car around, and I got her inside. I didn't say a word while driving, giving her a chance to work through things, to get calm enough to speak.

It took her a good five minutes, and when she did

speak it would have made a marine blush. She had quite a few names for Archy Grant, and an equal number of things that he could do with himself after he went to hell, along with several creative ways she would be glad to use to send him there. Her fury seemed to fill the whole car. I found an empty parking lot and pulled into the middle of it. Soon as we stopped, she said a terse thanks, then launched out and stalked up and down for a while, still cursing.

I held hard to the wheel and hunched down. She wasn't mad at me—God help me if I ever worked her up into such a state—but the force of it was such that all my instincts said to take cover until the storm passed.

Eventually the pacing in the cold April wind got her cooled down to the point where she could come back inside again. When she was settled in I shifted gears and drove toward her hotel at a sedate pace.

"Thanks," she said.

"You're welcome," I returned, with a touch of uncertainty.

"That's thanks for not asking anything obvious until I could talk without biting your head off."

"Am I safe now?"

She breathed in deep and let it out slow. "I think so."

I waited so she could draw in a few more gallons of air, then ventured to ask what had happened on the dance floor.

"You saw all the goings on up there?" she asked.

"The showstopper stuff, yeah."

"It was his way of flattering me. Get me out there, throw in a surprise, make me the center of attention so everyone thinks I'm really important."

"You *are* important."

"I know that, but I also know where I am in the world with it and how few people have actually heard of me. Archy was trying to improve things, which is great as far as it goes, but he's doing—doing—" She broke off, gulping a lot before hitting the side of her fist against the door. "I could kill that rat. I could dangle him over a vat of acid and lower him in an inch at a time. How dare he!"

We were getting close to the hotel. I took an early turn.

"Where're you going?" she asked, her flare of temper interrupted.

"Around the block until you're okay. You don't need to take this inside your home."

She gaped a couple seconds, then fell on me, planting a solid kiss square on my mouth. I nearly swerved up onto the curb, but hauled us straight again just in time. She seemed not to notice any of it, but was slightly more relaxed when she flopped back to her side of the seat.

"Now," I said, "what's the rest of it?"

"I can't quote him, it's jumbled up in my head, but he was smooth and amusing and really, really focused on me. If there's one thing a girl likes, it's to have a man act like that with her, but not so he's overdoing it. Archy knows just how to play that game and make it be like he's never tried it before with anyone else. He makes you feel happy inside about yourself. That's what he was doing to me, an A-one first-rate, head-to-toe seduction."

"All that during a short turn on the dance floor? With me looking on?"

"He's good, Jack. And it seemed like forever to me."

"What'd you say to him?"

"The way he did it, there wasn't a lot I could say. He didn't come right out and ask me to go to bed with him, but it was all hiding there under his words—like a worm under a rock."

That description was reassuring to hear.

"The way it ended I pretty much told him I needed time to think."

My reassurance wavered. "Think?"

"And talk to you. Oh, don't worry, I was just giving him a line, but I had to act like I was interested and leaving the door open."

"Until after the broadcast."

"Yeah. He's smart that way. He won't use the broadcast against me. It would be pushing things too much to say if I don't sleep with him, then I don't go on. He's going to use it to make me grateful to him instead, and then dangle other gifts under my nose to draw me on."

"Like more guest spots on his show?"

"Probably. If not that, then something else. I'm not going to go with him, but he *got* to me, Jack!"

I kept watching the road. "How so?"

"With all that. He knew *exactly* what to do and say to make me like him or at least be grateful and friendly. It was as if he'd been crawling around inside my head like some kind of a swami mind reader and picked out all my weak points to use them against me. Am I that transparent?"

"No, but he's had a lot of practice."

"I'll say he has. Everything he did tonight should have worked—would have worked. Most of the reason why I got so mad was that not so long back I'd have *let* him sweep me off my feet and to hell with the rest of the world. That's what happened with Slick, what he did for me. I was set up to do it all over again with Archy."

"But you didn't."

"I *might* have. That's what's so upsetting. If I hadn't met you, I might have."

I shook my head. "No, you wouldn't."

"Why d'you say that?"

"Because you're not who you were anymore. You've grown up past Slick and that kind of trap."

"With your help."

"Maybe I speeded things up a little, but you do it yourself, you just don't always realize it. The important thing here is that you nailed Archy on what he was up to, and you're not going along with it."

"Damn right I'm not. But he isn't going to like my answer. I've heard stories about how Ike LaCelle arranges things for him. All this tonight—he fixed it up. And I think it was my fault."

"It's not your fault he's a jerk."

"But it is that he knew where to find me tonight. He overheard me talking to Adelle about the date I had with you."

"He was at the dance rehearsal, too?"

She made a growl of exasperation. "He was everywhere today. He wasn't intrusive or anything, but just around, acting friendly, not overdoing it."

"What's Adelle think of this? She keeps a close watch on him."

"Not now. She's read the writing on the wall and shifted her attention to Gordy."

"Has Adelle got a diamond bracelet? A new one?"

Bobbi shot me a surprised look. "Yes, she was showing it off last night. What's that got to do with things?"

"I heard from Gil Dalhauser that that's Archy's standard good-bye gift to his girls."

Now it was a distinct snarl of exasperation, and she hit

the side of the door again. "So it's the queen is dead, long live the new queen—meaning me? How dare he expect me to fall right into line?"

"Because he's a rat?"

"If I'd just kept my mouth shut—"

"No, it's better this way. You know for sure he's a rat and can be on guard against him. I figure he told Ike where you'd probably be tonight and he got there ahead of us and arranged the whole thing with the band and the photographers."

"That had to be it. While that was going on I saw you talking with Gil Dalhauser and then Ike."

"Yeah, Gil tried to warn me to fade from the picture, then Ike came by to fix a deal with me to get out of the picture, but he changed his mind. He won't be fixing anything else for Archy with you."

"What'd you say to him? And how?"

"We came to an understanding. He's not going to do any more favors for Grant as far as you're concerned."

"Jack, you didn't—"

"Yes, my dear, I gave him a triple evil-eye whammy— but not one word of it had to do with your career."

She relaxed slightly.

I told her what Dalhauser had told me, then what I'd put into LaCelle's head. "He'll get with Archy and thoroughly discourage him about bothering you again, but make him think it's not coming from you at all. Or even me. Gordy's already warned Ike to leave us alone, but Ike decided to ignore him. This way it just seems like Ike is the one who changed his mind."

She thought that one over a long time. "It'll work fine for Ike, but I don't think so for Archy. If you'd heard the way he talked to me, you'd know. He's determined enough to not listen to Ike, I'm sure of it."

"I trust your call. Will you be able to put him off until after the show?"

"Since there's no need to worry about reprisals from Ike, yes."

"How in hell are you going to be able to work with Archy knowing all this?"

"Oh, that's nothing. It's just being professional. I'll get through it without a hitch. It's afterward that things will get sticky. He'll have expectations. I can handle it . . . but I don't want to. I can give Archy the air and do it easy so we're all friends, but it'd take a while. I don't want to be around him, have to play the game he's set up or give him the chance to know more about me than he already does. He'd just use it against me. Besides, whenever I think of him I want to knock his block off."

"Would you like a shortcut?"

She looked at me, big hazel eyes full of wistful appeal. "Yes."

My heart instantly turned into mush. "One triple-deluxe evil-schmevil, mind-changing whammy at your service, ma'am," I said. "If he's awake and sober—even if he's only sober—I can have him doing a tap dance on the Wrigley Building during a lightning storm."

"Holding golf clubs?"

"Wearing a suit of armor."

She threw her arms around me for another kiss; this time I prudently stopped the car.

9

WHEN I got up Tuesday night Escott had left the papers, unclipped and open to the right sections, on the kitchen table. They all had pictures — above the fold — of Bobbi and Grant dancing, smiling, and otherwise looking like they were having a terrific time with each other. The fruitier captions suggested that a new romance was brewing between Chicago's own radio celebrity Archy Grant and beautiful, talented club singer Bobbi Smythe. They even spelled her name right.

"Perhaps," said Escott, who stood in the hall doorway, "this fellow is operating under the belief that if one says an untruth often enough it will be believed, even by those who know better. From the evidence presented here I've assumed your evening out with Miss Smythe did not go as planned."

"You could say that. He bushwhacked us for a publicity stunt and Bobbi had to play along with it or look bad."

"How unfortunate."

"She's gonna kill him for this," I said, skimming a caption festooned with exclamation points and question marks.

"What about your own reaction?"

"I should have taken care of him last night."

"If I may ask, what were you planning to do?"

"Just a little mind changing. I wasn't going to punch him out; now I'm not so sure. On the other hand, Bobbi will probably beat me to it."

"Would you bring me up to date on this business? If she's going to assault the man, I'd like some background to enhance my appreciation of the event."

"The business will be all over after tonight."

"Then I should like to know what I've missed."

I brought him up to date.

He shook his head and tsked when I finished. "I must commend you for your singular show of restraint."

"Yeah, well, you won't be seeing much more of it. Publicity for his damned show is one thing, but this gossip about a romance is over the limit. Bobbi threw a conniption when he made his pitch to her; she's gonna boil right over for this."

"Which has likely already occurred since these editions have been out all day."

"Jeez, I better call her."

He went upstairs to give me privacy while I attacked the kitchen phone. I dialed the right number, but it just kept ringing unanswered. Bobbi must have been getting a lot of calls on this. Next time I dialed I let it ring once, then hung up and dialed again. It was a code we'd worked out long ago for those times when she wanted to be unavailable to the general populace.

"Hello? Jack?" She sounded both anxious and hopeful.

"Right here, angel. I just woke up and saw. You all right?"

She let out a long sigh. "Yes, I'm fine, but the phone's been going off since this morning. I never knew I had so many friends and that there were so many other people pretending to be my friends. There's also been reporters from every rag you can think of, a woman from *Radioplay* magazine came by the hotel trying to get an interview, and some cigarette company wants me to do an ad for them. I don't even smoke!"

"So? Just pose for the picture and pick up the check."

"I turned everyone over to my agent. This is driving me nuts. When I first saw the photos I laughed; now it's not so funny."

"I thought you wanted to be a star."

"I still do, but because I'm good at my job, not because they think I'm Archy Grant's girlfriend. That's what this is all about—him, not me."

"He's going to be taken care of tonight, I promise. You gonna be okay for the show?"

"That's the least of my problems. I can do that standing on my head."

"Wear some pants, then."

She made sputtering noises and dropped the receiver. I heard some strange, distant choking sounds, then something like a hen laying an especially large egg. A few clatters and clunks later she came back, breathless and with laughter still in her voice. "God, but I've missed you all day."

"You've got me for all night. I'll try and make up for it."

"Just hang Archy out to dry for me."

"First chance."

"I'm going to have to leave for the station in a few minutes. See you there in an hour?"

"Me and Charles both."

"Good, I can have one of you on each side to protect me from the curious public."

We said good-bye, and I went upstairs to get ready. It was to be the white tuxedo again tonight, but with a fresh shirt and tie. Bobbi and I had pretty much rumpled those the other night. I put on a pale, pearl gray topcoat and yelled toward Escott's room to ask if he was ready.

"I'm downstairs," he called from the hallway below. "And yes, I'm ready. I was just about to bring the car around."

"We can take mine."

"It's no trouble." I heard the kitchen door bang as he went out. By the time I was set, he'd brought the Nash up to the front door. I locked things, climbed in the passenger seat, and we were off.

"That's sharp," I said, nodding at his own topcoat. It was a rich dark wool and brand-new.

"Yes, I thought I would follow your example and augment my wardrobe as well for such an important occasion."

"Tuxedo, too?"

"Of course."

"I'm impressed." We passed a tavern with a red neon sign, and that reminded me of my visit to Moe's last night. After leaving Bobbi in the very wee hours, I'd swung by McCallen's house to check for him, but he was still gone. Before the dawn blotted everything out for me, I wrote another note to Escott and left it on the kitchen table. I mentioned Jim Waters and his guess that McCallen might be a communist. "Have you asked Miss Sommerfeld if she knows anything?"

"She's barely speaking to me. Our lack of progress is wearing thin with her, and we've come to the limit of the daily retainer she paid out, yet I feel honor-bound to present her with some sort of resolution."

"With McCallen making himself scarce it's kind of hard to wind the case up. We can go by his house after the party and see if he's decided to come home yet. If he has, then I'll finish things. It'll be good for the agency's reputation."

"I hope so. She's most unhappy with her hotel stay. Is Miss Smythe all right?"

I told him about Bobbi and her busy day fighting the phone and fame. "Archy gets his walking papers tonight, though."

"I'm delighted to hear it. What a uniquely sordid arrangement he must have with Ike LaCelle. Playing the procurer, indeed."

"Not anymore—at least with Bobbi. And Ike's no longer a problem. Him I was able to fix last night."

"Good. I remembered that I have a file on him in my office."

"Why does that not surprise me? What about Gil Dalhauser?"

"Oh, yes. I've quite a lot of information on him. We had a bit of a run-in about two years ago when I was working on a case that caused our paths to cross. To resolve my client's problem it was necessary to pass some bookkeeping information I uncovered on Mr. Dalhauser to the Internal Revenue people. He managed to avoid going to jail, but eventually had to pay them a whacking great fine. They've had their eye on him ever since."

"If he sees you at the party, is there going to be gunfire?" My question was only ninety percent joke. The other ten percent was entirely serious, inspired by past experience with my partner.

Escott tutted, something only the English can do right. "I hardly think so. There were no reprisals back then; I doubt any will be forthcoming after all this time. He might not even recognize me."

Parking in the heart of the city was a problem, as always. Escott found a place a block away, but the hike to the Wrigley Building was no real hardship. It was cool, but dry for once, taking the bite out of the wind whipping around the buildings. We arrived in plenty of time, and joined up with other polished-looking people riding the elevator to the studio's floor.

Unlike the restaurant there was no hitch about getting in; the tickets Bobbi reserved were ready and waiting, then we went in to find our seats.

She'd outdone herself and put us right in the middle of the front row. I looked around trying to spot anyone I knew and waved at a few faces from the nightclub. Gordy was not among them, but I figured his attention tonight would be on Adelle Taylor's performance in the review. You do not progress in a romance by ignoring the lady's interests.

Escott looked the place over as well. He had plenty of stage experience, but none in radio that I knew of, and seemed engrossed in what he saw. I got to play native guide for once and pointed out the sound booth and a few other things.

"What's that table over there that looks like a jumble sale?" he asked.

For English jumble, I translated American rummage. "Sound effects."

Escott had it pegged as looking strange. Set up within

easy reach of the soundman was a frame about a foot square with a miniature door set in it, but with a full-sized knob and latch. Nothing makes a noise quite like a shutting door as a door itself, I explained. A flat pan filled with cornstarch was a good imitation of footsteps in snow, and a pair each of men's and women's shoes stood ready on a square of wood to provide other footstep sounds. The rest of the inventory was just as oddball, including a small gun, a jug full of water and a big pail, a box of metal junk, another of broken glass, two unbroken glasses, a taxi horn, a large sheet of tin that could be the cracking thunder of a storm, and a typewriter. And those were just the larger objects, not counting bells, horns, whistles, and other debris necessary for building the illusions the script called for.

A sizable part of the room was devoted to the orchestra, otherwise known as the Variety Hour Band. They were making a chaotic din tuning up their instruments. All wore the same dark red coats with the letters *VHB* stitched over the breast pockets. Bobbi's accompanist, Marza Chevreaux, was at the piano, studying her sheet music. She was an angular woman with hair that was too black, and wore clothes too young for her forty years. The only time she smiled was when she was playing piano and when she dealt with Bobbi, of whom she was fiercely protective. Marza didn't like me much, and if she noticed me in the audience, she never let on.

Very unexpectedly Bobbi emerged from someplace backstage and all but skipped right toward us. No red dress with gold sequins as planned. Now she was wrapped snug in a deep blue clingy thing with a modest spray of rhinestones dotting her shoulders. She was happy and smiling, full of the kind of vibrant glow she always got while working. Escott and I made haste to stand.

She planted a no-nonsense kiss on my lips that everyone saw, perhaps to let all and sundry know the papers had gotten it wrong about her and Grant. I didn't mind. She finally let me go and turned her blinding smile on Escott. "Charles, I'm so glad you could come, how handsome you look."

She always seemed to affect Escott's ability to speak, but he looked pleased. His tuxedo was a conservative black style, no adventurous white coat for him, but it fit perfectly. He took her hand and made a little half bow to kiss it. I'd seen LaCelle and Grant do the same thing, but Americans just can't seem to get it right. Escott's version was all homage to and admiration for the lady, not some half-assed attempt to impress her for the man's own ends.

"And you are stunning as ever, Miss Smythe," he returned. "I'm quite looking forward to your performance."

"What's with the new dress?" I asked. I was worried that in spite of my best efforts I might have damaged the red one somehow.

"I had to get another for the show. All that stuff in the papers spoiled its debut."

I sort of understood that one.

"Besides," she continued, "after seeing the photos, I realized how overdressed I'd be. This one's much more appropriate."

We both told her she looked great.

"How're things backstage with you-know?" I asked.

"Just fine. He's all busy getting ready, no time for me. It's quite a relief."

"Still want to drop him in a vat of acid?"

"Not drop," she corrected. "I want to lower him in an inch at a time."

Escott's right eyebrow bounced. "My, we certainly are medieval tonight, but with justified provocation, I understand."

She beamed at him. She loved to hear him talk. "It's so good to see you again. You must come to the club before the review's run is over and tell me what you think."

"I shall endeavor to do so."

"And now I've got to get back before the director has a fit. See you in an hour." She directed this at both of us, squeezed my hand, and whisked away, leaving behind the rose scent of her perfume.

"Wow," I said, staring after her in awe.

Escott threw me an amused glance. "Indeed. Though his techniques are less than gentlemanly, one can understand your adversary's motivations."

"After tonight he's going to be just a bad memory."

The lights flickered, the orchestra's tuning efforts subsided, and the leader got them started on some bright dance music. It was a full ten minutes before broadcast time, but the crew that made everything work for the performers was still bustling around doing mysterious things with the equipment. The audience sorted and settled themselves, and usherettes in snappy red coats with lots of brass buttons saw to it that the last people found their seats. It was a full house. Grant's show was very popular.

Five minutes before things started, Archy Grant emerged, grinning and waving. A big cheer went up in response, louder than anything I'd heard for him yet, but this was an expected event, not something impromptu. He introduced himself and asked for the audience's help with the show, drawing their attention to some boxes hanging over the stage that read APPLAUD and LAUGH.

"I know you won't need any help from our director to know when to laugh," he said. "But he needs *your* help to make sure the show runs within its time limit. So when you see a sign lighting up, that's when you do what it says. When it goes out, that's him asking you to hold it down so we can get out the next line in the script. And trust me, you're all gonna love being in showbiz."

His delivery was exactly right so the laughs he got came easy. Escott and I were more reserved, Escott because that's how he was, and me because I still wanted to punch Grant in the nose.

Someone handed Grant a script, and he quickly introduced a number of people who came filing onstage holding scripts, including Bobbi. She got a little extra cheer of her own, accepting it graciously, though this recognition was more a result of the publicity in the papers than anything else.

Silent signals got tossed back and forth between the director and the players. The second hand on a huge clock swept up to twelve, and the band started in on the show's theme song the way it did every week. I used to enjoy hearing it and hoped I'd be able to again. Sometimes it's a bad idea to meet the person behind the celebrity.

Everything went smooth; the work they'd put into all the rehearsals paid off. You can mess up a line even reading from a script, but all the performers were in top form tonight, especially Bobbi. Though Grant was the main focus of the show, she easily outshone him, at least in the studio. Whether the spark of her personality was going out over the air or not, we wouldn't know until tomorrow's reviews. Then Escott, who was highly critical of performers who were less than the best, surprised me by leaning over while Bobbi was in the middle of a song.

"She really is wonderful, isn't she?" he murmured, his usually poker-faced expression softened and relaxed. Bobbi could do that to people.

"Amen to that, brother."

Bobbi finished to rolling applause, then the show paused for a coal commercial, and I thought of Gil Dalhauser and his trucking business. His trucks were the ones that hauled the sponsor's product all over the county. I started to look around for him, then changed my mind. If he'd been in the audience Escott would have said something. He'd trained himself to have an excellent memory for faces.

"Not too shabby," I said. "Better than you expected, huh?"

"Well, it is much more interesting to me to see how it's done rather than merely listen to the results at home. Also, it's easier to ignore the advertisements while in the studio."

Escott often got annoyed at the constant ads that paid for the shows and made a point of turning them down when he could. Unless he was especially interested in a program he often forgot to turn the volume back up again.

"There's something about Archy Grant that bothers me," he said.

"There's plenty about him that bothers me. What's your beef?"

His lips tightened and he shook his head. "He seems

very familiar in an odd way. He reminds me of someone, but I can't think who."

"Probably of himself. You've heard me listen to him a lot."

"That's not quite it or I'd have remarked on it before. The radio changes a person's voice as it filters through a speaker. But in person . . ."

The station break ended and the players stepped up to the microphones again to do a comedy sketch with Grant about a man trying to teach his dog how to drive. The sound-effects guy had his hands full, especially at the end, with the inevitable car crash and sirens.

"I know I've heard that voice before," said Escott, staring down at the brightly lit stage where Grant stood close by the microphone. "Now, I wonder who the deuce he could have been?"

He followed Grant's every move, concentrating on each line, laugh, and song, which is the wrong way to go about remembering something. The harder you try, the more elusive the memory becomes. He should have eased back so it could sneak up on him.

I left him to it and let myself enjoy what was left of the hour. It seemed to go by amazingly fast. Bobbi had often described the experience to me, saying it was a very intense kind of living. Sometimes she could remember everything in astonishing detail, and other times she went blank, depending on how much fun she was having. Then she'd have to ask me later how things had looked. Just in case, I took a lot of mental notes for her on this one.

The show ended, the applaud sign flared and faded, the lights went up for the audience, and that was the end of it. Escott said he'd go get the Nash and spare Miss Smythe the walk.

I waited for Bobbi, but not for too long. She was in a hurry to get to the Nightcrawler to catch Adelle's last performance of the review. I didn't want to miss it either, being curious to see how such a refined and graceful-looking woman would handle prancing about in a Chinese dragon head.

"Wasn't I terrific?" Bobbi demanded when she rushed up to me in the studio lobby. This would be one of those times when she'd recall everything. When that happened, she always knew the quality of her work.

"They'll have to make up new words for how good you were," I said, taking her arm, or trying to; she was so full of energy she couldn't hold herself still and had to dance around me a few times talking a blue streak about the fun she'd just had. In a way I envied her absolute joy and was a little saddened by the knowledge that it was something I couldn't give her. She'd made it for herself, using her own talent. The closest I'd been to what she had now was years back when I sold my first news piece to a paper, but that seemed small in comparison to her reaction.

People looked and smiled at her, whispering excitedly. A few came up and asked her to autograph their program books. This surprised and pleased her enormously.

"It was so scary, too," she said to me while scribbling her name with a borrowed pen. "Anything could have gone wrong. I mean, when it happens at the club, then only a couple hundred know the mistake, but on a national broadcast it could be thousands and thousands."

"Well, now they all know how great you are."

"Oh, I hope so, I really, really hope so!" she said,

looking so alive and beautiful that I felt something crack inside me. It was almost physical, the pain, and I was pretty sure it was my heart breaking.

If this guest spot did result in bigger, more important bookings for her, I might not see her so much, if at all. The big jobs were in New York and Hollywood. She could be gone for weeks, months at a time, traveling, working.

The press of people around her forced me to step back, and I wondered just how far I might have to keep stepping. Looking on from the edge of a crowd could be my new future with her, and I didn't think much of it. It gave me a tight feeling all over, like I was strangling, and I had to resist the urge to push through them all, to go to her and sweep her away before I lost her.

But that would have spoiled her moment.

This was Bobbi's time to shine, not mine to drop a cold bucketful of my own self-doubt onto her dreams.

I pinned a smile to my face and waited for the crowd's flood of adulation to subside. If I wanted to keep her, I'd have to steer clear of anything remotely resembling a leash and trust she would come to me when she was able to do so.

Not an easy thing to do, especially when all of me wanted to rush in for her.

For myself.

"Hey," she said, suddenly free of the autograph seekers and slipping her arm around mine. "Wake up, Handsome Hank. I thought you were going to protect me from the curious public."

"Anytime, anyplace," I told her lightly.

She leaned on me with a satisfied sigh as we walked toward the elevator. "Thanks for waiting."

"No problem."

Not the easiest thing I'd ever done . . . but certainly the smartest.

Escott would have played chauffeur right to the end by dropping Bobbi and me at the club then running off to find parking, but she persuaded him to turn his beloved Nash over to one of the valets.

"I'm not going to lose the chance to make a big entrance with two such good-looking men," she said.

I wouldn't have called Escott good-looking, but he was certainly distinctive with his height, lean face, and beaky nose, and, of course, a tuxedo always improves any man's appearance. He assented to her wish and gave up his keys.

We three walked in, with her in the middle, to be greeted in the outer lobby by those invited to the party who had been to or heard the broadcast. Once more I had to step back and give Bobbi to the crowd. Still not easy, but I knew she'd return, and that helped.

We'd arrived just in time for the review's intermission and threaded our way through the mob to get to Gordy's reserved table down front. He was there to greet us, and even his normally impassive face had a hint of a smile lurking under the surface. He shook hands with Escott, thumping him once on the arm in a friendly way. It was hard to believe that at one point they'd been on opposite sides of a gun, ready to kill.

"Good to see you. Sit. Have champagne," he ordered, so Escott sat and let a waiter pour him a glass.

"How'd the show go?" asked Bobbi.

Gordy nodded toward the darkened dance floor. The stage manager had sent someone out to sweep it clean, and he marched back and forth with a dusting mop a yard wide. "Pretty good. They liked her fine."

"Did you hear any of my stuff at all?"

"I had a radio in the lobby bar and listened there. Checked on the review during the coal ads. You were good, kid."

She heaved a big happy sigh. "Thanks for letting me do it."

"Be a crime not to." He turned to me. "That guy Waters came in. I took care of him like you asked. Red carpet all the way. People are thinking he's some kind of bigwig."

In addition to a paid-up cab I'd fixed it so Jim Waters could have whatever he wanted at the club and I'd cover it; he was my special guest. Escott warned me such an arrangement could be severely abused, but Waters struck me as being a gentleman and would behave accordingly. Besides, if I was wrong about him, then this would be a fast way to find out. "You're a brick, Gordy."

"I been called worse."

"Where is he?"

"He spotted some guys in the band he knew and went back to say hello. He looks like he's enjoying himself."

"Been keeping him company?"

"No time for it, but the girls have been checking on him regular, sitting at the table when they can, making sure he's happy. I think two or three of them are in love already."

"Great . . . I think."

"Is he as good a singer as you say?"

"You'll find out when I take away all your business."

"Not unless I hire him first."

The Melodians, finished with their break, came back to

warm up the new crowd. Jim Waters returned from his backstage travels and I introduced him around the table. Bobbi didn't have to turn her charm on for him, he looked bowled over just from sitting next to her. Our group emptied two bottles of champagne out fairly quickly and Gordy had more brought in, along with a tray stacked with finger sandwiches, caviar, and crackers. Escott dubiously eyed the latter, perhaps, as I was, thinking of our impatient client.

A thought suddenly started running in my head about writing a mystery story; all I had was a title — *The Case of the Impatient Heiress* — but no plot. It stuck me as being a good title; maybe I could do something with it. I borrowed a pen from someone and scribbled on a napkin so as not to forget, then tucked it away in a pocket. Maybe I'd have better luck with a regular mystery magazine than trying to write about man-eating spider gods for *Spicy Terror Tales*.

A waiter, noticing I was without, put a glass of champagne in front of me. I got a smirk from Bobbi and she whispered that she'd swap glasses with me when she'd finished hers off.

I'd been right about Escott and Gordy talking shop — either that, or each was trying to get information out of the other. News of anything going on in the city was like gold to them. Bobbi filled me in on backstage shenanigans at the broadcast, omitting Archy Grant's name from the stories until I asked about him.

She gave a little shrug. "He was friendly enough, but pretty involved with doing the show. When anyone mentioned the paper photos, he'd just say that we had a dance or two and that was it."

"Quite a difference from last night. I think my warning to him via Ike finally got through."

"Good, but I won't be completely comfortable about things until you've talked to him."

The orchestra changed its tune and tempo to the overture piece, and the lights went down over the dance floor. When the couples had cleared back to their tables, drunken Bill began making his rounds, asking people if they'd seen his lost love.

"Who's the guy that punches him?" I asked Bobbi as Bill went flying.

"It's a different man every night. The bouncers take turns—at least the ones we can trust to swing and not hit. During rehearsal one of the guys actually connected, so we had to let him go."

"Not permanently?"

"Nah, but he's never going to work in a musical in this town again."

The review proceeded without a hitch, and I had to admit that Adelle surprised me. She'd been so contained and elegant whenever I'd seen her and now capered like a veteran slapstick artist. To be fair, she had worked with Ted Healy on Broadway and some Mack Sennett comedies in Hollywood, so it'd be odd if she hadn't learned a few things about physical humor.

Lil and Bill made their triumphant exit in the rickshaw, then Adelle eventually returned for her solo, and again for the tea cup number. Bobbi watched everything intently.

I leaned close to her ear. "Don't worry, she's not going to take your place."

"It's not that. I'm studying what she does different

from me and trying to figure out why. It might make me
better at what I do when I go back."

"But you're already great."

"She's got a lot more experience than me. I learned a
truckload just doing the rehearsals with her. You can
never know too much about your craft. It's important to
study how others work at it."

I started to say something, then snapped shut. She was
so bull's-eye right, and it wasn't just for singing and
dancing. If I applied that to writing then maybe I could
get off my duff and sell a piece.

"What?" she asked, looking at me.

"Nothing. I just need to read more, is all."

Adelle's last curtain call brought her a few dozen
long-stemmed red roses. She spotted Gordy at the table,
waved hard, and blew a kiss at him. He applauded loud
and long, slapping his big hands together with bruising
force. Definitely a man in love.

Bobbi said she wanted to go backstage to congratulate
Adelle. I started to rise to go with her, but she patted my
shoulder and told me: "Uh-uh, girl talk."

No arguing with that. I sank into the chair and watched
her walking away. The blue dress did wonderful things
the way it slid around her hips.

"She's really something and no mistake."

I turned to the speaker, Jim Waters, and wholeheartedly agreed with him.

"Ever have days when you wonder what you did to
deserve her?" he asked.

"Everytime I wake up," I said. "The club look after
you all right? I'm sorry I couldn't have been here
sooner."

"I'm having a great time. It's nice to be attending a

party instead of playing at one, like I sometimes do. They carry my brand of beer, and the girls are friendly *and* cute. Not much else a man could ask for. That big guy who runs the place, I've seen his name in the papers connected with some shady stuff, but he's been a real gent."

"Glad to hear it. You got any problem with the shady stuff?"

"Huh. In this town you might as well have a problem with the railroads or the Stockyards. It's part and parcel of the life, so you might as well get used to it. What was that paper you were scribbling on? You had one hell of a look on your face just then."

"Paper? Oh, I got an idea for a title and didn't want to forget it."

"Title for what?"

"A story. I used to be a reporter, now I'm trying my hand at fiction."

"And opening a club, to boot. Lotta irons for your fire, kid. You finish anything in this writing of yours? The hardest part I used to have with my music was to sit down and finish something."

I fought against wincing. "A couple things. I've been kind of stuck for ideas lately."

Waters shook his head, laughing. "Sounds like you're in a block."

"Uh . . ." How the hell did he know? "Well, I've been busy . . ."

"Don't worry about it. When you want to write bad enough, you will. Just don't fool yourself into thinking it's all dreamy-eyed inspiration."

"It isn't?"

He snorted. "I write music myself, and if I had to wait

around for inspiration to strike I'd never get any work done."

"But isn't inspiration necessary?"

"Sometimes, but for the rest it's a nuisance. I can't sit and wait for the lightning to strike. If I get in a block, I shuck that one-percent-inspiration and start the ninety-nine-percent-perspiration part."

I was familiar with what Thomas Edison had said on the subject, and less than eager to want to believe it. "But don't you have to be in the mood to create and to be able to create anything that's good?"

"It helps, but never wait for it to come to you. Some days you just have to get the stuff out whether you feel like it or not, no excuses. Maybe what you produce stinks, but it's still good practice, and you can always make it better when you're done."

"I'd like it to be better to start with."

He chuckled, but with a serious, earnest look in his eye. "That *only* comes from constant practice. How good a musician do you think I'd be if I didn't play every day?"

"Not so good."

"You see my point?"

"Write every day? Sounds too much like real work." And I'd done plenty of that in the newspaper business.

"Exactly. But if you want something badly enough, what work you put in to achieve it is nothing to you. Whether you sell that work is less important than the fact that you finished it to please yourself."

"Though selling is good."

"Oh, I pretty much favor it. But never, ever wait for something as slippery as the mood to strike. That's either laziness or a lack of confidence in yourself. I had a friend

who once told me with a lot of smug certainty he planned
to have his first symphony finished within five years.
That was fifteen years ago. He should have decided to
finish his symphony the same day he thought about
starting it, then he might have had something for himself.
The only thing he got known for was making excuses to
himself and everyone else. If Mozart had had that
attitude we'd have never heard of him. He died at
thirty-five, you know."

I could feel my face growing longer. I'd died at
thirty-six. Prior to that all I'd achieved was to snag a few
bylines when the editors were feeling generous. And
after that . . . well, here I was at a party with a guy who
was essentially kicking me in the pants. I let him,
because he was right about all of it. "Your beer's gone,"
I said. "Lemme get you another so you can tell me
more."

We put our heads together at the table, and I threw
more questions at him and soaked in answers. Writing
with sounds and writing with words were more alike than
I'd ever suspected. Neither of us came up for air until
Bobbi actually tapped me on the shoulder. Waters stood,
balancing easily with his cane and told her how much he
enjoyed her radio work. He'd listened to the *Variety
Hour* in the lobby bar.

"But they need to get a better horn player for their
band," he added. "He kept cracking the same note over
and over."

"And here I was hoping no one would notice," she
said. "Would you mind if I steal Jack away for a
moment?"

He was agreeable to that, so she stole me away to

another table in a corner. She looked like she had things to say.

"What's up, angel?"

"I just got a little friendly advice from Adelle."

"This 'girl talk' stuff?"

"Yes, and then some. I had a feeling that after she saw the papers she'd want to speak with me. It's a good thing Gordy's making a solid case with her or she might have clawed my eyes out over Archy. She saw the papers and assumed the worst, but it's really all right."

"How's that? Because Gordy's softened the blow?"

"Exactly. She doesn't mind Archy having a new interest now that she's got one herself."

"I thought when you went shopping you told her you weren't after Archy."

"This is a case of Archy coming after me. She thinks I'm going along with it to further my career, so she gave me a little heart-to-heart."

"Kind of her."

"Practical, you mean. She's read the writing on the wall all right—and the diamonds in the bracelet. It's a nice piece, so she didn't do too badly, and she's still a regular on the *Variety Hour*."

"What'd she tell you?"

"Not to get between Archy and his audience, and when it's my turn to get the brush, go with a smile, but go. She said that was the lesson she learned with him. If the guy's not interested in you, you can't change his mind, though she tried. She kept hoping he'd come around back to her, but it's not going to happen."

"His loss, Gordy's gain."

"I thought hearing this would make you smile."

"Oh, yeah. I'm imagining the look on Archy's face when he realizes he doesn't have either of you."

She shrugged. "The sad fact is that there'll always be another girl out there for him."

"I could fix that, too."

"But not forever. Don't tell me you want to keep seeing him and Ike all the time."

I quickly admitted that I did not.

"Huh," she said, looking past me. "Speak of the devil."

Far across the room Archy Grant made a big and noisy entrance. The grin, the wave, lots of glad-handing and calling to friends. In his wake was Ike LaCelle doing much the same thing, and not far behind him stalked the more sober and undemonstrative Gil Dalhauser.

"Well," I murmured, "it's show time. I better catch him before he has any drinks." I stood, but Bobbi put her hand on my arm.

"You'll need some privacy, won't you?"

"That would be a help." And plenty of light, too.

"You won't get it here for a while, people will interrupt. Let me go to him, tell him to meet me in my dressing room in five minutes. I'll make sure he'll be there with bells on whether Ike warned him off or not."

"Angel, you're a devil."

"Just knock first to make sure Adelle's out."

Bobbi wasn't striving for extra attention when she walked over to join Grant, but she got it all the same. Her looks on top of the publicity linking them in a possible romance guaranteed that anyone interested was watching. Her face lit with a sweet unaffected smile, she put her hand out to him; he took it and drew her suddenly in close, but only pecked her on the cheek like a fond brother before putting a friendly arm around her. He was playing it careful, not too little or too much for the crowd.

"Ladies and gentlemen! My beautiful guest on the show tonight!" he called out, then stood back and applauded.

Bobbi took a bow, then turned to applaud at Grant herself. The mutual admiration display might go on for longer than five minutes; I took the opportunity to get an early start toward the backstage area. With everyone looking at them, no one noticed my quiet exit through the service door to the kitchen, and the staff there was too busy to bother with me. They were used to my mug anyway.

The back hall where the dressing rooms were was nearly cleared out. Just a couple chorus girls remained, and they were too involved talking to see me walk past. I gave Bobbi's door a snappy knock, but happily heard no reply. It was unlocked; I went in and turned on the light.

Flowers. Lots of fresh new flowers had been brought in, roses, big bronze chrysanthemums, humble bluebells, daisies, and I don't know what others turned the place into a crowded and fragrant greenhouse. They were different from the ones Bobbi had had, so I could assume these were all Gordy's doing. Adelle was going to have a tough job getting this load home—unless Gordy volunteered to help.

I made myself comfortable in a chair by the closet. It wasn't visible from the door, though I could see the whole room fine in the dressing-table mirror. Grant would not, of course, be able to see me.

My wait went on for longer than five minutes. Bobbi must not have been able to get Grant apart from the others long enough to deliver even a whispered invitation. He was probably milking the crowd for every drop of adulation he could get.

After about a quarter hour, though, I heard footsteps approach and pause outside, then the door was pushed open. It was welcome-to-my-parlor time.

Only the fly wasn't Grant, but Ike LaCelle. With no small disgust for the false alarm, I vanished just as he started to walk in. It made hearing more difficult, but I could follow the progress of his footfalls on the floor. He circled the room once, opened the closet, then checked on the tiny bath. Unhurried, he crossed back to the door.

"It's clear," he said.

Someone else came in.

"This is *not* a good idea," LaCelle continued.

"The lady wants to see me, who am I to say no?" said Archy Grant. He seemed to be in a remarkably good mood, even for a man whose business it was to be happy all the time.

"She's poison for you, Arch. Lemme fix you up with someone else."

"Tomorrow, maybe. First I find out what I'm getting tonight." Glass clinked on glass and I thought I recognized the sound of a bottle being set down.

"That boyfriend of hers is dangerous. I tell you there's something wrong with him."

"Gordy's just got you spooked."

"Fleming's the one who's done the spooking. You didn't have him looking at you like that, like the world was gonna end."

"Ike, you are not scared of some nobody kid like him."

"Damn right I'm scared. I know a creep when I see one."

"I've seen him and he's nothing."

"I just can't talk to you when you're like this."

"So we'll talk later—when I'm a lot more relaxed . . ." Grant trailed off into a long chuckle, sounding very pleased with himself. "Now get out before she comes. I don't want you spoiling the mood while she's in it."

"You said she wasn't so hot for you last night."

"She just changed her mind, same as the rest. All she needed was a taste of what it was like doing the show."

"Just like that? I don't think so. That broad's got more brains than you think. This is a setup, pal. Her creep boyfriend's gonna come busting in on you both and either he flattens you or they shake you down for dough."

"Then I'll lock the door."

"Archy—"

"I can take care of myself, Ike. And if the kid makes trouble we handle him like the others. Jeez, isn't it enough I let you come check things here first? Stand guard in the hall if you want, but get scarce."

Ike went out, grumbling.

"And don't let her see you," Grant said in farewell as he shut the door.

He walked back and stopped before the mirror. When I silently returned to solidity a few feet behind him he was inspecting his teeth and smoothing his hair back. He was a really good-looking man, maybe a little thick around the neck and shoulders, but with striking brown eyes, and an ingrained expression of pleasant humor. He looked like he knew the number on everything and would share it with you for a beer and a handshake. I'd been right about the bottle; he'd brought champagne and two glasses.

I stood very still, watching him for some time before

he started to feel it. Not that I have one of those airs of evil surrounding me; this was the sort of feeling anyone gets when they sense somebody's staring at them.

Grant straightened slow, and used the mirror to check the room, then turned slightly to look toward the door. That's when he glimpsed what just shouldn't have been there out of the corner of his eye. He twisted fast to face me, drawing in one sharp breath, eyes going wide, and backed hard away, bumping against the table. Things rattled and fell over. The image of the room in the mirror shivered.

His heart was banging fit to burst. I could hear its thudding ten feet away. I'm not like the undead in the storybooks and movies; I don't take pleasure in terrifying people—not usually. But for Archy Grant I found myself making a big exception. His pop-eyed expression of horror was giving me the kind of laugh he'd probably never before inspired in anyone. I couldn't help myself. It was probably just as well, too. Better this laughter than for me to be angry with him.

"Hi, Archy. Great to see you. I really enjoyed the broadcast."

"Wha . . . you . . ." His skill for ad-libbing had deserted him.

I fixed my gaze on him, smiling. "We're gonna have a little talk."

10

My head ached like a bum tooth, but it was worth it.

I'd thought everything out, all the stuff I had to make clear to Grant, all the changes I wanted from him. By the time I finished he no longer had any interest in pursuing Bobbi, though he still liked her—but only as a friend, as another colleague in show business. He would always treat her with respect and not do or say anything that would be detrimental to her career. My promise to Bobbi was intact. Maybe he wouldn't go out of his way to promote her, but he sure wouldn't arrange through LaCelle to destroy her.

In light of their conversation, I made sure Archy would be convincing to LaCelle about his change of mind for this particular seduction. I also planted a very strong suggestion that he and Ike stop playing their carrot-and-stick routine with women. The idea wouldn't last long, a couple weeks, maybe even a month. Suggestions that went against a person's normal behavior and inclinations tended to be short-lived and needed periodic reinforcing. If Grant and I crossed paths on a regular basis I would do it as opportunities occurred, but I wasn't counting on that to happen. It'd be up to chance, and I was content to let it remain so. Anything more and I'd be telling him how to run his life. I had my own life to worry about; I didn't have time for his as well.

The concentration necessary for what I was doing cost me, hence the thumping between my temples. I'd have to make a stop later at the Stockyards to balance the effort.

Of course, Grant remembered absolutely nothing about any of it.

He stood calm and blank-faced, staring at air until I got behind him, snapped my fingers, and vanished. I'd seen enough stage hypnotists to have picked up a few theatrical touches for myself.

When Grant quit the room, LaCelle—who had posted himself down the way as guard after all—saw and came over. I was floating unseen next to Grant and listened shamelessly.

"What? She stand you up?" LaCelle sounded relieved.

"I got to thinking about what you said and you're right. I've got no business going after her." Grant was doing fine, speaking almost word for word what I'd given him.

"What d'ya want me to do about her?"

"Nothing at all. She's a great talent, let her run with it. And lay off the boyfriend, too. No more guys following him around."

"But I thought you wanted to—"

"No more guys following him around," Grant cheerfully repeated.

And that was that.

Mentally dusting my hands, I took myself away to materialize in an unused corner, then went back to the party, feeling very satisfied about myself and the world.

Things had gotten noisier with the booze flowing so free, and the musicians decided to put in some extra playing time. It was much the same as it'd been on opening night, only the attention was divided between Bobbi and Adelle. Bobbi was busy for the moment, but I spotted Madison Pruitt at the chow line. I could take care of my business with him to fill the time until she was free.

Maybe he wasn't a creative type, but I did know better than to get between him and food and waited until he'd loaded a plate and carried it off to a table. He'd apparently been grazing for a while, as his area was crowded with empty plates containing identical remains of what he was now digging into. When Madison found something he liked, he stuck with it.

"How you doing?" I asked, walking over.

He looked up, mouth full, and said something unintelligible, but friendly in tone, gesturing for me to sit. For the amount of food he was always packing away he was ever on the gaunt and gangly side. His loose clothes were informal tweeds, lots of them, with two knitted vests under the coat. Either he was cold all the time or trying to pad out his thin form. I hadn't seen him for the last few months. He'd been injured by scabs at an auto-plant sit-down strike, who gave him a concussion and broken arm. Both seemed healed up; he wore no cast, but there was a white scar over his left eyebrow that hadn't been there before. He looked a little older, a little more worn.

"Heard you had some bad luck with strikebreakers," I said. "Glad to see you're up and around."

He pushed his thick-lensed glasses back with a knuckle and bobbed his head. "Yeah, that's what happened. They were animals in the pay of the fascist overlords. I tried to tell them about being exploited, but they wouldn't listen. Too busy hitting me."

I knew what I'd let myself in for, but was resigned to it and listened as he gave me a very thorough account of his assault. He was grimly proud of it, and stopped eating long enough to show me the scarring on his left arm where it had been broken during his clubbing. I could admire him to some extent; qualities in him that could be seen as faults had given him a kind of obtuse courage. Maybe I thought he was nuts for what he was doing, but at least he was out doing it. I winced appreciatively for what he'd been through and told him he'd been badly used. He wholeheartedly agreed, and that led him off on another tangent about the parallels between the strikers and the Spanish Civil War. It was pretty convoluted, and he talked too quickly for me to even try to follow. When he paused for breath I broke in to bring the conversation around to where I wanted.

"Ever heard of a guy named Jason McCallen? He might be a member of the party."

Madison looked cagey. "Why do you want to know?"

"I'm just trying to get a line on who he is. Someone told me he might be a communist, and from what I've seen he's probably a good one for the cause. He's a big guy, very intense, Scottish accent."

"A Scotch communist?"

"Scots," I said, parroting Escott. "Scotch is a drink."

He thought for a bit, then shook his head. "I've never met him, but then the meetings can be pretty large. We don't all know each other."

I shrugged. "Okay, it was a long shot."

"I could ask around."

One thing I didn't need was Madison accidentally putting his foot into a bear trap. He'd been banged up enough. "That's good of you, but don't bother."

"Why you want to know about him?"

"Just a little business deal I'm thinking about. I wanted to see how steady he was."

"Business deal?"

"It's nothing. How's the American party doing these days?"

The subject change was all I needed to keep him from asking more questions. He bent my ear until I happened to notice Ike LaCelle watching me from a few yards away. I didn't think he'd heard anything, but wouldn't put it past him to read lips. He broke into an instant smile and strolled up. Despite my having spooked him, he never once let it show and glad-handed me like we were the best of friends. I wondered what the hell he wanted.

"Fleming! Good to see you!" His booming greeting had its effect on Madison, startling him so he paused a moment in his plate grazing to stare. LaCelle was practically sparkling with fond fellowship. "That was a hell of a show tonight, wasn't it?"

"Which one?"

"Why, both of 'em, of course. Bobbi's on the ladder to stardom, I'm sure of it, and Adelle's never been better, don't you think?"

I agreed and introduced him to Madison, who stopped eating again long enough to shake hands.

"I've heard of you, Mr. LaCelle," he mumbled around his latest mouthful.

"Oh, yeah? Well, don't believe a word of it, I was drunk at the time."

Madison stared, uncomprehending. "I didn't mean to imply anything about you in a negative sense, far from it.

Marza—Bobbi's piano player—told me what an important and influential man you are."

I could almost hear the acid in Marza's voice were she to hear herself described as a mere piano player.

"I've got the ears of a few people here and there," said LaCelle. "Mr. Fleming can tell you."

To be agreeable, I nodded and resisted asking what other things besides ears he might have as trophies. He would not have been able to appreciate it.

"Then you're just the sort of man that's needed to help further a truly great cause," said Madison. He put down his fork, which was a dangerous sign. "Have you ever given serious thought about the contributions that the American Communist Party has made toward the betterment of the workers right here in America?"

LaCelle seemed nonplussed for a second, but recovered quick. "No, Mr. Pruitt, I can't say that I have."

"I think you'll be surprised to learn just how much influence we've had on improving conditions in every . . ."

Oh, he was on a roll, all right. LaCelle listened and nodded in the right places, and damned if he didn't pretend to be interested, but then he was already putting on a perfect sham of friendship toward me. Instead of hanging around actors, he should have been one. "Yes, you do have a point there, Mr. Pruitt. But tell me, doesn't your family own Canuvel Steel?"

Madison's turn to be nonplussed. He wasn't secretive about his background, but didn't exactly shout it to people. "Only a controlling interest, but—"

"Really? I think we've got a lot to talk about, then, but I can't do it dry." He turned to me, holding hard to his old-pals act. "Fleming, you look like a man who needs a drink, too. Lemme get you something."

"Thanks, but I'm fine."

He didn't listen, though, and signaled a waiter. "What'll you have? Grain or grape?"

He was in a jovially insistent mood. It was easier not to argue. "Champagne's fine."

He snagged three glasses from the waiter's tray and shared them around. "A toast, gentlemen. In memory of a very successful evening for two lovely ladies, Bobbi and Adelle."

I couldn't get out of that one, and he was too close for me to only pretend to sip. Madison gulped his down, LaCelle took a healthy swig, then smiled expectantly at me. I did the same, though it was like trying to drink gasoline. He grinned as though he'd accomplished something, and I wondered if he suspected anything about me being a vampire. It didn't strike me as likely, but better to be a little paranoid than a lot sorry.

While the champagne went to war with my picky digestive system, I smiled back and tried to pin him with a look. His nose was pretty red and his eyes had an unfocused cast. Damn, but he was too far along to be an easy mark; even Madison would notice the effort I'd have to put into it to get past the booze. I'd have to try some other time—when I had more time. If I didn't move soon, things would get very embarrassing.

Before Madison could resume his proselytizing, I stood and excused myself, saying I had to go see Bobbi about something. LaCelle's eyes flickered with amusement like he didn't believe me, but nuts to him. Right now I had to leave and quickly.

The men's room was in the outer lobby, just go up a couple tiers and turn right. For me it was like a hike up the Matterhorn, and I had to do it casual in case LaCelle was watching. I also had to try keeping a normal face on so no one would notice anything was wrong. In the meanwhile the stuff I'd taken in rolled around my guts like red-hot marbles. Only just in time did I push the door open and stagger blindly to a stall so my body could reject what was now pure venom to me. A tearing cramp doubled me over, and I retched hard.

The noisy unpleasantness was all done in less than a minute. Someone in another stall asked if I was all right, and someone else laughed and observed that I just couldn't take it. I flushed the toilet, then washed my hands and got out before either man emerged to find the mirrors ignoring me.

I was annoyed with LaCelle, but even more annoyed with myself for allowing him to steer me around as he'd done. Instead of suspecting me of being supernatural, maybe this was some kind of payback for scaring him last night. Having gotten him to do something he didn't want, he'd just returned the favor. I'd have to start getting smarter about avoiding such pitfalls in the future.

Still shaken and angry, I went back to the party in the main room, and it was pretty much as I'd left it, loud and full of life and music. Oddly enough, LaCelle had stayed to talk to Madison Pruitt, and I didn't know which of them to feel sorrier for. LaCelle looked past Madison toward me, his head slightly cocked like a man waiting to see something. If he thought I'd come back for more manipulation, he was in for a disappointment.

Gordy's prime table by the dance floor had other people sitting there, smoking and talking as they drank more of his booze. Escott was up on the second tier with a group gathered around Archy Grant, who was telling a very animated story that was getting him a bushel of laughs. Escott wore a strange, tight smile through it all, as though he wanted to get the joke, but couldn't quite. At least he wasn't off in a corner alone.

Then I spotted Gil Dalhauser staring intently across the room at Escott. Dalhauser was statue still amid the movement of the others around him. The look on his face as he concentrated on my partner was nothing less than murderous.

This evening was getting too complicated.

Making my way across so Escott could see me, I gave him a subtle high sign, then waited. Grant got to his punch line, and his crowd exploded with laughter, except for Escott. He continued with the smile, but no more than that as he broke away from them. It couldn't have been because of not understanding the point; he must have had something else distracting him, and I had a good idea what it might be.

"Dalhauser's trying to fry you with his eyes," I told him.

"He has not escaped my notice. I've been doing a reasonable job of pretending not to see him, though. He seems content to simply glare."

"That'll be Gordy's doing. He put the word out that we were strictly hands-off in this town. Ike was ready to take a chance, but maybe not Dalhauser."

"The test will be how that policy holds up should either of us ever choose to travel outside the bounds of Gordy's protective influence."

"You want to ask him about it?"

"No, I prefer a little uncertainty in my life."

Well, if he didn't want to worry about it, neither would I.

"Are you all right?" he asked, peering at me.

"I couldn't get out of joining in on a toast. Had to go get rid of the stuff I drank."

"It certainly doesn't agree with you. You seem very pale."

"Well, I am what I am, you know." I wasn't about to say "vampire" out loud, even if nearly everyone around us was drunk.

"That's just it, you usually have better color."

Even as he spoke I felt my stomach going into a knot. "Jack?"

I resisted giving in to it and gulped hard. From here we were closer to the backstage rest rooms than the ones out front. I pushed away from him and down toward the dance floor, crossing it and ducking into the wings. Escott was right at my heels.

Bobbi's dressing room was closest. I hurried in and made it to the toilet in time as the next cramp hit. Nothing came out but spit. It tasted vile and was colored with blood. I used the sink spigot to rinse my mouth out and still couldn't lose the taste. Escott hung close and watched, his face stitched up with concern.

"Get your coat off," he said. "I'll help you."

"Huh?"

"Just get it off."

There didn't seem to be any reason not to, and I wanted to loosen my tie anyway. He hung the tux jacket in the closet, then got a towel and wet it.

"Run this over your face," he ordered, handing it to me.

I did so. It came away red. "Shit, I'm sweatin' blood. What the hell is this? Poison again?" My body had done the same thing once before.

"That depends on what was in the drink you had. Alcohol is a toxin, after all."

"It was champagne. Just a little champagne."

"Then you've a deucedly poor reaction to carbonation—"

"No, it wouldn't hit me like this. No wonder he was looking so pleased. That son of a bitch Ike put something in it!"

Escott asked a few more questions, and in between cramps and spitting into the sink I told him about what I'd overheard from Grant and LaCelle and the knight-in-armor bit I'd done on Bobbi's behalf. I wiped bloody sweat from my face and neck, having taken off my shirt and undershirt to keep from staining them. The symptoms were subsiding, though. Each bout was shorter and milder than the last.

"If he meant to croak me he's in for one hell of a surprise," I said, holding the towel under cold water to wash the red away. I swabbed it around my face and neck, and for once it came away clean.

"I think you were given something nonfatal but inconveniencing. If you suddenly dropped dead, Mr. Pruitt would surely remember drinking that toast with La-Celle."

"Don't bet on it."

"Yes, but LaCelle wouldn't know that. I'll wager what he slipped you was nothing more than an old-fashioned Mickey Finn, meant to publicly embarrass you when you passed out, apparently the worse for drink. A pretty little retaliation, don't you think?"

"I'm gonna hang him out in the wind for this."

"By all means, and I'd very much like to watch you do it. Do you plan to tell Gordy?"

"Only if he asks. This is between me and LaCelle."

Escott went out front while I finished cleaning up and dressing again, making sure there was no trace of blood on anything. Whether he was drunk or not, LaCelle was going to hear from me, either with hypnosis or a sock in the jaw. Or both.

Madison's table was empty, and I couldn't spot him or LaCelle in the crowd. I started toward the casino room, but Bobbi called to me, hurrying over.

"Where've you been?" she asked. Her expression went from pleasure to puzzlement when she got a close look at me.

"A little cleanup work. You seen Ike LaCelle?"

"Not lately. Jack? What's wrong?"

"He hasn't given you anything to drink? Sent any to your table?"

"No. Why?"

That was a relief. "If he ever does, don't have any."

"Why not?"

"He tried to slip me a Mickey."

"*What?*"

I explained a few things to her until she wanted to take a pop at LaCelle herself. "It's my fight," I said. "I gotta be the one to take care of him."

"Can I still be mad at him, too?"

"All you want, angel, just don't mess up your career."

"Guys like him shouldn't be anywhere near show business."

Now, there was an idea. I wondered what the climate was like in Greenland this time of year.

"How'd it go with Archy?" she asked, knocking over my train of thought.

"I think you'll find any future work with him to be a lot easier. From now on everything will be strictly platonic as far as you're concerned."

She was delightfully grateful, her expression of it improving my outlook considerably, but she wasn't up to her usual energy.

"You're tuckered out," I observed as she leaned against me.

"Much more of this and I'll need to prop my eyelids open with toothpicks. Is it too early to take me home?"

"Not after the work you've done tonight."

"But the show was only an hour long, and I didn't have to dance."

"And I saw you putting out three times more of yourself than you've ever done before."

"Okay, I'll have one of the guys find me a cab."

"Not on your life. I'll get you home."

"But you want to see Ike—"

"Who doesn't seem to be here. Tomorrow night's soon enough for him. I'll go find out if Charles wants to leave."

Escott had returned to the group around Grant, close enough to listen but far enough back to leave without drawing attention. Grant still noticed when I came up, and watched as we left, but never once paused in his latest story. When he was holding court he probably hated losing even one audience member.

Once Escott understood I'd given up trying to find LaCelle and was going to drop Bobbi home, then return for him, he opted to leave, too. He wanted to stop at the office before going home himself, and that went along with my pausing to tank up at the nearby Stockyards. We got our coats and said good-bye to a lot of people, and I made sure about Jim Waters getting a ride home. Bobbi slumped against me on the front seat of Escott's Nash and went right out. I put an arm around her to keep her from sliding around.

Escott gave her what I could only call an envious look. "How I wish it was that easy for me," he murmured.

"Gonna be one of those nights again?" I asked, not without some sympathy.

"Possibly. God knows I tire myself out, but my dark sleep is often elusive."

"Your what?"

"My dark sleep, the true sleep, the absolute rest that comes when one is completely unconscious and dreamless. Most nights I don't really fall off the edge into it. I merely doze. Some part of me is still stubbornly awake and aware. Hours and hours of it until morning comes."

"I've had nights like that. The ones where you just drift and sort of dream?"

"Yes, unfortunately. Does that still happen for you?"

"Only if I'm caught away from my home earth." When that happened, the dreams weren't nice, either. In fact, they were usually pretty hellish, so I took care never to get caught out.

"Perhaps I should send off to London for some earth and see if it might make a difference," he mused.

"Worth a try," I said with a snort. "Why don't you take a sleeping pill?"

"I used to, but they stopped working for me. I had to take more than was safe to have any effect, and they made me so sluggish I could barely get out of bed the next day."

He rarely opened up like this. His profile under the passing street lamps was hard to read, but he seemed sober enough, nowhere near the Shakespeare-quoting stage. "When was that?"

A pause before answering. "A long time ago. A different life."

"Back when you were acting?"

"Yes, back then."

His tone was light, but with that vague reply I knew I wouldn't be getting any more from him on the subject. He usually clammed up about anything to do with his early life, only occasionally telling an amusing story about his acting career with a traveling stock company in Canada. He said he'd left them to turn private agent because it allowed him to eat regularly. I always had the feeling there was more to it than that. Coldfield once hinted I was right, but said it was up to Escott to tell me when he was ready.

Bobbi woke when we stopped, and I walked her in and up to her suite. Escott had said to take what time I needed, lighting his pipe for something to do. Given the circumstances, none of it took long. I was still light-headed, an aftereffect of the Mickey, and though triumphant, Bobbi was bone-tired.

The blue dress wasn't nearly as complicated to get off her as the red one. She draped it carefully over a chair. Looking at her naked body as she turned made me sorry things had turned out the way they had, but it was never as good when she was too sleepy to respond to what I was doing. I needed to know she was enjoying things, too.

Tucking her in bed with a kiss would have to do for tonight. She was asleep before I left the room.

Between condensation and the pipe smoke, the inside of the car seemed to have its own private fog bank. Escott had taken on a distracted mood, which I was used to, meaning he was working on some inner problem. I hoped it had to do with the Sommerfeld case, but didn't interrupt to ask. He drove the nearly empty wee-hour streets without a word, probably without knowing what he was doing. When he got like this his body worked like the automatic pilot of an airplane.

As we apporached the office I ventured to put in a request that he drop me at the Stockyards. I hadn't had time the night before to feed, and was really starting to feel the hunger. He nodded and made the right turns, then parked and cut the motor, again telling me to take my time. I shed my pale gray topcoat and the tuxedo jacket, unwilling to put them at risk with the cattle. It was cold out, but that wasn't anything I worried much about anymore.

My trip in was quick and the cattle blood satisfying as always, taking care of any lingering trace of my hypnosis-induced headache. Fully alert and refreshed, I hurtled back to the car, materializing in the passenger seat. Escott was still puffing on the pipe and hardly reacted.

"You know audiences would pay good money to see something like that," I said.

"Indeed, but can you juggle?" He started up, put the car in gear, and got us to the office, parking a few steps down from the stairwell opening.

"What do you want here?"

"Just to look into a few things in the files. It won't take long."

"Gil Dalhauser?"

"Among others, then we can make a check on Mr. McCallen's place."

I was interested enough to want to look into a few things for myself. It beat sitting in the car watching the signals change. I followed him up the stairs. He unlocked and walked in. The light was on, but he always left it that way. It discouraged intruders, and at night he wisely preferred entering a well-lit room.

Close behind, I almost bumped into him on the threshold, he stopped so abruptly. Looking past, I saw what had put him on guard: cigarette butts in the desk ashtray—he always emptied it before leaving—and a file-cabinet drawer not quite closed. Those were locked tight each night without fail.

"I shan't be but a minute, Jack," he said in an unworried, conversational voice. "I think I left it in the desk."

He crossed the room, his steps on the wood floor making too much noise for me to hear if anyone else was still present. From his actions he'd assumed we had company, which was a prudent thing to do until proved otherwise. He put the pipe down and reached toward a drawer that contained a loaded revolver. I started forward to do an invisible check of the inner room. Neither of us achieved our goals. The other door was hauled open before I could vanish.

Jason McCallen emerged, holding a little revolver in his big fist. It was a .22, and I had the idea that it may have come from Mary Sommerfeld's house. He'd probably paid her place another visit despite her new locks.

He swung the muzzle first on Escott, who halted in mid-movement, his arms slightly raised, then to me. I gingerly finished walking in, stepping away from the door and leaving it wide. McCallen's dark eyes were hard and his posture tense. When a man looks that nervous it's best to give him a clear path out.

"What the devil do you think you're doing here, man?" Escott demanded, all irritation. I winced.

The gun came back toward him. "I'm trying to find where you two took her."

"By breaking into my file cabinets? The ones here are only for old records. Current cases are stored elsewhere. You'd have had better luck if you'd simply made an appointment." Escott put his arms down.

McCallen looked baffled a moment, but recovered, scowling. He didn't brandish the gun around, giving me to think he knew how to shoot. "Don't try me, mister. You know where she is and you'll be telling me or I'll use this."

"To maim or murder?" For all the fear Escott showed, McCallen could have been threatening him with a flyswatter.

"You just take your pick." McCallen fired once, snapping a shot about five inches left of Escott's skull. The balloon-pop explosion was loud inside the confines of the little room. Escott didn't move, but I flinched and surged forward. McCallen aimed at me again. "Don't tempt me, laddie."

Like he had all the time in the world, Escott turned to inspect the small, eye-level hole by the window in disgust. "Well, there's another damned repair job for me."

"Charles," I said warningly.

His mouth twitched as he glanced at me, his gray eyes dancing with inner excitement. He was *enjoying* himself, for Christ's sake.

I put my full attention on McCallen, moving to draw his gaze. "I want you to *listen* to me."

"You'll be the one to·do the listening," he said, sighting down the short barrel at my nose.

I'm fairly bulletproof, and therefore should have been the calm one here, but having been shot too many times, I was understandably gun-shy. It took concentration to get anyone hypnotized, and that little muzzle pointed my way was a hell of a distraction.

Escott made a small warning gesture for me to hold off. "Now, Mr. McCallen, I'm willing to be reasonable about this. You will please put your firearm away, sit down, and talk with me like a civilized man."

"So you can try to flimflam me with more insulting money offers? Not on your life—and that's what it'll be if you don't tell me where she is."

"You're an intelligent fellow, Mr. McCallen. Were our positions reversed, would you betray her to a madman with a gun? Is that your plan? To find her and kill her?"

McCallen made a kind of outraged choking sound. "All I want is what's rightfully mine. You're the bastards that broke into my house and took it away."

"I confess we did bend the law a bit—"

"Bend!"

"But from what we've been told it was in a good cause."

"The woman's a daft spoiled brat and she'll ruin it."

"Ruin what, exactly?"

"My chance of a lifetime to—"

"Jason! *Jason!*"

From the stairs came the sound of several men galloping noisily up, shouting in fear. McCallen's odd-ball cronies from the bar crowded into the room, with Paterno leading the way. He stopped and gaped at the tableau.

"What the *hell* are you doing?" he bellowed at Mc-Callen. "We heard a shot—"

"I'm trying to get this damned fool to talk. Now stand out of the way so I can get on with it."

Paterno was all wide-eyed shock and nerves. "You're out of your mind! You don't just shoot people for something like this."

"You want the goods, don't you?"

"Not like this! Put that thing away and let's go before someone calls the cops."

"But he knows where Mary is!"

"She'll turn up sooner or later. You might as well face it, it's over with her."

"She's probably hiding out with that toad of a prince. Is that it?" Eyes glittering, he turned the gun on Escott again. *"Where is she?"*

Paterno must not have been thinking clearly, for he rushed forward and grabbed at the gun. Everyone else froze, various expressions of horror on their faces. Paterno and McCallen struggled back and forth, cursing. I caught Escott's coat sleeve and yanked him over and hopefully out of the line of fire. The gun muzzle went every which way in the scuffle.

Then it resolved to unexpected quiet. Paterno managed to get both hands on McCallen's gun arm and push it down against the desk. McCallen stopped fighting him. Both glared at each other, breathing hard for several moments. With a snarl, McCallen shook him off. He didn't put the gun away, but he wasn't pointing it at anyone.

"Come on then, y'pack of louts," he growled, then shouldered his way past them all to stump down the stairs. They looked a lot cowed by what they'd seen, but followed.

Paterno straightened his rumpled coat with shaky dignity and grimaced at me and Escott. "Gentlemen, I apologize for this. Jason's been under a lot of strain lately."

"So it would appear, sir," said Escott. "Thank you for your intervention."

"I'll try to talk some sense into him about Mary."

"Please do—Mr. Paterno, is it?"

His mouth popped open. "How do you know my name?"

"It *is* my trade. Perhaps you will be so kind as to tell me—"

Paterno shook his head and darted for the door. "Some other time, sorry. Gotta go."

Escott made no move to stop him, so I didn't either. We watched his hasty exit, then I closed up after him.

"You okay?" I asked in the abrupt silence.

"Quite fit, thank you."

"What were you thinking, arguing with the man? He could have killed you!"

"But he didn't."

I could have gone through all the stages of exasperation and anger with him and yelled till I turned blue, but we'd been through it before, and he wasn't going to change. For an instant I very seriously considered hypnotizing him to make him behave with more caution, or at least apologize for being such an idiot, but gave up the notion. It was too much against his nature.

"I'm getting some air," I said, and went out, not slamming the door too hard.

It was a figurative excuse, since I no longer breathed regularly, but I had to be clear of that office and away from Escott until I calmed down. Muttering a lot about things I couldn't help, I took a swift turn around the block, consciously pumping my dormant lungs to flush them clean and work off the adrenaline. Hatless and coatless, I didn't feel the cold, only noted that the wind had altered direction from the Stockyards so the stink was gone.

McCallen, Paterno, and company were also gone. They had to have parked out of sight of the office, but not out of earshot while McCallen was doing his Burglar Bill routine. Everything *seemed* normal now. I made another circle, just to be sure. The cars in the immediate area of the block were familiar, the others I wasn't so sure about, but I felt marginally better for the exercise. I could return and not be tempted to give Escott a punch in the nose for his own good.

"What's the damage?" I asked him when I walked in again.

He was at the desk with a spread of papers in front of him, puffing heartily on his pipe. "Minimal. Our Mr. McCallen must have some lock-picking skills, for that is how he had to have effected his entry to both the office and the files. He'd gone through all the ones under *S*, but of course did not find anything on the case. My current notes are in the usual spot, safe and sound."

He'd built a trick medicine cabinet in the washroom

that swung out to reveal a hiding place in the wall. "Is that the file he wanted?" I nodded at the desk.

"Dear me, no. I was just refreshing my memory about Mr. Dalhauser and that other fellow, LaCelle. Not much on the latter, I fear, nothing further than ten years back. Do you think you could find out a bit more from Gordy? I tried to have a chat with him but his mind was rather focused on the charming Miss Taylor tonight."

"Did you get to meet her?"

"Briefly. I recalled enjoying her performance as Titania when one of the local stations undertook to do a version of *A Midsummer Night's Dream*. Very sprightly she was, though I thought she'd be taller."

"Why do you want to know about LaCelle?"

"Knowledge is power. Perhaps you could also inquire about Grant, too."

"Still think you know him?"

"I'm not sure. I'm quite good at faces, and his is not familiar to me, yet there's something about him . . . well, there's nothing for it tonight. I'll look into things tomorrow. Now about concluding things with Mr. Mc-Callen . . ."

Despite the cooling-down walk, I still had to bite my tongue at the mention of that lunatic. The only one loonier was my partner. "After I drop you home I'll go look him up. If he goes back to his house, he's not going to be a problem anymore."

"Excellent. But I'd like you to find out exactly what is in Miss Sommerfeld's mysterious envelope. I should have had a look before when you got it back, but she was so adamant about her privacy I chose to respect her confidence. Not an error I plan to repeat, but who knew then that it would become such a nuisance?"

"Tell her it might help speed finishing the case."

"That could work. I'll also ask if she knows this Paterno chap. Right, then. I've got all I need for the time being. I should like to go home and study this over some hot brandy." He squinted through the pipe smoke at my shirtsleeves. "Aren't you just a bit chilly?"

"Gimme the keys, I'll go warm the car up."

"I doubt that it's had time to cool, but here, and thank you." He tossed me the ring and began shuffling his papers together.

The Nash was still warm, but I had it idling smooth, and the air coming from the heater was nice and hot. He'd have a comfortable ride home. It'd only take Escott a minute to lock the office, for all the good it seemed to do. I turned the headlights on so he could see better, and far down the street another car's lights also bloomed.

I was still rattled about McCallen, but didn't think he'd have ditched his friends for a return bout so fast. The possibility existed, though. I leaned across the seat and opened the passenger door, calling to Escott to get a move on. From the top of the stairs he said something in reply, but I couldn't catch it; the wind brought only the sound of itself and the fast-approaching car.

Bad. I didn't like the feel of this at all. Scrambling out, I hurried toward the stairwell opening just as Escott emerged onto the sidewalk. I yelled at him to duck, to get out of sight.

He saw the car coming. It was still distant enough not to be a threat; he had time to move but did not. He must have been trying to get a look at the driver. Impossible in the dark.

I called out again.

Then I heard a loud, sharp *crack* off to my left, and

realized my mistake. The threat was not from the car, but from across the street. A man came out from the deep shadow of a doorway, arm extended and pointing at Escott. The wind caught a tiny puff of smoke from the gun in his hand and carried it away.

Escott made a fast, abortive move toward the protection of the Nash, but not fast enough.

The gun made a bright flash—several bright flashes—of fire and smoke. The vicious noise of the shots bounced off the surrounding buildings.

Five shots. Very quick.

Two caught Escott square in the chest.

I saw it so clear it was like a still picture of the instant.

He jerked and made a strange breathy grunt, then dropped straight down like his knees had been cut from under him.

11

BRAKES squealed as the car came to a rolling stop between me and the gunman. He ducked and dove inside, his form hidden by the bulk of the vehicle. The driver hit the gas and gears and hurled off, taking the first corner on two screeching wheels.

Escott sprawled facedown on the sidewalk. Very still.

Not fair. It's just not fair.

The thought rolled over and over in my mind, blocking out everything else. I could not see for a moment; gray mist enveloped me. When it cleared I was kneeling by him with no memory of how I'd gotten there. I just couldn't take it in, only feel an overwhelming black sickness washing over me like a wave of icy lake water.

I reached out, took his shoulders, and eased him over.

Not fair.

"Charles?" It was someone else's cracked and frightened voice, not mine.

He was still alive. Mouth open. Trying to breathe. Looking up at me.

"God, Charles, I'm sorry."

He struggled, his whole body shuddered from the effort. Struggled. And drew in a ragged, shallow breath.

Not enough. It rushed right out again. He labored for another gulp of air.

"I'll call for help."

But when I started to move, he flailed a hand, catching my arm. He shook his head, lips forming the word "no."

"But I've—"

"No," he coughed out. He mouthed the word once more, shaking his head.

"You've got to . . ."

No. His paper white face made a ghastly smile as he fought for air.

"—wait a second."

He feebly patted his chest, nodding.

And I suddenly understood him. "You . . . you god-damned son of a bitch."

He relaxed slightly and closed his eyes. The next breath he took was less shallow, and he held on to it longer.

"You goddamned *bloody* son of a bitch!"

Still wearing that rictus of a smile, he made a sound like a tiny laugh. I wanted to belt him, but he'd been hit hard already. Trembling head to toe, I stood and paced, unable to stay in one spot. I wanted to yell or punch holes in brick walls. Only by using up a ton of self-restraint did I manage not to do both.

"Thought you knew," he wheezed out a full five minutes later. He made motions that he wanted to stand.

"I forgot," I said through my teeth. I had to clench them tight to keep them from chattering in the aftermath of the adrenaline. It left a metallic taste in my mouth, and my guts churned with nausea. Helping him up, I felt the thickness of his bulletproof vest through his clothing.

"Could have. Noticed lack. Of blood."

Of all people in the world, I *should* have noticed. But the only thing that had stuck in my brain was the sight of my best friend falling, and the thought that it wasn't fair for him to die. I made a choking sound he took for a response.

"Understandable. Heat of. The moment. All that."

"You scared the shit out of me," I finally snarled. The two of us staggering like drunks, I got him over to the car. "You going to be all right?"

"Just. A bit. Winded," he said, leaning heavily on the fender and puffing. "Knocked it. Out of me."

I looked him over and didn't care for what I saw. "Just how hurt are you?"

"Don't know. Chest heavy. Bruised."

"I'll find a hospital."

He shook his head. "Not that bad. Need rest. Not questions."

I thought of an alternative for him, a doctor who would not ask about the bullet holes. "Okay, inside the car. We're getting out of here."

He nodded, and I got him past the door and in so he could collapse onto the seat. I slammed things shut, went around, and slipped behind the wheel. The big motor was still idling smooth; I worked the clutch and gears and shot away without looking back.

"My pipe's on the walk," he said in a faded version of his normal tone.

"For Christ's sake, you'll get another." And live to break it in, thank God.

"I creased the files rather badly." He indicated where he'd rolled them up and stuffed them in his inside pocket.

"We'll send them to the cleaners for ironing."

He make an abortive sound in his throat suspiciously

like a laugh, then subsided, holding his arms crossed over his chest. He wasn't completely recovered. When he breathed in too deeply it came back out as a cough.

"You break any ribs?"

"Don't think so." He was getting some color back, though there was a sheen of sweat on him. "Bruised. Never had the wind knocked so thoroughly from me before. Thought I'd pass out."

I thought I'd pass out, too. "Did you see who it was?"

He shut his eyes, thinking, then shook his head. "When you shouted I was looking at the car. It was probably meant to be a distraction from the shootist. When he appeared all I saw were the muzzle flashes. Did you—"

"Same thing. Hat and muffler covered him up, but he was big, well built. I think it was McCallen. The car looked like his Ford, but—" All I could remember of it were the headlights dazzling my sight. And after the shooting started my memory blurred. Only the sharp image of Escott dropping remained.

"The car was not unlike his," he said. "The gun I'm not sure about. McCallen fired once in the office. I counted six shots in the street."

"You *counted* them?"

"Strange how the mind will fix on the most absurd things in a crisis. I was thinking if he would only just run out of bullets without hitting anything vital—and counted them. Six. Not just five. McCallen's revolver was a six-chamber model, and he'd already used a bullet."

"So he reloaded. Or had another gun."

"But a motive?"

"He's crazy."

"Even mad people have their reasons. Why kill me before finding out what he wants to know?"

"That's something we can answer tonight."

He didn't ask what I meant, not after he realized where I was driving. A short detour first, then I'd find him some medical help—if he'd accept it.

"This should be most interesting," he said sometime later when I parked the Nash in front of Jason Mc-Callen's modest residence.

His car was on the street and lights showed behind the house's drawn shades. "Looks like he's home," I said, setting the brake.

"Which is a most foolish spot to hide himself if he's guilty."

"Not unless he's packing to leave. I'll change his mind."

"I'm coming as well."

I nearly argued with him, worried that he was too fragile yet, then thought of how I'd feel if it'd been me. I got out and went around to the passenger side to help him. He was moving as little as possible and slowly, for which I could not blame him, and briefly took my arm for balance until he was clear of the running board. Then he settled his clothes into place, pausing as he fingered the holes made by the bullets. They were larger than a .22 would have made. One was on the right, the other just left of center over his heart. Either of them would have been fatal.

He looked at me with a tight smile, a corpse's smile. "Could have been quite nasty, don't you think?"

I pushed a return of that icy-black sickness away. "I'm glad it wasn't worse. Come on, let's get this bastard."

He followed, waiting on the sidewalk as I ghosted up

the steps to try peering through the windows. I returned a moment later.

"Can't tell if he's there or not. I'll go in first and unlock the door. Give it a few minutes, then you come in. I want to see his face when he finds out you're alive."

"As do I."

I disappeared fully and slipped between the cracks around the door, re-forming just inside. The living room looked the same as the last time, but with a few more newspapers added to the pile around the chair by the radio. A man's topcoat was flung on another chair. Listening hard, I heard an irregular clinking noise from the kitchen. McCallen must have worked up quite an appetite. After fixing the door for Escott, I went transparent and silently drifted down the hall.

As I guessed, McCallen was about to feed his face. He'd made a sandwich and was in the process of pulling a bottle of beer from the icebox. His cat meowed plaintively, circling his legs.

"All right, y'greedy little bugger, here's another bit, but that's the last one." He pulled some small item out for the cat, who devoured it with a purr I could hear even in my present state.

I made myself solid and stood framed in the doorway. McCallen was partially turned from me. An easy enough mark.

He straightened, saw me, and gave a satisfyingly startled jump, but recovered lightning fast. He set his feet, hunching his shoulders forward, and very deliberately set down the bottle of beer. There was murder glowing in his eyes as he glared at me.

"Now I've got you," he rumbled. "You'll be leaving here in a box by the time I'm done with you, laddie."

His reaction was all wrong. He was surprised, but it was not the surprise of a guilty man.

"Where's the gun?" I asked.

"I won't need a gun for the likes of you."

He bulled forward. I stayed put. He threw one very quick right. I went transparent for exactly how long it took his fist to travel through me, went solid, and caught him a smart punch in the gut. I pulled it, not wanting to damage him too much. He doubled over with an *oof* and staggered back, clutching his midsection. He crashed against the table, and went down. As he sat on the floor trying to get his lungs to work, Escott walked in.

Most of his color was back, concentrated in two spots high on his cheeks. His gray eyes had a hollow, haunted cast to them. He'd just looked his own death in the face; it would leave marks. "Mr. McCallen," he said after a few moments, sounding quite normal.

McCallen squinted up at him and sneered. "So the two of you have come to gang up on me? Brave of you."

Escott frowned mightily, glancing once at me. "Jack, we have the wrong man."

"I think you're right." McCallen was pissed as hell but not shocked. "Well, if he didn't shoot you, who did?"

"I'm not averse to discussing that subject, but elsewhere, if you please."

McCallen looked back and forth between us. "What are you two gits on about? I never shot you—only your damned wall."

"Indeed, and were I not distracted by a greater problem, I'd have you arrested for it."

"Why, you—" He started to gather himself, but I made a swipe with one foot, knocking his legs from under him. He sat down again with a thud.

"Hey! What the hell is this?" Paterno appeared behind us, shoved his way past, and went to McCallen. "You all right?"

"Where the hell were you?" McCallen shrugged off Paterno's offered help.

"Taking a leak. What's going on here?"

"It's two against two now, that's what." He started to get up.

But Paterno grabbed him and told him to wait a minute, then looked at my partner. "You—you're Escott, aren't you? The agency?"

"That is correct, sir."

"Hey, I'm sorry about the stuff earlier, but I think you should leave. Jason's got a grudge on, and you don't need to be here."

"I quite agree, but not before my curiosity is satisfied about the contents of that envelope."

"The envelope?"

"The one my friend retrieved for Miss Sommerfeld. I know you're familiar with it."

"Some other time—"

"Now," Escott said firmly.

I took a half step closer and tried to look intimidating. McCallen took it as a challenge and made another move to stand. This time I caught his eye and told him to sit still and be quiet. His jaw sagged as though he was mildly startled, and he abruptly sank back to the floor.

Paterno stared down in puzzlement at his amazingly cooperative friend, then at me. I switched and gave him a brightly encouraging smile.

"The envelope?" Escott prompted.

"Uh—yeah."

"It would seem to be the source of all conflict."

Paterno snorted. "You can say that again. Listen, haven't you got some kind of confidentiality pledge in your line, like a doctor?"

"Not precisely, but I can keep a secret."

"We just don't want any of this getting back to Mary's family." He waited for some kind of promise, but Escott only raised an eyebrow. Paterno wearily gave in with a short sigh. "It's nothing illegal, but they could throw another monkey wrench into the works."

"What works?"

"What Mary and Jason have—or had—when they were working together. Since they hit the last scene in the third act it's been nothing but fight, fight, fight."

It was Escott's turn to do puzzlement. "Third act? As in a play?"

"That's it. A play."

"A play?" Escott looked like he just found half a worm wriggling in an apple he'd bitten.

"A play," Paterno confirmed. "They've been working on it for the last year."

"Miss Sommerfeld and Mr. McCallen are writing a play?"

"*Were* writing it."

"Until her family stepped in?"

"Nah, before that. The third act, like I said." He looked doubtfully at McCallen, who was sitting still just as he'd been told. "See, they were working on it just fine, and she's got connections in the theater and managed to get a copy of the first draft to Helen Hayes, who went nuts over it, so then this producer gets really hot to see it, 'cause with her in on it, he figures they've got the greatest thing to hit the boards since *Hamlet*."

Escott nodded slowly. "*Hamlet*? Indeed?"

"The trouble is Jason and Mary got this problem with the third act. He wants a happy ending, she don't. They both got good reasons for either one, but neither of 'em gives an inch to the other, then it was fight, fight, fight all the time. Her family didn't know about any of this until Mary starts going to the plant to talk with Jason a little too often, then meeting him at the bar to work some more. The folks don't know about the play, but they figure their little precious is getting too friendly with the wrong kind of guy, so they send her to Europe, which really delays things."

"And when she returned . . . ?"

"She finds Jason's been tinkering with the play without her being there to argue with him about the changes. She gets mad and sneaks it away from him, then he sneaks it from her, then she hires you to get it back."

Escott looked at me. You could almost see the other half of that worm dangling from his open mouth. I shrugged and said consolingly, "At least it's not a divorce case."

He looked back at Paterno. "And just where do you fit in the plot of this little vignette?"

"I'm their agent. And I've got a producer and these big-money investors all lined up. Do you have any *idea* how hard it is to get one of these birds interested in an original work by two unknowns? It's next to impossible! This may be their only chance. The investors option the play, whatever the ending, and produce it with Helen Hayes starring in it, but they won't wait forever. All we gotta do is get Mary to sign the contract, only she's not where we can find her, thanks to you two. And Jason."

"Maybe . . ." I said, clearing my throat. They both looked at me; Jason was still playing zombie. "Maybe you could have both endings. Play each one on alternating nights. People would pay to see it twice over, then."

Paterno put on a beatific expression. "My God, but that's one we never thought of. It could make theatrical history! You hear that, Jason? Now, *that's* something that could work. Jason?"

Escott shut his eyes and pinched the bridge of his nose. "It's late, and I suddenly feel very tired."

The beleaguered agent swung his attention back to his last hope of success. "So, would you please tell us where she is? A phone number, a post-office box—anything?"

"Is she aware of this pending contract?"

"Yeah."

"Then why is she not interested in signing if the ending doesn't matter to the producer? That dispute could surely be worked out afterward."

"Because this big lug on the floor got her mad the way he handled things, so off she went. Besides, she's a rich kid. She has no idea what it's like to be hungry, so she's got no need to be in a hurry about anything. But me and Jason do, so I'm begging you, give us a hand here. She don't even have to see Jason; I can do all the go-between stuff like I'm supposed to do."

"Very well. I shall contact her tomorrow and see what I can arrange. Have you a number where you may be reached?"

"Here's my card, and thanks! Thanks a million! You hear that, Jason? We got some light at the end of the tunnel. Jason . . . Jason?" Paterno gave his friend a shake, jarring McCallen out of his trance.

"I heard," he muttered sluggishly. "I want to talk with her."

"Only after the contract's signed. You let me do my job and we'll all be rich and famous."

Escott cleared his throat. "Miss Sommerfeld's recent experience with Mr. McCallen has been such as to give her the strong impression that she was in fear for her life. His behavior toward her—"

"He was only giving as good as he got. But he won't do any more of it, I promise. Right, Jason?"

McCallen growled.

Escott regarded them one at a time, his gaze finally resting on Paterno, the negotiator. "My contacting Miss Sommerfeld is on condition that Mr. McCallen give his word of honor that he cease and desist all harassment of her."

"Say yes, Jason, and sound like you mean it," pleaded Paterno.

A louder growl from McCallen that trailed off into muttering. "Very well. I'll leave the proud baggage alone if that's what she wants. She can have her toad of a prince for all I care." His cat, which had been hiding under the icebox, emerged and delicately walked over to butt its head against his leg. He petted it roughly, which it seemed to like. "As God is my witness, the more I deal with women, the more I like my cat."

"Communists," I grumbled, hauling the steering wheel around.

Escott hugged his chest and braced with his feet as I took a corner too sharply. He hissed in pain, but it wasn't my driving that hurt him, it was his own laughter. He'd started to dissolve into it as soon as we left McCallen's, and he couldn't seem to stop.

Paterno had let us know the odd-looking crew that hung out in the back room at Moe's was little more than a bunch of would-be writers. The "speeches" the waiter had overheard were passages from whatever novel, story, or play was being read aloud so the other members could critique it. The critiques often got vocal enough to be mistaken for arguing.

McCallen, because he was the oldest, had the most forceful personality, and had even published a few short stories, was their unofficial leader. He also held a steady job and could often stand them a round of beer. The rest were either students at the university or still living with their parents while they worked to make their fortune as writers.

"Perhaps they're exactly what you've been needing to stimulate your own literary efforts," Escott suggested.

"I don't think McCallen would stand for it."

"You've the means to get around him. The only foreseeable problem would be your not partaking of a beer with them, but you could get around that as well." Then he must have thought of the communist angle and again began chuckling and groaning at the same time.

I let him wheeze on without comment. He needed the laughs. Whether he'd ever admit it or not, the near miss of his own murder had shaken him, and this was a release from the tension.

After a few miles he eased up on the hysterical humor when he saw the direction I took would not bring us home.

"Why here?" he asked as I made a decisive turning into the Bronze Belt.

"Because after McCallen, Gil Dalhauser is my next choice for a suspect. If it was him, he'll have connections all over the city—except here."

"Dalhauser?"

"You know how he was staring at the party. He was throwing hot needles at you. And he's tall enough to fill the bill."

"True, but to be that angry after all this time, and then to do the shooting himself seems a bit of a stretch. Even were he so murderously minded, I should think he'd be more likely to employ muscle in his stead."

"Not if he wanted to keep it quiet. There's also the personal touch to think about. After all the grief you gave him—are still giving him since the tax guys aren't letting up—he'd find it a lot more satisfying than fobbing it off onto another."

"A most logical argument—but to wake Shoe up at such a late hour . . ."

"I don't think he'll mind. You need a place to lie low."

"I'll be safe enough at home—"

"Like hell."

"—because Dalhauser will think I'm dead. He saw me fall."

"But there won't be anything in the papers on it, the cops won't have a report, and no hospital will have heard of you. He'll be watching for those. When he doesn't see 'em, he'll figure he missed or only just wounded you and we got away."

"Very well, I'll concede those points. If he is the one, and if I am the target." He touched the holes in his clothing lightly. "These could very well have been meant for you. People have mistaken us one for the other before."

"Not this time. The shooter had plenty of chances to see me coming and going when I took that walk, and in my shirtsleeves he'd be able to tell me from you easy enough." Knowing that, I still had to suppress a shudder. He'd been standing dark and unmoving in the deep shadow of that doorway watching the whole time, patient, patient, patiently waiting. "Besides, I don't have anyone mad at me, except maybe Archy Grant, only I took care of him, so he's no threat. Ike LaCelle had a beef but slipping me a Mickey was his payback. He wouldn't expect me to be up and around to be shot. Unless you can think of anyone else you might have mortally offended at the club, it must have been Dalhauser coming after you."

"At the club? Oh, yes, of course, whoever it was would have followed us from there. But why kill me and leave you alive to spread tales?"

"Gordy warned him off."

"But both of us are under his protection."

"Me more than you because of the business with Bobbi. Dalhauser must had thought if he let me go, Gordy might allow him to get away with bumping you off. The score he tried to settle tonight dates from long before Gordy's order."

Escott frowned over that one. "It's not impossible, but I don't see it as very likely. He would surely expect you to avenge me or for you to demand that Gordy do so."

"Maybe. By doing that, then all bets are off. If I went after him he'd be able to kill me, claiming self-defense."

"It does make for a neat package. But still . . ."

"What?"

"If he'd shot both of us at the same time, then no one would be left to accuse him in the first place. We'd have simply been the targets of some other person's revenge."

He had a good one there. "Meaning maybe it wasn't Dalhauser, but someone who would know I'd suspect him?"

"Then either you or Dalhauser or both of you would eventually be removed. I'm sure he has plenty of enemies who would like him out of the way, and one of them could be clever enough to use you to do it."

"That's just too complicated and open-ended. But if a mug in mob business is going to be killed, always look at his friends first for a motive, not his enemies. It's a little something I learned from Gordy."

"Wise man. I shall have to speak to him tomorrow about it."

I pulled the wheel left, then right, and eased off the gas. The Shoe Box Nightclub was just half a block away. It was dark, but there would be people on watch to notice our arrival and let us in. "You know, it could be someone completely outside of all this, the club, and the rest. Who else would want to kill you?"

"Not many, actually."

"I thought in your work you'd have hundreds lined up."

"The advantage of being a private agent rather than a conventional investigator is that most of my cases have nothing to do with life-and-death matters. Certainly I have enemies, but they're more likely to do me a minor ill turn such as LaCelle tried with you, not risk hanging to kill me."

"You can't think of anyone?" I found a space by a fireplug and parked.

"Not at the moment. Give me a bit of time." Escott shifted on the seat. "Damn. It feels like a bowling ball's been smashed into me. I hope Shoe has an aspirin on the premises."

Since he owned a bar, Coldfield had something better than aspirin available; it was just too bad for me I was unable to have any. I could have used a nice, numbing drink.

We were semifamiliar figures to some of his people, but two white guys turning up in the dead of night still inspired a lot of caution. We were in the process of being given a slap-down search when their boss arrived and called them off.

"What the hell's wrong?" he demanded, hurriedly descending the stairs from his rooms on the second floor. He wore a bathrobe and his feet were bare, but he looked alert and ready to take on anything.

"We've only a minor favor to ask—" Escott began.

"Don't try that crap with me, Charles. There has to be something mighty wrong for you to come this late looking like you do."

"It was my idea to come here," I said. "Check his shirtfront."

He checked and his eyes widened. "Shit, Charles."

Escott gave him that corpse's smile. "Fortunately my extra insulation against the cold came in quite handy."

"Are you all right?"

"A little sore . . ."

"He's a lot sore and needs a safe place for the night," I put in.

"He's got it, but I want to know what happened."

"I'll give you the goods if you can get him off his feet."

Coldfield took over from there, dismissing everyone

but Isham, who was still dressed and accompanied us upstairs. He took a chair by the door and watched and listened as I related the evening's main event to his boss and what had led up to it. Coldfield wanted to send for Dr. Clarson to give Escott a once-over, but the patient turned him down.

"This can wait until morning, Shoe," Escott insisted, then swallowed four aspirins with a big glass of water.

"You could have a broken sternum."

"If I did, then I'd be in considerably more discomfort than I am and would readily agree to an examination. Right now all I want is a place to lie down and no one shooting at me for a few hours."

"It's yours, but first thing tomorrow you see the doctor."

To that Escott gave in. He actually looked like he might get some sleep for once. Isham escorted him out to settle him in a spare room.

Coldfield turned to me. "What about you? You going or staying?"

"Going. I should keep an eye on the old homestead. I'll be safe in my hideaway."

He had reservations about that, and also wanted to talk more. I spent an hour discussing all the stuff with him that Escott and I had covered. Coldfield knew Dalhauser, having had some dealings with him through the unions.

"He's dangerous," said Coldfield, "but he's nothing near to stupid. Standing around waiting to shoot Charles like that is plain stupid, and crossing a man like Gordy is just as dumb. You sure he's the gunman?"

"Neither of us got any kind of a real look, but Dalhauser's the most likely. Tomorrow Charles will call Gordy and let him know somebody's not listening to orders. The two of 'em might come up with a better choice for idiot of the year, and when they find him I'm gonna wring his neck."

"Shouldn't that be Charles's job?"

"Not if I get there first. I honest to God thought he'd been killed, Shoe. And the only thing I could think of was that it wasn't fair for him to die. Like he'd been playing a game and was counted out too soon by a crooked umpire. It sounds childish."

"It's called grief," he said.

"But Charles didn't die."

"Don't matter. The grief is for what might have happened. It don't hurt the same, but it still hurts. Say you're standing on the edge of a cliff and a gust of wind pushes you over, but at the last second someone grabs you back to safety. You're alive, but you're going to be shook up for a while about it. About what might have been. Charles is going to be feeling that stronger than you are."

"And doing his best not to show it."

He heaved a great sigh. "Oh, yeah. But there's gonna be a reckoning before this is done. I just hope he doesn't tear himself apart over it."

"What do you mean?"

"He's had some shit thrown at him in the past. He didn't handle it too good."

"What was it?"

Coldfield shook his head. "Not my story to tell."

I'd hit that wall before, and knew better than to try to get more out of him. Isham returned, and Coldfield told him to drive me home in Escott's Nash, then bring the car back.

"Keep him here until I'm awake?" I asked Coldfield.

He snorted. "Do my best. But you know what he's like."

Isham hung around long enough for me to ascertain that no ambush lurked in the house, then drove off in the predawn light. I wondered if he ever slept, but not for long. The pale graying in the east was already starting to hurt my eyes. Funny how artificial things like candles and lightbulbs didn't affect me as powerfully as the sun. I hurried inside, dumped my tux coat and topcoat carelessly on the couch, then vanished to enter my basement chamber while I still could. If I waited too long, I lost the ability to vanish and would have to use the trick trapdoor, which was a pain to bother with when I was rushed.

My limbs stiffened up even as I sank onto the earth-padded cot. When my head hit the pillow I was gone for the day.

The next night I woke to the sound of the kitchen phone ringing, and knew it must be for me. Someone had been waiting for sunset, probably Coldfield; Bobbi always gave me a few minutes to stretch out the kinks. I shot up through the cracks and materialized, snagging the receiver and cutting off the annoying bell.

"Yeah?"

"It's Shoe."

"What's wrong?"

"Nothing that I know of, but I thought you should know that Charles took off around noon, so be on the watch for him."

"He took off? I thought you were going to—"

"You ever try to stop him when he really wants to do something?"

"Yeah, like trying to catch air in your hands. Did he say anything to you? Any idea where he went?"

"We had a late breakfast and he said he was going to do some poking around. I thought I'd talked him into waiting for Clarson to see him, but I had to think again. The son of a bitch."

"How was he feeling?"

"Good enough to slip away without me noticing—and I'd been expecting him to try something like that."

Great, Escott was on the hunt with no forwarding address, running on the edge of the cliff again. I hoped he'd not get so focused on his prey that he'd lose his footing. "The man's got a lucky star, he'll be all right."

"You saying that to convince me or yourself?"

"A bit of both, my friend. If he drags in home I'll call you at the Shoe Box."

"And I'll call you if he shows here," he said, and hung up.

I took a look at myself and decided I was a mess that needed to be swept under a rug. Just as I started for the stairs the phone rang again. This time it was Bobbi.

"Hi! I just wanted to thank you," she said, sounding fresh and bright, everything I wasn't.

"Uh . . ."

"You awake yet?"

"Yeah, sweetheart. But what'd I do again?"

"You fixed things with Archy, remember? And have you seen the papers yet? The reviews for both shows are fantastic."

"That's good. I'm glad something's going right."

"What's happening there? You sound off. You can't be having a hangover."

"Some stuff came up for a case Charles is working on,

and it's got me distracted. Just as well you called, I might be busy tonight. If I'm not there by the end of the last show, can you get a ride home?"

"No problem. What case? That blackmailer?"

"A new one. Tell you later. What's the deal about Archy? You saw him today?"

"Adelle invited me to come to the *Variety Hour* rehearsal so we could have lunch and shop afterward, and Archy was a perfect gentleman to me. No double meanings under the jokes, no trying to impress me with extra attention. I mean he was friendly, but that's where it ended. You're a miracle worker, Jack."

"I'm glad to be doing something right."

"It was great, even Adelle noticed what a good mood he was in."

"Is she still solid with Gordy?"

"She's coming to the club for dinner with him tonight."

It was good to know where he'd be later if I had to find him. Escott would have talked to him, and he might have a line on where my partner had taken himself.

Bobbi had to leave to get ready for her first show, so I was soon dropping the receiver back on its hook, free to finish the trip up to my room. I stripped and bathed and was just doing the last button on a fresh shirt when I heard a noise downstairs.

I went to the landing and saw a man's shadow moving against the frosted panes of the glass inset of the front door. His hat obscured details, but he had height. Maybe the gunman had decided to come check on me, the one he'd ignored. I vanished and reappeared in the lower hall, tucking my shirttails into my pants, listening with interest as he fumbled noisily with the lock. He apparently wasn't worried about alarming anyone. The knob turned, and he pushed the door open. It swung back hard and banged against the wall, rattling the glass. The man swayed on the threshold, then lurched a few unsteady steps inside.

It was Escott.

"Charles?"

He didn't seem to hear me, and plowed toward the stairs, hand out to grab at the banister. He missed it by a mile and overbalanced, stumbling forward to sprawl gracelessly onto the treads. I went to him, got him turned over. For an awful moment I thought he'd been shot again, this time for real—until I caught a whiff of the booze. He reeked like a bum on Saturday night.

He looked at me earnestly, but didn't see me at all. He was drunk out of his mind, and his eyes were wild. In a pleading tone I'd never heard from him before, he slurred out, "Din' do it, Shoe. I swear I din' do it."

12

"DIDN'T do what?" I asked, too flabbergasted to do more than gape.

"Was Raymond, cou' o'ly be him. O'ly one. Swear it."

"Who's Raymond?"

"Not my fault, but my fault. 'F I'd jus' *been* there!" He pushed me away and tried to stand, then winced and sat again. "'S wrong. Hurts." He gingerly rubbed his chest, puzzled by the pain.

"Yeah, I know. Come on with me, we'll fix things." I got an arm around him and hauled him up. He groaned with the movement, but didn't fight as I guided him upstairs.

"No good," he said sorrowfully, his feet dragging. "No good at all."

We made it to his room, and I got him to the bed. He lay down flat, staring at the ceiling, and still mumbling nonsense. He wouldn't or couldn't answer any of my questions.

His tuxedo was well creased, same as his topcoat, like he'd been in them both too long. His tie was gone, and his shirt gaped open around the neck. He hadn't shaved since yesterday and the uncharacteristic stubble, along with his present crazed state of mind, put fifteen years on him.

"I'm sorry. I'm so sorry," he said again and again.

"It's all right," I told him. "It's all over now." Whatever it was.

I got his shoes off and pulled the bedspread across his body. He kept a carafe on the night table. I filled it in his bathroom, poured water in a glass, and managed to get him to drink most of it down. There was a storage closet in the hall. I rummaged and found a bucket, placing it next to the bed in case he woke up sick, which was very likely. Having survived a number of hangovers myself, I knew what a long trip it could be to the bathroom when your gut's unhappy and your legs aren't working.

"They proved it," he said earnestly. "You know they proved it." He was talking to the ceiling.

"What did they prove?"

"Tha' I din' do it."

"Do what?"

"'S was Raymond. O'ly one."

"Charles? Charles, you hear me?"

"Mm?"

"You need to sleep now."

He shook his head over and over. "Bad stuff then. No dark sleep. No real . . ." He'd drifted off, mouth open, filling the air with the smell of stale booze.

I stared down at him and could not believe that he'd done this to himself. He was always sober and in perfect control. What the hell had happened to make him do this?

A few times in the past he'd pulled shenanigans like disguising himself, taking on completely different characters and acting them well enough to fool even Coldfield. This wasn't one of those times. Escott had gotten himself well and truly plastered, and there was no figuring the why of it until he woke up.

At least he wasn't having trouble with insomnia tonight.

I went downstairs and checked the street. He'd parked the Nash crooked, leaving the lights on. No surprise there, but I was astonished, not to mention thankful, that he'd not killed himself getting home. I just hoped he'd not killed anyone along the way. With the armor plating on that buggy, it'd be hard to tell if he'd run over some luckless pedestrian. The keys were still in it. I drove to the alley in back and put it in the garage, sieving into the house through the kitchen door. Going straight to the phone, I dialed Coldfield and told him what was going on.

"He's drunk? What do you mean, drunk?" he demanded.

"Just that. He's a lot more than three sheets to the wind."

"You sure?"

"It's no act." I'd listened to the sound of Escott's heartbeat, something he couldn't fake, so I knew for certain he was genuinely unconscious. "He's passed out in his room."

"Good God."

"He was babbling a lot. Kept calling me by your name and saying that he didn't do something, but he wouldn't say what. He said it was a bird named Raymond. What does that mean?"

There was a long silence on his end.

"Shoe? Who's Raymond?"

"It's—it's . . ."

"What?"

"Oh, sweet Jesus on the cross. I'm coming over."

"Then I'll—oh, hell." Catching a movement out of the corner of my eye, I snapped my head around.

Shep Shepperd stood in the hall doorway, still wearing his slightly too large overcoat—and aiming a gun at my midsection. Because of my hypnotic help he'd forgotten all about our first encounter and wasn't the least bit afraid of me.

"Don't get funny," he said in a very soft voice so the phone wouldn't catch it. "Say good-bye and hang up."

"Jack? What is it?" Coldfield hadn't heard anything, but he sounded very alert to the fact that something was amiss.

"No, angel. Don't you worry your pretty little noggin about it."

"What'sa matter? You got company?"

"Yes, yes, I know, sweetheart," I said in a tender, understanding tone. "But I gotta take care of something. I'll be all right, I promise. You just look after yourself when you get there, and I'll see you as soon as I can."

"Damn right you will," he growled ominously as I dropped the receiver into place.

I turned to face Shep, thinking I'd been wrong about Dalhauser, and Escott had been wrong about the gunman's target. That, or this guy was here to finish off the one witness to the shooting.

"Who sent you?" I asked. "Ike LaCelle?"

He showed no obvious reaction. When he was in charge of things, Shep was quite a different man from the terrified goof who'd fled from me before.

"Or is it Gil Dalhauser?" I was already lining things up

on how to take him, but he backed away a step and gestured with the gun.

"Get your coat," he said.

"Why?"

"Going for a ride."

"A ride to where?"

"To see someone."

"Who?"

"Get your coat and find out."

I could have given him the evil eye, but that might take time, and it was likely his prizefighter partner was waiting for us. Neither of them needed to find out about my helpless partner upstairs. The front door was open— I'd forgotten to lock it—and I could hear a car's engine chugging nearby. Weighing up the options—and there weren't many I wanted to bother with—I decided to go along with them. Coldfield was on his way and would keep a watch on Escott. With any luck, I could deal with whoever was behind the shooting and find out the why of it.

I shrugged into my old topcoat, jammed on a hat, and let Shep usher me outside. He shut the door, doing a quick check of the street. No one was around, but he kept the gun close to his body so its outline was less visible. He made me get in the backseat. Ace, the prizefighter, was in the front passenger side of the Buick. He also had no memory of our initial encounter and, poker-faced, covered me with his own revolver while Shep drove. I wondered if Ace missed his machine gun very much.

Hunching down against the door so Shep wouldn't notice any problem with the rearview mirror, I paid attention to our route. They didn't seem worried about me seeing anything, giving me to think this might be one of those rides made famous by the Chicago gangs. If so, then the man behind it all had no fear of Gordy's edict.

If it was a man. For a fleeting moment I seriously considered Adelle Taylor as being the brain running things. I'd faced a hellishly effective female gangster not so long back; I had a right to be paranoid about it. Additional thought cured me of my lunatic suspicions. Most of them, anyway. Adelle had no motive to kill Escott—at least none of which I was aware—so I dismissed her from the lineup. For the time being.

The drive was long, taking us into one of the city's many seedy sections. The road paralleled some train tracks, and with every mile the area around got more dismal and deserted. Closed factories, warehouses with broken windows, deserted businesses, it was an industrial zone with no industry; any that had been there had been sucked dry by the Depression, leaving only their bones behind as poor shelter for vagrants. There were few cars around, and all of them were going in the opposite direction from us.

Then even the buildings thinned out in the flat landscape, giving way to weed-choked empty lots protected by peeling no-trespass signs. Just one structure loomed ahead, a big three-story job protected by a tall, netted fence with barbed wire along the top attached to struts that slanted outward. The warning signs posted to tell people to keep out were many and large.

Shep took us around to the front entry, going unchallenged past a small gate kiosk and the guard inside it. His only acknowledgment was to wave once as we went by. As soon as we were in, he emerged to close the gate behind us.

On one end of the vast yard were oversized gas pumps,

on the other a railroad siding where freight cars could be unloaded. In between, dozens of trucks were parked in orderly lines, patiently awaiting their drivers to return to take them on their rounds throughout the city. They were all coal trucks belonging to the business Gil Dalhauser supervised for the mob.

Shep drove to the big building, which was the repair garage. One of the huge doors yawned wide; he took us right in. Only a few service lights were on, leaving the rest of the cavernous interior thick with black shadows. Several trucks were in various stages of disassembly, their guts revealed, the stink of their greasy insides tainting the cold air.

We stopped and Shep cut the motor. Silence flooded in.

"Out," he said, opening his door.

I got out along with the fighter, and they guided me to some metal stairs.

"Up," Shep ordered.

Up I went, but they did not follow.

A tall man waited at the landing two flights above. Gil Dalhauser, with his hands in his pockets. I finished the climb and joined him on a metal catwalk where he stood by the rail, silhouetted against a wide bank of windows. He made a hell of a vulnerable target, but that along with his hands being out of sight gave me to understand he wanted to talk, not shoot.

"Good evening, Fleming," he said. No lights were on up there, but you could see the whole of the garage and the most of the yard, depending which way you faced. He was in a position to cover both.

"Depends. What's this about?"

He made no reply, only looked out at the trucks standing in silence below, then turned toward the windows. The pale glow from the night sky washed color from his face and turned his blue eyes transparent.

"What a truly awful place this is," he murmured in a soft, hollow voice. It did not travel far past me. The dusty air around us seemed to swallow sound. "Do you see it?"

"Yeah, I see."

"I don't think so. Come over here and look at it. Just stop a moment and really study what's before you. It's completely different in the daytime. There's hundreds of men about, all the shouting and truck noise and phones ringing, but for a few hours in the night it's like this . . . utterly deserted. So dirty and dark, cold and quiet . . . like the grave. Now . . . do you see it?" He sounded like he'd made this observation before, and enjoyed saying it so he could watch how it affected his audience.

He was giving me the creeps. "Why'd you bring me here?"

"Because it's discreet, and you can see people from a distance when they approach." He stared unblinking out the windows. "And it serves to make a point."

"Which is?"

"You are quite alone, and vulnerable."

I didn't think he meant that in its more obvious sense. "What is it you want?"

"To tell you that you should take Escott's shooting as a serious warning."

"What do you know about it?

"Enough to say you should both leave town for good. Vanish."

I paused over that one.

He glanced at me. "Oh, yes, I know your friend somehow survived the shooting. He was seen today, quite hale and hearty, nosing around where he shouldn't.

If you don't get him out tonight, he will be dead before dawn. That's a guarantee. They won't stop until he's dead. Until both of you are dead."

"Why both of us now and not last night?"

"I'm not sure. I think last night you weren't seen as a threat. If Escott hadn't survived, you'd probably be free and clear, but I suppose he thinks Escott's been talking to you."

"Who's after him, and why? Why kill us?"

He frowned. "Escott's not told you?"

"He doesn't know himself." Though from his condition when he'd come home, I could figure Escott may have found out.

Dalhauser chuckled softly in his throat. "Now, isn't that ironic?"

"Why is he a target?"

"I've no idea. I was hoping you'd be able to tell me."

"Come on."

He turned those expressionless eyes on me. "I really don't know why. I only know that he's been marked, and his adversary is determined past all limits of caution."

"Why the warning, then?"

"Self-interest. I'm doing what I can to comply with Gordy's order about you two."

"Why don't you tell Gordy what's going on? Have him step in and stop things."

"Because this goes beyond his influence. The mobs in this town leave you alone as a favor to him or because he controls them. But not everyone is under his control or cares about doing him any favors. Not everyone is smart enough to listen."

"Ike LaCelle, for instance?"

No surprise from him at my mention of the name.

"Ike's a flamboyant starstruck pimp, but don't underestimate him. Below the surface flashiness he's also a smart, tough, fast-thinking son of a bitch."

"But he can overstep himself?"

Dalhauser nodded agreeably. "If he thinks the risk is acceptable. Like that dose he slipped you last night."

"He told you about it?"

"He laughed for hours thinking he'd one-upped you. Only you didn't get as sick as he'd hoped. I've told him also not to underestimate you. And you may believe it or not, but I've tried talking him out of this course of action."

"Have you, now?"

"For my own ends, of course. If he gets himself into real trouble, I'm going to feel it in the pocket sooner or later. Gordy's hands-off is still in effect for me, though I'd not shed a tear if Escott got rubbed out. But I'm a cautious man; Ike is not."

"What's Ike's beef with Charles? You must have some idea."

"He didn't confide anything of it to me, and I have asked many times. What I know for certain is that he is determined to kill you both. While I won't actively participate, I won't stop him, either. Outside of my business interests, none of this is really any matter to me, but when I see a train wreck about to take place, it seems only prudent to let the engineers know there's trouble ahead. There's no telling where the damage could go or how far before—"

"Does this have to do with Archy putting the moves on Bobbi?"

He looked puzzled.

"Because if that's it, then it's all over and done. Archy's not interested in her anymore."

"Yes, I heard, and I'd like to know how you managed that. But I think you're on the wrong track there."

"Where's LaCelle?"

"He could be anyplace. I'd tell you if I could."

"What's his plan? Another shooting?"

He shrugged. "Maybe. Only this time he will make sure of his target. So . . . are you going to be smart and leave or stay and die? I won't find out for some time. I'm taking a little trip to a card game in Cicero to have a solid alibi for the next few days."

"I'm staying."

His mouth tightened slightly at the corners. "You're really not afraid, are you?"

"Not for myself, no."

"Interesting man. I can see why Gordy respects you."

"You got a way of contacting LaCelle?"

"Since I don't know where he is, I can only pass along word and hope it reaches him. Why?"

"You've warned me, you can warn LaCelle in turn. I could scrag him for what he almost did to my partner, but I won't if I don't have to. I don't like killing very much."

Dalhauser's brows twitched as he took that in. I could see he thought I looked too young and guileless to be a killer.

"Tell him I want to talk. He can pick the time and place; I'll come unarmed."

"Talk?" He looked at me like I was the biggest fool in the world. "You'd only make it easier for him to bump you."

I knew I could survive most any trap Ike cared to set

up. Probably. If he decided to come after me with wood instead of lead, then I was out of luck. "He plans to bump me no matter what, right? At least this way I can find out why."

He shook his head. "I'll put a word out. But it may not get to him in time."

"You know when he's planning to do something?"

"Just that it will be late tonight. He may have people watching your house by now."

"Waiting for me to come back?"

"Yes. You're really not leaving?" When I didn't answer he moved past me and started down the stairs. "Then I wish you luck. It's been nice knowing you."

"That's it?" I asked, annoyed.

He paused, not turning around. "You've been warned, you choose to ignore it, so I'd say, yes, that is very much it."

Dalhauser continued down to the garage floor, then on outside. A motor started up, and from the window I saw him driving toward the gate, raising a thin cloud of dust that quickly settled.

I half expected Shep to follow and leave me stranded, but he and his friend waited and drove me back, neither of them sparing a word in my direction the whole trip.

As we neared the house I asked, "You two going to see Ike LaCelle later?"

They exchanged looks and did not reply. I'd figured these birds to be working both sides of the fence or simply available for whoever might be hiring.

"Good. Tell him Jack Fleming wants to talk with him before the shooting starts. He might hear something to his advantage." It was a sweet phrase lawyers liked to use before they started charging you for services rendered, and seemed appropriate here. "You got that?"

"I got it, punk," said Shep, unimpressed.

He dropped me at the corner, so I had to walk half a block, but it was just as well. I spotted an unfamiliar car with two men inside watching the house. Being direct always appealed to me, so I just went up to the driver's side and opened the door.

The element of surprise is always a good thing to have working for you. That and enough light. They could see me well enough to succumb, and less than a minute later they were hanging on my every word. I asked if there were any others spying on the house. They were the whole show. I gave them the same message I'd given Shep and stood out of the way so they could drive off to find their boss.

Maybe I should have gone with them, but there was a big Nash parked just behind my car out front, meaning that Coldfield was here, which was a huge relief. He'd be in six kinds of fits wondering what was going on after so long a wait. I wanted to talk with him and make sure Escott was all right. For all I knew, LaCelle might have hopscotched his own boys and come in through the back.

Making noise as I cautiously walked in, I called to Coldfield, holding myself ready to vanish at the first sign of gunfire. He yelled an answer that he was upstairs. He sounded impatient and irritated—that is, normal. I went up and found him in Escott's room sitting by a lamp with a newspaper in hand.

He tossed the paper aside and rose to face me. "What the hell's going on? Where've you been? That phone call—" He made no effort to hush his voice, but none of it disturbed Escott. He was exactly as I'd left him, soddenly asleep and snoring. The room's air had a decided tinge of his alcohol-soaked breath to it.

"Gil Dalhauser sent some muscle over to pick me up," I said. "That's what interrupted things during my call. Seems he wanted to talk, but without drawing attention to it. Apparently Ike LaCelle is behind the attempt on Charles, but Dalhauser couldn't say why." I crossed to a window and opened it a few inches. The draft coming in was cold, but helped to disperse the sour sickroom smell.

"How could he not know why?"

"It wasn't for lack of trying. Ike wouldn't tell him."

"Then you tell me what you know."

I looked at Escott. "I will, but I want to find out what's in his head. Come on, and I'll make some coffee that could float a horseshoe."

"You can drink coffee?"

"Nah. These nights all I can do is smell it, but we're going to get him up and sober and find out just what set him off."

Coldfield followed me to the kitchen, where I had to play hide and seek trying to find things, since cooking was not something I did anymore. Once in a while I made a sandwich for Escott when I was in a kindly mood, but that was pretty much the limit. The coffeepot was easy enough, being too large to conceal itself for long, but cups and spoons took longer. After locating the necessities, I made the concoction triple strength. While the stuff brewed, I told Coldfield all about my trip to the truck yard, finishing up with the orders I'd given LaCelle's watchdog lackeys.

"You mean you just let them go?" He was outraged. "You outta your mind to do that."

"Glad you think so. LaCelle might think the same and be curious enough to set up a meeting."

"He'll set up a shooting gallery."

"I've survived those before."

"But Charles is in no shape for any of that."

"Then let's go get him into shape."

I got the pot and a cup and carried both upstairs.

Between the two of us we stripped Escott down to his skivvies and carried him to the bathtub. I pulled the curtain partway around to minimize splashing and opened the tap wide for a cold shower. He was sound asleep for a full minute before the icy water finally got to him, and he started fighting it. First trying to push it away, then sputtering and cursing. Coldfield held his feet, I held his shoulders, keeping him in place until he seemed more conscious than unconscious.

Escott's skin was a nice shade of blue and violently puckered with gooseflesh when I took pity and shut off the flow. He shivered like an earthquake and readily accepted the cup when I put it under his nose. He tried to take it but couldn't get his hands to work right. I held it, and he slurped some in, making an unhappy noise as it burned his tongue.

"He won't be able to keep that down," Coldfield observed.

"Which is why he's in the tub and I'm out here," I said. Sure enough, the coffee made a sudden reappearance. I turned the cold water on again and flushed everything clear.

Escott squinted blearily at me. "Damn your eyes."

"You know who I am?"

"Damn your—oh!" He leaned forward, coughing. I kept the water running, but twisted the tap on for the hot.

He eventually stopped shivering. I cut the water and offered another cup of coffee. He drank it down, then lay back in the water spray and groaned.

"You awake now?" I asked, drying off with a towel.

"Yes, unfortunately."

"Sick?"

"Please don't say that word."

I poured more coffee.

"This is wretched stuff," he complained.

"Sue me. Drink."

He choked more down.

"You need any help getting dressed?"

"I want to sleep."

"What a change. You can sleep later. In case you haven't noticed, we've got company."

Coldfield waved at him from the door. "Hi, Charles. You look like hell."

Escott glared at him, then dropped his gaze, his shoulders slumping. "Nothing changes."

"Oh, yes, it does. Are you gonna pull yourself together and get off your ass or do I have to come over and kick it for you? Maybe you've forgotten, but you told me a long while back to do exactly that the next time you got stupid. This sure looks to be one of those times."

"Very well," he said wearily. "Leave the coffee. Let me work on this."

I thought he would still need help, but Coldfield signed for me to come along. He was right. Escott had had enough self-induced humiliation for one evening; he didn't need us around to help him pull on his socks.

We tramped down to the kitchen. Coldfield expressed regret at not snagging a cup for himself.

"I can go up for the pot," I offered.

"No, give the man some privacy to recover. I'll make do." He found a shallow pot, put some water in it, and set it on the stove to heat.

I sat at the kitchen table and watched as he raised the flame on the gas ring to its highest level. Yellow tongues licked up the sides of the pot.

"You've seen him like this before, haven't you?" I asked.

"Too many times to count."

"When? Back when you were actors?"

He shook his head. "Later. It's a long story." He pawed through a drawer and found a tea strainer, setting it next to a coffee cup. "He used to get drunk all the time because of something that happened in Ontario about a dozen years ago."

"You think it's related to what's happened to him now? The shooting?"

"I don't see how it could be."

"Something set him off. Tell me. It's time I heard."

"That's up to Charles."

"Not anymore. Not after the shooting and what he's done to himself today. Not after the way you reacted when I asked about 'Raymond.' Who is he, and why does Charles keep saying he didn't do something? What's he talking about?"

"It's not up to me to tell."

"Charles can't and probably won't, so you're the only one left. Is it connected to Ike LaCelle?"

"I don't know. Maybe. I read over those files Charles got from his office. LaCelle didn't catch anyone's notice until some ten years back. It's not impossible he's involved."

I resisted prodding him again, though the wait was

making me crazy. He was working his way around to finally talking; he only just needed to get used to the idea.

The water started to steam. He waited for it to boil, cut the heat, then dropped in a big spoonful of coffee and stirred it around a minute. He poured it into a cup through the tea strainer. From where I was, it smelled good, but it would have a hellish kick for drinking.

Coldfield sat opposite me and grimaced. "I really don't see how his shooting could have anything to do with what happened back then, but the only times he *ever* got this kind of stinking drunk was when he thought too much about it. He hasn't been like this for years, though."

"Then something today must have brought it all back to him. Come on, tell me what's going on that I should know about."

He put his hands around the cup as though to warm them, staring down into the coffee, and heaved a long-drawn, defeated sigh. "All right."

13

Ontario, Canada, April 1924

THE sausage sandwich had been a mistake.

The afternoon stop of the Hamilton Players at Elkfoot Flats for petrol included just enough time for a late luncheon. Charles W. Escott, second youngest member of the troupe, lavished several coins from the grouch bag hung around his neck on a meal that was meant to last him the rest of the day and into the next. Since joining the acting company six years before, he'd long grown accustomed to the vagaries of touring and knew the only meal you could count on was the one you'd just finished. He ate heavily and well for the money he'd spent, but was now having second thoughts about the last sandwich. Though it had looked and smelled quite toothsome in the tiny café, the sausage had had an odd taste to it, but at the time he'd put that down to the spices. Hunger won out over his usual caution in regard to road meals, and he'd finished every bite.

Now, as the first ominous tendril of nausea caressed his insides, he swallowed thickly and knew things would get worse before they got better. There wasn't much he could do about it, either, except sweat it through. They were all due to play in Ottawa the following evening and could not be delayed just because of an upset stomach.

Charles was one of the drivers in the little caravan of four cars and a large truck, a job he usually enjoyed. He continued at it, saying nothing about his growing sickness, for the activity kept his mind off the discomforts of his body. Besides, if he stopped, he'd likely lose his place in the car, having to give it up to one of the more senior members of the troupe. That meant bouncing around in the back of the truck with the properties, costumes, and extra luggage, something he literally would not be able to stomach.

The road between Toronto and Ottawa should have been in better condition, but winter had had its way with the surface, creating whole sections to challenge even Mr. Ford's indefatigable motor cars. About an hour after the last stop, two of them broke down within a mile of each other. One from a cracked axle, the other with bent wheel rims.

The grumbling passengers wearily redistributed themselves into the remaining vehicles without much discussion and proceeded on toward the next village where they hoped to find aid for their stricken transportation. It was crowded in each of the remaining cars as seven people packed themselves into a space more suitable for four. Those that were left had to make do crushed together in the cab of the truck or perched uneasily on top of things in its back.

Spirits were fairly high, though. Their last run had paid well, and the group in Charles's car entertained themselves exchanging plans on how they would spend their cash once they hit town. Bianca Hamilton, half owner of the company and also its pay mistress, longed to have her hair washed and styled. Cornelius Werner, one of the older leading men, spoke fondly of getting thicker socks. He often voiced complaints, his most frequent one having to do with his constantly cold feet.

Being an actor who suffered from such a condition usually invited numerous obvious jokes from his peers, but for once none of the others indulged in them. During the day there had been a hint of spring in the air, but now with each mile the sky grew darker and the air a lot colder. They huddled together in their coats, with blankets tucked all around. Outside, wide patches of unmelted snow still covered the ground under the trees, and the scent of it was in the rising wind.

"I think we're in for it, children," said Bianca, staring out as the first fat flakes of a new storm spattered wet against the windshield.

Charles kept driving, peering hard through the clacking and inadequate wipers. He turned on the headlights and tried to ignore a cramp twisting his guts. No one noticed the grim cast to his face; they all looked grim. He had to slow as the snowfall got heavier, and he couldn't see to avoid the more obvious potholes. The overloaded car lurched and swayed along, and after an hour of it they'd barely covered twenty miles.

"This is ridiculous," Bianca stated. "I'm getting seasick."

"Freezing and seasick," said Cornelius, next to her in the front seat.

"It's a freak blizzard," added Stan Parmley, whose looks had earned him young romantic leads.

"This late in the season?" asked Bianca.

"That's why it's freak. We may have to pull over."

"Then we'll freeze to death," said Cornelius.

Until Bianca ordered otherwise, Charles would continue, though by now his cramping was uppermost in his concerns. He knew he'd have to stop before very long, and that it was likely to be unpleasant and embarrassing.

The wind vigorously buffeted the car, and he had to fight to keep it on the road—which was rapidly disappearing under the fresh layer of snow. After half an hour he could only discern its surface from the rest of the murky landscape because it was somewhat less bumpy.

"Slow down," said Bianca. "I see a signpost."

Charles slowed, easy enough to do, but because it was full dark and the headlights were thwarted by thick flurries, he was compelled to get out and walk to the sign to read it. The needle-sharp wind was painful on his exposed face, and the sting did not go away when he returned to the car.

"It said thirty-seven miles to the next town along this stretch," he told them, raising a disappointed groan. "That's two, perhaps even three more hours of travel. If I recall correctly, the hamlet of Moose Welts consists of a postal office and a small dry-goods store—both in the same building."

"No hotels?" asked Raymond Yorke, who had signed with the company only a month before, supplanting Charles as youngest member. Like Stan, he was handsome, but in a rugged American way despite his English-sounding name. He was always in a relentless good humor even in the worst of times. Now he looked soberly apprehensive.

Bianca shook her head, sighing. "We've been on this road more than once and have often passed Moose Welts. If you could see it you'd understand why we kept going."

"I fear our two courses of action," said Charles, "are to continue all night in this, or turn back. The wind would then be behind us. There's also a chance the snow might thin out the farther south we retreat from this storm. We can stay at the last village and try again in the morning."

"I vote we go back," Cornelius muttered.

"We can't," said Bianca. "We have to be at the play-house or lose our contract."

"The contract has an 'act of God' clause, doesn't it? This would seem to qualify. No one's going to come see us because they'll all be snowed in."

Bianca still had more argument left and made use of it while the others shivered. Charles leaned against the door in nauseated misery until woken from it by a sharp rapping from outside. He cranked the window down. Clarence Coldfield, the only colored man in the company, peered in.

"What's the holdup, Bianca?" he asked.

"It's under discussion."

"Well, discuss it fast because I'm turning the truck around."

"You can't do that!"

"It's not exactly my decision. Everyone's cold, tired, and in a bad mood. Henry got out and saw how far to the next stop and started a mutiny. They're all going back to Elkfoot Flats whether you want it or not, and I might as well be driving them as freeze out here. Your sister's going along with the rest." That the other owner of the company was joining the impromptu exodus lent a certain legitimacy to it.

"Just let me talk to them a minute."

Cornelius put a hand on Bianca's arm. "Now is not the time for debate. A vote has already been taken."

This resulted in more animated discussion initiated by Bianca. Clarence frowned at Charles, who was his best friend in the group. "You all right? You look awful."

"Bit of a bad stomach, is all."

"It must have spread to the rest of you, then. Listen, don't wait for Queen Bianca to make up her mind, just turn and follow us out. Henry was already bringing his buggy around."

Charles nodded and rolled the window back up. A mile later Bianca was still obliviously arguing with Cornelius.

The blizzard seemed to ease with the wind behind them, and Charles could better see out the windshield since the snow was no longer hitting them head on. Countless flakes sailed ahead of them, their swift dance in the headlights mocking the car's snail pace. Charles followed in the tracks left by Henry's car, and could see nothing at all of the properties truck.

Bianca finally noticed their change of direction, pursed her lips, and sat back in the seat, her body rigid with anger. She was not one to fast forgive when she lost a fight, particularly when she was in the wrong. Everyone else was relieved, though the laughter was somewhat forced when Raymond launched into one of his funny stories. Since he was still new, the others hadn't yet heard them all. Charles didn't care about any of it. He would soon have to give in to his cramps by making a short trip to the woods long before they reached Elkfoot Flats.

Then the brake lights of Henry's car flashed, and Charles had to stop.

"Now what?" asked Stan. They were surrounded by threatening trees swaying in the wind like drunken giants. He was a child of the city and most things to do with the forces of nature made him nervous.

Henry himself came to deliver the bad news. "I lost the truck."

"What do you mean? Did it break down, too?"

"I mean I lost its trail. Clarence got too far ahead of me, and the snow filled in the wheel ruts I was following. I thought I was still on the road, but we're on another road and have been for a while."

The language inspired by this announcement was much less than polite, for when it came to cursing, no ship full of sailors could surpass a company of highly annoyed actors. Charles abstained, having excused himself from the car while the opportunity was available. He knew Bianca was good for at least ten minutes' worth of recrimination.

Going far enough into the thin woods for some privacy, he was surprised—and highly thankful—to find a looming shape in his path that proved to be an outhouse, complete with a copy of last year's Sears catalog. He made hasty use of both, and, upon emerging, looked around for any other buildings he reasoned might be nearby.

He returned to the others to report that not all was hopeless. The road Henry had mistakenly taken for the main route actually led someplace, halting at a small, but sturdy hunting cabin. No one occupied it, but there was a store of wood stacked by the door and a substantial fireplace within.

"You broke inside?" asked Bianca, aghast.

"It wasn't locked. There's nothing of value there, but it *is* shelter, and this *is* an emergency. I suggest we take advantage of it before frostbite sets in."

His suggestion was universally accepted, for by now even Bianca was too cold for further argument. The two cars plowed through another hundred feet of snow and came to stop in the yard before the cabin.

"How rustic," Bianca commented, walking in. It was constructed of logs and looked old, but the cracks were well chinked up and the roof was sound.

Space was short in the small structure; there was barely room for the fourteen of them to lie down on its bare plank floor, but that made it faster to heat once a fire was started. After that, everyone's humor improved, except for Charles, who could now well and truly succumb to his case of food poisoning.

Someone noticed, of course. Like any other family the members of the company were sensitive to each other's moods. Several of the more lively girls volunteered to play nursemaid, but Bianca shooed them away and administered a practical bicarbonate of soda in melted snow. She told Charles to stay close to the door so he could escape to the outhouse when necessary. He rolled himself under a borrowed blanket, shivering in a cold sweat but counting his blessings.

He'd been nineteen, recently demobilized from the army, when he'd walked into a London theatrical agency six years earlier looking for work. Times were bad and there were a lot of other young men with the same problem; the chances of an inexperienced hopeful getting a job were nearly zero.

Bianca Hamilton, then a forceful woman of thirty, had just formed The Hamilton Players acting company with her sister Katherine, and both were determined to see it succeed. They were looking to hire a man who was smart, self-possessed, willing to work for a percentage of ticket receipts, and travel to Canada. Their chances were also nearly zero.

Charles had been the only one to come in that day who seemed qualified and able. He was told to pack and be ready to sail by evening. Whether he could act or not was a side issue, for the sisters were of the opinion that it was a teachable skill.

On the voyage over he got to know the people who would become his new family, and they him. Working and training with them, he soon discovered he was clever with props and character makeup, had a gift for memorizing dialogue, and an excellent mind for solving whatever problems arose. In the world of the theater, things went wrong all the time, so he soon became their miracle man.

The membership of the troupe was not a constant thing. Some came and went, depending on their fortunes, others were fixtures for year after year. Charles had become one of the latter. For all the irregularities, mishaps, poor pay, and often dismal living conditions, he loved his work and the people who worked with him. He could not imagine himself doing anything else with his life.

Now he lay curled on the floor of the log cabin with most of those people, listening to their laughter and talk, and was thankful not to have to be alone.

A resourceful lot, some of them had brought extra food supplies, mostly tea, biscuits, and an occasional discreet flask of spirits. The Hamilton sisters were not against drinking, but they forbade it prior to a performance and abhorred drunkenness.

A search of the cupboards turned up a large cooking pot, suitable for stews and soups. They had no makings for either on hand, but one bright soul had bought a remarkable quantity of beans. When asked why, Raymond Yorke said they represented a fortnight's worth of eating and had been cheap. As the youngest and newest member of the group, he was often the butt of much ribbing, but was now hailed as the hero of the hour. The pot was scrubbed clean of dust and hung on a convenient fireplace hook. People took turns fetching snow to melt in it. The evening meal would be rather plain, without any salt pork for flavoring, but no one would go hungry.

In honor of his genius and foresight, Raymond was given the first plateful when the beans were ready. He pronounced them edible and took it upon himself to play server to the others. Plates and utensils were short, but no one minded sharing.

Charles, still in the thrall of food poisoning, could not bring himself to join them. Raymond noticed and insisted he at least have a cup of tea.

"You're very kind, but I shan't be able to keep it down," said Charles.

"You need to flush out your pipe works," Raymond told him with a grin. "Even if you can't keep it down, you'll still get some cleaning done."

That had a certain logic to it, and Charles wanted to be rid of the bland taste of the bicarbonate of soda he'd taken. He drank the strong, too sugary tea and resumed his fetal position, quietly alert to the least internal change that would signal the tea's reappearance.

About ten minutes later his patience was rewarded— so to speak. He slipped out the door and found a spot away from where the other actors had been digging snow. At the conclusion of his business he felt worse than before, dizzy and heavy of limb, and his head hurt. He dragged back inside the warm cabin, resuming his spot by the door. The drone of his friends' talk lulled him into a dull doze.

Though the necessity of roughing it lent an almost festive air to their gathering, the day had been long and hard. Soon after dinner they all fell one by one into slumber. Some snored, but the noise did not disturb the others. Raymond alone sat up, tending the fireplace. Charles woke slightly to see him adding more wood to the blaze, then finally dozed off.

He woke again some while later, with the groggy feeling that he'd heard something but surfaced too late to identify it. After a moment's thought he was fairly certain someone had merely passed him going out the door. Another wakeful soul in search of the facilities, no doubt. He noticed the fire was very low, being composed more of deep red embers than flame. Raymond had probably retired long since and was one of the many lumps crowding the floor.

Charles suppressed a groan as he once again felt the need to hurry outside. He'd hoped to sleep through his nausea, but it was back and decidedly stronger than before. His head pounded as he stood, and he nearly fell over from a sudden swoop of dizziness, only catching himself just in time. He found he had to break every movement down into a single separate action in order to accomplish anything. It was like an acting exercise Katherine Hamilton had taught him. She was elsewhere at the moment, having been in the properties truck with Clarence and the others. They'd be wondering what had happened to the cars by now, worried sick . . .

Bad word, that.

Carefully, bracing against the door frame with one hand, he lifted the simple wooden latch. Opened the door. Stepped out. Closed the door. Looked around. Where was that damned outhouse? There. Just follow the beaten trail the others had left earlier.

Now—walk toward it and try not to fall down.

The snow had stopped; the wind had died to nothing. His boots crunching through the white drifts made the only sound except for his ragged breathing. His breath hung on the air, almost solid enough to cut. He knocked on the outhouse door, but got no response from within. Perhaps he'd been mistaken about someone preceding him.

No matter. The nausea was bubbling up in him again along with another cramp. He grabbed at the door handle and hurried in—and only just in time. As the door—which was balanced to swing back into place—shut, he thought he heard yet another sound coming from the direction of the cars. He's seen that they'd been shrouded with snow, but not badly. The digging out in the morning would not be too arduous. The person who had gone before him must have forgotten some necessary bit of luggage. Charles couldn't think what anyone would need at such an hour.

He sat in the cold little house, leaning against its cold wooden side, but strangely unmindful of the chill. He sat and sat and tried very, very hard to think of something anyone would need from the cars. This seemed to take him a terribly long time, but it distracted him from his internal wretchedness.

What was the time, anyway? Charles fumbled with his coat, trying to find the pocket where he kept his watch. He kept working at it until he realized he was trying to find a pocket that was not there. This struck him as very amusing, and he wanted to tell someone about it . . . but of course he was alone. It would have to wait.

He stubbornly continued his search, finally opening his outer coat. It was important that he do that so he could . . . find . . .

. . . his watch. Yes, he wanted his pocket watch.

When he did draw it free he had to stare at it awhile, trying to remember how to open the thing. He knew he'd done just that thousands of times, but then he'd not had to pause and think about the action. Everything was so much more difficult when you had to *think* about it.

He was ready to give up when he recalled the matter of the tiny catch on one side and pressed it. That was much better. He angled the timepiece to catch a stray slice of outside light and got a fleeting glimpse of the watch face. It was either ten after midnight or two in the morning. He couldn't be sure about the minute and hour hands; his eyes weren't focusing too terribly well.

That accomplished, he wondered why it had been so important to know the time. In retrospect, it had been singularly unimportant. He snorted in disgust and spent several minutes putting his watch away.

Through it all, a small part of him was aware that something was quite wrong. It knew that sitting out in such cold for so long was dangerous, and he most likely had a fever. It told him—over and over and with growing alarm—to wake up and go back to the cabin before he froze to death.

But he was still sick, and couldn't bring himself to move just yet. He dozed off, a very light doze, because his eyes were still open. He was cold, but still did not really feel it. The danger, the frantic voice inside said, was when he started to feel warm. Well, that hadn't happened yet, so he was all right. Quite all right, thank you very much.

Raymond Yorke finished his work on the older of the two cars, making sure it would take some hours before any members of the company could bring it back to running order again. He wasn't stranding them forever, just long enough to prevent their being a nuisance.

He wiped grease from his hands with a rag and quickly pulled on his gloves. It was damned cold, but that would also help him. Since the company was twenty miles out in the middle of nowhere and uncertain where they'd left the main road, no one would be too anxious to try walking to find help. Besides, if the properties truck ever reached Elkfoot Flats, Katherine Hamilton would raise a royal stink about coming back to find her sister and the others. A minor hardship for them and too bad, so long as things worked out in his favor.

Still, he knew he faced a hellish risk, trying this stunt with all the snow. Farther down the road it could be drifted up too high for the car to get through, but such a golden opportunity might never present itself again. He was willing to take advantage of it. He'd been waiting and waiting for the right moment to come, and now that it was here he would not pass it up.

Raymond walked back to the cabin, easing quietly inside, though it was unlikely any of them would wake at this point. The dose of morphine he'd stirred into the pot just before serving had them all ready to audition for the part of Rip Van Winkle tonight. All he had to do afterward was tend the fire and wait. It hadn't taken long; he'd been very generous with his portions and the drug.

The only hard part had been to keep a straight face as he watched them dropping into dreamland one by one.

He stepped carefully over their sleeping forms to get to the fireplace, and built it up to have light to work by. That done, he started at the far end of the small cabin, going to each man and woman, emptying the contents of their grouch bags into his own. Worn around the neck and under one's clothing, the old theatrical tradition was an excellent way of keeping your valuables intact—so long as you were conscious to defend them.

This job's haul was especially large. The receipts from the Toronto performances had been their best since he'd joined the company, and tonight he had the luck to snag most of their earnings before they could spend it.

And that didn't even count the watches and jewelry.

Once he got back to the States and sold the stuff to connections he'd made in New York, he'd have more than enough to keep him in fine style for the next year or so. By then, the hue and cry would have cooled down and he could plan for his next little party.

Happy almost to the point of humming, Raymond collected it all, from Mr. I'm-such-a-great-artist Cornelius Werner, to Miss I-invented-Shakespeare-myself Bianca Hamilton, and all the rest in between. He did not forget to take the car keys from the snoring Henry.

"Raymond?"

He froze. Absolutely, completely froze at the sleepy, inquiring voice. It was Bianca's.

"Raymond? What are you doing?"

"Just making sure everyone's tucked in." Christ on a stick, was that the best he could think up? He turned slowly, wearing a guileless smile.

Bianca sat up, rubbing her face. "What's wrong?"

"Everything's all right, go back to sleep." For some people morphine was unpredictable. They could hold a lucid conversation, eyes wide open, and still be asleep, not remembering anything when they woke later. He hoped that held true for Bianca.

She did not take the suggestion, and struggled to her feet, shedding her blanket. "No . . . you're doing something. What are you—"

He quickly covered the few steps to get to her—one fast clout to the jaw would take care of her nicely— except she had time to scream, and she managed to duck. It was more of a fall out of the way than a controlled movement, but it served. She screamed again, calling at the others loud enough to break through to some. Cornelius stirred with a sleepy grunt and squinted around, confused.

Raymond had to nip this in the bud. He reached down for Bianca, who was trying to crawl away, slapping a hand over her mouth and another around her throat. She fought him frantically, still trying to call out, kicking, beating, and scratching at him. This was too much. He lifted her—she was a small woman—and slammed her head against the edge of the fireplace flags. *That* stunned her. She instantly went limp.

Cornelius was his next problem, and far more formidable. He may have been complaining and fussy, but he had size and thirty years ago had been an excellent rugby player. He tackled Raymond bodily and started hitting hard. Their scuffle carried them into others, rousing them.

Raymond punched back, but with little effect. He managed to roll the groggy actor toward the fireplace, flailing out for a weapon. His hand closed on a piece of firewood. He heard the crack and felt the impact go up his arm without realizing what it meant. Only after Cornelius suddenly collapsed did Raymond understand. Blood ran down the side of the old man's skull. A lot of blood.

One of the girls who had been sleeping near Bianca cried out. Stan Parmley was stirring, nearly awake, mumbling questions.

It was too much. Robbery was one thing, but they'd never let him get away with this. He had to think, but they weren't going to let him think. If they'd only just shut up a minute . . .

The girl opened her mouth again. Raymond lashed out, using the piece of wood like a club. It proved to be very effective at making her quiet. He whirled on Stan. The first swing was a glancing blow, the second far more solid.

Then came the third, the fourth, the fifth . . .

Just to be sure.

He *had* to be sure.

And he had to be sure about *all* of them.

It took an amazingly short time to finish the task.

Noise. Not too distant. Sluggishly surfacing from his daze, Charles eventually identified it as the cabin door slamming shut. Someone must be in need of the facilities. He'd have to leave.

Easier thought of than accomplished.

He was still not cold, but very stiff from sitting in one place for so long. Shifting himself sparked off lots of painful clamorings from his joints and especially from his legs. The pins and needles marking the return of circulation to them slowed him down.

Another sound came to him: that of a car motor starting up. What a good idea. A good idea to start it so it wouldn't freeze up and fail to run in the morning.

A state that was likely to befall him if he didn't get up and move around soon. As he forced himself along, he noted with some confusion that the sound of the car was gradually fading. That couldn't have been right. Perhaps his fever was distorting things.

Pushing on the door put him back in the snow again, in the utter stillness. Not one whisper of wind now stirred the surrounding trees, though in the distance he could just catch the determined rumble of the car. Certainly one of their Fords, for only one remained in the yard. Showing clear in the pristine snow were the tracks and ruts where the driver had turned the second vehicle and taken it away.

Why? Had some of the members decided to leave once the storm was past? That hardly made sense—unless it was to find the properties truck and let the people with it know the rest of the company was all right. Bianca might sanction such a trip. She and Henry must have taken off, since the missing car was the newer one Henry always drove.

Charles trudged toward the cabin, feeling frail and sick, though not so bad as before, and very, very tired. He wanted to sleep for a few months. And later, take a very hot bath. And never, ever have another sausage sandwich as long as he lived.

He quietly let himself in, noting that someone had built the fire back up. It was very warm inside and now that he had something to compare it with, he realized how truly cold he'd become, after all. He picked his way carefully over to the fireplace, afraid of waking those he passed.

None of them stirred, though. He sat in front of the blaze and thawed out his hands. His feet were icy as well. He'd have to go with Cornelius to find extra socks for himself if this kept up.

God, but it was so *still* in here—as though for some reason everyone held their collective breath. The last time he'd felt anything remotely similar had been in the aftermath of his first battle. The only sound had been his own heartbeat and the only movement were the flocks of ravens come to feed on the dead.

He pushed that thought out, as he always did. The war was past and done, and he was free to forget its horrors. He'd seen to his patriotic duty and survived.

And yet it was so bloody *quiet*. Had Stan Parmley forgotten how to snore? He was so infamous for it that none of the other men ever wanted to share a room with him.

Charles turned from the fire, peering about, waiting for his eyes to adjust to the dimness. As his attention shifted to the others, additional details emerged: some of them weren't lying in a normal manner, arms were raised above their heads, or flung out to their sides, resting on those next to them. Nothing really alarming, just odd. But there was a smell in the air, like rusted metal, and very strong beneath it the stink of urine and feces . . . just like that damned battlefield. When death took the soldiers their bodies relaxed and . . .

No. He was imagining it. His fever was bringing back one of his really bad memories and casting it upon his friends here.

Then his gaze was finally drawn to Bianca, who lay just a few feet from him. She often played the doomed Queen Gertrude when they did *Hamlet* and always died

quite well in the arms of the young prince. Now she
seemed to have achieved a similar stillness, that same
slight arch of torment to her body. But Bianca always
closed her eyes for that scene. However dramatic an
open-eyed death might be, sooner or later you betrayed
yourself to the audience by blinking.

This time, however, Bianca did not blink. Charles
stared at her a full minute, waiting.

He gave up and looked away, not wanting to understand what was before him. He turned toward Cornelius,
who lay on his stomach, his head pressed against the bare
floor in what must be an uncomfortable position. He
usually played Polonius, but never did he die at the hands
of Hamlet in such a pose. He usually sank slowly down,
managing to instill even that action with a hint of comic
pomposity. He never just gracelessly dropped.

Then Charles saw the blood, saw that it was everywhere, on everyone, on *every single one of them*—and
the dread comprehension he'd refused to accept broke
upon his numbed mind like an avalanche.

Hours later in the too bright light of morning, the
properties truck lurched into the yard and paused next to
the remaining Ford. Clarence Coldfield got out and went
around to help Katherine Hamilton down. They'd left
Elkfoot Flats at dawn to search for the lost members of
the company, and Clarence had spotted tire tracks
coming out from a side road that cut into the woods.
Being the only available clue, they decided to follow it
and it had unexpectedly paid off.

Both walked toward the small cabin, calling out to
announce their arrival, but getting no answer.

Chicago, 1937

Shoe Coldfield improvised another cup of coffee for himself with the cooking pan. I didn't think he really wanted to drink it so much as have something to do with his hands.

"That's pretty much it," he said, sitting again. "That's what we pieced together from what Charles told us and the guesswork on what we knew about Raymond and the investigations the cops did. At first they thought Charles had done it and threw him in jail, but Katherine Hamilton raised holy hell and made the police go to work. That's when they found all the money was gone, then they traced the car to Ottawa. The only member of the company who was missing was Raymond Yorke, and a man fitting his description had sold the car that afternoon after the murders."

"Then he skipped?"

"Christ in heaven, he vanished off the face of the earth. Not easy to do, because everyone was after him. The papers up there called it 'The Cabin Killings' and played on it for weeks, demanding action, but nothing came of it. We had no picture of Raymond to pass around, and when we tried to trace his history nothing came of that, either. His description fit half a dozen con men and thieves from all over. He'd made himself up from head to toe when he joined us and tossed the role away when he left."

"What about Charles?"

He shook his head, looking down at the coffee. "The doctors said it was like shell shock. He was in a bad way.

Crazy and scared out of his mind. Soon as I walked in the door and saw, I shoved Katherine back and made her stand out in the yard. I wasn't raised in what you would call a nice neighborhood; I've seen a lot of bad, but not then or since have I ever seen anything as bad as what was in that cabin. Twelve of my friends, twelve good and harmless people . . . I heard a moaning sound over by the fireplace, and found Charles just sitting there, and the look on his face . . .

"I asked him what had happened, and that set him off. He screamed, just shrieked out at me that he didn't do it, and that's all we could get out of him for a time. Of course he didn't do it, but he felt guilty all the same. I got him out of there and then had to tell Katherine and then had to keep her from going in. She didn't need to see.

"The whole thing was one wicked mess after that, what with the cops accusing him and his condition adding to their suspicions. They thought he'd gone crazy and killed them all. There's probably a few up there who still think he did it. When the smarter ones started looking for Raymond, things eased up, but didn't improve much beyond that."

"What happened to the company?"

"With her sister dead Katherine didn't have the heart for it anymore, so it broke up. The rest of the players moved on. Some of the bodies were shipped off to relatives, others with no families to claim them were buried side by side at Elkfoot Flats. It was the worst thing that had happened up there in anyone's memory. The town church always has a special mass every year for those dead on the day they were killed. People still stop at the cemetery to look at the markers and hear the story. The man who owned the hunting cabin eventually burned it. Said he couldn't stand to go inside for thinking of what happened there, and no one blamed him for it."

"What about Charles?"

"Charles had what you would call a breakdown. Hell, he was only twenty-five, just a kid. He'd been in the war, but this was different. This was like his family was dead, and he felt guilty for being alive. My God, while they were being murdered he was outside half asleep in a damned shithouse."

"But he was sick and drugged. The tea Raymond gave him—"

"Yeah, it had a dose of morphine, too, only it didn't stay in him long enough to have as strong an effect. We all figured that in the heat of the moment Raymond didn't make a body count, and that's how he overlooked Charles. Or maybe he remembered and thought Charles would get some of the blame, which did almost happen."

"What sort of breakdown did he have?"

"The kind where a man's sorry he's alive. He used to say he should have been with them, either to save them or die with them as well. It tore him up in his soul, and he couldn't shake free of it. The authorities finally put him in a sanitarium, and the doctors there shot him full of morphine to keep him quiet. When I found out no one was really helping him I asked Katherine to see about getting him released. I took him home with me to Chicago, tried to find a doctor who could help, but it turned out the best doctor was time. Once the morphine got cleared out of him, he seemed to get better, started sounding like his old self again. He even found an acting company here that he joined for a time. I think it was mostly to prove he could go back to the work, not because he really wanted to. But every so often he'd save up, buy a few bottles of booze, and try to kill himself with it."

"Good God."

"He knew what he was doing. I finally got fed up with it and beat the hell out of him one night. That opened his eyes. Maybe it scared him, maybe he was angry. A couple days later he tells me he's going back to England, and off he went. I never expected to see him again, but a few years later he turned up in the Belt asking after me. By then I had a start looking after my business, and he tells me he's doing insurance investigation work. Said it was something like what his father did. When Charles got enough experience behind him to get his investigator's license he broke away and opened his own agency. Considering what he'd been through, he's not done bad for himself at all. Leastwise until now."

"And if this bender he went on *is* connected to the shooting, you think he found Raymond?"

"I think it's more of a case that Raymond must have found him."

"And Raymond's calling himself Ike LaCelle?"

A third voice, very subdued, cut in to answer. "No. No, he is not."

Startled, we both turned toward the speaker. Charles stood in the hall doorway, looking bad. He still hadn't shaved, though he'd otherwise cleaned up and dressed. His face was fish-belly gray, his eyes haunted pits, and he swayed slightly. He'd sobered up some, but not completely; it hurt to see him like this. Coldfield rose and brought him over to the table. Escott slumped into the chair and groped for the coffee. He choked on it at first, but got half of it in him.

"Can't either of you learn to brew a decent cup?" he complained. "Tastes like ashtray leavings."

"Did you find Raymond?" Coldfield asked.

"I did."

"And he's not LaCelle?"

"No, but he is very good friends with the man. You see, Raymond's name these days is now Archy Grant."

Coldfield stared at him a long time, his mouth open. I did the same. "Oh, sweet Jesus, are you sure?"

Escott laughed, a dry whisper of sound without mirth, without joy. "Yes, my friend. I am very sure. I am as certain of that as I am of death itself."

14

"How can that be?" I asked. "I mean, *how*? He's Archy Grant. He's famous. Everyone knows who he is."

"Who he is, not who he was. His life history, prior to ten years back, is but a sketch, and, I'm sure, entirely fiction."

"What's your proof? I mean, you gotta have something solid to take to the cops before they'll do anything."

More of that whispery laughter. I wanted to hit him to make it stop.

Coldfield stepped in. "Come on, Charles. Tell us what you found out."

Escott gave up laughing and just stared ahead, but without seeing. "The irony of this is that I was not looking for Raymond Yorke at all. I was looking for the man who shot at me. Gil Dalhauser was the most likely suspect, but when I let him see me today he scowled, but wasn't particularly surprised. The man is doubtless an excellent poker player; he did not so much as flick an eyelid. So I dismissed him from my list and sought to test the lesser probability that Ike LaCelle represented."

"Did you tell Gordy any of this?" I asked. "Warn him someone wasn't listening to his orders?"

"I'd planned to call him, but only after I ascertained the identity of the guilty party. I made other calls and learned what I needed to know. Ike LaCelle usually spends his ample free time in the company of Archy Grant, perhaps because it affords the opportunity to meet new celebrities. Grant was having a rehearsal today for his show next week, something LaCelle usually attends, so I went to the studio."

"Bobbi was there, she didn't mention seeing you."

"That is what you may expect when I do not wish to be noticed. I sat in the back and did not draw attention to myself, wanting to have the full effect on LaCelle when I finally confronted him."

"So he could shoot you again?"

"I still wore my vest. It was a reasonable gamble."

"Reasonable?"

Coldfield waved a warning hand at me from where he stood just behind Escott and mouthed the words "Let him talk." I recalled what he'd said about our mutual friend's desire not to live, and suddenly all those times Escott had risked himself made sense. "Go on, Charles," he said. "What did you do?"

"Waited until the end of rehearsal. I watched them working through things, making changes, suggestions, laughing, arguing—it quite took me back to old times. Grant had piqued my curiosity last night. I couldn't help but think I'd met him before, yet his face was unfamiliar to me. But sitting so far in the back of the auditorium, where his face was only a small pink oval, I paid more attention to his body movements and his voice.

"I did not grasp it at first, and then I told myself I certainly must be mistaken. It's been thirteen years since I last saw Raymond, and he'd only been with the company for a month, but some details do stay in the brain, hidden deep and difficult to coax forth, but there all the same. The longer I watched Grant work, the more the past came back to me. I remembered how he carried himself, that cocky I-own-the-world walk, the shape of his head, his laugh, patterns of speech, and accent. All of it.

"By the end of the afternoon, they finished the rehearsal and everyone left. I took myself around to the exit Grant was heading toward and waited for him on the other side. He was alone for the moment, but LaCelle was not far behind. Grant came through the door, saw me, and stopped. Stopped and simply stared at me. He didn't say a word. Neither of us did. But I knew. I knew. And so did he.

"LaCelle came through just then, with a crowd of hangers-on, but I turned and walked away before he could notice me and react. I had what I wanted, the name of the gunman and the reason why he tried to kill me. Then I had to leave before . . . before . . ."

"You went nuts and killed him?" asked Coldfield.

"Yes. Exactly that. I began shaking all over and couldn't seem to stop. Thought I'd pass out in the elevator down to the street. It came right back to me again, the rage. I had to calm myself and try to think."

"So you went out and got drunk."

"I don't remember much of that part. I suppose I must have, for the both of you to make such a fuss, and I don't feel at all well."

"But you did it, Charles. You found that son of a bitch. You got what you most wanted."

"Except for proof, my friend. I've no admissible proof against him." He breathed out one short puff of air to express defeat. "No proof. There's no way to prove he did the shooting last night or that he was ever Raymond Yorke. All I have is inside my head, and you cannot set a personal conviction on an evidence table in a courtroom."

"Fingerprints," I said. "The cops must have taken fingerprints back then. It wouldn't be much to—"

"There are no prints of his on record from the scene. He wore gloves."

"Come on, he must have left some for them to find. Did he wear gloves the whole month he was with the company?"

"Certainly he did on the night of the murders. He also wiped down everything he'd touched in the cabin and the car. Even the cup of tea he gave me had been polished clean. As for other items he may have handled, any prints he might have left were obscured by those of the other company members."

"He was one careful bastard," said Coldfield.

"There's still your testimony," I said. "And a lot of circumstantial evidence to go with it. If you found other members of the troupe, they could probably identify him just as you did."

Escott shook his head and finished the rest of his coffee; from the grimace he made it had gone cold. "Believe me, I've thought this through, and even under the most favorable of legal proceedings, it is not enough to hang him. I did not actually see the crime take place, and was in the partial thrall of morphine at the time. Any attorney he hired would get the case thrown out. Grant's too well protected, by the passage of time and his own fame."

He didn't sound like himself at all. He was still

carrying a load of liquor, though, maybe that was why he was so readily giving up before even starting.

"He's not protected from me," I said. "We get him to confess. I've done that before. Give me ten minutes with him, and he'll be marching straight to the nearest station house to give himself up. Hell, I could have him drive straight to the Elkfoot Flats station if you wanted."

Escott stopped staring at nothing and focused his eyes on me. They were the eyes of a man who's been to hell and back and still has the stench of damnation clinging to his soul. "Oh, my dear friend, this is not your fight."

"It is now, because I've practically invited Ike LaCelle to come over here. If I'd known about *any* of this, I'd have gone to see him first and stopped things."

"It's progressed too far for that."

Between this and what Dalhauser told me, I was ready to agree, but not give up. "Okay, maybe so, but at the moment you're in no shape to deal with him. When he gets here anything could happen, so you two get scarce. Go to the Shoe Box and I'll phone you there when I've got news."

"I think we're about to get a firsthand report right now," said Coldfield. "That was the front door, wasn't it?"

"Stay here and keep quiet." I hurried past him to the hall.

He'd called it right. LaCelle was just stepping inside. With him were Shep and the prizefighter, who were already in, their guns drawn. All three turned to face me.

LaCelle grinned. "Hey, Fleming! Good to see you, I got your message. What's the something I can learn to my advantage?" He'd put on his usual pose of a hearty good mood, but under it all was the sly confidence of a man who knows he has all the best cards in the deck. He wasn't afraid, and he should have been.

"Take me to see Raymond Yorke."

His grin faltered, and he cocked his head inquiringly. "Who?"

"Can the let's-pretend game, Ike. You may hang around the talent, but none of it's rubbed off. We both know what's going on and how it's going to end. Before it does I want to talk to Yorke or Grant or whatever he's calling himself now."

"What a lot you seem to know—or think you do."

"What I know or not doesn't matter, you're going to take me to him."

"Okay, okay. I'm glad you're making this easy on yourself. But that partner of yours who doesn't know how to die is coming, too."

"He's not here."

"Now who's playing pretend? His Nash is sitting right outside."

"That's my neighbor's car. Take me to Grant. After I talk with him he won't be interested in Escott."

LaCelle snorted. "That'll be the day."

Somewhere behind me I heard a thump followed by a grunt and a soft thud. What the hell . . . ?

"What was that?" LaCelle had heard it, too.

"Don't move!" Escott snapped. He stood in the parlor looking out at us, and in his hands was his granddaddy crossbow. He had a bolt loaded in it, and the string was pulled back, ready to shoot.

"Ike?" Shep, uncertain of the change in the situation, aimed his gun at Escott.

"Hold it, both of you," Ike said, also bringing his gun

around. The fighter continued to cover me. "No shoot-ing."

"Yes," Escott agreed. "Let us all behave as gentlemen and no one will get hurt."

"What the hell's that thing?" asked Shep. "Some kinda cockeyed bow and arrow?"

"It's as deadly as any gun," Escott informed him. "And has the added advantage of being nearly silent."

"It's three to one," said LaCelle cautiously. "And we've got more shots."

"True, but my one shot is aimed at you, and I'm an excellent marksman."

"He is," I added. "He practices all the time."

LaCelle thought hard, then eased back slightly. "Okay, what do you want?"

That was all I needed. "I want you to look at me, and I want you to listen to me."

"No, Jack," said Escott, breaking my concentration before I made any kind of progress. "Not that way."

"It'll be easier for us."

"I'm finishing this alone. This is my fight."

"Where's—" I bit it off. Maybe Coldfield was work-ing his way around the outside of the house to take them from the front door. No need to reveal anything about having another player in the game.

Escott said, "Gentlemen, I shall get my coat and we will leave. You will take me to see Archy Grant."

"Charles, they're not going to do any such thing, they'll kill you first."

"I think not. Because of Gordy's protection, isn't that correct, Mr. LaCelle?"

Nonplussed at such cooperation, he gave an uncertain nod. "Yeah, that's right."

"Which is why during the shooting last night you drove the car, but did not actually pull the trigger. You left that for Grant to do, did you not?"

"Sweet, ain't it? Gordy can't hold your getting scragged against me."

I snorted. "I think you're smart enough to know Gordy won't fall for any hairsplitting like that."

"He'll have to. In the scheme of things Archy's a lot more valuable property than either of you. Archy's show's a gold mine to my bosses and damn near legit. They're gonna want to keep him around and working. My job is to keep him happy, and he won't be happy until the both of you are bye-bye."

"But not until he talks to me?" asked Escott.

"Oh, yeah, he wants that, too."

Escott looked like he wanted to talk some himself. He had a lot of years of it saved up. Coldfield might need more time, though, for whatever he had planned. "This little job gives you quite a hold over Archy, doesn't it?" I put in. "Must be nice."

LaCelle seemed genuinely surprised. "What hold? We're friends from way back. He helps me, I help him. Tonight I help him clear up an old mess, so tell your friend to put down the fancy Robin Hood gag and you two come along quiet."

"Okay. You heard the man, Charles. Let's go for a ride."

Escott shook his head. "Not both of us. Only myself. I'm going to ask you to arrange things with this fellow so that you stay here." There was a strange note to his voice that put a chill in my spine. "And I truly mean stay here, Jack. No covert following."

So he didn't want me tagging invisibly along. Like hell

I wouldn't. Not when he looked like that. "Grant wants to see both of us. Isn't that right, LaCelle?"

LaCelle had picked up on the unspoken interplay between Escott and me and was cautious. "That's what he wants, yeah."

"Get your coat, Charles."

"This is *my* fight."

There was something seriously wrong going on inside his head. I could see it and even feel it, and it was important enough for me to break my number-one rule concerning friends. "Charles . . . *listen* to me."

A change came over his face, and he looked sad. "I cannot. It has to be done my way."

Oh, hell, I'd forgotten about all the booze still sloshing around in his blood. Of course he'd be able to resist my influence. "You're not going without me."

"But I *must*." He was blinking a lot, and his voice was thick.

"Charles—"

"I'm sorry," he whispered. He suddenly shifted his aim and pulled the trigger on the crossbow.

No—

Too late.

The bolt slammed into my chest, knocking my last draw of breath right out. I fell against the stair banister and dropped, sprawling. Pure fire blossomed through me. My helpless body twitched and spasmed, heels cracking against the floor, arms thrashing from the agony. I heard a terrible strangling, hissing sound and realized I was the one making it.

LaCelle yelped some exclamation of surprise, and I was distantly aware of his hasty backing away.

Bloodsmell. Mine.

I clawed at the thing jutting from my ribs, but couldn't get my fingers to grasp it, pull it free. The blinding pain slowed me, finally paralyzed me. The convulsions abruptly ceased; my hands slipped down at my sides, and I lay staring at the ceiling, corpse still, but fully conscious.

Burning.

Please God, make it stop!

Burning inside.

"Ike?" Shep's voice. Scared. "What do we do, Ike?"

"Gimme a minute." LaCelle. Badly shaken.

"Did you *see* what he did to him? He's crazy!"

"I know, I know! Just shuddup an' lemme think!"

They shut up.

Screaming.

Charles, help me!

Screaming in my head.

No one to hear.

But he knows. He must *know!*

Escott said, "I'm putting this down now and going to get my coat." Very calm.

No one moved as he followed through. On the edge of my blurring vision I saw him shrug on his heavy topcoat. He paused by the hall table for a minute.

"What're you doing?" LaCelle demanded.

"Just writing a little note for anyone who finds him."

"You lemme see it."

"Of course."

Paper rustled as LaCelle grabbed it from him. " 'Please remove bolt as quickly as possible—C.E.' What is this? Some kinda sick joke?"

"He's crazy, Ike. Get away from him." Shep. Nervous.

"My good man, I am not crazy, merely drunk. May I

have my note back? Thank you." Escott knelt by me, his gray, hollow face coming into my line of view, and pushed the paper partway into my shirt between the buttons. "I don't expect you to ever forgive me, but after tonight that won't matter. Talk to Shoe. He'll help you understand why." He brushed his fingers over my eyelids to close them, then stood. "Might I ask where we'll be going?"

LaCelle gave a brief, sickly laugh. "Someplace cold, dark, and quiet."

"Sounds like a grave."

"Yeah, it does. Come on."

They all trooped out, leaving me where I had fallen. My body was inert, but my senses and mind were all too aware. Unable to act or react, but aware and furious. The only thing hotter than my anger at Escott was the searing bolt lodged between my ribs.

He was going off to die, and he knew it.

He was going off to kill.

Himself and one other—if he had the chance.

For when he came into my view he'd been tucking his pen away. It was that damned fat-bodied pen with the hidden hypodermic needle, and God knows what he had in the thing.

No way to tell the time.

Pain distorts it, slows it down, turns a minute into an hour.

I couldn't tell how many seeming hours oozed by before I heard a faint groan from the dining room. Other less identifiable noises followed, then a couple of unsteady footsteps.

I knew when Coldfield reached the hall by his sharp intake of breath.

"Sweet Jesus, kid, what did you *do*?" he choked out.

You've got no business blaming me. This is Escott's fault.

He came closer, cursing softly, and I felt him lift the paper free of my shirt. "What the hell? Is he crazy?"

Yes, very. Now just do what he said to do.

"Aw, shit. God in heaven, this ain't fair."

Damn right. I didn't deserve this.

"Not . . . fair."

Hurry, Goddammit!

The fire around the bolt, which in a strange way I'd nearly gotten used to, flared white-hot—hotter—all over again. I couldn't cry out, not until he pulled the thing free, and he wasn't doing a very good job of it. I thought his hands were shaking. He kept muttering unhappily to himself.

Then he snarled, and I felt something unholy tearing my chest apart, and suddenly the damned thing was out.

The aftershock flattened me like a lead brick. I could move but didn't want to; the one thing I could do— couldn't help but do—was vanish.

Surprised, Coldfield cursed loud and at length. He hated, really hated being surprised. This one couldn't be helped. The damage was too much for me to hold out against; my body did what was best for it and took itself away to an instant release from the pain.

I floated in the comforting bliss of nonfeeling for a while, trying to ignore Coldfield's increasingly noisy demands that I come back. He sounded angry at first, then apprehensive, not knowing what exactly had become of me. Far too soon for my recovery of spirit, I made myself fade back to solidity again, but took my time.

Coldfield watched, wide of eye, as I gradually reappeared, sitting weary to the bone on the stairs. It felt like a few dozen elephants had been jumping on me, and I hunched forward, hugging myself.

"You doing that slow for dramatic effect?" he asked after a minute.

I laughed once, and was amazed that it didn't hurt. "Just being careful. I wanted to make sure everything was working."

"You all right?"

"I think so." I ventured to straighten and checked myself over. There was a lot of blood on my clothes, but it could have been much, much worse. The one time I'd been truly staked by someone determined to kill, I'd lost too much blood to simply vanish and heal. Tonight had been different, though, because Escott had missed hitting my heart. On purpose. He'd wanted to stop me, but not permanently.

I unbuttoned my shirt. Coldfield stared at the spot where he'd pulled the bolt out. My skin was stained, but the hole was all sealed up like new. He next stared at the bolt itself where he'd dropped it on the floor. Spatters of blood radiated out from it.

"What happened to you?" I asked. We both needed our minds to be elsewhere.

"Charles clocked me when he got that crossbow down from the wall." He shrugged himself away from wherever he'd gone and gingerly touched the back of his head behind one ear. "Not too bad. I've had tougher knocks sparring with the boys. But you—how did—"

"He's on a real bender." I peeled my ruined and bloody

shirt off and told him what happened. I expected him to
not want to believe Escott's shooting of me, but he
accepted it quite readily. After all, Escott had cracked his
skull without a second's thought. "He's off and running
on the edge again, only this time he'd going to go right
over."

Coldfield watched as I strode purposefully upstairs,
stumbling only once. "You got a plan?"

"No, just a clue and not much of one," I called back
while snagging a fresh shirt from my room. A black one.
I pulled it on as I hurried down again. His coat and hat
were hanging from the hall tree. I tossed them at him and
continued buttoning. "It's something LaCelle said. I
think I know where they're taking Charles."

"You *think*? And if you're wrong?"

"We both know the answer to that."

Coldfield was still pretty shaken, so I did the driving
while he slumped in the passenger seat and tried not to
look sick.

"How hard did he hit you?" I asked.

"Enough so he's going to regret it when I get in
swinging distance of him again."

"Seriously, you got any double vision, ringing ears,
stuff like that?"

"It just hurts. Doc Clarson can check me over later.
You just step on it."

I stepped on it, going along the route Shep had driven
me earlier. It seemed to take longer this time, or more
likely impatience and fear were distorting my perception.
I cut through lights and doubled my speed when I could,
knowing I could take care of any traffic cop who stopped

me. None did, though, and we were soon sailing next to the wire fence of the truck yard.

"This is Dalhauser's place. Why here?"

"Something he said to me that LaCelle pretty much repeated. It's isolated and Dalhauser's off in Cicero making an alibi for himself. Seemed like a good place for them to bring Charles so no one would interrupt."

"It doesn't take long to kill a man."

"I know." I hit the gas for one last spurt and rounded the corner to the road that ran past the little gatehouse. I pulled into the entry. The gate was shut. The watchman was there, and he was alert. He came out, on guard for trouble, but unprepared for a smile and a fixed gaze from me. Seconds later and he was opening the gate for us. He'd readily told me that two cars had gone in not long ago, but he hadn't checked inside them. Sometimes it's best not to notice certain faces. I told him his shift was over and that he should go home. He thanked me and left, whistling as he drove off in a battered Ford. He wouldn't remember anything of the last few minutes for a long time to come.

"Cripes, I need you to be working for me," said Coldfield. "I'd have a lot bigger territory and run it more smoothly if I could talk people into things the way you do."

"You don't want the headache." I shifted gears, fed it some gas to get speed, then let the big car coast quietly forward.

"Seems to me it'd be worth it."

The door to the cavernous garage was shut, and I recalled Shep leaving it open. Above and to the left of it were the wide windows Dalhauser had used to survey the yard, and I discerned the form of a man standing in almost the same place.

"We've been made," I said. "There's someone up top who must have seen the gate guard pass us in. Maybe we can make them think we've got business here, too. Keep them busy while I go in."

"I'll ask for Dalhauser."

"Great, but if they give you trouble, take off."

"Okay."

He gave in to that a little too readily, but I didn't have time to argue. I braked in front of the door, rolled down the car window, hit the horn a few times, then vanished. Unsused to it, Coldfield said "shit" in reaction. I flowed out and over, and went right up the side of the building.

It was made of sheet metal, which is damned dense for getting through. I wasn't even sure I could get through it. In the past there'd always been a convenient crack or an open seam. Now I just kept going until I felt a subtle change in the surface that marked where the windows began. I didn't like going through glass, but could if I had to.

Just when it seemed like it was about to break, it didn't, and I was inside. I cast around, trying to locate the man I'd seen, but he wasn't on the upper landing anymore. That, or I'd miscalculated and drifted the wrong way. Very slowly I took on form, balancing it just right so I had enough of me solid to the point where I could see, but hopefully not be seen. It made me semitransparent, and the result was alarmingly like a Hollywood movie ghost.

I got alarmed myself when I realized I'd risen too high, and was some ten feet above the landing.

I really hate heights.

Easing down to the floor diffused my near panic, then I unexpectedly went solid. There was a fluttering behind my eyes, and a fog of weakness wrapped around me. It was the blood loss, and there'd been no time to stop at the Stockyards and replenish. It was bad, not fatal, but I didn't like the uncertainty. What if I had to go invisible and suddenly reappeared at an inconvenient moment? What if I couldn't reappear at all?

The man at the window was neither Shep nor the prizefighter. I'd hoped that LaCelle would hold down the numbers of his goons, but apparently he trusted them to keep their mouths shut. This mug's mouth was definitely shut when I got through with him. His eyes, too. I dragged him over to a patch of shadow by the outer wall and rolled him face in so he wouldn't be noticed right away, and relieved him of his gun.

The service lights were out, so there was a whole lot of darkness above and below, and though I could see fairly well, I didn't like it. It might mean that they'd already killed Escott and no longer needed illumination to work by.

I held still and listened. Outside, Coldfield was arguing with two men, trying to convince them that he had a meeting with Dalhauser. They didn't sound like they were buying his story, but he stubbornly held to it.

Moving farther inside, I tried to pick up any other voices. Nothing. Not up here, anyway. I tiptoed along the walkway to the other side of the building and used the second set of stairs there, reasoning that everyone's attention would be focused toward the front.

I had better luck on the ground level and saw two men standing by the entrance, watching the others with Coldfield. They looked like Shep and his boxer friend.

Parked near them were two cars, which gave me an idea of the odds. There could be from eight to ten men here, including LaCelle, Grant, and Escott. Four were occupied, one was unconscious, leaving maybe one or two others lurking about.

A line of what looked like offices ran along the right-hand wall beneath the walkway. Lights showed under the closed doors of one. A man paced up and down before it, out of boredom rather than any sense of making rounds, I thought.

If I took him out, it would be noticed by the two up front, but I was reluctant to spend the energy going invisible and staying that way, which I'd have to do once in the room. I thought of a compromise, though. Vanishing, I hurried forward and slipped under the door next to my target. When I came back to solidity the weakness hit me again, but much worse and I nearly made noise stumbling against a table. I was using myself up. Damn Escott for complicating things.

The dim room I stood in was an office with the usual stuff in it. I pressed an ear to the wall it shared with the lighted room.

The first voice I picked out was Ike LaCelle's. "Yeah, it's nothing. Some guy came here by mistake. They'll get rid of him."

"You sure about that?" Archy Grant.

"It's fine. Now you gonna finish this or stay here all night?"

"Oh, I'm finishing it, but he's gotta tell me a few things first. Isn't that right, Charlie-boy?"

"Then you're gonna be here all night," said LaCelle. "I know that kind of look, and you ain't getting squat from him without a fight."

"I don't have to fight, not while I've got bolt cutters handy. You see these, Charlie-boy? They're great for snipping off fingers, noses, and even itty-bitty toeses. Maybe I should start with that honker of yours. What do you think?"

"I'd rather you didn't," said Escott, sounding tired and more sober than before.

"Of course, and I'd rather I didn't, either. It'd make such a mess, and I just paid for this suit, you know."

"How much did that face cost you?"

"What?"

"The plastic surgery. When you lean close I can just see the scars. It is an excellent job, they're barely noticeable."

Grant chuckled. "Yeah, the doc did do a good job. Made me even more handsome."

"But you could not change or hide your walk, the set of your shoulders, the shape of your head. Your *voice*."

"It still threw you for a while, though. God, what a laugh you gave me sitting with the rest at that party, staring and staring and not being able to figure it out."

"Obviously it was not a very long laugh. I'll wager I also made you sweat, else you'd not have tried to kill me in such a hasty and ill-planned manner last night."

"It woulda worked. I thought it had worked, but, jeez, how many guys are crazy enough to wear a bulletproof vest to a goddamned *party*? You take the cake, Charlie. But never mind that, right now I want to go down memory lane with you. What's the old gang doing these days? I want to know what happened to them."

"I'm sure you do. You're becoming quite famous, aren't you? The last thing you need is to have another someone like me turning up and identifying you as Raymond Yorke."

"That's it in a nutshell. I want to know where the rest of them are, the bunch that was in the truck. You know, don't you? You'd make it your business to keep track of them. How about we start with Katherine Hamilton? Where's she keeping herself?"

"She went back to London and succumbed to influenza a year after you murdered her sister."

Grant was silent a moment. Thinking, maybe. "You know, I didn't really mean to kill Bianca, so it's not really murder. She just hit her head too hard. It was an accident."

"And the others? Were the other eleven also accidents?"

"It's funny, but I don't remember much of any of it. That was a lifetime ago. I'm a completely different man now."

"You remember all right. Not as I do, but you remember it all the same. Every second of it."

"I was just a kid." Grant's tone was light, dismissive.

"And you simply made a mistake?"

"The only mistake I made was making too much noise. If I'd been quieter I wouldn't have woke up Queen Bianca. She's the one who started it all with her fussing. The one thing I did right was not getting caught. What's so funny?"

Escott made that dry whispery sound. "Your boundless honesty."

"I'm telling you, Archy, he's off his rocker," said Ike, who seemed to be on the far side of the room. "You weren't there to see, but he shot down his partner just like that." The sound of a finger snap. "Didn't even blink.

Dead as a doornail. I've asked him why, and he says it was to keep his friend from trying to save him. He's crazy."

Archy made no reply. I could imagine him giving Escott a good long look.

Escott said, "And what is your interest in this butcher, Mr. LaCelle? You two met some ten years past, did you not?"

"More like twelve. I helped him get the new face."

"And he began doing comedy work in the vaudeville houses? Became successful at it? He turned out to be a good investment for your time and efforts on his behalf, and you benefited him with connections to people who could advance his career. Quite a fortunate symbiosis for you both. How many others have had to die along the way?"

"Hey, I don't have to talk to a crazy man if I don't want to, and I don't want to. Archy, if you're going to do something, do it."

"Yeah, yeah. Okay, Charlie, what about Klopner? You remember him? Where's he?"

"He died three years ago of a bad liver."

"And Eric Lynd?"

"He was in a motoring accident in Buffalo and died with three others."

"Coldfield, is he dead, too?"

"No, but you'll never be able to get to him. He's like you, too well protected. On the other hand, he doesn't know who you are and likely never will. He never listens to comedy shows."

Escott was smart to admit to Coldfield still being around because LaCelle probably knew enough to catch out a lie.

"So everyone in the company is either dead or un-reachable, huh?" Archy sounded doubtful.

"Yes, that's it exactly."

A sharp cracking sound. A slap. "How many teeth you want to lose before you die?"

"That's the problem for you. You don't yet realize it."

"What?"

"I'm already dead, Raymond. I died a long time ago with them. I *should* have died with them. Part of me did."

"He's crazy, I'm tellin' you," said LaCelle.

Another slap. "Do the dead feel pain, Charlie? I can put you through an awful lot of it."

"You already have. There's really nothing more you *can* do to me."

A series of slaps, then the unmistakable sound of fist against body, and Escott's rasping breath. He didn't have to put himself through this. He must have thought out a way around it. Then I realized this was his way of punishing himself for surviving the murders.

"You're going to tell me where the others are, and no crapping around about their being dead," said Grant. "I don't have to kill you tonight. I can keep you alive for as long as it takes."

There it was, that dry laugh again. The laugh of the damned. "Yes, I suppose you will."

More fist work. I started to vanish, to go help him. It didn't happen. Dizziness swept over and through me. I fell against the table, making noise, but no one in the other room seemed to notice.

Grant's voice was thick with anger. "You want I should start with the bolt cutters next or how about some pliers for your teeth?"

"That won't be necessary," Escott murmured. I could

barely hear him. "If . . . if you will allow me some paper, I'll write . . . write out what you need to know."

"Now suddenly you're cooperative?"

"Disappointed?"

"Write any lies and Ike will find out."

"Keeping me alive until you confirm my information? Wise of you. Very well, now some . . . some paper, if you please. Thank you, but I've my own pen."

He's going to do it, I thought. *The son of a bitch is going to do it.*

Then the door to my dark office opened, and the lights flicked on. Someone else had heard me. The pacing man, his gun ready. For all that, he was still hellishly surprised. Even more so when he discovered how fast I could move. Maybe I couldn't vanish, but I still had a store of speed and strength left. It made more noise, though, disturbing the others.

"Ike! Go tell those bozos to hold it down," Grant snapped.

Even as the thug hit the floor I hit the light switch. No time to shut the door. LaCelle was already out and looking around. I softly backstepped into the sheltering darkness and waited for him.

He went right instead of left, though, having spotted the knot of his men still gathered around Coldfield.

"What is this?" he wanted to know. "What's going on?"

Damn. Coldfield was outnumbered five to one. Escott had the best chance with just the one man to face, but was handicapped by his beating and the leftover booze. But Grant wanted him alive to give information. Coldfield won my mental coin toss.

No time or ability to be subtle about it. I took another

gun off the thug I'd aced and slipped out the door, hiding my approach in the shadows of the huge trucks. LaCelle was just in the process of figuring out who the unexpected visitor was when I slammed the butt of the gun against the side of his head. He dropped fast and made noise as he did, drawing the prizefighter and Shep inside for a look. The fighter didn't know what hit him, but Shep came in ready for trouble and fired at me.

The shot cracked too close to my ear, and I dodged fast, hurling around to put the massive body of a truck between us. The last thing I wanted was another wound taking away what little blood I had left. I crouched and waited for him, deciding not to shoot back. It would have given him a muzzle flash to aim for in the dark. Besides, he was using up bullets.

Some kind of activity was happening outside with Coldfield, and I thought I heard Grant impatiently calling out again from the office. He wanted to know what was going on. Hell was breaking loose all over the place.

Shep fired in my general direction again while on the run. He took cover behind a ten foot tall stack of oversized tires, which would have worked for him except for my night vision. He probably couldn't see anything of me except my pale face, and I was keeping my head down. After a few moments he yelled a question to his friends outside, but they must have been too busy to answer. His next question was aimed at anyone else in the garage, demanding they reply and help him, but I'd already taken care that those soldiers wouldn't be awake for some while.

Just him and me and a stack of tires.

I quit my shelter behind the truck and cat footed toward him from an angle, pocketing the gun. It was just as well I'd put on the black shirt; the tires were damned dirty as I pushed hard against them.

Shep must have figured what was coming and tore from his cover like a flushed rabbit just a thin second before the avalanche would have buried him. He was fast, but I didn't let him make it to the door. He ended up on the greasy cement next to LaCelle and the fighter, but in no condition to complain about any of it.

Coldfield came in just as I was going out, and we almost didn't stop in time. He swung his gun away at the last instant and wilted with relief even as I pulled my fist in.

"Where's Charles?" he asked, a little out of breath. His coat was on crooked and his shirt torn open.

"In one of the offices with Grant. Stay low. I don't know if I got them all."

"There's two by the car you don't have to worry about," he said, following me.

I looked all over, but didn't see any other men wanting to risk open battle. We paused on each side of the closed office door, and I listened hard. The light was still on, but nothing stirred within. Maybe Grant was listening hard himself, wondering what was going on.

With Coldfield covering me, I kicked the door in. It flew back and banged off the wall, but by then I was inside.

The layout was the same as the room where I'd hidden, with the same kind of furnishings and not much space between them. No one was there. On a desk lay a blank sheet of paper and some bolt cutters. No trick pen. I didn't know if that was good or bad.

"Grant must have taken him," I said.

Coldfield cursed, then left, with me close on his heels.

He ran toward the front, heading for the cars. I turned and went deeper into the murk of the garage.

This far in and things were dim even for my eyes, so I listened again and almost immediately picked up the sound of footsteps above me. They were on the catwalk. The other stairway was closest. I tore across to it.

The upper landing on this side was clear; all the action was at the far end. Against the bank of windows I saw the silhouttes of two struggling men. I recognized Escott's lean figure, Archy Grant's sturdy form. Grant looked to be winning. As I hurried toward them, Grant wrestled Escott around and got a choke hold on him from behind, trying to lift him off his feet. Escott's swollen face was going red as he clawed frantically at Grant's unmoving arm.

"Grant!"

He paused, startled by the interruption, snapping his head toward me. I didn't know him. The ever-confident, wisecracking entertainer was gone. What was left behind still possessed a ready smile, though, and the exhilarated madness of it was enough to stop me cold.

"I'll break his neck," he said cheerfully, and to illustrate, he hauled back a step, dragging the weakened Escott along.

I put my hands out, palms skyward. "Don't."

"Hey, it's you. Well, how do you like that? And here Ike said you were dead. It's not like him to get things so wrong."

Easing closer, I prayed there was enough light coming in the windows for me to be able to work on his mind. I didn't think there was, and with him gone crazy to boot . . . "Let him go, Archy."

"Nah, I don't think so. How 'bout you get outta my way and I just leave? I'll let him go later."

Not alive, I thought.

Grant kept smiling. "You don't think I will? Hey—I'm Archy Grant. Anyone'll tell you. There was no trusting old Raymond, but *my* word's good."

If I could only vanish, get next to him. I tried. Nothing happened for me.

Escott made a wheezing noise, straining to breathe. His face was puffed and bloodied from his beating, and for a bad second I couldn't tell if he recognized me or not. Grant increased the pressure. "Take it easy, Charlie-boy. We'll have our little talk soon enough."

Escott's knees gave out; he stopped pulling at Grant's arm.

"That's better. Act nice and I give you some air."

"Grant—" I began.

"No, I'm not talking with you, I'm telling you—*back off!*"

I could rush him, but what kind of damage could he do to Escott in the second it would take for me to cross the few yards between us? Then I saw Escott's hand flapping feebly against one of his pockets. His bulging eyes were staring at me, pleading, but not for help. He wanted time. He wanted Grant distracted.

"You hear me, punk?" Grant hadn't noticed anything yet.

"I hear you," I said. I went back a pace to show him I was also listening to what I heard.

"Who's the other guy with you?"

"He's nobody. I'll get rid of him."

"No, you call him up here. I want both of you where I can see."

"Okay, just don't—"

His thick arm came up half an inch, tightening. "Don't what?"

"If you kill Charles you'll have nothing to stop me from coming for you. Think about it."

His smile faltered, then he nodded, all good natured. "Yeah, that makes a lot of sense, but you still do what I say or I give your buddy a lot more misery. Call the other guy. Make it fast, Charlie-boy should be getting pretty blue by now."

I yelled at Coldfield, but didn't use his name, just calling out to him where we were. He yelled back that he was coming up.

"He got a gun?" asked Grant. "I heard shooting. I bet he's got a gun. He leaves it down there."

Coldfield was almost to the stairs. "Jack? What the hell's—"

"No guns," I said quickly. "He's got Charles. He'll kill him if you . . ."

Coldfield got the idea and told me he was putting his gun down. I didn't know whether that was true, and Grant didn't look to be buying it, either.

Escott had reached his pocket. He got the pen out. Nearly fumbled it.

I tried not to stare and instructed Coldfield to come up slowly with his hands high. He grumbled and growled, but did just that. He reached the landing and stood next to me, glaring at Grant.

Grant's eyes went wide. "Well, trot out the band and let's have a parade, if it ain't old home week! I was just thinking about you, Coldfield. Good to see you again. Still got that shoeshine box?"

Coldfield went still. I couldn't tell if it was from the question or if he'd spotted what was happening.

Escott's long fingers had unscrewed the cap of the pen. It dropped away, making a small noise on the rough cement floor.

"Yeah, Raymond, I still got that old box," said Coldfield. "You need a shine?"

Grant laughed once. "I bet you'd love to hear me say yes. You did the work, but you didn't much like it, did you?"

"Not much. Got a different line, now."

Escott looked to be gaining ground. Maybe he was getting more air, but he didn't seem to be able to find the trick catch for the needle. He couldn't see what he was doing.

"Got my own place, a nice little club," Coldfield continued. "Remember me talking about that? You should come over sometime. We got some great music there."

"Do I look like a sucker? We all know how this has to end. I want the two of you to start backing up. You don't come near me or Charlie does his act with the angels from now on. Go on."

Hands out, we reluctantly retreated. Exactly one step.

It didn't sit well with Grant. "I know you both want to kill me, but it's not in the cards. You try and Charlie goes first. If I lose, he loses, too. You got that? You got any of tha—"

Escott jabbed downward with the pen. There wasn't much force behind it, but it was enough to stab the needle into Grant's leg. Grant snarled and jerked against the sudden pain. Before I could get to them, Escott twisted partially free and buried his elbow into Grant's side. He set himself, then violently pushed them both backward toward the windows.

One of the big lower panes shattered as Grant staggered against it. I was there in an instant, reaching for Escott. Grasping his coat, I hauled him out of the way. He fought me.

"Let him!" Coldfield shouted.

I let go, dimly understanding. Escott wrested clear of me. He swayed, coughing, but was able to stand alone.

Grant managed to recover his balance and kept himself from going through the window. He braced a moment against the bent frame, staring wildly at us to see what we'd do. No one moved. He looked down and saw the body of the pen sticking incongruously out from his thigh at a right angle. He swatted the thing away, and cursed at the new pain it caused him.

Panting, Escott raised a shaking hand at Grant. "I think . . . I think things are more even, now."

"What'd you do to me, Charlie?" he demanded. "What was in that—"

"It won't take long. But it will be . . . extremely unpleasant while it lasts."

"Charles," I said evenly. "What was in the needle?"

He gave a thick laugh that turned into another cough. "Just a little strychnine."

"Oh, my God," Coldfield whispered.

Grant shook his head. "No, it's not. You can't get stuff like that. They control poisons, so it can't be—"

Escott wore an awful smile. "There are small amounts to be found in certain kinds of rat poisons. You can extract a good concentrated dose of it if you know how. And I do."

"No, you're lying—"

"We'll see. It should start very soon. The convulsions are the worst. You'll break your own bones from the thrashing about. You won't be able to talk, but you *will* be aware. Every terrible moment of it, you'll feel . . ."

That was too much for Grant. He lunged at Escott, who ducked his head and met him halfway, ramming his shoulder into the other man's body. There was a solid thump and both grunted from the effort and impact.

I started to step in, but Coldfield yanked me back. "It's his fight. Let him."

Escott got in one sharp jab, a good one. He may have been handicapped before, but now he was operating on pure rage. Years of it. He cut loose with another few deep punches before Grant tried to get away. As he turned, Escott caught him around the shoulders and, whether by accident or design, steered him toward the window. Grant bucked against this. Escott let him, but hung on, using Grant's force to carry them around. They swung in a full circle, ending up with Grant crashing into another sheet of glass, breaking it. Grant yelled something, fighting wildly to push himself back. Escott snaked his arms under Grant's elbows, locking hands behind his neck to hold him in place with a full-nelson. Grant tried to slide sidways out of it. He had the muscle, but Escott had the height and used it for leverage.

He smashed Grant's forehead hard onto the metal frame. The stocky man abruptly slowed, obviously stunned by the blow. Escott gave him no time to recover. He released his grip and got his hands behind Grant's shoulders, shoving him down. Hard. Against the shards of glass still sticking up from the frame.

Grant's unprotected throat caught it all. The more he fought, the more pressure Escott applied to hold him in place. Bloodsmell blossomed in the cold air. Grant shrieked and gagged, damaging himself further with his struggles. Escott put all his weight into holding him down. It went on for one minute, two, as Grant's fight slowly drained out of him. His kicks and flailings got weaker, less controlled, then subsided to reflex twitching, then to no movement at all. A few moments after that, Escott seemed to fold in on himself and sagged away, slipping heavily to his knees.

"Charles?"

He wouldn't turn to meet my eye, just wearily shook his head. Maybe he expected me still to be mad at him for the crossbow bolt. I just might be, but it would keep until later.

"Holy shit," said Coldfield, going over to kneel by him. "We gotta get you out of here, so come on. Can you stand?"

Escott made no reply, but allowed himself to be helped to his feet. He was a real mess. Grant had fought hard to keep his life, but Escott had had thirteen years of rage stored away, waiting for release. It was all used up. He tottered now, frail as an old man even with Coldfield's help.

From the floor I retrieved the fat-bodied pen. The hypodermic was wickedly visible. I found the protective cap and carefully returned the thing to a relatively harmless state again.

"You really got poison in this?" I asked Escott.

He blinked at me a few times, he might have been in shock. "What?"

"Is there strychnine in this like you said?"

He shook his head, his puffed mouth spasming once. "Just . . . just some saline solution."

"It's only a bluff?"

"Under the right. Circumstances . . . the power of suggestion . . ." He looked at Grant's body. "Too easy."

"Easy?"

"Too. Fast a death."

After a moment Coldfield said, "You got that right. I could wish you'd left some for me, though."

Escott's unexpected laughter was dust dry with hardly any breath behind it. I'd never heard anything like it before and never wanted to again. It was the laugh of a damned soul. But this one had managed to crawl out of the pit for another chance.

15

JUST getting Escott out to the car wasn't the end of it. We had a body, a famous one at that, on our hands, and though it would have been easy enough to sink what was left of Archy Grant/Raymond Yorke into the lake, it wouldn't have been too smart. His disappearance would have raised too many questions and left an open case on the books. I wasn't so sure what we arranged was particularly smart, either, but it would have to do.

As soon as we left Escott dozing in the Nash's backseat, Coldfield and I dealt with the wounded. We found a breakroom and dragged them all inside so I could go to work. Reviving one man at a time with a splash of cold water, I'd put him under again and made sure that whatever he remembered about the last couple hours did not include me, Coldfield, or Escott. I was tired, and the work made my head ring, but it was either this or the cops on our doorsteps.

There was a problem with Ike LaCelle, though. I hadn't been as careful as I should have been when I'd hit him. The side of his skull was black with blood, and was spongy. No amount of cold water would ever wake him up again.

Coldfield scowled at the body and spared a hard look at me.

"You okay?"

"No."

But I'd feel bad about it later. I got an idea, and he helped me lug LaCelle upstairs next to Grant. We found a box of grease rags and used them to wipe down everything we might have touched in the joint, and I cleaned my prints from the gun I'd used for the clubbing. I put it in Grant's lax hand, while Coldfield tried to place LaCelle's hands around Grant's neck.

"No one's going to believe this," he said. "If someone was strangling me I'd shoot, not hit him with the gun."

"It's a semiauto," I said. "Grant just forgot to flick the safety." I reached across and made sure the safety was indeed on. "He's a radio star, what does he know about guns?"

"The evidence is all wrong and they'll know it. The cops won't buy this for a minute."

"They don't have to, so long as they never find out about us being here."

"But those other mugs . . . what you did won't last, will it?"

"It'll last a few weeks. Long enough. By the time they recall anything useful, they'll know to keep shut about it or else get dragged in by the law." I'd put that suggestion in their heads as well, along with the idea that they should just leave the country altogether. They were all still in the breakroom, having a nap at the lunch table. I did not envy their waking when it did come, knowing what they would find on the upper landing.

It was bad. The blood from Archy's torn throat made a spectacular flow down the building's metal side to soak into the bare earth below. The scent of it was a constant torment to me. My corner teeth were out, and I had to fight a near-constant fluttering behind my eyes. I was weak and in need. If I'd been there alone, I might not have been able to fight off the urge to feed from the unconscious men. I didn't care to use people in the same way I used cattle, but had done so before when forced by necessity. Things weren't that dire for me yet, but the likelihood of my losing control increased the longer I delayed going to the Stockyards.

Coldfield's presence helped me to keep focused, but I knew I wouldn't be able to hold out for too much longer. I told him to hurry, but didn't say why.

We were careful and thorough, though, knowing we could never risk coming back to fix some forgotten detail.

The last thing Coldfield did before we left was to spit on Grant's body.

"Too fast," he muttered, turning away.

The story hit the city and then the rest of the country the next morning like lightning, or so Coldfield told me that evening when I got up. Every paper had a different account about the shocking deaths, which I took to mean either the cops couldn't make up their minds or the editors were improvising to fill space under the screaming headlines. Probably both.

I'd called Gordy the night before to warn him of what was about to happen. He didn't have a lot to say, only that it'd be tough on Adelle, and he'd take care of things. He never asked the why of it, either. It said something for the measure of trust he had in me; that, or he'd already had some inkling of what was going on. I wouldn't put it past him. He kept close tabs on nearly everything in his corner of the world.

He had some pull with the city and a lot with the thugs—who'd taken one look at the artistic tableau on the landing and run like hell. He said we wouldn't see any trouble if he could help it, but to keep our heads low anyway. LaCelle had been well-liked in certain quarters.

As the days passed with no progress for the cops, local citizen groups began demanding action from their politicians. If a famous and popular man like Archy Grant could be killed by the mob (it was widely assumed he was defending himself from LaCelle), then no one was safe, so ran their logic. The fact that most of those politicians were virtually owned by the mob didn't come into it.

Grant had many admirers, allowing him a magnificent funeral. Bobbi attended to help Gordy with the stunned and grieving Adelle. Their pictures got in the papers, but that was only to be expected. They were all questioned by the cops and the press, but were unable to shed light on the mystery.

Lots of people thought it sad Grant had no family to mourn him. Somebody suggested starting a charity in his name using what money he'd left, but there wasn't all that much of it. He'd bought a lot of women diamond bracelets, after all. LaCelle was buried someplace back East with a lot less fanfare and fewer photographers.

Through Gordy, I heard bits and pieces of what was really going on. Gil Dalhauser, ever neutral, was keeping quiet. The cops knew it all for a setup and didn't believe in it for a minute, but quiet pressure from above eventually got them to close the case. They gave a special release to the press stating they were satisfied that for reasons unknown LaCelle and Grant had had a falling-out and killed each other. They repeated the lie loudly and long enough until everyone got tired of hearing it, and the nine-day wonder got replaced by other crimes and disasters.

Not one word surfaced connecting Grant or LaCelle to the Cabin Killings. They'd been carefully silent about that to shield themselves, and it served now to shield Escott and Coldfield. And me.

Escott decided to stay home from his office until his face healed up. Coldfield spent time with him during the day, and I hung around at night to keep an eye on him. For a guy who'd killed an old enemy with his bare hands he was acting pretty normal, which worried me. I had Coldfield and Gordy and Bobbi to talk to if I wanted, but Escott just went on like nothing had happened, never mentioning it.

He did apologize for shooting me, though. I told him he was a son of a bitch and never to do it again. He took that to mean he was forgiven.

Two days after, he got a frantic call from Mary Sommerfeld. Jason McCallen had broken his promise to stay away and was driving past her house again. Escott told her to call the cops, but she said she didn't dare because of the adverse publicity it might generate. She pleaded with him to come help her.

Escott still looked like a car wreck, so I told him I'd handle it. The woman was genuinely scared, and I wanted to be out of the house for a while. Bobbi was working until late on the club show; there was plenty of time for me to deal with one crazed playwright.

I didn't think McCallen would do anything stupid, but I changed my mind fast when I pulled into the street and saw his Ford parked before the Swiss chalet house. Bailing fast out of my Buick, I hurried up to the front door and found it had been broken open. She'd changed the locks, but one good kick had turned them into so much junk and splintered the frame.

Beyond the threshold all was dark. I slipped in quietly with my heart in my mouth and listened.

Then I heard a crash from the back and Mary's muffled scream, followed by the deep, aggressive rumble of McCallen's voice.

I'll kill the bastard.

Another crash, much louder than the last, and Mary cried out. I rushed toward the back, toward her bedroom. The lights were out there as well, but I had no problem seeing every detail.

There was a broken lamp on the floor, and a table had been toppled over. The real damage was the bed, which had collapsed under their combined weight and exertions.

Mary screamed again, quite caught up in the moment as she beat and clawed McCallen's broad back amid a tangle of sheets and discarded clothing.

"Yes! Yes! You big hairy Scotsman! Oh, God, *yes!*"

Deciding she didn't need my help after all, I got the hell out as quickly and quietly as I could, though neither of them was in a state to notice much of anything except each other.

Returning to the house I found Escott in the parlor where I'd left him. He looked up startled from a paper that still bore headlines about Grant's death. "That didn't take long. False alarm?"

I dropped into a chair and put my feet on the coffee

table. "Sort of, but you can close the Sommerfeld case for good."

"Really? How did you manage?"

"Let's just say she worked out her differences with McCallen." If she called later asking for me—which seemed very unlikely—I planned to give her a song and dance about a flat tire. "How's the riot going?" I asked, nodding at the paper's bold print asking questions that, with any luck, would never be answered.

"As well as one can expect."

"How about yourself?" Simple words with a lot behind them. Whether the action is justified or not, taking a life is going to have its effect on the soul. I should know.

"I'm fine," he replied after a moment. "Just a little tired."

"Yeah?" Usually he just said he was fine and left it at that.

"I think I shall take some time off and go on a little trip."

He *never* took trips. Not unless they were connected to his business. "Where to?"

"Toronto."

That caught my attention. "Why Toronto?"

"Miss Katherine Hamilton settled there. Some of my other old friends are there as well. I'd . . . like to see them again."

See them and maybe let them know Raymond Yorke had met with his judgment. I almost offered to tag along, but kept it to myself. If anyone went with him it should be Coldfield.

"Sounds like a good idea," was my only comment.

"Sometime in the next few days I'll make arrangements, then."

"I'll hold the fort. Stay as long as you want."

He nodded and went back to the paper, but after a few minutes folded it onto the pile on the table, wished me good night, and trudged upstairs.

I sat and didn't do much of anything, just listened. The house was very still, and when I concentrated I could hear its every tick and groan. It didn't take much to follow Escott's muted progress as he got ready for bed.

Upstairs, he opened and shut his closet, then a drawer. I could follow the padding of his bare feet as he crossed and recrossed the room. For a while I feared it would be another of those nights where he'd pace and pace, but this time he got into bed. The springs creaked as he lay back with a sigh. Then he clicked the light off.

I sat and listened, and waited and hoped.

And after a few infinite minutes heard his breathing gradually lengthen and deepen.

I sat and listened and offered up silent thanks.

He'd found his dark sleep at last.